HISTORICAL

Your romantic escape to the past.

Miss Anna And The Earl
Catherine Tinley

The Lady's Bargain With The Rogue
Melissa Oliver

MILLS & BOON

MIX
Paper | Supporting
responsible forestry
FSC® C001695

Published by
Harlequin Mills & Boon
An imprint of Harlequin Enterprises (Australia) Pty Limited
(ABN 47 001 180 918), a subsidiary of HarperCollins
Publishers Australia Pty Limited
(ABN 36 009 913 517)
Level 19, 201 Elizabeth Street
SYDNEY NSW 2000 AUSTRALIA

Cover art used by arrangement with Harlequin Books S.A.. All rights reserved.

Printed and bound in Australia by McPherson's Printing Group

Miss Anna And The Earl

Catherine Tinley

MILLS & BOON

Catherine Tinley has loved reading and writing since childhood and has a particular fondness for love, romance and happy endings. She lives in Ireland with her husband, children, dog and kitten and can be reached at catherinetinley.com, as well as through Facebook and on X @catherinetinley.

Books by Catherine Tinley

Harlequin Historical

A Waltz with the Outspoken Governess

The Triplet Orphans

Miss Rose and the Vexing Viscount
Miss Isobel and the Prince

Lairds of the Isles

A Laird for the Governess
A Laird in London
A Laird for the Highland Lady

The Ladies of Ledbury House

The Earl's Runaway Governess
Rags-to-Riches Wife
"A Midnight Mistletoe Kiss"
in *Christmas Cinderellas*
Captivating the Cynical Earl

The Chadcombe Marriages

Waltzing with the Earl
The Captain's Disgraced Lady
The Makings of a Lady

Visit the Author Profile page
at millsandboon.com.au.

Author Note

I hope you have enjoyed The Triplet Orphans series. I had great fun writing Rose's, Izzy's and Anna's stories and bringing all the threads together for this, the grand finale!

I'm already working on my next Regency romance, involving an identity switch between an heiress and a maid. Watch out for that one, coming soon!

For Clodagh
Welcome to the world

Prologue

Elgin, Scotland,
1797

'Mama, tell us the story about ZanZan and Milady!' Anna gazed at her mother adoringly.

Mama laughed. 'Again? I declare it is your favourite story. Very well, but you must promise to go to sleep immediately afterwards. Now, move over a little, and I shall sit on your bed.'

The triplets—Anna, Izzy and Rose—shuffled over in their large, comfortable bed and Mama stretched out beside them, smoothing her simple dun gown. There was an ink stain on her hand from her long hours clerking that day.

'Once upon a time,' she began, 'There were three little princesses. They lived in a beautiful castle—'

'Not like our cottage!' declared Izzy, briefly taking her thumb from her mouth.

'No, indeed. Our little cottage is beautiful in its own way, though, and we are very grateful for it. Now, the princesses lived in a beautiful castle with their dear friends—'

'Milady!' Rose jumped in with the name.

'And ZanZan!' added Anna. ZanZan was her favourite.

'Yes, the princesses and their mother lived with ZanZan and

his mama in the beautiful castle. It had nearly a hundred rooms, and the children played and laughed all day long.'

'There was a big, big staircase,' said Rose, lifting her little arms and spreading her hands to show how large the staircase had been.

'And a piano!' said Izzy.

'And secret places. Tell us the part about the secret places, Mama!' Anna could see some of them in her mind's eye: the bookcase in the library that was really a door; the hidden drawer in Mama's desk that would pop open when she pressed the third carved flower from the left; the loft in the stables that no one would know was there. She remembered *everything*.

'And another time,' Mama said, and there was a different tone to her voice, 'The mother of the princesses stayed in an inn for three whole weeks!'

'Why, Mama? Why did she stay there?'

'It was when the princesses' mother was getting ready to be married to their father. Her husband-to-be stayed in a different place, as was proper, and each Sunday the minister read out their names in the church to see if anyone might try to stop the wedding.'

Anna was fascinated. 'Why would someone do that?'

'His family did not wish him to marry. But they did not find them.' Mama shook her head. 'It was a happy time for them both.'

'Like now, Mama?' asked Rose.

Mama smiled. 'Yes, like now.' There were more stories then, until finally Mama said, 'Now, let us sing *The Lady Blue* together, and then we shall say our prayers. But remember, you are never to speak of your father. Now, promise me!'

'I promise, Mama.'

Chapter One

> *The Lady Blue she points her shoe*
> *You find the line to find the kine*
> *The key is three and three times three*
> *The treasure fine is yours and mine*

Cross Keys Inn, Kelso,
Saturday 8th August 1812

I promise, Mama.

Anna awoke, her cheeks damp, her heart aching, and her head full of vague images of churches and danger. What had she promised? She could not recall. Her dream had included a wedding, she remembered, but there had been some danger attached to it.

Her sisters' weddings? Both Izzy and Rose had married recently. But there had been a strange feeling to the dream—a sense of menace.

I promise, Mama.

Her own words still hovered in the morning air. Had she dreamed of her parents' wedding, perhaps? Sighing, she recognised that her disturbed sleep had its origin in the eternal restlessness that haunted her.

There was no proof their parents had ever married, although Mama had been known as Mrs Lennox. As an adult, Anna suspected that had been pivotal. Something had made Mama run away from home and bring up her daughters in a sleepy town in the far north of Scotland, perhaps? But surely such scandal would have been quelled by marriage, even if it had taken place after Mama was with child?

Mama's death from a wasting disease when her triplet daughters had been just ten years old was a loss from which Anna had never recovered. It also meant Maria Lennox's daughters now had no way of having their questions answered, no way of knowing who they truly were. As the years went by, the moments of grief were less frequent, but no less painful.

Never having known their father, losing their mother had been a terrible blow for Anna and her sisters. Thankfully Mama's employer, Mr Marnoch, had become their guardian, and years later his sister, Lady Ashbourne, had sponsored the triplets for a London season.

And now the season had ended, and Anna was on her way to a country house in Scotland for a *ton* summer gathering—still occasionally wondering how she and her sisters had managed to attract such good fortune. They had enjoyed balls and soirées, had been to the theatre and to places of interest in London.

They had even attracted the favour of the Queen herself—as well as disfavour from some of the more critical ladies of the *ton*. Anna's heart sank a little, recalling the antipathy of people such as Lady Renton and Mrs Thaxby, both of whom had disapproved of three nobodies without family connections being feted by the *ton*. Both ladies, and their husbands, had been invited to the upcoming party in Lammermuir House, and Anna anticipated some tense moments during the next three weeks.

Maybe, Anna mused hopefully, the animosity towards them from certain people would now be reduced, given recent events. Anna's sisters had both made excellent marriages towards the end of the season. The youngest triplet, Rose, had wed James, Viscount Ashbourne—their sponsor's nephew, and Izzy had recently married Prince Claudio of Andernach, a distant cousin of the Queen.

Despite being the eldest of the triplets—by a full twenty minutes!—and being identical in looks and figure to her sisters, at least, to an unfamiliar eye, Anna had not attracted so much as a single proposal of marriage.

Which was why she was sleeping alone in this comfortable bed in a well-appointed room in the Cross Keys Inn, with a serving maid on a truckle bed beneath the window to protect her reputation, while her sisters slept in nearby chambers in their husbands' arms.

As Anna rose and began to prepare for the final part of their journey, she reflected on this. It was hardly surprising, she supposed, that she was the one still unwed. As the eldest, she had always carried the weight of unseen responsibilities, and as such felt herself to be a little less impulsive than Izzy and a little more practical than Rose, whose dreamy head was often stuck in a book.

Anna was self-contained by will, and design, and intention. Not for her the flirtatious arts; she could no more be arch, silly or full of smiles than she could fly—which was to say, not at all. And, while she had developed a foolish *tendre* for the Earl of Garvald, who was hosting the upcoming summer gathering, she was much too practical to take such a notion seriously.

Recently, the triplets had managed to establish that Mama's maiden name had been Maria Berkeley, and that the formidable Lady Kelgrove was in fact their great-grandmother. She had chosen to recognise the connection, yet Anna knew some high sticklers in the *ton* continued to sneer at the Lennox triplets behind their painted fans.

As she descended to the parlour for breakfast, Anna distracted herself by going over again in her mind some of the faint, precious memories she had retained of her childhood. She remembered the years in their little cottage in Elgin before Mama's death—a house now sadly changed beyond recognition. A local farmer had taken it on, building outwards and upwards until it bore no resemblance to the humble cottage that had been their happy haven while Mama had yet lived.

There was also the wonderful place they had lived *before* the cottage, in some place other than Elgin—the place she remembered as a fairy-tale castle with a huge staircase. She and her sisters had been born there, she knew, for Mama had told them so, many times.

At least I know that much, little as it is.

They had been five when Mama had moved them to Elgin, and ten when she had left them all, to live in heaven. Anna still had happy memories of their life in the castle, though she was now one-and-twenty, which meant that sixteen years had passed.

The Lady Blue, the little song Mama had made up, was haunting her this morning.

Was it in my dream too?

Anna and her sisters had each been given a ribbon by the midwife at birth, tied around their wrists to help Mama distinguish between them—blue for Anna, green for Izzy and pink for Rose. Later, Mama had always sung *Greensleeves* for Izzy, while Rose's song had been *Ring a Ring O'Roses*. Anna's song had been *The Lady Blue*. Eventually the girls had realised that, while both Izzy's and Rose's songs were well-known, no one had ever heard of *The Lady Blue*, and so it had felt even more special to Anna.

There were actions to each of the songs, too—clapping patterns and movement. When they were little, they had loved pretending to sneeze, then throwing themselves to the floor for the 'all fall down' part of Rose's song. For *The Lady Blue* they had followed different actions for each part, first pointing the toes of their right foot as they made a sweeping curtsey, arms outstretched in a grandiose way. They had then woven in and out around each other three times before they'd all finally clapped hands together and against each other's palms as they had chanted about the treasure.

It had been silly and meaningless, and Mama had told them afterwards she had made it up—cleverly crafted in iambic tetrameter, Anna realised later. But in Anna's mind it encapsulated Mama's vivacity and creativeness, and the fact that her girls had been the centre of her world. Even after their tenth birthday, when she had gradually become so weak that she had spent all her days and nights in bed, and Mr Marnoch had sent one of his own maids to help care for them all, she had asked them to sing *The Lady Blue* for her.

'The true treasure,' Mama had told them once near the end, when she had been sleeping most of the time, 'Is the love that we share. Never forget that, Annabelle, Isobel, Rosabella: my belles.'

Anna never had. After the funeral, and Mr Marnoch's awkward kindness in telling them he had arranged for them to live at Belvedere School for Young Ladies on the edge of Elgin town, Anna had known that the three of them needed to look after one another through whatever might befall them.

And now her sisters were married, and she would have to get used to being without them. Rose and James, her viscount, had married in Elgin, in the same chapel where Mama's funeral had taken place. Izzy and Prince Claudio had travelled to Shropshire for a couple of weeks after their London wedding. This had reduced the triplets to pairs, different pairs at different times, and Anna had not yet had to suffer being without them both at the same time. Thankfully they were now all back together, travelling to Scotland for the Earl of Garvald's country-house party.

Anna and her sisters were now one-and-twenty, and so much time had passed that her precious memories were now reduced to impressions and feelings, rather than images. But each time she entered a new building Anna's mind would search out similarities—a door, window, or the sweep of a staircase that vaguely reminded her of the castle. Whitewashed walls, flagstone floors, and large open fireplaces always reminded her of the cottage where they had lived so contentedly.

Last night, the wooden beams in the ceiling of her chamber in the inn had brought to mind their bedroom in the castle. Sadly, the memories were fading by the day, the month, the year. Soon, she knew she would have only the merest glimpses in her mind of Mama, and of the places in which they had lived with her. Too much time had passed.

She had been very little when they had moved to Elgin from the castle, but Anna recalled being happy. In her memory it had been idyllic: games with her sisters and their friend ZanZan; her first piano lessons with Mama and Milady; and even some

memories of riding a pony. While she had enthusiastically continued with piano, gaining good proficiency during her years at
school after Mama's death, she had not continued to ride, and
now suffered from quite a fear of horses.

If we had stayed there, perhaps I...

But no. Anna knew herself to be sensible, practical, logical.
There was no point in imagining what might have been. Rose
might dream of an idyll, and Izzy might demand and seize
every opportunity, but Anna would simply accept her lot. As
she always had.

Lammermuir House, Scotland

William Alexander Edward Henderson, Earl of Garvald,
entered the breakfast room where a slim, good-looking lady in
her middle years was delicately nibbling on some toast, a dish
of chocolate by her elbow.

'Good morning, my love,' he announced, bending to kiss his
mother's cheek. 'My, you are looking fetching this morning!'

'Do you like it?' Lady Garvald glanced dubiously at her day
gown of figured muslin. 'The dressmaker has assured me that
my new gowns are based on the latest fashion plates. Not having travelled to London since before you were born, I have no
idea of current fashions. Our guests will arrive today, and I
know I have made all ready with the staff, but I do not wish to
disgrace you with dowdy gowns, Will!'

'You could never do that. And, I assure you, your gown is,
er, all the crack!'

She sniffed. 'Well, I am glad to hear it, though I feel I should
not approve of such an expression.'

'Ah, but that is why you are a darling, Mama. For you do not
chastise me—you simply feel that you *ought* to do so!'

'To be fair, even as a child you rarely needed to be chastised—apart from that horrible year when you turned nine.'
Her brow furrowed. 'You were so unhappy, as was I, and I did
not know what to do with you!'

Will grimaced. 'To this day I can recall my anger. Children
cannot, I suppose, understand such matters.' Mama had sunk

into quite a depression at that time, and had not the energy to deal with a deeply unhappy eight-year-old boy. But that had been a long time ago. It would do no good to think of it now. With an effort, he smiled, asking, 'But surely I gave you some grey hairs while at university?'

She rolled her eyes. 'Even in rural Scotland, the tales of your antics reached my ears. Many young men must kick off the traces for a while, I know, but deep down I was certain that such larks would be short-lived. And I was right!' She sent him a sideways glance. 'I imagine you will marry soon. It will be wonderful to have children again in this big house.'

'Now, Mama…' He raised a quizzical eyebrow. 'Do not hold such expectations, for they are sure to be dashed. I am but five-and-twenty, and have plenty of time for such matters.' They had had this conversation many times, he evading what he knew to be his responsibility to marry and produce an heir. It was perfectly reasonable to be unmarried at his age. And since the notion of marriage filled him with unease, he was clearly not ready to tie himself to a bride. At least, not the *wrong* bride.

'Your bosom bows, Lord Ashbourne and Mr Phillips, have both married this year, have they not? Even the prince will bring his new bride to our party—and he is younger than you are!'

He clapped a hand to his chest. 'A hit, Mama! I cannot deny it. But just because they have wed it does not follow…' His eyes widened. 'Did you just *snort*, Lady Garvald? How unladylike! Ah, that is more like it!' She had dissolved into helpless laughter. 'Now, breakfast!'

'I am worried about Lady Kelgrove.'

Izzy, Anna's younger sister, had joined her at the breakfast table in their well-appointed private parlour in the inn.

Anna's heart lurched. Their mama's elderly grandmother had welcomed the triplets into her family, her home and her heart with alacrity and generosity.

'Oh, no! She is unwell?'

Izzy nodded, then clarified, 'Tired, perhaps—too tired. When I called to her room just now, she was in a crotchety mood, talking of her rattling bones and an aching head.'

'Lord, we knew the journey would be too much for her. I do wish she had stayed safely in London.'

'Safe? She is not a person who wishes to be safe.' Izzy thought for a moment. 'It is, I believe, one of the most admirable things about her.'

Having been included in Lord Garvald's invitation to the party at Lammermuir House, and on hearing who else was to be invited, Lady Kelgrove had instantly announced her firm intention to travel. Anna recalled their futile attempts to dissuade her.

'Watch me!' she had challenged, at their protestations. 'I may be eighty-four, but I am not yet underground! Lady Garvald, the Earl's mother, is, as I recall, a pretty-behaved girl with sense between her ears. Such people are rare and must be celebrated. Besides,' she had mused, 'I have a notion to observe certain of the other guests.'

'Who, Great-Grandma? Who?'

'Whom!' Lady Kelgrove had corrected, a wicked glint in her dark eyes. 'It is to do with your father, but we will have plenty of time during the house party to tell you what I know, what I suspect and what I mean to discover!'

This had been decidedly intriguing, given that Anna and her sisters had only recently discovered their mother's family, and Lady Kelgrove had once hinted she had suspicions about who their father had been. Lady Kelgrove seemed to thrive on intrigue, and had once told Anna she liked to keep information for herself as long as possible

'So,' Izzy continued, 'I suggested staying on here for another day or two. The Cross Keys is among the best of the inns we have stayed in so far.'

'Has she agreed?'

'She has, which is both reassuring and concerning.'

Anna knew exactly what she meant. 'Is she breakfasting in her room?'

'Absolutely not! She is indomitable!'

Sure enough, half an hour later Lady Kelgrove appeared, accompanied by her personal maid, Hill. A quick glance towards this loyal servant gave no clues as to her mistress's health, and

Anna suppressed an inner sigh. Why must servants always be so unreadable?

They were joined by Prince Claudio, Izzy's doting husband, who sent his wife a warm glance as he seated himself opposite her. Izzy's title was now Princess Isobel of Andernach— decidedly strange, when said princess was one's own sister who had used to pull Anna's hair when she'd lost her temper as a child. As Lady Kelgrove was taking her seat, the parlour door opened, admitting Rose, the youngest of the triplets, along with her husband, the Viscount Ashbourne. His aunt, the dowager viscountess, had declined the invitation, and was instead planning a visit to her brother in the coming weeks.

'I have decided,' announced Lady Kelgrove, after the customary greetings had been exchanged, 'To stay in Kelso for a couple of days. It looks a pretty sort of town, and I am pleased with this inn. Although I have, naturally, brought my own linen, Hill assures me that the beds are spotless!'

At this, they all concurred about the quality of the inn, the pleasantness of the town and the prettiness of the surrounding countryside. No one mentioned, nor did they need to, the gruelling journey they had made thus far from London, nor the fact that only one more day of travel would take them to Lammermuir House. This being Saturday, their intention had been to complete the last forty miles of their journey, for one did not travel on a Sunday. If they did not continue on today that would mean two further clear nights of rest for the elderly lady—a plan of which Anna heartily approved.

But, when they all expressed their support for the entire party delaying their onward travels, Lady Kelgrove would have none of it.

'Absolutely not! Lady Garvald expects us today, and so you must all travel on without me. For one guest to be tardy may be thought an inconvenience, but for such a large party to be delayed would be insupportable! It would be deeply insulting to our hostess, as I should hope my dear Maria's daughters would understand.' She sighed, adding, 'The Kelgrove estate is not entailed, you know.'

They exchanged puzzled glances, but she elaborated. 'My

long-suffering lawyer had no need to search through the lesser branches of my husband's family for a male heir when he died, for I inherited all of it—as will you girls. You are all now substantial heiresses, you know, and as such must come under the critical eyes of the *ton*!'

Anna's jaw dropped. Not having thought about the matter much until now, she understood immediately that she did not need to be an heiress, for her sisters had both married well. Of more concern was Lady Kelgrove's hinting at her own demise. Was she more unwell than she was pretending?

Izzy—as ever the quickest to form a response—instantly declared herself to have a headache and, since she had recently recovered from influenza, this could not be gainsaid.

'I do not feel well enough to travel,' she complained, perjuring herself without a blink. 'I am actually relieved that you are staying on, for it gives me exactly the excuse I was searching for!'

Lady Kelgrove sent Izzy a sceptical look but thankfully did not dispute this, and so an hour after breakfast Anna found herself in Lord Ashbourne's coach with Rose, her husband alongside them on horseback. Izzy, Prince Claudio and Lady Kelgrove would follow them in two days.

'Thank goodness our great-grandmother will have some rest before the rigours of the Earl's house party!' Rose commented. 'And wasn't it clever of Izzy to think of a way to remain with her?'

'Indeed!' Anna shook her head slowly. 'Izzy's quickness of mind has proved useful yet again. I could not think of anything to say once she had called into question our understanding of how to go on!'

'It is still so strange to know who Mama was.'

Anna thought for a moment. 'Even stranger to think that in the coming weeks we are likely to discover more about our father—if Lady Kelgrove is correct in her suspicion that she knows his identity.'

'We already know Mama's family has turned out to be wonderful.' Rose frowned. 'Well, Lady Kelgrove is wonderful, at least. Her husband, our great-grandfather, seems rather harsh, based on what little we know of him.'

Anna shrugged. 'All we know is that, rather than telling his wife that their only living grandchild had run away, he pretended she had died in the smallpox outbreak. Perhaps he was trying to spare her feelings, or cover up the scandal.'

'Perhaps. But why did Maria run away to begin with? She cannot have been in the family way, for we were born nearly a full year later. And, even though we came early, she still would not have been with child until at least a couple of months *after* she ran away.'

'We may at least hear more of our father soon. From that we might be able to reason why she ran away.'

Rose's expression brightened. 'True! And Mama always spoke warmly of our father, so if Lady Kelgrove truly suspects who he may be then I am eager to learn more of him—what sort of man he was.'

'A servant, perhaps, or tradesman.' Anna had long since concluded that Mama's sweetheart might have been deemed unsuitable by her family. 'Though our surname—Lennox—seemed unfamiliar to Lady Kelgrove.'

'It is likely to be someone like that, yes. Perhaps a temporary servant by the name of Lennox. Otherwise why not simply marry him, with her family's approval?'

'Exactly. And why did Lady Kelgrove say that she wished to observe some of the guests at this party, do you think? Might it be connected?'

'I have no notion, but I did think it an odd thing for her to say.'

Anna chuckled. 'Our great-grandmother delights in being odd, and cryptic, and even eccentric, I think! She will certainly add colour to this party!'

'And we are to meet Lord Garvald's mother. Did you note Lady Kelgrove's praise for her?'

Anna nodded. 'Since Lady Kelgrove does not often give praise, we must suppose Lady Garvald to be all that is good.'

'That is indeed encouraging, for I confess her son quite intimidates me!' Rose grimaced. 'Oh, I know I should not say so, for he is one of my husband's closest friends, but…' Her voice tailed away.

Anna nodded sympathetically, but found herself unable to reply, for in truth she had no idea what to make of Lord Garvald. Gazing out of the carriage window, she pictured him as she had last seen him, in the Ashbourne drawing room two weeks ago. His strong form and handsome face were clear in her mind's eye—dark hair, strong jawline and his eyes a shade of blue that sometimes spoke of the sky, sometimes the sea.

Blue was Anna's favourite colour, and she usually chose it to trim her white muslin gowns with embroidery and ribbons—partly because using their preferred colours helped others distinguish between her sisters and her, but partly because blue was genuinely the best colour in nature, in her opinion. The hint of blue in a cloudy sky was hope. The blue-green murmur of the sea at Stotfield or Garmouth, during an occasional excursion from Elgin during her childhood, had always fascinated, calmed, and impressed her with its vastness. And she never forgot that the colour had become hers when she'd been born and the midwife had placed a blue ribbon on her wrist so that Mama could distinguish her from the other babies. Yes, from birth she had been destined to prefer all things blue.

Lord Garvald's coat had been of blue superfine, that last day, she recalled. It had suited him. It had been two whole weeks since she had seen him, and she was no nearer to understanding why he affected her so. During her season in London she had frequently been in his company—at balls, soirées, musicales and the like. The *ton*, after all, was not so large. He was urbane, well-respected and sober, without being staid. He had seriousness, dignity and, occasionally, a hint of dry humour. Yet from the first, Anna had sensed he was playing a role. And from the first, he had had a strange effect on her senses. Each time he looked directly at her, his eyes—those blue, blue eyes—had seemed to search out her soul.

No one else had commented on it, responding to him with joviality, warm politeness or simple courtesy. A few, like Rose, found him forbidding. But only Anna seemed to feel this strange affinity to him. Each time she was with him, her heart seemed to melt and he took up all her attention.

Once again, she told herself she was being nonsensical. Of the triplets, Izzy had always been the one to let her imaginings run away with her, Rose the one most likely to be lost in dreaminess. Anna's approach was simple, straightforward and unaffected by flights of fancy.

Maybe that is exactly why I am drawn to Lord Garvald, she mused now. The Earl seemed equally immune to the fancies, exaggerations and scandals of the season as she.

Perhaps, she thought now, *we share a love for practicality, and nothing more.*

She was certain being in his company for most of the next month would serve to resolve this riddle in her mind. And perhaps she had imagined that he disordered her senses, for she had not seen him in a full fortnight, and could think of him as she did now, without any effect on her senses beyond a barely discernible fluttering in her innards and a slight increase in the intensity of her pulse. Yes, there was nothing out of the ordinary about it. Nothing at all.

Chapter Two

'Welcome, friends.' Lord Garvald bowed formally, then half-turned to the lady by his side—a lady so like him in looks that she could only be his mother. 'Mama, you remember my dear friend, Lord Ashbourne? May I present his bride, Lady Ashbourne…?'

As Lord Garvald began the formal greetings, Anna's mind was in quite a degree of turmoil. The carriage had turned into the entrance somewhere after Haddington, and as the house had come into view her innards had gone into some sort of frenzy—a development as unexpected as it was unwelcome.

His eyes had met hers briefly just now, and a jolt had gone through her, just as though she had been struck by lightning. What on earth was happening? While this was the first time she had ever had the opportunity to attend a *ton* country house party, she had been acquitting herself well in the ballrooms and drawing rooms of Mayfair all season. That being the case, this sudden attack of nerves had caught her by surprise.

Or was it to do with the man himself, and her earlier reflections that he affected her in some particular way? The notion was unwelcome. Yet she could not deny that her attention was almost entirely given to the tall, dark-haired gentleman currently leading the introductions.

Why should she be so affected by seeing him again? The impact was certainly potent. After just two weeks without being in his presence, the urge to allow her gaze to rove hungrily over him was so strong, she had to deliberately quell it, distracting herself by swiftly taking in the facade of Lammermuir House.

Something about its form instantly reminded her of her castle childhood home—although that castle had been much bigger than this one. Despite this, the Earl's home was substantial, pleasing to the eye and well-built. It was square, solid and... reassuring somehow, Anna thought fancifully. Judging by the architecture, she guessed some parts dated back to Elizabeth's reign, while others were clearly more recent additions.

'And this is Miss Lennox.'

Anna made her curtsey, reassured to see a kindness in Lady Garvald's eyes that was not always there among *tonnish* people. The Earl's mother was petite, warm and engaging, and she had clearly passed her eye colour to her son. They were much alike, which would account for the stab of familiarity that had struck Anna on first seeing her.

Viscount Ashbourne was now explaining that Lady Kelgrove, Prince Claudio and Princess Isobel would arrive on Monday, two days later than planned, and that he hoped it would not put Lady Garvald out too much.

'Not at all, my lord—our guests may arrive according to their own preferences. And it is far easier, after all, to have *fewer* for dinner than to add extra people, do you not agree?' Her eyes danced, and Anna felt herself relax a little. Given the Earl's habitual stiffness, it was a relief to find his mother to be so engaging.

Viscount Ashbourne agreed most readily, and their hostess led the way indoors.

'Lord and Lady Renton have already arrived,' she offered. 'As have Mr and Mrs Thaxby. The Thaxbys came directly from their house in Edinburgh—a delightful mansion, by all accounts. They plan to return there following our little party. Now, then, I shall introduce you to Gibson and Mrs Lowe.'

She indicated the elderly butler and the housekeeper standing inside the hallway. 'I am sure you are all desirous of a rest before dinner, so Mrs Lowe will show you to your rooms.'

After expressions of thanks and gratitude had been properly made by the party, Anna followed the rest up the wide staircase. It had two turns, windows along the middle section and an archway along the landing—a common arrangement, and one that definitely stirred something in Anna's memory. Her castle must have had something similar, perhaps. Lord, would her life always be like this—always searching in vain for a time that was past? *Now* was what mattered, surely?

Yet, as Mrs Lowe led them along the upper hallway containing the guest bedrooms, a small door on the right caught Anna's eye. It was just a door, narrower than the others and with a traditional latch, yet something inside Anna made her keep her eye on it as they approached then passed. She shivered, realising she had had a sudden attack of goose flesh. Scottish castle architecture from mediaeval times until the present day had clear commonality; Lammermuir House must date from the same era as the place where she had been born.

'Here you are, miss.' The housekeeper opened the door to what would be Anna's bedchamber. 'Your maid will ensure all your things are unpacked.'

'Thank you, Mrs Lowe. What a pretty room!' The bed was large, ornately carved in dark wood and with a canopy. A matching screen, side tables, desk and chair completed the set, and there was a soft armchair positioned by the small fireplace—an arrangement almost begging for Anna to sit and read in comfort. The hangings were of blue and gold, the wall coverings a gentle golden hue.

Once the housekeeper left, Anna made her way to the window. Outside was the front of the house, and she leaned forward to see the hum of activity below, the servants removing the trunks from the various coaches.

Sally, Anna's own personal maid, had accompanied her from Ashbourne House in London. Anna had never had the services of a maid until this year and was most heartily glad. Sally knew how she liked her hair to be dressed, and which gowns were most suitable for which occasions. Anna was determined not to let herself and her family down during her stay at Lammermuir House.

It was also important that she look her best at all times. Something about this thought bothered her, for she was unused to particularly caring about her appearance. Pushing the thought away, she kicked off her slippers and dropped her reticule onto the chair. Yes, she would be comfortable here. She just knew it.

'Tell me, Miss Lennox, have you been to Scotland before?'

With some effort, Anna focused on the young gentleman beside her. Mr Ashman was the son of Sir Walter Ashman, the local magistrate, and both he and his father had been invited to dinner, presumably to counterbalance the fact that both she and Lady Kelgrove were 'extra' ladies in the party. Given that Lady Kelgrove's arrival had been delayed, the dinner group had ended up imbalanced anyway—a fact to which Lady Garvald had airily referred, then dismissed as they were all being seated. She was at the foot of the table facing her son, as was correct, and Lord Garvald had Rose and James on either side of him, they being the highest-ranking guests present. The honour would be passed to Izzy and Claudio after Monday. Regardless, Anna was unlikely ever to be placed beside him at dinner. Not that she cared about such things.

'My sisters and I actually grew up in Scotland. We attended Belvedere School in Elgin until this year.'

His eyebrows shot up. 'Indeed? I have heard Elgin described as a fine town, though sadly I have never visited it.'

'We are very fond of Elgin.' There was a silence. Knowing her obligations, Anna added. 'And what of you, Mr Ashman? Have you always lived in the district?'

'I have, and like you with Elgin, I am fond of it. There is something most agreeable about maintaining a connection with the place of your birth, is there not?'

'Indeed—but I must tell you that I was not born in Elgin. We lived somewhere else for the first five years of our lives.'

A gleam of humour lit his eye. 'Am I permitted to know where? Somewhere else in Scotland?'

'Yes, definitely Scotland, but in truth I do not know where exactly. Such information was lost when my mother died.'

'I am sorry to hear that. My own mother is also deceased.'

They shared a momentary glance, acknowledging the connection, then he moved on to begin telling her about the beauties of the district. Anna's gaze flicked briefly to the head of the table, as it had frequently during dinner, and her jaw sagged briefly as she met the Earl's gaze. How long had he been looking at her? Had he been listening to her conversation with Mr Ashman? And why did he look so displeased?

Rose said something and he turned his attention to her, just as the footmen began serving the next course. This was the signal for Lady Garvald to turn the table, so Anna turned to her right to converse with Lord Renton—an affable gentleman, quite undeserving of such an acerbic wife—and the conversation moved on.

Afterwards Lady Garvald led Rose and Anna out of the grand dining room, along with Lady Renton and Mrs Thaxby, into the yellow drawing room which she explained was where she and her son usually conversed after dinner. The gentlemen left to their port would join them in due course, but this was Lady Garvald's moment. Anna chose a satin-covered sofa near the piano, glancing at the instrument covetously. She loved to play, and wondered if Lady Garvald might permit her to practise on what looked to be a fine instrument.

Glancing around, Anna subtly eyed the others as they took their seats. Rose was nearby, glowing with contentment in a pink silk evening gown—her recent marriage undoubtedly the source of the contentment. Lady Renton had marched straight up to claim a wing-backed armchair near the fireplace, quite the most comfortable seat to be had, and probably normally occupied by their hostess. Anna would not have dreamed of doing such a thing, but Lady Renton clearly had no such qualms.

Anna's gaze roved on. Mrs Thaxby was eyeing the furnishings and art with an assessing air, her habitual frown in place. No doubt she would shortly have something to say about the decor, the paintings or some such thing. Finally, Anna met the gaze of their hostess, who smiled warmly.

'I cannot tell you how delighted I am to have guests in the house again! I often receive my neighbours, but it has been an age since I welcomed old friends and acquaintances from London. And of course new friends too!' She gestured towards Anna and Rose, and would have said more, but was forestalled by Lady Renton.

'I remember being here around fifteen years ago,' she announced, rearranging her silk skirts. 'As I recall, my daughter did not travel, being unwell at the time. I had left her in the safe hands of her nurse, for who wants a small child hanging on one's skirts while trying to enjoy an extended house party?' Her gaze became unfocused. 'I always thought I would have more children.' She brightened. 'Still, at least I was not barren.'

No one quite knew how to respond to this—particularly since everyone present knew Mrs Thaxby had no children.

After a brief silence, Lady Garvald offered, 'Like you, Lady Renton, I have only the one child, but a son such as Will is all a mother could wish for. I am so proud of the man he has become, though I sometimes miss the boy he used to be!'

So the Earl's given name was Will. It did not suit him, somehow. It was at once too...too *informal* and too *English*. One of the things Anna genuinely admired about Garvald was his pride in being Scottish at a time when all things English were thought by the *ton* to be innately superior. And the Earl's general demeanour was rather more characteristic of a *William* than a *Will*.

Naturally this brought her thoughts back to the way he had seemed to glower at her earlier. She shrugged inwardly, shaking off the discomfort at the notion he might be displeased with her. Somehow it had mattered briefly that he approved of her, but such notions contradicted her knowledge that her worth lay not in the approval of any individual—even a glowering Earl who was far, far too handsome. Instead, her value was in knowing herself to be Anna—a good sister, friend and, in this situation, house guest.

Besides, she must have imagined anything *specific* in the Earl's expression, given that it was Garvald's...er, *William's*... habit to glower. And William was a Scottish name too, she reminded herself: William the Lion; William Wallace.

'But would you not have wished for a daughter, Lady Garvald?' Lady Renton once again spoke with a particular bluntness.

Lady Garvald's gaze flicked briefly to Anna, then Rose. She nodded. 'I would, but sadly my husband died soon after my son's birth.' She smiled. 'I pray Will chooses a suitable wife, for she will be the nearest thing to a daughter I shall ever have.' She touched the diamond bracelet on her wrist. 'I shall be delighted to pass this heirloom to her.'

'A pretty piece, to be sure.' Mrs Thaxby's eyes gleamed with hardness. 'Have you had it valued?'

'No, I have not,' Lady Garvald replied firmly. 'Its true value lies in the meaning it has for this family.'

Mrs Thaxby gave a short laugh. 'Its true value rests in those stones, Lady Garvald, and in the gold they hang upon. We had a similar treasure in my family—the Fletcher necklace. A cluster of diamonds around a large, pear-shaped sapphire. Unfortunately, it was stolen many years ago and was never seen again.'

Clearly shocked, Lady Garvald asked, 'And did they ever catch the thief?'

Mrs Thaxby shook her head. 'All that wealth, gone forever!' Muttering, she added to herself, 'That necklace was worth a dashed fortune!'

Anna's jaw hardened. Mrs Thaxby cared only for wealth, and the *ton* knew it. But was there nothing of sentiment in her for a family heirloom lost after who knew how many generations?

'Does your son seek to marry, Lady Garvald?' For once, Anna was glad of Lady Renton's plain-spoken manner as well as her tenacity, for she too wished to know the answer to this particular question.

'Oh, no. But he will marry eventually, of course.' Their hostess gestured vaguely. 'This place, and the family name, require it.'

I had not thought he might marry!

Anna was conscious of a strange tension within her. The word 'eventually' was reassuring, though. The sudden anxiety began to drain out of her, even as her mind caught up with her nonsensical reaction. Why should she care when the Earl married, or whom?

'And if you were to choose his bride, what would you require in the next Lady Garvald?' Mrs Thaxby's tone was piercing.

Lord, what a pair!

Anna exchanged a brief glance with her sister. Lady Garvald was facing quite the inquisition.

'Oh, I should not dare to meddle in such matters.'

'Ah, but it is hardly *meddling* to ensure our children make good marriages—that they choose someone of consequence, with clear lineage and an air of distinction, yes?' Lady Renton was persistent, that was certain.

Mrs Thaxby gave a sweet smile. 'Your daughter, of course, is lately married, Lady Renton—to Mr Phillips.' She added, in a confidential air, 'Dear Lady Garvald, you may not know Mr Phillips, not being part of the London set.' She tilted her head to one side, as if considering the matter. 'I am not sure Mr Phillips could be said to have an air of distinction, but he clearly met your standards, Lady Renton.'

Ouch! Lady Renton had not been pleased with her daughter's choice and the *ton* knew it. Anna was conscious that her shoulders were now decidedly tense.

Lady Garvald's chin lifted. 'I have met Mr Phillips here on a number of occasions, and I think him an excellent young man. As to whom our children marry, that is a matter for them, I think. For my part, I should much prefer if my son chose a lady of character. Family background is of course important, yet we generally judge people by how we find them, do we not?'

Lady Renton sniffed, her eyes flashing fire. 'I must disagree with you there, Lady Garvald. I most certainly judge people based on their connections. Those with…shall we say *questions* about their paternity…in particular can never be fully accepted by right-thinking people, no matter how well they marry.'

Shocked—for this barb could only be aimed at her and her sisters—Anna froze, noting that Mrs Thaxby was attempting to hide a smirk at Lady Renton's words.

Lord, they care not who is hit by their arrows!

The two ladies constantly baited one another, as well as casually striking anyone else within earshot.

Lady Garvald intervened with an air of calmness. 'I must clarify something, Lady Renton. You were here *sixteen* years ago, not fifteen. I remember it well, for my son was eight years old that summer—almost nine. That was also the last time I saw a dear friend.'

My, she is bold!

She'd corrected Lady Renton so smoothly, and diverted attention from anyone in the room with questionable parentage, all in one sentence. Anna felt a surge of admiration for their hostess. Though unused to the viciousness of the London drawing rooms, Lady Garvald was clearly both formidable and quick-thinking.

'You are correct, Lady Garvald.' Mrs Thaxby took the opportunity to lob another rock in the general direction of Lady Renton. 'I was also present at that house party, and I remember it was 1796. But, tell me, who was the dear friend whom you never saw again? I recall the Kelgroves were also present, and of course Lord Kelgrove is since deceased, but he cannot have been your *special* friend, surely?'

Something about her emphasis on the word 'special' set Anna's teeth on edge. The woman's insinuation was obvious, and highly insulting.

Why on earth has Lady Garvald invited these two odious women to disturb her peace?

It made no sense—unless perhaps the ladies had been kinder sixteen years ago. Reflecting, Anna doubted it. Lady Renton's character was well-known, and the lines on Mrs Thaxby's face signalled a lifetime of grievance and complaint.

'Of course not!' Lady Kelgrove's tone was sharp, but she continued with a milder manner. 'She was a friend who moved away. She was not part of our party.'

'I find female friendship to be unnecessary,' declared Lady Renton. 'While I have many acquaintances among the ladies of the *ton*, I should not describe any of them as *friends*, I not think.' Anna's jaw sagged again at Lady Renton's statement. The woman seemed entirely oblivious to the fact that the principal reason for her lack of friendships was her own demeanour, nothing more and nothing less.

'I, on the other hand, have more friends than I can count,' declared Mrs Thaxby, making Anna blink. While the Thaxbys were received everywhere, given their lineage and wealth, Anna would struggle to identify anyone who might call Mrs Thaxby a friend.

'Including the Dowager Viscountess Ashbourne,' Mrs Thaxby continued, 'Who is a dear, *dear* friend.' Anna caught her breath at the sheer scale of the falsehoods being presented. 'I am *so* disappointed she is not here. As chaperone for Miss Lennox, she really ought to be.'

Now they were all looking at Anna. 'My sister, the new Lady Ashbourne, is more than capable of chaperoning me, I think,' she offered quietly.

Lady Renton sniffed. 'In my day such a young woman could never be held to be an adequate duenna. My, you are *exactly* the same age!' She laughed at this, just as though she had said something witty.

Anna resisted closing her eyes in despair. The weeks ahead stretched out endlessly. Perhaps they should never have come. But Ashbourne and Garvald were bosom bows, and Anna had secretly been pleased at the notion of spending the summer here in Garvald's home—partly because she wondered if she might see another side of him here. Now though, with the Thaxbys and the Rentons disturbing everyone's peace, it did not seem worth it.

Thankfully, at that moment the door opened, admitting the gentlemen. Instinctively, Anna's gaze went to Garvald. As their eyes met he frowned, as if sensing something of her distress. Instantly she veiled her emotions, smoothing her expression into what she hoped was inscrutability. His gaze immediately went to his mother and his frown deepened.

'Will, here so soon!' Was there something of relief in Lady Garvald's tone? Anna certainly thought so. Glancing about, she realised that both Mrs Thaxby and Lady Renton seemed oblivious to, or uncaring about, the air of tension in the room.

'We could not stay away!' declared Lord Ashbourne gallantly, making straight for his wife and kissing her hand as he took his seat beside her. Mr Thaxby and Lord Renton chose seats as far away from their spouses as was possible in the drawing room, while Garvald sat with his mother, and Mr Ashman and his father joined her on the satin settee.

What on earth has happened?
Will sensed the tension in the room immediately. Miss Lennox was on edge, as was his mother—although both ladies had hidden it behind a veneer of politeness.

Taking the empty seat next to Mama, he hoped the return of the gentlemen might alleviate any tension among the ladies. He knew the Rentons and the Thaxbys of old and, of the four of them, the beleaguered Lord Renton was the only one he had any time for.

'We have been discussing Garvald's lands,' Lord Renton informed him. 'We can hope to ride every day, so long as the weather holds up.'

At this, Miss Lennox exchanged a rueful glance with her sister.

What does it mean?
Mrs Thaxby, it seemed, had also spotted their exchange.

'What? You do not like our plans, Miss Lennox?' Mrs Thaxby sent her a piercing look, quite matching the tone of her question. Will began to suspect the character of the conversation prior to his entering the drawing room.

'I am afraid I and my sisters do not ride, Mrs Thaxby.' Miss Anna's tone was calm. 'Still, no doubt we shall find other diversions while you are all out.'

'Not ride?' Lady Renton was all astonishment. 'Young ladies who do not ride? My, what is the world coming to?' She shook her head sadly. 'Once again I must be proud of my own daughter's accomplishments.'

'Including her stellar marriage?' This was clearly a reference to Lady Renton's daughter having married Mr Phillips.

Mrs Thaxby never failed to miss her mark, Will thought, watching as her husband handed her a glass of wine procured from one of the impassive footmen flanking the fireplace. Will had hinted to his butler a few days ago that Mrs Thaxby's relationship with wine was perhaps more focused on quantity, not quality.

'I am very happy with Mr Phillips as a son-in-law.' Lord Renton spoke firmly. 'As sensible and responsible a young man as I ever encountered. Our daughter chose well.'

Mrs Thaxby's mouth tightened but she subsided.

Well said, Renton!

As host, Will found himself biting back one of his usual acerbic remarks. Mama had warned him to have a still tongue, and he would do all he could to promote whatever harmony could be achieved among the guests.

Briefly, he glanced at Miss Anna, and together they shared an instant's wry acknowledgement at the recent exchange. As he met her gaze, her blue eyes brimming with humour, he was disturbed to find his heart suddenly pounding and his mouth dry.

How does she do that?

'I shall teach you to ride, my love.' The affection in Lord Ashbourne's tone was plain as he looked adoringly at his new wife. 'And your sisters, too.'

With a small cough, Garvald drew his friend's attention. 'I have a couple of quiet mares that would suit Lady Ashbourne and her sisters. They are at your disposal, Ashbourne.'

'Oh, no!' Rose protested. 'I would not keep you from your sport, James!'

'We shall speak of it later, then,' Lord Ashbourne assured her, clearly undeterred.

The group was now large enough to enable multiple smaller conversations and, as people began speaking informally to those seated nearest, Will was able to share a few words of reassurance with his mother.

Miss Anna was sitting with Mr Ashman and Sir Walter, he noted, and they seemed to be conversing easily and naturally together—so much so that he noticed her shoulders loosening and her smiles become natural rather than forced. While he could only be pleased that she was feeling comfortable, something within him could not help wishing that it had been he and not the Ashmans who had taken the trouble from her brow.

Eventually, tea was served, and then they all dispersed—
Will to the billiards room with some of the gentlemen, Mama
accompanying Miss Anna to her chamber. He watched them
go, his heart a mix of worry, hope and delight. What would the
coming days and weeks bring?

Anna climbed the stairs to her room alongside her hostess,
relieved the evening was at an end. While Lady Garvald and
her son had been pleasant hosts, and the Ashmans delightful
company, the bickering warfare between the Thaxby and Renton
ladies had unsettled her.

In addition, the news that riding was to be the main day-
time occupation was concerning. She and her sisters would
be sorely disadvantaged, and she was daunted by her brother-
in-law's offer of lessons. While Anna would dearly love to
be able to ride, the thought of learning—of being near those
large, prancing, unpredictable creatures—made her decidedly
nervous. Rose would be fine if her doting husband was there,
for James would ensure she came to no harm. Given the way
the Ashbournes were so fixated on each other, though, Anna
doubted that James would even remember her own presence,
never mind her safety.

'Is your chamber to your satisfaction, Miss Lennox?'

'Oh, indeed, my lady. It is pleasant, and comfortable, and
with as beautiful a view as I have ever seen!'

'I am glad.' She paused. 'My son tells me you have always
lived in Scotland until this year—Elgin, I believe, and another
place before that?'

'That is true.' She could not recall ever speaking to Garvald
directly about it, but it was no secret. 'We moved to Elgin when
we were just five years old and have no clear memories of the
place we lived before that.'

'I see. There is something I wished to say to you. Many years
ago, I had the——'

'My lady!'

They both started, turning on the stair.

'Sincere apologies, my lady.' It was Mrs Lowe, the housekeeper. 'One of your guests has just requested a bath—at this

time of night! I dunno how I'm supposed to get gallons of hot water up three flights of stairs at eleven o'clock at night. Most of the servants are already in bed, for I shall have them up at five to see to all the extra duties!' She did not look pleased.

'I see.' Lady Garvald's brow was creased, as well it might be. 'Please excuse me, Miss Lennox.'

'Of course!'

As Lady Garvald descended with her housekeeper, Anna shook her head ruefully. Although she could not know for certain, she was willing to guess that the identity of the demanding guest could be narrowed down to two people: both female. And, what was more, it was likely that Lady Renton or Mrs Thaxby—whichever one of them it was—had demanded a bath deliberately, in order to test Lady Garvald's servants, hospitality or patience.

Outrageous!

If only she could help in some way! But, no, there was no role for her in this. She could help best by going to her room and staying there—and not requesting a midnight bath!

Chapter Three

The breakfast room at Lammermuir House was as pretty as the rest. Morning sunlight slanted through the tall windows, setting patterns dancing on the gleaming silverware. Indeed, the whole house had a warm, welcoming feel to it. Adhering strictly to the time set out by their hostess the night before, Anna arrived around five minutes after nine, smoothing her day gown of fine embroidered muslin as she entered. Surprisingly—or perhaps not, now she came to think of it—Lady Garvald was as yet the only person there.

'Good morning, Miss Lennox!'

After exchanging greetings and confirming that she had slept very well, Anna took her seat, requesting eggs, toast and porridge with honey.

'Ah, a woman after my own heart!' observed Lady Garvald, indicating her own bowl of oatmeal. 'The London chefs have not persuaded you to have fish or meat for breakfast, then?

Anna shuddered. 'No, indeed! I find I must breakfast lightly—especially since my sisters and I were raised on plain food.' She frowned. 'Please do not think me ungrateful, for I assure you our dear Lady Ashbourne—the dowager, that is—has been so welcoming and so generous.'

Lady Garvald smiled. 'Naturally! I understand she is your

guardian's sister and that he is a solicitor in Elgin. Is that correct?'

She is remarkably well-informed.

'Yes. My mother clerked for him for five years and rented a cottage near his office for us to live in. She often spoke of her gratitude for his kindness.'

'Some people,' mused Lady Garvald, 'Being kind themselves, seem to attract kindness wherever they go. While others...'

They shared a look, knowing there was no need to finish the thought, for they understood one another perfectly. Just then, the door opened and the Earl entered, causing the usual response in Anna's foolish innards. As she responded to his greeting, she was conscious of her cheeks burning with heat—quite why, she could not imagine, but it was dashed inconvenient.

Lady Garvald, watching, seemed briefly to still, an arrested expression in her eye, before responding to her son.

'How was the billiards last night, Will?'

He grinned. 'With Ashbourne abed, there was no one who could beat me. Still, I let them play one another.'

'How generous of you!'

He laughed. 'As host, one must suffer these indignities!'

Anna joined in, enjoying the wry, self-deprecating tone. She and Lady Garvald shared a similar sense of wit, it seemed. What surprised her was that Will—that the *Earl*—had the same sense of humour. In London he had only ever been stiffly remote—which was why she could never fully understand why he, of all gentlemen, had sparked such an inconvenient *tendre* within her.

Her gaze swept over him briefly. Yes, he was handsome. Thick dark hair, strong jawline, deep blue eyes—all were present and correct, as was his fine form, currently displayed to advantage in buckskins, a crisp white shirt, cravat and a morning coat of deep-green superfine.

She suppressed a sigh. It was unfair that one man should be so...so *beautiful*! Particularly when he was so habitually closed—closed, unreadable, inscrutable... Briefly considering her new brothers-in-law, she reflected that both James and

Claudio were much more transparent to her in their thoughts and feelings. Unlike the Earl, who...

Actually, to be fair, thought Anna, his current repartee with his mother was showing her an entirely different side to him.

Perhaps it was a good idea, coming here.

Anna had long recognised the Earl's intelligence, worldly knowledge and insight, but now she was also developing an understanding that, like her, he seemed to share a love for absurdity. This was a side to him that was decidedly lighter. Briefly, she remembered the look they had shared last night when Lord Renton had put Mrs Thaxby firmly in her box, and once again her heart skipped a beat. Clearly, he and his mother shared true affection, a notion that gave motherless Anna a brief pang—which she ruthlessly ignored. But his affectionate tone, open expression and relaxed good humour were entirely new—and entirely welcome. Perhaps, after all, he could be a Will rather than a William.

The conversation continued, Lady Garvald apologising for stifling a yawn at one point, which made Anna wonder just what had happened with the requested bath last night. Waiting until the room was briefly empty of servants, both footmen having been dispatched on errands, she asked with an innocent air, 'Was your housekeeper able to solve her dilemma last night, my lady?'

'Eh, what's this?' The Earl glanced sharply at his mother. 'Did something occur after we left the drawing room?'

'Oh, it was nothing, Will. One of the guests requested a bath, that is all.'

'A bath? A *bath*? At near midnight?'

'Oh, no, more like eleven o'clock.'

His jaw hardened. 'Never tell me that Mrs Lowe had to drag servants from their beds at that hour of the night!'

'Actually, no. I was able to persuade the guest in question to wait for morning. Even now, the extra footmen are processing to that bedchamber with hot water.'

He rolled his eyes. 'Lord save us! Good for you—your powers of persuasion are legendary!'

She gave him a rueful look. 'Not always, Will. Not always.'

There was a pause, Anna frowning in confusion as some meaning passed between them. 'But, in this instance, yes.

'Miss Lennox,' she continued, 'I shall speak plainly, for I think we understand one another. I care not whether I fail some arbitrary test of hospitality set by a demanding person. The request for a bath was an opportunity to show my teeth, and the boundaries beyond which I and my servants will not go. And I took it.'

'I am glad to hear it,' Anna replied. 'And I must tell you how much I admired your ability to hold the conversation after dinner, despite the missiles being flung about!'

'Missiles? What missiles?' The Earl's curious look was soon replaced with rueful laughter as they informed him of some of the verbal barbs being hurled around his drawing room while the men had been at their port.

'Lord!' he declared. 'I did wonder what had been said when we first joined you. There was an air of disquiet, I think.' He shook his head. 'The viciousness of the *ton*, exported to rural Lothian! Still, so long as we choose to be entertained, their arrows cannot pierce too deeply.'

'A good tactic, and one which we employed last evening, I think!'

'I do hope you will enjoy your time here, Miss Lennox.' His tone was curt, reverting to the familiar cadence she knew from London. 'It is important to me,' he continued, 'That you—that *all* our guests—may spend a pleasant few weeks at Lammermuir.'

'You love this place very much, do you not?' Anna's tone was low, her throat strangely tight.

He nodded, eyeing her directly. 'Aye. As a house, and my home, it is special to me.' Their gazes held and something between them swelled and resonated, taking the breath from Anna's lungs.

'You should take Miss Lennox on a tour of the house after breakfast, Will.'

Startled, Anna broke his gaze and looked at Lady Garvald. For an instant, she had forgotten Will's mother was present.

'Indeed,' the lady continued, humour dancing in her eyes, 'I insist on it.'

And so half an hour later Anna found herself walking by his side through room after room, covering every nook and cranny of the ground and first floors, until she was quite dizzy with it all. The building was a random collection of older parts and more recent additions, from thick, stone-built castellations to an elegant modern wing. As usual, some of the sights reawakened hints of old memories: the winding staircase to the castle tower; the library with its numbered sections outlined in gold paint; one of the drawing rooms done out with green hangings; even some paintings—a still life, a rural scene with a herd of cattle and a portrait hung above the fireplace in the Earl's study.

'My grandmother,' he explained, seeing her focus on it. 'A strong character, they say. I had it moved here. I quite like having her with me as I work on my documents and accounts.'

'Her strength of character is obvious,' Anna murmured. 'Just look at the vivacity in her eyes!'

The lady had a tall coiffure, an elaborate gown *à la française*, and a familiar diamond necklace on her wrist. No doubt Mrs Thaxby would have commented on the latter. Instead, Anna stood there, studying the portrait more attentively.

As was customary the artist had contained multiple details hinting at the life of the sitter: a book on the table beside her; a harpsichord in the background; a window revealing an idyllic scene of fields and sky. There was even a little dog peeping out from behind the lady's cerulean silk skirts. It all looked decidedly familiar, and a search for the painter's name provided an explanation.

'Gainsborough!'

'Yes. My grandfather hounded Mr Gainsborough until he agreed to paint her portrait. He was, I understand, already busy with multiple commissions, but my grandfather had his way in the end. He was excessively fond of my grandmother, by all accounts.'

'Gainsborough's style is so distinctive, I almost feel as though I have seen this painting before.'

He seemed to freeze in place. 'Many *ton* houses contain

Gainsboroughs.' He paused. 'Do you remember anything of your first childhood home?'

'Almost nothing.' She shook her head sadly. 'Even my memories of the cottage we lived in afterwards are fading.' She pressed her lips together. 'It is all we have of our mama, those memories.'

'But—Lady Kelgrove...?'

'Of course, we are delighted to discover our connection to her. She has begun to tell us of Mama's childhood—though has said almost nothing as yet of the time when she ran away. Previously she had told my sister Rose how Mama's brother died— killed by brigands on the Heath, and his friend left for dead alongside him. She lost her daughter, then both grandchildren.'

He shook his head. 'Lady Kelgrove has had much tragedy to deal with.'

'Which is perhaps why she is so delighted to have found us.' Anna frowned. 'I just hope that her insistence on travelling does not make her too ill. She was determined to come here, you know!'

'Perhaps having another rest day today may aid her?' He opened the door, indicating she should precede him back out into the hallway.

'I do hope so. Oh, are we to go below stairs?' He had pressed something in the panelling, opening a hidden, narrow doorway off the main hallway which she realised led downstairs via a simple stone staircase. Again, she was reminded of the similar door upstairs. Why it had stayed in her mind, she could not say.

His eyes danced. 'I always abhor those who show only the public rooms. As master, I am responsible for ensuring the kitchens and storehouses are adequate for their purpose—just as much as I am responsible for ensuring the acquisition of art and furniture with which to grace the drawing rooms and library! A tour should of course show the inner workings of a house, I always think. And, as master, I am prodigiously well-informed about such matters as ovens and chimneys!'

Fascinated, Anna followed as he showed her through kitchens, sculleries, wine stores, dry rooms and even the laundry. Everywhere they went they encountered startled servants who curtseyed and bowed, and who seemed to find it highly unusual that the Earl was showing a young lady around the servants' quarters. Perhaps, despite his protestations, he did not get the opportunity to show visitors around very often.

'Apologies, sir!' The housekeeper bustled towards them, a hint of outraged dignity about her. 'If I had known you wished to inspect our work below stairs, I would have made all ready!'

'Not to worry, Mrs Lowe.' He smiled. 'Just an informal walk about, that is all.'

His calm tone seemed to mollify her a little, and she glanced towards Anna, as if taking in the Earl's companion for the first time. Her eyes widened briefly, a gleam of speculation in them. 'I hope you find everything to your liking, Miss Lennox.'

What an odd thing to say.

'The house is delightful, Mrs Lowe. And everything is very clean and well cared for.'

She preened a little. 'Well, we do have a good group of hard workers here, that I will say, miss. Of course, we have added extra staff for the house party, and they are still under my eye, I assure you.'

'I have no doubt that you and Gibson have everything in hand, Mrs Lowe.' The Earl's tone was firm.

Seemingly satisfied, she nodded, asking if she might assist them with anything else.

'Oh, no, no,' he assured her, opening yet another door. 'Now, Miss Lennox, this staircase will take us directly to the upper floors of this wing.'

Smiling a farewell to the housekeeper, Anna followed him up a long, dimly lit staircase, pausing to let footmen pass with empty jugs. Presumably they were still engaged in filling the bath for Mrs Thaxby or Lady Renton—whichever of them had so outrageously demanded such a privilege at nearly midnight.

Gasping in surprise as they emerged on the landing where the bedchambers were located, Anna observed, 'We are so far up! You know, I think my childhood home was rather like this—lots of hidden staircases and passageways.' Out of the corner of her eye she saw the narrow door, wondering if he would take her through it, but instead he led her down the landing.

He shrugged. 'Most larger houses have a warren of runs for the servants to move about unobtrusively. Now, let me show you the chambers we have set aside for Lady Kelgrove, and for the prince and princess.'

The bedchambers were like her own, comfortable and richly furnished. She made appropriately admiring noises, then, as they began returning to the main staircase, commented, 'Thank you for showing me around. I believe I have seen everything!'

He laughed. 'Not quite, for we have not visited the attics or the outbuildings. Another day, perhaps.'

Attics. So her instincts were probably correct, and the narrow door must lead up to the top level of the house. 'Do you know,' she offered, 'I believe this is the longest conversation we have ever shared? How strange!'

He shrugged. 'London events do not facilitate conversation, I find. At least, not meaningful conversation. And I myself have not the happy knack of being an easy conversationalist in company—which I have no doubt is commented upon frequently.'

'Oh, no,' she lied politely. 'But surely everyone is more able to be open and at ease in their own home?'

'That is certainly true. Now, we are back at the breakfast room.' He indicated the door, surely the hundredth they had just passed through. 'Let us see,' he added softly, leaning down to speak softly in her ear, 'How many of our lay-abed companions have managed to rise, for it must be nearly ten!'

She gave a short laugh, quickly stifled. His breath was on the side of her cheek, his lips so close to her ear...

Dash it all! Now her heart was racing, her senses tingling, and no doubt she would be flushed again, just as they were about to engage with company. The weather was fairly warm, to be fair, so hopefully no one would think anything of it.

Fixing a polite expression on her face, she stepped inside where the whole party was present, save Lady Renton. It seemed Lady Garvald had already informed them that she was being given a walk around, and some of the others immediately clamoured for the same privilege. Laughing, the Earl agreed, and it seemed to Anna that he had never looked more handsome.

Taking her seat, she joined in the general clatter and hum of breakfast and conversation, remaining when the Earl left with Rose and James, the Thaxbys and Lord Renton, leaving only Anna and Lady Garvald along with Sir Walter and his son. Lady Renton, she deduced, was currently enjoying her bath.

The day passed in a mixture of conversation, food and wine. The party attended church in the little chapel on the grounds, and once again Anna was struck by a sense of familiarity— something about the layout, perhaps, or the way the light came in through the glorious stained-glass windows. Walking out with Rose in the late afternoon to explore the pretty gardens to the side of the house, Anna took the opportunity to speak to her sister about the strange feelings she had been experiencing since their arrival.

'I think wherever we lived for those first five years must have been very like this house, Rose. I have half-memories all around me here. Have you felt it too?'

Rose shrugged. 'Not really. But you were always the best at remembering things from long ago, Anna.'

Anna frowned. 'There must be many such houses, but this one has a decidedly Scottish feel to it. The architecture is distinctive, I think.'

'Which means we probably lived in Scotland for those first five years.' They shared a look. 'I am glad.'

'Me too. Although Mama was English, and in all likelihood our father was too, I have always felt Scottish in here.' She jabbed at her chest.

'As have I.' Rose frowned. 'Now you come to mention it, I did think there was something familiar about the main staircase. The one here is much smaller than the one in our castle, but something about the turns and the windows...'

'I thought exactly the same! And yet, there are only a limited number of ways in which one can design a grand staircase, so we must not read too much into it.' She sighed. 'I am glad of anything that connects us to memories of Mama, no matter how vague.'

Rose slipped a hand into the crook of Anna's arm. 'We three

will always have each other. We are all Mama's daughters, and while we remember her she will live on.'

'And now we also have Lady Kelgrove.'

'Who believes she knows something of our father!'

'That is true. While we might never discover our first childhood home—for Lady Kelgrove cannot know of it—would it not be wonderful to know who he was?' She giggled. 'I suggest he was a handsome groom, turning Mama's head with his strong body and his oh-so-handsome face!'

Laughing, Anna joined in the speculation, suggesting an earnest vicar with a lively mind and a loving heart.

'Yet,' Rose objected, 'Mama was never *pious*, so I hardly think he could have been a vicar!'

On they went, Anna enjoying the simple pleasure of spending time alone with Rose who, naturally, had been distracted by her recent marriage. Emerging from the pretty rose garden with its statues of Poseidon and Athene, they turned a corner, entering what was clearly the kitchen garden. Two gardeners were currently engaged in harvesting vegetables—vegetables which would no doubt grace their table today. One of the best things about being back in the country was the freshness of the food—from garden to fork in just a few hours. Anna was convinced it tasted better.

Seeing them, the gardeners paused their work to bow and await their passage. Anna and Rose nodded smiles in their direction and carried on. Ahead, in the small yard between the kitchen garden and the house, a laundry maid was vigorously scrubbing something made of linen—a petticoat perhaps— while a valet or footman was beating a reddish-coloured coat.

Curious, Anna looked closer, wondering if it was Lord Garvald's, but a pang of disappointment went through her as she realised the coat was too small to belong to the Earl, who was a head taller than both Lord Renford and Mr Thaxby.

Lord, I am even interested in his coat! Really, this fixation was proving mightily inconvenient! She had no thought of marriage, no indication that he liked her, nothing—only her own random notions.

Like the gardeners, both servants paused politely as the girls

passed. Strangely, Anna wondered for a brief instant if the valet
wished to say something to them. The way he looked at them
seemed rather intent. There was nothing sordid about it; it was
just a look. She eyed him curiously. He was a trim, well-pre-
sented man with grey hair and a face filled with lines, suggesting his age to be more than sixty. He held himself well, with a
quiet dignity. A servant, naturally, could not address a guest of
the family without a clear reason to do so, but...

They walked on towards a small orchard. Just as they reached
the first trees—the apples beginning to ripen nicely on their
low, twisted branches—Anna's thoughts about the owner of
the coat were confirmed. Mr Thaxby stormed round the corner, making for the valet, and seemingly unaware of Anna's
and Rose's presence.

'John! Why did you not come when I called?'

The valet bowed, his brow furrowed. 'I apologise, sir.' He
indicated the coat. 'I am readying the mulberry jacket in preparation for this evening, as you requested.'

'As my valet—my *current* valet—you are expected to understand and anticipate my needs.' Lifting a hand, he slapped the
man hard on the side of the head. Anna winced and stepped a
little closer to Rose.

'Do you understand me?'

'Yes, sir. How may I serve you?'

'We have decided to ride out. Bring my boots to the room
near the servants' quarters where the others are already making ready. Well, why are you still standing there, gaping at me
like the feeble-minded ninny you are? Go!'

'Yes, sir.' The man went, briefly rubbing his left ear, which
surely must still have been ringing with the force of his master's blow.

Anna and Rose remained stock-still until Mr Thaxby had
disappeared around the corner, then shared an angry look.

'Only the worst of men abuse their servants so!'

'He hit him as hard as he could, knowing the valet could
not fight back.'

'And John—the valet—had done nothing wrong! How was
he to know they would go out riding?'

'One thing puzzles me...' Rose's brow was furrowed. 'Why did he not send another servant to fetch him?'

They eyed each other in dawning horror. 'Because he wanted to do it himself.'

'Because he wanted to hit him.'

Anna shuddered. 'I have always heartily disliked the Thaxbys. Now I have even more reason to do so.'

On they walked, and it took some time for the sick feeling in Anna's stomach to subside. Eventually, though, they spoke of other things, their conversation eventually circling back to Anna's half-memories revived by aspects of Lammermuir House.

'Now,' declared Rose, 'This seems familiar to me!'

She indicated the stables with a hand, and Anna chuckled. 'Well, naturally, for most stable blocks look the same to me. I do recall you were particularly enthusiastic about learning to ride when we were little.'

'Whereas you were nervous around the ponies at first—though, as I recall, ZanZan was very patient with you.'

'He was.' Anna sighed. 'So, you do still remember some things, then.'

Rose shrugged. 'Very little. Not like you. I do wish I could recall more of Mama.'

Anna squeezed her hand. 'Me too, Rose. Me too.'

Chapter Four

Descending via the main staircase later, clad in an elegant evening gown of white silk adorned with tiny blue rosebuds along the hem and sleeves, Anna took particular notice of the elements of Lammermuir House that seemed familiar: the layout of the turns in the stair; the position of the windows... Yes, this staircase was smaller, but surely she remembered peeping through banisters like these at a hallway below?

Lost in thought, she made her way to the drawing room, there to await the dinner gong. Entering, she was surprised to find the Earl and his mother deep in conversation.

'But you *must* tell them, Will, and soon. After all, that was the whole purpose in bringing them all here.'

The Earl had a definite air of agitation about him, Anna noticed. *How curious!*

'I shall, Mama, once they are all here. Indeed, I wondered if Miss Lennox—'

'Miss Lennox!' intoned the footman, and mother and son whirled to face her.

'Miss Lennox!' echoed the Earl, covering any confusion he might have experienced by striding towards her and taking her hand. 'You look delightful this evening. Does she not, Mama?'

'I suspect,' offered his mama with only a hint of dryness,

'You would find Miss Lennox to look delightful even should she come adorned in sackcloth!' She indicated a nearby settee. 'Come, my dear, and sit with me. Did you enjoy our gardens earlier?'

'I did, my lady,' Anna confirmed, even as their earlier words were sinking in. *What must he tell me? And what was Lady Garvald's purpose in bringing us here?* 'The roses are exquisite!'

Naturally, she could say nothing of the incident involving Mr Thaxby. Dropping the Earl's hand—which left her own feeling bereft—she moved to sit with her hostess, who beamed.

'You have hit upon exactly the right thing to say to my mother, Miss Lennox.'

His eyes met hers, and as usual there was a sense of breathlessness within her. 'How so, my lord?'

'The rose garden is my mother's particular pastime, and I believe it fair to say it owes as much to her as to the efforts of the gardeners.'

'Oh, stuff!' retorted his mama inelegantly, but a telltale flush stained her cheeks. 'I only do a little.'

'Every day!'

'Well, yes, but one absolutely must keep deadheading to keep the flowers coming.'

'But your dedication means you can take at least some of the credit for the garden!'

'I suppose. Have you any interest in gardening, Miss Lennox?'

'Truthfully, I have never had the opportunity to try.' She thought for a moment. 'But I see how it could be fascinating, working with one's hands, doing something which leads to the development of such a beautiful garden... Yes, I believe I could have an interest, given the opportunity.'

'Your true interest is music, is it not?'

Now it was Anna's turn to blush.

My, she is well-informed on everything! He must have...

'I do enjoy playing—although having to play at *ton* recitals and musicales is quite the most terrifying thing I have ever experienced.'

Lady Garvald indicated her own piano. 'Feel free to practise or perform any time while you are here—or not to perform, if you truly do not wish to.'

'Oh, no, I am happy to play if you wish it.'

She nodded, satisfied. 'Perhaps after dinner, then.'

'You are in for a treat, Mama. I have heard Miss Lennox play, and her talent is remarkable.' Anna's eyes flew to his face, seeking any evidence of polite exaggeration. But, no, he seemed entirely sincere. Swallowing, she realised abruptly his opinion mattered to her. It mattered very much.

'Lord and Lady Renton!' They turned at the footman's announcement, Anna inwardly bracing herself for whatever level of acerbity Lady Renton would unleash tonight. By the time greetings had been made, Rose and her viscount had arrived, and before long the whole party was assembled and the gong sounded for dinner.

Afterwards, they retired to the drawing room—first the ladies, the gentlemen joining them relatively quickly. Mr Thaxby was wearing a mulberry-coloured jacket, Anna noted. Anna played and was complimented by everyone—even Lady Renton, who for once had no caveat or indirect insult with which to shadow any words of praise.

Relieved that her performance had gone well, it was only when she was climbing the stairs for bed at nearly midnight that Anna recalled the Earl's strange conversation with his mother earlier.

That was the whole purpose in bringing them all here...

Lady Garvald's words made no sense. Unless...

Anna stopped halfway up the stairs, uncaring of the footmen below, who must surely think her behaviour odd. Bending, she peeped through the banisters as she might have done as a small child. Of course, the proportions would seem different. To a four-or five-year-old, this staircase would have seemed positively enormous.

Sally was waiting in Anna's bedchamber, and Anna submitted to her ministrations while inwardly her mind was awhirl. Was it possible? The library, the chapel, the paintings... Images whirled through her mind like leaves in autumn. The mysterious door on the landing... The staircase...

The maid left and Anna went to bed. If this *was* the idyllic first home of their childhood—which of course she could not say for certain—that would mean that Lady Garvald was 'Milady'. *My lady.* Yes, that would fit.

And was ZanZan... Milady's son? Will was probably about the right age and ZanZan, her dearest friend, had had dark hair. Had his eyes been blue? She could not recall. She only knew that she had missed him terribly after they'd gone to Elgin. A loss that had become part of her, compounded by Mama's death five years later. Loss rippled through her, a familiar pain sharpened by what were no doubt fanciful notions.

Had she not spent a lifetime unconsciously searching for her first home and the happiness she had enjoyed there with Zan-Zan? The yearning within her might well be making her mind wish for things that simply were not true.

Another notion struck her. If the Earl had recognised them on their arrival and presentation in London, why had he not said something? No, the mysterious matter his mother was urging him to speak of must be something else.

Anna took a deep breath. She was no dreamer, like Rose. Nor was she passionately romantical, like Izzy. She was Anna—plain-spoken, logical and always practical. She should not be dreaming of impossible things, for the very reason they were impossible. That way led to heartache and yearning, and the reopening of deep wounds that were slowly scarring over.

No. She must put all speculation from her mind. Just because she was in a house that was architecturally similar to one she had lived in a long time ago meant nothing, really, nothing at all. Blowing out the candle, she turned on her side and allowed sleep to claim her.

Will lifted his glass, idly noticing how the glow of the brandy was enhanced by candlelight. When the others had retired he had sat on, needing some solitude and quiet before seeking his own bed. A reckoning was coming—probably tomorrow, when their final guests arrived. Was he ready for it? He did not know.

Since Anna and her sisters had made their presentation earlier in the year—astonishing the court by being identical triplets—he had been on edge. There were so many questions, so much riding on the answers. What if he was wrong to have done things this way?

Ah, but what if I am right?

So far, the house party was going exactly as one might have predicted. Anna and Rose were perfectly well-behaved, Mrs Thaxby and Lady Renton rather less so. The gentlemen were a mix of bemusement, indulgence and studied ignorance. Why his mama had invited these others was not entirely clear to him. Obviously they had needed to invite enough guests to make the thing a party, but there were some surprising specimens among them. While Lord Renton was generally well-liked— and rather pitied at times—he knew no one who genuinely liked the Thaxbys.

Sighing, he took another sip. It was late. Riddles could wait.

She is peeping through the banisters.

The staircase is enormous, the central feature in this house-like castle. Or is it a castle-ish house?

Below, Lord Garvald glowers at her. Shrieking, she runs upstairs, making for the narrow door. On she goes, up and up to the top floor, where there is safety.

The corridor is narrow, daylight pouring in from the two skylights. She opens the door on the left and dashes inside, to the safety of the nursery. Her sisters are there, and ZanZan.

'Oh!' She feels surprise. 'Were you not just downstairs?'

Anna awoke, her mind and heart racing. Without thought, she sat up, leaving her bed. Feeling for the unlit candle on her side table, she made her way across the room and opened the door. The house—*or was it a castle?*—was quiet. Clearly, everyone had retired. Lighting her candle from the large candelabrum illuminating the landing, Anna hurried towards the narrow door. It was not locked, and she lifted her candle to survey the narrow stairs leading upwards. *Yes!* Her heart pounding, she ascended, her bare feet making no sound on the wooden steps. At the top she lifted her candle again, surveying the ceiling above. There were two skylights, now wreathed in darkness.

The door on the left loomed into view. With a shaking hand, she opened it and stepped inside.

Yawning, Will made his way along the landing. That last brandy had hit the right spot, and he now had every hope of sleeping tonight, despite the worries that plagued him. The Lennox sisters. His mother. Anna.

He stopped. The door to the attic floor was open. Frowning, he took the branch of candles from the side table and made his way up the narrow staircase. The door on the left was open, the one that led to the nursery, and a glimmer of candlelight shone from within. With a sense of inevitability, he pushed the door wide open.

She whirled around, candle in hand. Her eyes were wild, hair unbound, face as pale as her thin nightgown.

'What is your name?' Her tone was demanding, though her voice cracked.

'William. Will.' His throat felt tight, and it seemed as though his heart would leap from his chest at any moment.

This is the moment. It had finally come.

'No. Your *full* name.'

'W-William Alexander Edward Henderson.'

'Alexander. Xander. Was that your mother's childhood name for you?'

'Yes.' He took a breath. 'You called me ZanZan.'

Chapter Five

He stood immobile, silence stretching between them as his words sank in. His heart was thundering; his breath caught. She reached out a trembling hand, and all the while her eyes searched his face.

'ZanZan.'

Their eyes locked. 'You—you remember me?' His throat felt tight, his voice cracking. Everything, his past and present, revolved around this.

'I do now. And I have never forgotten—' She broke off, putting her free hand to her forehead. 'Oh, lord, I feel strange. I…'

As her knees buckled he managed to catch her with one hand, wrapping his arm around her and setting his candelabrum down on the dresser to his left. Her own candle had fallen to the ground, and he stamped on it to snuff it out while simultaneously wrapping his other arm around her. Her head lolled awkwardly against his arm, and his stomach felt a little sick at the wrongness of it.

She was clearly unconscious—well, why should she not be, given the shock she had just experienced?

Dash it all, I should have told her before!

Glancing about him, he realised he had few options. The three wooden bed frames that had served the triplets so long ago were still there, bare of mattresses and looking sadly neglected. But then, no one ever came in here. He himself had avoided the place, associating it with the dreadful sense of loss he had felt for years after they had gone away.

His only option was to sit on one of the small beds and hold her on his lap. He was not prepared to lay her on a hard, dusty floor, and carrying her downstairs might lead to dramas neither of them would wish for. A shudder rippled through him as he briefly imagined what the Thaxby or Renton ladies would have to say about such a shocking turn of events! No, somehow he had to keep this private, and hope she would be well again soon.

He sat gingerly, but the bed held their combined weight without protesting. Although it was furthest away, he had chosen the bed to the right of the small fireplace, and as he readjusted her on his lap he understood why. This had been her bed. How many hours had they all played here together, here and throughout Lammermuir House? Anna, Izzy and Rose had been more than companions to him. They had been friends and family in one. And he and Anna...

Afterwards he had tried to explain it to his mother. Through the tears and distress of an eight-year-old boy, he had expressed outrage that Anna had been taken away by her mother.

'She—she is my twin!' he had protested.

Mama had tried to understand. 'Do you mean that, of the three of them, Anna is the one you liked best?'

'Yes! But no! I like all of them. B-but they are t-triplets. And me and Anna are the *same*. We are triplets together—I mean t-twins. And I am going to m-marry her when I g-grow up.'

'Speak slowly, Xander. You're tripping over your tongue.'

At this, he recalled stamping off in frustration. And it seemed every time Mama had told him to 'slow down', 'take a deep breath' or think about what he was saying, his stammer became worse. He'd known she was trying to help, but it had only made him more aware of it.

By eleven, there'd been times he could barely get a word out, and his time at boarding school had been dominated by boys, and occasionally teachers, mocking his speech. At fifteen, realising that his own name was one of the hardest things to say, he had retired the name Alexander and adopted his birth name of William. He had also dedicated himself to practising his speech, realising that he could be completely fluent while reading aloud or singing, and building confidence from there.

Despite working on his speech, Will's wounds from the loss of the Lennox girls had only faded, not healed. When they had left, his mother had sunk into low spirits for a long, long time, compounding his hurt. Somewhere deep within him, he had known one thing: *people leave*.

By the time he had left university, most of his friends had not even realised he had a stammer, so adept had he been at managing it—including covering it up by changing a word if he knew it would trip him up. He rarely relaxed his guard—except with his mother and a few close intimates—and had developed something of a reputation for being closed and distant. Aloofness was now part of his nature—partly to hide his speech defect, partly because he could never seem to risk being hurt. He had male friends, good friends, but until recently he had never allowed a woman to touch his heart.

It did not bother him—most of the time. But, when it came to *wanting* to be open, wanting to speak to a certain person about the fact they had known each other as children, it had proved impossible. The very thought of speaking the truth to Anna had caused his body to tense in fear. Naturally, he had had no way of knowing how she or her sisters would react— they might well have been delighted to meet someone from their past again. But none of them had recognised him. To be fair, their names and the fact that triplets were so unusual had made him certain: Anna, Isobel and Rose Lennox, the triplets.

To them, though, he was an unremarkable gentleman whose given name—if they even thought to ask someone for it—was apparently William, not Xander. And their mother had clearly never told them their first home had been Lammermuir House, the seat of the Earl of Garvald. Given all of that, why should she—*they*—have realised?

Yet *something* had brought Anna to her old bedroom tonight. He had deliberately shown her around the house, hoping she might recognise something. He had not, though, had the courage to bring her up here, for the nursery had barely changed in the sixteen years since they had left, travelling by Mama's coach to meet the stage at Haddington. That was a strong, clear memory for him—the sight of their coach disappearing down the drive. It was the last time he had seen them—until they had appeared in the Queen's drawing room as beautiful young ladies, leaving him briefly stupefied.

Their beauty—Anna's beauty—had quite knocked him back, his mind and heart swirling in confusion as they'd made their curtseys before the Queen. Afterwards he had danced with her, incapable of much speech, bowled over by the knowledge that the beautiful woman holding his hands was none other than his very own Anna.

Refocusing on the present, he felt the warmth of her body against him. There had been no sign of recognition in her earlier. Once again, the thought could not be denied. Something must have sent her here, to her old chamber after midnight. *She remembers!*

Gently, he smoothed back her hair from her face. She was breathing evenly, and had it not been for her extreme pallor he might have been able to pretend she was asleep.

My, how beautiful she is!

Eight-year-old Xander had had no point of reference, but twenty-five-year-old Will knew that objectively Anna and her sisters were beautiful—the Queen's diamonds, no less.

She stirred, lifting a hand to her head, then her eyes opened. There was a brief moment of what looked like—was that *wonder*?—then she struggled to raise herself up.

'My goodness!' Her voice trembled. 'Did I faint? I never faint!'

He helped her to sit, but now her face was close to his, her bottom pressed into his lap. *Too close.* 'You did! Let me help you.' He smoothly lifted her off him and placed her carefully alongside him on the small bed, exhaling in a curious mix of relief and disappointment.

'Now, are you feeling faint again? Perhaps sitting up so quickly was too much.' His hand was still on her back, in case she should once more be overcome, and he could still feel the warmth of her skin through the thin nightgown. Now that she was recovering, his treacherous body had decided to notice every detail: the swell of her bosom hinted at in the warm candlelight; the delicious scent of her beside him; the sight of her kissable lips.

Sending a stern rebuke to his nether regions, Will focused on her health. Such concern, he hoped, would prevent his body from fixating on other matters.

'Yes, I... But I shall be well presently. Let me just sit a moment.'

'Of course.'

She looked at him, and he at her. Time seemed to stand still. The urge to kiss her was becoming unbearable, but before he could lean in she shook her head, as if to clear it from confusion.

'You are ZanZan.'

'I am. I am relieved you remember me.'

She clasped his free hand, declaring fiercely, 'I would never have forgotten you! Never!'

He swallowed, unsurprised to find his eyes stinging. 'I knew you all from the first, at your presentation.'

She nodded thoughtfully. 'The Lennox sisters. Triplets.'

'You are fairly distinctive, to be fair. I danced with you that day, but you clearly had no idea who I was.'

Her hand was still on his, and now she squeezed it. 'I am sorry, Zan—I mean Will. I mean, my lord.'

He waved this away. 'I am delighted to be ZanZan again.' He smiled. 'Or Will, if you prefer. Anything but "my lord". We have too much history between us for formalities.'

Her brow was furrowed. 'Looking back, there was always something about you. When I saw you at soirées or balls, I always... But I did not... I think,' she finished slowly, 'That something within me half-recognised you.'

'Perhaps.'

She smiled at him through eyes wet with tears. 'You were our best friend, and Milady like a second mother to us.'

He flinched inwardly. Something about her emphasis on the word 'friend' was bothering him.

'And your mama, Mrs Lennox, was so good to me. Why...?' He swallowed. 'Why d-did she leave, take you away?'

She frowned. 'We do not know. Some danger, never speci-fied.'

His jaw loosened. 'Danger? Here?' *What on earth...?*

'I know. It seems unlikely.' Shrugging, she squeezed his hand. 'ZanZan! It is—it feels like a miracle to find you! I missed you so much, and for so long!' Her eyes searched his face, as if seeking to find whatever faint memories she had of the boy and map them to the man. 'My recollection is that you and I...' she faltered.

'That we were *particularly* close? Yes, we were. I told my mama after you left that you were my twin.' He thought for a moment. 'She never understood it.' His face twisted. 'And your departure affected me for a long time. I felt abandoned.' He rolled his eyes to lessen the sting, but she caught her breath.

'Of course you did! I had Izzy and Rose, and we each had our mothers, but you lost your three best friends. "Abandoned" is exactly the word.' She bit her lip. 'No doubt you were angry with us.'

'Angry is an understatement,' he admitted ruefully. 'I was lost in rage for a time. But all is well now.'

'It is.'

There was a silence as they simply stilled for a moment, his heart swelling with a fierce mix of unknown emotions. They rose then by unspoken agreement and he walked her back to her room. Somehow her hand stayed in his all the way. At her door he bowed and kissed her hand.

'Sleep well, Anna,' he murmured.

'You too, ZanZan.'

Walking down the landing, he felt compelled to look back. She had not moved, and at his turning she smiled. Heart soar-ing, he matched her, and continued on to his chamber feeling as though he were walking on air.

Anna awoke, realising from the light at the edge of her cur-tains it was morning. *Finally.* All night she had slept in brief snatches, being too full of astonishment, emotion and *questions* to rest deeply.

She was suddenly, unexpectedly, angry with Will. Or Zan-Zan, as she now knew him. He had known, all along, for months. Yet he had never so much as hinted at the truth, leaving Anna and her sisters in the wilderness of ignorance all this time.

I thought him a stranger. Was he playing games with me?

Thank goodness Izzy would come today, for one thing was certain: her sisters must know as soon as possible! Should she tell Rose this morning or wait and tell them both together? Might Izzy feel left out?

Recently, at the request of both Lady Kelgrove and Lady Ashbourne, they had held secrets for a time, to be revealed at a key moment. The *ton* liked its drama. And so they had delayed revealing the fact they were identical triplets until their presentation, not leaving Lady Ashbourne's house until their day at court. Later they had also allowed Rose and James to share the news of their marriage. And just a few weeks ago Lady Kelgrove had held a ball for the express purpose of revealing that the Lennox sisters were her great-granddaughters. Was that so different from what ZanZan had done—keeping the secret of their connection all this time?

Yes. A few days, a couple of weeks…not months. They had been presented in March, more than five months ago. And, she now realised, his mother had clearly been urging him to tell them yesterday. Yet he had not. And, if she had not realised and gone to the nursery, she would still not know the truth.

Still, for now it would be good to keep this news to herself, so as to tell Rose and Izzy at the same time later today.

Keep it to herself and ZanZan.

I must speak with him.

Rising, she twirled about the room to the sounds of an invisible orchestra. Joy was everywhere—inside her, in the air about her, in the beautiful day now beginning. She opened the curtains, gazing at the gardens below with a fresh eye. Should she have recognised the view? It mattered not, for her search was over. She had found Lammermuir House. Found Milady. Found ZanZan. Even though she was cross with him, it did nothing to diminish her joy at having rediscovered her first home. It was as if she'd found a missing part of herself.

I was born here.

Yes, she would tell Izzy and Rose together, later today. Oh, how wonderful it was going to be! But first she should write it down. Something this momentous must not be forgotten. Sharpening a pen, she sat at the small desk in the corner of her bedchamber, committing to paper the astounding sequence of events which had unfurled last night. As she wrote, she realised she was addressing it to her mother in the form of a letter. She told Mama all about it—Lady Garvald's warm welcome, Lammermuir House itself and the Earl who was really ZanZan. Mama had always encouraged her girls to keep a journal, and Anna was well used to writing about the events, thoughts and feelings she was experiencing.

Eventually, she was done. Crossing the room, she rang the bell for the maid, then returned to the window and the beautiful day outside.

Half an hour later she was in the gardens—alone, for of course it was terribly early and only the servants were about. Softly humming to herself, she wandered amid tall gladioli, proud hollyhocks and Milady's roses until he came, as she had known he would.

'Good morning, Miss Lennox.' Her heart stilled, then raced. How handsome he looked! His coat was blue and brought out the colour of his eyes.

ZanZan has blue eyes.

The knowledge satisfied something deep within her. Joy at seeing him warred with the crossness within her, and joy won—at least for now.

She made a curtsey. 'Good morning, my lord.'

They laughed then, and he stepped towards her. 'Anna!'

'ZanZan!'

Taking her hand, he placed it in the crook of his arm. 'Let us walk together.' He leaned towards her. 'I saw you, from my window.'

She sent him a sideways glance. 'I hoped you might.'

'But you have a dimple!' Raising a finger, he touched her

cheek. 'How did I not know this? And why have not seen it before?'

'Ah, my elusive dimple! It is one of the few things that distinguishes me from my sisters. It apparently only appears when I adopt certain expressions.'

'Very well. I shall endeavour to make a study of it, for I wish to know everything about you. And I mean everything.'

'As do I. About you, I mean.' She exhaled, her earlier anger briefly forgotten in the face of his warmth. 'How fortunate we are to have found one another again! Dear friends reunited.'

Was he frowning? Perhaps not, for his tone was even as he offered, 'I know I really should have made myself known to you from the first. I...'

'Yes, why did you not say something? All this time you knew, yet you said nothing.' Inwardly, Anna recognised that what she sensed felt almost like betrayal. No wonder she had been angry earlier. This was ZanZan, and he had said nothing. Why?

'Well, at first I was in shock, and you clearly did not recognise me. I was, to be honest, at a loss—and I am unused to being out of control in that way.'

Interesting. Control was clearly important to him.

'I suppose,' she offered, 'It would have been very difficult for you to casually mention in conversation: *by the way, did you know we grew up together*?'

'True. But there is more to it than that.' He took a deep breath, and Anna abruptly realised he was about to say something of significance. 'When I told you before I am not blessed with the happy knack of being an easy conversationalist in company...'

'Yes?' Her attention was entirely on him, so much so she was almost holding her breath.

He grimaced. 'The truth is that I have a s-stammer, which I manage to hide fairly well most of the time.'

A stammer? She had had no idea. She nodded thoughtfully. 'I see. So is that why...?'A number of things now came to her: his aloofness; his reluctance to speak to a larger group; the air of tension she had sensed in him at times.

'It is.' He smiled. 'I do not even know for certain what you are trying to say. I just sense that you understand.'

For answer, she nodded and squeezed his arm. She did. So much made sense now.

'So,' he began in an entirely different tone, 'Are we to tell the others? My mother already knows who you are, but I think she will be delighted to hear that you have remembered.'

'I would prefer to tell my sisters first—before the Thaxbys and Rentons, I mean.'

'This afternoon, then, when the prince and princess arrive?'

She nodded. 'And perhaps we can tell Lady Kelgrove and your mama at the same time?'

'A capital notion. Let us attempt to contrive it, then.'

The next few hours were a heady mix of joy, wonder and frustration. Thoughts flew through Anna's mind like a river in torrent, bustling and roaring over one another so that she hardly knew what was what. Somehow, she made it through breakfast, a walk in the woods and a long and dreary lecture from Lady Renton on the freedoms allowed young ladies now that would never have been permitted in her day. It was little wonder Mama had run away, if that had been the case, thought Anna dryly.

Rose naturally sensed something different about Anna. To be fair, Anna thought, the air of suppressed excitement within her must be apparent to anyone who knew her well. But, when Rose sent her a questioning look when no one else was watching, she only shook her head and gave a look which she hoped was mysterious and mischievous in equal measure.

Late in the afternoon Prince Claudio and his bride arrived, followed a few moments later by Lady Kelgrove in her large and comfortable travelling coach. Their servants had already arrived and were currently engaged with Lord Garvald's footmen in bringing trunks and bandboxes to the respective bedchambers. Standing on the drive with the others, Anna took part in the exchange of greetings with a strange feeling. What she had to tell her sisters would change all their lives forever, for it had changed hers.

Once inside, Lady Kelgrove requested tea in her bedchamber, making Anna exchange a look with Will. Anna then sent him a nod to indicate they should go ahead with sharing the news regardless, and Will sent her an answering nod. In that moment it did not occur to Anna to notice how attuned they were.

While the others were engaged in conversation, he took the opportunity to ask Anna in a low voice, 'Well? Shall we await Lady Kelgrove's return?'

Anna shook her head. 'I can barely wait a moment more. We can tell Lady Kelgrove later.'

He nodded. 'I suggest the morning room in…ten minutes? I shall bring my mother.'

'Agreed.'

The conversation had been swift, but they had understood one another perfectly.

That is because Will—the Earl—is my ZanZan. She hugged the notion to her, enjoying the excited warmth within her chest and stomach. *Happy butterflies.*

Ten minutes later, Anna led Rose and Izzy to the morning room by the simple expedient of bidding them to accompany her. Rose looked a little confused, to be sure, but since Izzy was currently dominating their conversation with an account of how their coachman had almost missed the entrance to the estate, even though it was perfectly obvious, the moment passed without any precipitate questioning.

Lord Garvald and his mother had clearly just arrived, for as they entered she was saying, 'I really should not be away from my guests, Will. I must ensure Lady Kelgrove has all she needs— Oh!'

She blinked as the three Lennox sisters entered, bringing a hand to her chest. 'Your Highness! Lady Ashbourne! Miss Lennox! My, you are so alike! I know I commented upon it outside, but it really is quite striking!' Pausing, she turned to her son. 'What is amiss, Will? For this looks suspiciously contrived.'

He laughed. 'As sharp as ever, Mama.' He took a breath. 'Nothing is amiss. Indeed, what I have to say will, I hope, be received was good news. Yesterday Miss Lennox and I…'

'Oh, my goodness!' Izzy clapped her hands, even as it dawned on Anna what she must be thinking. She stood helplessly in horror as Izzy clattered ahead with her customary lack of foresight. 'Are you to be *married*?'

Chapter Six

Izzy looked from Anna to the Earl and back again, delight apparent on her face. 'How wonderful! I—'

'No!' Will cut her off, then grimaced ruefully. 'I apologise, Your Highness. It might have seemed as though that was the announcement I was about to make.'

Anna was frozen to the spot, overcome by mortification. The way his mama was looking at her…and as for Izzy!

How could she?

The Earl was still speaking, and belatedly she returned her attention to what he was saying… 'She felt as though she half-recognised some of the parts of Lammermuir House.' He paused, looking at her expectantly.

She took a breath. 'Lord Garvald has now confirmed that a lady called Mrs Lennox lived here for five years. And she had triplet daughters.' Her words dropped into the silence like stones in a well. The impact was deep, resonant, and shocking.

'What—here?'

'This is where we lived?'

Izzy was quick to make the connection. 'Then you are Milady, Mama's dear friend!'

'I am,' said Lady Garvald tremulously. 'I missed her dreadfully when she went away.'

'Wait,' Rose said thoughtfully. 'So are you the boy who was our friend?'

He grinned. 'You called me ZanZan.'

He used exactly those words last night.

A shiver of something tremendously powerful washed over Anna at his statement. His words had immediately proved to her who he was, for no one else could have known their childish name for their friend.

'ZanZan! Oh, my goodness!' Izzy enveloped him in a brief hug, then turned to his mother. 'Milady!'

Lady Garvald opened her arms, and Izzy embraced her. Rose and Anna did the same, Anna feeling in that moment a strong connection not just to Milady and her son, but also Mama. Rose also hugged Will, but Anna did not even move towards him. Well, how could she, when it was clear her moment of revelation with him had already passed? And, besides, much as she wished to embrace him, something within her did not want an audience—particularly after Izzy's recent, mortifying assumption.

'This is astonishing!' Izzy eyed Will. 'When did you realise, my lord?'

'When the Queen's major-domo announced the three Misses Lennox at your presentation and you walked towards her, as alike as peas in a pod! *And*—' he emphasised '—I danced with each of you that day, and not one of you recognised me!'

Rose's hand flew to her mouth. 'How dreadful! I apologise, my lord!'

He waved this away. 'Call me Will. Or ZanZan, if you prefer.' He gave a rueful laugh. 'Realising there must be some reason for it, I said nothing, but immediately wrote to my mother, who was, naturally, delighted.'

'All season he has been keeping me apprised of your progress, my dears,' said Lady Garvald. 'As well as details you revealed of your life in Elgin, as the *ton* came to know of them. I heard of your tremendous success in society—the Queen called you her "diamonds" at your presentation, and I can understand why. My dear friend Maria would be so, so proud of you!'

'You are too kind!' Izzy took her hand. 'But I am so happy

to see you again after all these years. I remember little of this place, but I remember it as a happy time.'

'Yes.' Anna's voice was little more than a croak, so she coughed briefly before continuing. 'I recall this was a place of love and of safety. We were happy here.'

Lady Garvald gave a look that was half-glad, half-sorrowful. 'Your mother was happy here too—until that day when she was suddenly *unhappy*, and agitated, and declaring she must go. Nothing I said could persuade her to stay.'

'But why? Did she say why?'

'Not enough for me to fully understand, no. I was hoping you might be able to enlighten me. Did she ever explain it to you?'

'No. But she told us bedtime stories of this place, and both of you.' Anna swallowed. 'She wanted us to remember you both with fondness.'

'And did you?' Will was looking at her directly, and the yearning in his eyes sent a feeling of weakness through her. 'Did you remember us with fondness?'

'Oh, yes!' Izzy replied fiercely. 'In her stories, Mama described us all as princesses, and you the young prince.'

'And now you have married a prince and become a princess in real life!'

Izzy giggled. 'I know. Astonishing, is it not? As astonishing as finding Milady and ZanZan after all these years.'

Anna was still holding on to a previous thread. 'What reason did Mama give you for wanting to leave, Milady?'

Lady Garvald took a breath. 'That she and her girls—you three—would be in danger if she stayed.'

Exactly as Mama had hinted to them. On the occasion of Rose's marriage, Mr Marnoch, their dear guardian, had shared a letter from their mother with them—a letter containing words of love and sorrow. A letter which Anna nearly knew by heart, for she had painstakingly copied it from Rose's original, and had read it dozens of times. In the letter, Mama had said:

There were people who wished us harm...

And:

*The old danger had returned, and so I had no choice but
to flee again.*

There had been no further details as to who the people were,
or what form the harm might take, but clearly Mama had judged
it to be clear and imminent enough that she had been forced
to leave the sanctuary of Lammermuir House and begin a new
life with her children, cutting all ties to her dear friend Lady
Garvald.

Anna's sisters were clamouring to know more. What had she
meant? What danger? What had made her leave?

Lady Garvald looked thoughtful. 'I had been planning a
house party, much like the one I am hosting now. It was to be
the first party I had hosted since my husband's death, as I worry
dreadfully about such matters. Maria had gently encouraged
me to host small soirées with the neighbours, so I had decided
to be brave, inviting some of the leading members of the *ton*.

'I had thought to surprise Maria with the details, assuming
she would be excited to be receiving *ton* visitors. I showed her
my list of guest names and she immediately went pale. She then
looked at me—I shall never forget her stricken expression—
and said she had to leave.

'And she did, the day before the guests were due to arrive.
During the two weeks in between, she would tell me nothing
of her motives, nor where she was going. Indeed, I believe she
did not know where she was going, for she had lived here as
my companion for five years by then. My coachman brought
her—brought you all—to the staging inn at Haddington, but
I knew not whether she would travel north to Edinburgh or
south to England.'

'How curious!'

Danger! Anna's stomach felt a little sick. There it was again.
What troubles had poor Mama faced? To what lengths had she
gone to keep herself and her daughters safe? And why?

Lady Garvald's eyes were distant, as she recalled her friend's
words from long ago. 'I remember she said to me, "I hope to re-

turn one day. Or perhaps my daughters shall. I have left something of myself here and I hope that it will endure"…'

'Poor Mama! To have to run away not once but twice!' Rose had tears in her eyes.

'But running from what? Or whom?' Izzy's expression was fierce, as if she would avenge Mama's pain right then and there.

'We cannot know that now,' Anna offered with her usual practicality. 'What we do know is that this was our home for a time.' She turned to Will. 'Now that we have realised this, I should like another tour please. May we?'

'Absolutely.' He turned to bow to Izzy. 'Perhaps after you have rested after your journey, Your Highness?'

'Stuff!' declared Izzy inelegantly. 'As if I could rest now! Lead on, ZanZan!'

So once again Anna made her way through the house, which was distinctly castle-like in parts, this time accompanied by her sisters as well as Will, while Lady Garvald went to check on Lady Kelgrove's comfort.

ZanZan is Will. Will is ZanZan. There was something perfect about it—about finding her dearest friend again after so many years.

A notion struck her and she caught her breath. *That must be why I was so drawn to him in London!* Although her mind had not recognised him, something deep inside had known him.

Not a *tendre*, then. Good, for that made more sense. Why would she have developed a *tendre* for a gentleman so reserved? In reality her feelings for him had been present from the moment she'd met him again in London, for he was her dearest childhood friend. And she was far too practical to daydream and indulge nonsensical notions.

The Earl's reserve, too, had been explained. ZanZan's speech impediment as a child had affected Will's demeanour in social situations in adulthood. It made perfect sense. And there was something about the fact he had told her about it—something moving, and precious.

She stole a glance at him. His face was relaxed, his expression open as he laughed with Izzy about her ongoing expressions of shock, surprise and delight. Something inside her warmed at the sight. *He can be open and easy with us, for we are his childhood friends.*

On they went, Rose and Izzy exclaiming at half-memories in key places. 'These cattle look decidedly familiar,' Rose mused, standing in front of the bucolic painting in the library. 'Although I may well be putting notions in my own mind.'

Anna's heart skipped. 'I thought that painting seemed familiar, too! That one, and another—the one in your study, my lord.'

'Will.'

She tutted at herself. 'Will.' Although she knew it, somehow her mind was still slowly accepting that Lord Garvald was ZanZan and that their previous connection gave her the right to use his given name. Warmth ran through her at the thought, and she shook her head. 'It still seems so strange.'

He grinned. 'Strange, but delightful.'

She smiled back. 'Agreed.' A moment later, she realised that there had been a silence, and that her sisters were exchanging a glance.

What?

'Shall we go there next?' she babbled, suddenly unsure. 'I should like to know if my sisters are drawn to the other painting.'

On they went, and by the time they had reached the Earl's private study she had managed to regain control of her mortification. Her sisters—themselves both recently married and strongly enamoured of their husbands—were seeing things that were simply not there. Yet to speak to them of it might make it seem more real, for they could pretend that it was she who was raising the issue and possibility.

She frowned, remembering confessing to Izzy a few weeks ago that she had something of a *tendre* for Garvald. Perhaps she should say something, for Izzy might not otherwise understand that it was not a *tendre* after all but something entirely different.

'Here she is!' Will indicated the Gainsborough above the fireplace. 'My grandmother.'

'She is beautiful!' Izzy's eyes searched the painting.

'And formidable,' added Rose. 'I am not certain... There is something about it...'

'The dog! I'm sure I remember that little dog!' Izzy remarked, eyes shining. 'How wonderful!'

'Really?' Anna's heart skipped in hope. 'Then, like the rural scene, perhaps we do remember these somehow.' She took a breath. 'There is somewhere else—a place that I have recognised with certainty.' She looked at Will. 'May we go to the nursery next?'

He assented, and as they made their way to the narrow doorway leading to the staircase Anna could feel excitement build within her. Even if Izzy and Rose failed to recognise the room, she had, and besides there was no real need to search for proof, as they now knew for certain they had been born here in Lammermuir House. Still, when they entered the room, she took in the familiar scene with a quick glance, her gaze flicking to the wooden beams overhead. Just days ago the beams at the inn had reminded her of this very room.

She need not have worried about her sisters' memory. 'Oh, my goodness! This was my bed!' Izzy marched straight to one.

'Yes! And this one was mine!' Rose pointed to the bed to the left of the fireplace. 'Mama used to sit in an armchair just there at bedtime. We said our prayers and sometimes she would tell us stories.'

'Yes!'

'And our clothes were kept in that cupboard.'

'And we had books! They were kept in there.' Marching across to a corner, Izzy opened the door of a small cupboard, then shrieked with excitement. 'Look!'

She held up a dusty tome which Anna recognised straight away. '*Tales of Mother Goose!* Oh, Lord, I remember!'

'*Little Red Riding Hood!*' Rose added, her voice trembling. 'And the one about the glass slipper!'

The gates containing the emotions within Anna abruptly gave way, and she found that she was crying and smiling all at once. With perfect timing her sisters too were overcome, and they gathered together in an embrace, heads touching and arms around one another, while Will stood to the side, grinning with joy.

After hugging and making use of their handkerchiefs, the

sisters returned to the book, exclaiming at the illustrations and the stories within.

Will, who had been silent throughout, now commented to say that he remembered clearly Mrs Lennox reading the stories to them. 'I used to sit on the small carpet before the fireplace.'

'Yes!' As he said the words, the memory came clearly to Anna—Will listening intently, his dark hair and serious expression as he sat by Mama's chair. 'I can picture you in my mind.'

'This is…this is wonderful.' Rose's voice trembled. 'I cannot tell you how happy I am to find this house again—the place that was our first home.'

'You are welcome here any time. Lammermuir House will always, in some way, be your home.' Will's voice was gruff, and Anna's throat tightened at the emotion in it.

'Thank you.'

They lingered then, sharing memories and hearing Will's stories of their time with him. Every word was vital, and Anna focused intently, feeling as though she were an incomplete painting slowly being coloured with wholeness.

Chapter Seven

Eventually they left the nursery, Izzy clutching the dusty book tightly to her chest. The servants informed them that Lady Kelgrove was taking tea with Lady Garvald in her chamber, so they all made their way there, including Will.

When their great-grandmother heard what they had to say she was all astonishment and delight. 'So this—' she sent Lady Garvald a piercing look '—is why you have convened this house party. To meet the triplets again.'

'It is—and it is not only that.' Lady Garvald again told the story of Mama's abrupt decision to leave and Lady Garvald's assumption that it had had something to do with an earlier house party, sixteen years before.

'I wondered if bringing the same people back together might help us all unravel the mystery.'

'Hmm…' Lady Kelgrove's brow was furrowed. 'Her grandfather and I were among your guests, but it would make me sad to think Maria saw herself as being in *danger* from our discovering her.' She sighed. 'My husband could be…difficult. Family pride was everything to him. But I like to think if he had found Maria again—alive and well, with three beautiful daughters—he would have forgiven her for running away. Although, he had put it about she had died, so perhaps…'

Her gaze swung to the triplets. 'I am glad for you, my dears. I have no doubt you were safe and happy here, and how wonderful that Lady Garvald realised who you are!'

'It was not especially difficult,' Lady Garvald offered dryly. 'Triplets, surname Lennox, exactly the right age... My son realised straight away at their presentation.'

'Of course he did.' Lady Kelgrove sent Will a sharp glance. 'Yet you said nothing.'

'They did not recognise me and I wished to proceed with caution.'

Lady Kelgrove gave a nod of agreement. 'That was sensible, given what we now know—scant as the information is. Bringing everyone here—a place full of your own loyal servants, a place that is well-known to you—was entirely fitting.'

Anna felt the hairs on her arms stand to attention. Lady Kelgrove was not suggesting there was present danger to them, was she?

No, I must be imagining it.

'No doubt you girls will be ranging all over the house, seeking memories. But you must not inconvenience Lady Garvald!'

Anna was now smiling inside. Lady Kelgrove was acting as though they were eleven, not one-and-twenty. But it was heartwarming to have a family member to chastise one, after so many years when they had only had each other.

'I honestly do not mind, my lady. The girls are welcome to treat Lammermuir House as their home, for once it *was* truly their home.' She sighed. 'I had a great fondness for them, and for Maria.'

'Did she ever speak of the girls' father?'

'Yes, but not in a way that I might work out who he was. He was a gentleman, that I know, and he died just before she arrived here.'

Anna exchanged glances with Izzy and Rose.

A gentleman! Not a servant, then. So why...?

'I had suspected it.' Lady Kelgrove's eyes held a faraway look. 'I even suspect I know his name. But the young gentleman in question was perfectly eligible. So why did she run away from home?'

Lady Kelgrove's words speared through Anna. *She knows who our papa is!*

Lady Garvald shrugged. 'Something to do with his trustees.'

'Was he under-age?'

'Yes.'

'Hmm.' She pursed her lips. 'As I thought.'

'They married in Scotland, Maria said.' Lady Garvald frowned. 'Indeed, I vaguely recall her suggesting they had wed somewhere near here.'

'So they were properly married.' Lady Kelgrove grew thoughtful. 'That may be significant. No proof, of course.'

Izzy was clearly unable to contain herself any longer. 'Who is our papa?'

Lady Kelgrove sent her a look that was half-sympathy, half-mischief. 'I shall tell you of my suspicions soon, I promise. You must be patient, child. You have waited twenty-one years. You are perfectly capable of waiting a little longer, for there are matters I must confirm.' She frowned. 'One cannot simply make allegations without some modicum of proof.' She rose briskly. 'You must all leave me now, for I have some urgent letters to write.'

Having been summarily dismissed they departed, exchanging wry glances at Lady Kelgrove's autocratic demeanour.

'She is such a forceful character,' Rose mused. 'I wonder if that is where Mama got her strength from?'

'Not just your mother,' Will murmured. 'You all have it. By the time you are in your eighties, I have no doubt the *ton* will be in awe of all three of you!'

Izzy tossed her head. 'People often recognise that I am strong. It takes perception to see the strength in my quieter sisters.'

He eyed her steadily. 'We all knew each other as children. Perhaps there is something in that.' His gaze moved to Rose and Anna. 'When you all left, my mother and I were like vines whose tree had blown down in a storm. We had each other, but missed you all dreadfully.' He pressed his lips together. 'It took time, but I re-grew myself.'

A pang of pain went through Anna as she tried again to imagine how bereft he must have been. 'I am sorry, Will. We still had a sense of family, since there were four of us. You and your mother had only each other.' The words seemed inadequate, and she had said them before to him. Still, it was all she had.

He shrugged. 'I took no permanent harm.'

Anna was not sure she agreed with this but, while she was trying to think of a response, he continued.

'What of Lady Kelgrove's assertion she knows the name of your father?'

'Yes!' Izzy's eyes were ablaze. 'We shall soon know of him!'

'She said she *suspects* it, Izzy.' Anna's tone urged caution. 'She did not say she knows for certain.'

'But Milady's account seemed to match her suspicions entirely.' Izzy ticked each element off on her fingers. 'A gentleman, under-age, eligible...by which we must assume her family would have eventually supported a match.'

'So perhaps it was *his* family who did not approve.'

'Maybe.' They all stood for a moment, realising they lacked the information with which to consider or guess further.

'We shall simply have to wait,' said Anna, knowing it fell to her to contain the speculation.

'Oh, Anna!' Izzy's brow was creased. 'Why must you always be so *practical*? This is one of the most exciting days of our lives, and all you can tell us is that we must wait! Well, you know how dreadfully poor I am at waiting!'

Anna touched her arm. 'I know, love, and, believe me, I am just as excited—and just as frustrated—as you are. I too wish we did not have to wait.'

'Lady Kelgrove has some plan in mind—that much is obvious.' Will's deep voice was reassuring, yet Anna's innards responded to it just as they had all year—with butterflies and a racing heart. Clearly her body had yet to catch up with the news that he was *not*, after all, simply a handsome eligible gentleman for whom one might develop a *tendre*. Instead he was her dear childhood friend, and the connection she shared with him was because of that, nothing more.

It was important that she not let her feelings and notions run away with her, for he too would see her as a friend. Just because she was surrounded by newlyweds should not encourage her to allow herself to be overcome by sentiment.

They discussed Lady Kelgrove's cryptic comments for a moment more, then parted on the landing—Rose and Izzy to find their husbands and share the news, Lady Garvald going in search of her housekeeper.

Anna and Will, left standing together, walked to the front door by unspoken agreement, and from there to the gardens to talk, speculate and wonder together about recent events. Anna even told him about the incident between Mr Thaxby and his valet—a tale that left Will frowning.

He glowers to great effect, she thought, laughter bubbling up inside her.

But his words sobered her. 'A man who abuses his servant is no gentleman. The valet had no choice but to take his chastisement—even though his master was quite clearly in the wrong.' He frowned. 'I would never have invited them—it is only because they and the Rentons were to be part of the original list.'

'The one that made my mother take us and run away...'

'Yes.' They were silent for a moment.

'Might they be something to do with our father?'

'Or the danger?'

She nodded. 'Or both?'

'And what of the Rentons? Lord Renton is a good man, and sensible. His lady is outspoken and rather single-minded, but I cannot imagine any harm in her. I could, however, imagine her threatening to cut off a young man who wished to marry someone not meeting the lady's approval. She would be of a similar age to your mama, I expect.'

'Had Lord Renton a brother, perhaps? A brother considered too young for marriage? But Lady Renton would not have been able to prevent a marriage, surely?'Anna shuddered. 'Family connections are everything to Lady Renton. Why, as you know she objected to her daughter marrying Mr Phillips, who is one of the kindest, smartest gentlemen I know.'

He sent her a quizzical glance. 'So you find kindness and intelligence to be important qualities in a gentleman.'

'Does not everyone?'

He shook his head. 'There are some who would have mentioned Mr Phillips's connections and fortune first.'

'Sadly, I believe you are correct.' She sent him a sideways glance. 'And what of young ladies? What are their important attributes, do you think?'

'As what? As a friend? A bride?'

Something within her almost choked at his choice of words, but she managed to respond. 'Is there a difference then? Or are there some attributes a young lady must aspire to irrespective of the relationship?'

He considered this for a moment. 'The core qualities apply to both gentlemen and ladies—kindness and discernment being chief among them. But I suppose most men would seek something *more* in a bride that would certainly not be present in a friend.'

'Something more? Is friendship not then enough of a basis for marriage?'

'Some marriages undoubtedly are built on a firm friendship—and are all the better for it. But many of the current generation have a notion for…for *love*.'

The word hung in the air between them, and Anna's heart was now pounding.

'My sisters,' Anna offered, speaking firmly for fear of an unbecoming tremble in her voice, 'Have both married for love. And I believe they will be happy.'

'Agreed. Prince Claudio and the viscount are both lucky, I think.'

The hairs on the back of Anna's neck were standing to attention.

What…what is he saying?

Laughing lightly, she offered, 'Rose will always be pleasant and even-tempered, that is for certain. Prince Claudio, though, will soon discover that our Izzy has strong opinions on many matters, and it is difficult to steer her from her course once she has fixed on something. But she adores him, so they will do very well together.'

He gave a bark of laughter. 'Oh, you may be certain that Claudio knew *exactly* who Izzy is when he married her. Indeed, I believe it is the reason why he married her.' He thought for a moment. 'Knowing one's spouse is rather important, do you not think?'

'Undoubtedly.'

'And, of course, you and I...'

'My lord!' A young page was hurrying towards them.

'Yes?' Will's tone was a little brusque, as though he had not welcomed the interruption. 'What is it?'

The page bowed. 'Her ladyship requires your presence, sir. In the drawing room.'

'Very well.' He offered Anna his arm. 'Shall we?'

She assented and they walked together in perfect harmony, making their way to the drawing room to have tea with the Thaxbys and Rentons—whom Anna had almost forgotten were here, in the excitement of the last two hours. No one mentioned the rediscovered connections—it was all too new, and they needed time to understand it. With some difficulty, Anna managed to quell her inner agitation, and by the time her sisters and their husbands joined the party she felt perfectly calm inside.

Having enjoyed a brief hack earlier with the other gentlemen, it seemed her brothers-in-law had been playing billiards together. The raillery between them—which Will now joined with wit and enthusiasm—warmed Anna's heart, for Claudio had only recently befriended the other two gentlemen.

They are alike in so many ways, mused Anna now, glancing from one to the other. Good men, with handsome faces, lively minds and kind hearts.

Her mind went back to her conversation with Will.

My sisters have married well.

She did not finish the thought, for something about it was unsettling, and soon afterwards the party dispersed to dress for dinner.

Chapter Eight

Dinner itself was uneventful. Sir Walter and his son attended once again, and tonight Anna found herself seated between Prince Claudio and Sir Walter, so was able to enjoy perfectly cordial conversation with her food.

When the gentlemen came to join the ladies in the drawing room, young Mr Ashman made directly for her, pulling up a chair next to hers and engaging her in light, pleasant chat. Mr Thaxby brought her a drink—he often served the ladies in this way, even in London, despite the fact that there were always footmen aplenty ready to provide wine or ratafia on request. Privately, Anna had frequently wondered if it was because Mrs Thaxby was excessively fond of wine but did not like to single herself out by requesting a refill very often.

'It is a delight to see you again, Miss Lennox.'

Smiling politely, she thanked Mr Ashman, a little concerned that his attentions were particularly towards her. In the general hubbub of conversation there was no need for concern that others may read anything into his attentions, surely? While he spoke in detail about the new book he had lately received from Hatchard's, she subtly glanced about...

She froze. Will was glaring at her—at them! But why? Nothing untoward was occurring, and Mr Ashman must be perfectly amiable since Lady Garvald had invited his father and him to dinner for the second time. Perhaps she had imagined it, for as their eyes met briefly Will's expression became masked, then he bent his head to listen to whatever Mr Thaxby was currently saying to him. Her eyes went to Thaxby, sporting a familiar maroon jacket, and she swallowed.

'Do you not think?'

'Oh, undoubtedly,' she offered, hoping it would suffice.

'I knew you would agree, Miss Lennox! I shall make the arrangements with Lady Garvald, then, and we will enjoy a delightful excursion!'

An excursion? *To where?* Naturally, she could not now ask. Lord, what had she agreed to? She was not normally so scatter-brained.

From across the room, Lady Kelgrove hailed her. 'Annabelle! Please play for us.'

'Of course!' With a polite smile of farewell to Mr Ashman, she made her way to the piano, thinking about what she would play. As her fingers touched the keys, she knew. Here was a piece she knew by heart—one of Mr Mozart's beautiful, mellow piano sonatas. Mama used to play it on the dilapidated little piano they had had in their cottage, and Anna had practised and practised it after Mama's death until her fingers knew it by instinct. Closing her eyes, she lost herself in the notes, feeling as though she were bringing Mama back into the room with them.

The music soared and softened, and she felt every emotion, every need: Mama's struggles; she and her sisters, orphaned too soon; Lady Kelgrove, who had spent years alone, believing she was the last of her family; Will and his mother, who had grieved when they had gone.

Her heart sore, she now played with hope. Love was here, and people reunited. This place was her first home, and her soul felt it. As the last notes died away, she allowed herself to return to the present and opened her eyes.

There was a silence. Bewildered, Anna looked around her. Will's gaze was fixed on her, his throat working with emotion. She swallowed, breaking his gaze. Both her sisters, as well as Lady Garvald, were making use of their handkerchiefs, while

Lady Kelgrove was gripping the arms of her chair so tightly that the knuckles were showing white.

'Brava!' Lord Renton applauded, supported with enthusiasm by Sir Walter and his son, and with politeness by Lady Renton and the Thaxbys. 'A virtuoso performance, Miss Lennox!'

Anna, still shaken by the feeling that Mama had been right beside her as she played, could only manage a tremulous 'Thank you,' before making for the nearest empty seat, next to Lady Kelgrove.

'Your mother loved that piece.' Lady Kelgrove spoke softly.

Lady Garvald managed a sad smile. 'She often played it here as well—and on that very piano.'

'What is this?' Lady Renton's tone was sharp. 'Maria Berkeley visited here?'

'More than that,' replied Lady Garvald calmly. 'She and her girls lived here for a number of years.'

'Indeed?' Lady Renton's gaze jumped from one to another, presumably in an attempt to assess who had been privy to the information. 'How interesting! I knew her a little. Did you know her, Mrs Thaxby?' Her eyes gleamed as she threw what sounded like a challenge to her rival.

'I did not. At least... I believe I met her on only a few occasions.'

'You must have known her, Mrs Thaxby, for she had a season. But perhaps you did not then move in those circles?'

'I always moved in those circles, being a Fletcher!' Mrs Thaxby, her lips white, continued in a calmer tone, 'I knew Maria's brother, Mr Richard Berkeley, who was then heir to the barony. He and my brother George were great friends.'

Lady Renton, clearly undeterred, continued. 'You must tell me more, Lady Kelgrove. I remember your Maria was a *sweet* girl!' Lady Renton's attention was engaged, for she leaned forward with an interested air. 'But how did your granddaughter come to be living here, in the middle of nowhere?'

Anna flinched at the implied insult to Lady Garvald, her son and the entire Scottish nation, before another notion struck her. A sweet girl? If Maria's love had been a member of the Renton household, and the young Lady Renton had wished to prevent a marriage, there was no sign of it in her honeyed tones. Unless—and this was entirely possible—Lady Renton was extremely accomplished at pretence and dissimulation.

'No.' All eyes swung back to Lady Kelgrove. 'Tonight I wish to speak not of Maria, but her brother—my grandson, Richard, whom Mrs Thaxby referred to just now.' Her voice trembled a little. 'He always loved that piece when Maria played it.' Sitting straighter, her tone now became brisk. 'Your uncle, my dears, was as promising a young man as ever lived. He died very young, you know.' She paused. 'Murdered.'

Something strange was happening, Anna noted. While most people's expressions signalled shock, Mrs Thaxby's bearing had gone rigid, her eyes glassy, almost frozen. *What on earth...?*

'Is that not correct, Mrs Thaxby?' Like a hawk swooping on its prey, Lady Kelgrove's tone and words were directed with arrow-like precision at Mrs Thaxby.

As Anna watched, fascinated, the woman mastered control of herself. With a sad sigh, she nodded. 'Indeed, Lady Kelgrove. A *dreadful* tragedy. Dreadful.'

'And your brother was involved, was he not?'

Now Mrs Thaxby's brow was furrowed. 'Involved? I am unsure of your meaning, my lady.'

'He was there that night, I understand, on the Heath. When the brigands attacked your coach.'

'My coach? I was not there!'

'How clumsy of me! I meant to say, your *family* coach, with its rather distinctive crest. The Fletcher crest.'

'Well, yes. Richard and my brother George were great friends, as you will recall. They were going to a card party at Kenwood...' She made use of her handkerchief and, as if on cue, Mr Thaxby crossed to sit with her, taking her hand with a sorrowful sigh.

'If only they had dined with us that night,' he said, shaking his head slowly, 'Instead of insisting on travelling out to Hampstead.'

'So you knew of their intentions? They had spoken beforehand of this card party?'

'I do not recall exactly...' His face took on a sorrowful mien.

'But Mr Berkeley died that night, and George was seriously injured by those thieves.'

'They even murdered the coachman and groom, did they not?'

At Mrs Thaxby's nod, Lady Kelgrove leaned forward. 'Did you not think that strange?'

'I... What are you saying?'

'Robbers do not normally *murder* their victims—particularly not when those victims are gentlemen of consequence, riding in a crested coach. The risks would not be worth it. Nor do they typically murder the servants. The coachman's weapon was still in its place, indicating they were taken by surprise. Indeed, George said so afterwards.' She shook her head. 'I have ruminated over it many times over the years. It simply makes no sense.' Her gaze swivelled to Mr Thaxby. 'Did you not wonder at it, Mr Thaxby?'

'Well, I...that is to say... I had not thought of the possible significance. I...'

'We were grieving, Lady Kelgrove!' Mrs Thaxby's look held something of triumph, mixed with relief. 'We could not even think clearly at the time. Our poor, dear George had been left for dead and took many months to recover.'

Lady Kelgrove nodded regally. 'This I know. Some of his recovery took place at my country home, where as I recall he felt happy and safe.'

The hairs were standing to attention on the back of Anna's neck as a preposterous notion formed within her mind. Instinctively her eyes sought Will's. His look was steady, and she understood she should not give voice to any suspicions just now. She dared not look at her sisters. Besides, Lady Kelgrove seemed to be managing the situation masterfully. It did not occur to her to notice that, once again, she and Will had communicated without words.

Mrs Thaxby, whose jaw had dropped at Lady Kelgrove's last words, now brought a hand to her forehead. 'I declare I am feeling decidedly unwell! These memories are awakening old wounds.'

'My dear!' Mr Thaxby was all solicitousness. 'I shall take you to your chamber immediately.' Helping his spouse to rise, he bowed to the assembly, then slowly walked his lady to the door.

The door closed behind them and Lady Kelgrove nodded.

'Exeunt stage left!' she murmured, but with an air of satisfaction. 'Mrs Thaxby,' she announced with a casual air, 'Was several years older than her brother George. Indeed, she and her husband were trustees for his fortune until he could come of age, along with a very elderly lawyer. Of course, George Fletcher died just before he reached his majority. And, since he died unmarried and childless, his fortune went to his sister and her husband.'

Anna's mind was working furiously. *Trustees... Fortune... Murder... The Kelgrove country estate...* And something else: *danger.*

'But let us speak no more of this!' Lady Kelgrove's tone was firm. 'Anna, play something lively and light-hearted, if you please!'

With some initial difficulty, Anna complied. By the time she had played two more pieces, and various members of the party had performed a song, the Thaxbys' presence was no more than a ghost among the assembly. Later, after tea had been served, Anna and her sisters managed a brief conversation about Lady Kelgrove's comments.

'Was George Fletcher our father?' Izzy, naturally, went straight to the point.

'That was my thought too.' Rose's expression was full of wonder. 'I recall Lady Kelgrove telling me how Mama and Richard and George were great friends, and that George spent every summer at Kelgrove Manor. She also said that Mama nursed him through his recuperation after Richard died.'

'After Richard was *murdered*,' Izzy clarified. 'And Lady Kelgrove seemed to be suggesting—'

'Hush!' Anna glanced about. 'People may hear you. Let us speak of this another time.'

Satisfied they were aligned in their thinking, Anna returned to her seat, where Mr Ashman proceeded to regale her with tales of his university days. He was an entertaining companion, and made her laugh more than once. Thankfully, he then made reference to his suggested excursion in a way that gave her clear information. They were to travel out to a place called Gifford, two days hence, and would walk through some woods to see a ruined castle.

At length he and his father departed while there was still light in the sky, and Anna was gratified by his making a point of kissing her hand—a gesture which he did not perform for anyone else. While she would not wish to give Mr Ashman the wrong impression, she did like him, and had been grateful for his entertaining company in helping dissipate the uneasiness following Lady Kelgrove's probing questions. Should she ever marry, perhaps someone like Mr Ashman... But, no; something within her rejected the notion. Besides, despite her sisters' recent nuptials, she was in no hurry to marry. There were more important matters to be resolved first.

The remaining young gentlemen, including Will, made for the billiards room soon after, and no sooner had the doors closed behind them than Izzy rose, beckoning her sisters. 'Excuse me,' she announced to the remaining assembly, 'But my sisters and I must go. There is something I wish to show them.'

Ignoring the speculative look in Lady Renton's eye, and the disapproval—or was it concern?—in Lady Kelgrove's, Izzy took them by the hand and ushered them out of the door.

'Quickly!' This was Izzy at her most excited.

What on earth...?

'Where are we going?'

'To ZanZan's study. I've just had the most tremendous notion!'

Allowing herself to be propelled along, Anna was almost breathless when they reached the room. Sunset lent the view outside a rosy glow, and the room itself was twilight-dim. Izzy had snatched a branch of candles from the hallway as they entered, and now she thrust them aloft, illuminating the painting above the fireplace.

'What is it, Izzy?' Her eyes searched the Gainsborough, Zan-Zan's grandmother's eyes seeming to be dark and mysterious tonight in the half-light.

'What colour is her dress?' Izzy demanded, her voice tight with excitement.

Rose was frowning. 'Blue. Why?'

The hairs on Anna's arms were suddenly alive, and standing to attention. *'Blue!* And look, her right foot is peeping out from under her skirts.'

'Oh, my goodness!' Rose's hand flew to her mouth. 'She points her shoe!'

'"The Lady Blue she points her shoe…".' Izzy was all excitement. 'I do not know why it suddenly came to me. Something to do with this place, and Mother Goose, and Lady Kelgrove's probing. Can Mama have been thinking of this painting when she made up the rhyme?'

'Yes! It is obvious now!' Anna's heart was pounding. 'I felt close to her earlier, when I was playing piano. This just adds to it. I feel like we are finding her all over again.'

'But do you not see? There is a message in it!'

'In what? The rhyme?' Even as she spoke, distant memories were coming to her, including those triggered by wooden beams in an inn. '"The treasure fine is yours and mine…".She often spoke of hidden treasure, but always in an oblique manner. Can it really be a message?'

'She always said how clever we were, and how she knew we were skilled at solving riddles. Do you recall at Christmastide she often made up little rhymes and riddles that led us to sweetmeats hidden somewhere in the cottage or the garden?'

'Yes! And *The Lady Blue* is very similar to those, now that I think of it!' Rose's eyes were shining. 'But what treasure?'

'We know she was not wealthy…' began Anna, thinking it through, 'And she often talked about our little family being her most precious treasures… Perhaps a letter, like the one she left with Mr Marnoch for us?'

'That would be wonderful—but we must not dare to hope!'

'First,' Anna asserted, trying to focus on logic, 'We must solve the riddle—if indeed it is a riddle. Then we will know the form of the treasure.' She frowned. '"The Lady Blue she points her shoe…".It seems clear now that Mama refers to this painting. Next is, "You find the line to find the kine".'

'*Kine* is cattle. Are there cattle in the background?' Izzy held the candles higher but, disappointingly, the countryside visible to the left in the painting showed only fields and sky—a few birds the only living creatures outside.

'Points!' Rose indicated the delicate satin slipper emerging from beneath the wide skirts of ZanZan's grandmother. 'She *points* her shoe!' Whirling round, she assessed the invisible line created from the angle of the shoe. It led directly to the window opposite. 'She is pointing outside!'

As one, they rushed to the window. Below was the rose garden. '"Find the line to find the kine",' breathed Rose. 'Finding the line from the pointed shoe leads...' She looked back at the painting, then outside again, carefully assessing the angle. 'It leads *there*!'

Chapter Nine

'What is that exactly?' asked Izzy, as they peered at the object at the end of the path, following the line of Rose's pointing finger.

'It's the statue of Poseidon,' said Anna. 'But what has that to do with cattle?'

There was a silence. 'Let us go down. We shall have to inspect Poseidon. Mama will have left us another hint; I know it!'

Anna sighed. 'Should we not wait until morning? No, do not give me that look! But it is nearly dark, and we... Oh, very well!'

A few moments later they were hurrying through Lady Garvald's precious rose garden, Poseidon and his trident looming above them as they reached the end of the path.

'What's the next line? "The key is three..."'

'No.' Anna interrupted Izzy's enthusiasm. 'We know how Mama's riddles worked. We cannot move on to the next until we have fully solved this one. We must find the *kine*—the cattle—first.'

'She is right, you know,' Rose agreed, bending down to peer more closely at the plinth. 'We dare not think about the numbers until we know we have found the cattle.' Straightening, she made a frustrated sound. 'Nothing. No engravings or letters.'

'None that we can see, leastways,' said Izzy. 'Too dark for such a detailed search.'

Resisting the urge to say *I told you so*, instead Anna offered in a conciliatory tone, 'It was worth a try. Let us meet in the morning before breakfast and search again.'

All in agreement, they turned…to see a trio of handsome young gentlemen standing at one of the large windows, laughing fondly at them.

'The three husbands!' said Izzy, blowing a kiss to the prince.

'Er—no.' Anna spoke flatly. 'Two husbands and a friend.'

'At present that is the case. But who is to say what may happen in future?' She and Rose exchanged a sly glance. 'It would be perfect if you and Will—'

'Stop right there!' Turning to face them, Anna put her hands on her hips. 'Such foolishness is not to be tolerated—and especially when we have just learned that Will—that the Earl—is our dear friend ZanZan!' She took especial care to emphasise the word 'friend'.

Her sisters, however, were having none of it. 'What has that to do with anything?' Rose's expression was one of genuine puzzlement. 'Will is our friend, yes, but he is also a man. A man who is not a relation, and so is perfectly eligible!'

'Exactly!' Eyes blazing, Izzy put a hand to her heart. 'Oh, it would be just *perfect* if you married him, for he and Claudio are becoming fast friends.'

'And of course James and Will are already bosom bows!' Rose cast Izzy a sideways glance before continuing. 'Naturally, we would not wish you to marry where your heart is not engaged, but it seems to us that you and Will are ideally suited.'

'And so you told me yourself!' Izzy asserted triumphantly.

'I did not!' Anna retorted hotly.

'Well not, perhaps, in so many words. But I clearly recall a day a few weeks ago when we were walking in Green Park and you confessed to feeling a *tendre* for him!'

I knew she would mention that!

Anna waved it away. '*Pfft!* That is nothing. A maiden is perfectly entitled to feel a passing fancy for any good-looking young man and then change her mind if she chooses.' She tossed her head. 'And I do so choose!' Deep within, she sensed fear—fear of believing them. Of daring to hope, then finding such hopes crushed.

Izzy laughed. 'Some maidens may, yes, but you are *Anna*—always cool-headed, always sensible! For any man to capture your fancy he must indeed be special.'

Anna rolled her eyes. 'Logic was never your strong point, Izzy. Have you not thought that there may be another explanation for that *tendre?*"

'Another...? What on earth do you mean, Anna?'

'Yes, speak plainly.' Rose added her urgings to Izzy's.

'Simply this.' She ticked off the points on her fingers. 'First, my memories of our childhood have always been stronger than yours. Agreed?'

They nodded.

'Second, my...*curiosity*...about Will goes right back to the day we first met him at our presentation to the Queen. There was something about him, *something* that made me look at him more, or focus on him more, than anyone else. That *something* was clearly that I remembered him, not that I felt...*feelings* for him. Why, I did not even know him!'

Her sense of triumph was short-lived. Making an exasperated sound, she asked, 'Why the knowing smiles?'

'You were drawn to him.'

'You *looked* at him more.'

'But no, I—'

'You were beginning to love him, even then.' Rose's gaze grew distant. 'It was the same for me, when I was beginning to love James. My heart fluttered and my mind raced every time he was near.'

'And I thought of Claudio constantly, even when he was not present.'

Anna's eyes widened. Some of what her sisters described was disturbingly close to her own experience. *Lord, I hope they are wrong, for I do not wish my heart to be broken. To love is to be vulnerable...*

'In fact,' Rose concluded firmly, 'I loved James even when he vexed me.'

'And I loved Claudio even though I despaired at his hedonistic lifestyle. So, you see, it is all a hum. For you to have a *tendre* for Will is entirely perfect, as we said.'

'But he is just a friend to me!'

The words came out with more vehemence and volume than Anna intended, but at least it had an effect. There was a brief moment of shocked silence during which Anna had the satisfaction of seeing both her sisters' jaws drop, even if she wondered briefly if she had just told an untruth—to herself, as well as them. It was an unwelcome thought, so she swiftly banished it.

'Just a friend? But...'

'Well, naturally that is how *we* see him, but *you*... A friend...' Izzy looked decidedly crestfallen. 'Oh, dear.'

'What? What "oh, dear"?'

'Well, he may not see you as simply a friend.' Rose's tone was tentative. 'And so he may be disappointed—hurt, even. I would not like him to be hurt.'

A pang went through Anna at the thought of Will suffering any hurt from any source, alongside wild hope. But there was nothing—*nothing*—to suggest that Will saw her as anything other than a friend. Why, he did not even offer her gallantries, such as Mr Ashman did! Yes, he had kissed her hand after bringing her to her bedchamber on the magical night when she had found the nursery. But that meant nothing, for they both had been overwhelmed by her discovery. Will was reserved and unreadable, but he was also her own dear ZanZan. Surely she, who knew ZanZan so well, would be able to tell if Will liked her in a particular way?

No. It cannot be.

She shook her head. 'I am certain of it. So you need not be concerned that he will take any hurt from me. Now, let us go inside, for it is becoming chilly!'

Head held high, she led the way, almost *hearing* the dubious looks being exchanged by her sisters behind her back and conveniently ignoring the fact that the late summer air was anything but chilly.

* * *

Next morning after breakfast the sisters reassembled in the rose garden, this time accompanied by the three gentlemen—the two husbands and a friend. Anna had awoken determined to stop thinking too much about complex matters over which she had no control, and which made her feel decidedly confused. She did not like to feel confused, and had always valued her own mind over what some people might fancifully describe as their 'gut'. No, logic and order ruled the day.

And Anna's mind was busy with the puzzle of *The Lady Blue*. It was her own rhyme, and she therefore felt under an obligation to solve the riddle of it—regardless of whether there was treasure at the end. Feeling connected to Mama again was treasure enough.

Izzy had made the first discovery, and together they had followed the invisible line from the direction indicated by the lady's satin slipper. Today's task was to solve line two—the elusive cattle. The home farm was not near, and Will had said that cattle would never have been near the house. He remained rather mystified about what was causing the three sisters to babble so incoherently on their way outside, so as Izzy and Rose forged ahead with their husbands it was left to Anna to explain.

'Mama always wrote riddles for us, leading to little surprises like sweetmeats—especially at Christmastide. There is a rhyme that we used to sing, and we know she devised it. We now believe it is a riddle based on this place.' She gestured about her. 'That is why Izzy was asking if cattle were ever allowed near the rose garden. We believe the statue of Poseidon is the first sign, and we are seeking the second, which is something to do with cattle.'

'How intriguing! So what is the part of the riddle related to the statue?'

'It says,"You find the line to find the kine".' She laughed lightly. 'Perhaps it sounds foolish to you, but for us it is an unexpected opportunity to solve one last puzzle set by her.'

'Not foolish in the least! And, remember, your mama was important to me too.' Their eyes caught and held for a breathless moment, making Anna's heart pound in her chest. What if her sisters were correct and he too…?

His forehead creased. 'But what makes you certain the statue is the correct starting point?'

They had reached the statue. Just then, Izzy asked, 'Will, has this statue always been here? Might it have been moved since Mama's time?'

Her words struck Anna with the force of a thunderclap, making her gasp. 'Will! Where was your grandmother's portrait hung before you had it moved?'

'Excuse me?'

'You said you had it moved. From where? Where was it during our time here?'

His eyes widened. 'The library. On the right-hand side. Nothing else has been moved or changed in that room.'

'The library!' Anna spun to face her sisters. 'The room where we saw the painting of the cattle!'

Then they were off, skirts flying in their wake, accompanied by the gentlemen. Anna's pulse was now racing for entirely different reasons. The portrait would originally have been hung opposite the rural scene. It had to be the solution to the second line.

Breathless, they raced to the library, making directly for the idyllic painting showing a herd of highland cattle grazing contentedly amid trees and ruins. A craggy mountain was visible in the background, and a river to the left. There was nothing unusual about the painting, and the gilt frame looked entirely usual.

'I *knew* there was something about this!' declared Rose. 'I just knew it!'

Anna's eyes, having searched the scene, were now looking at the space held by the painting. It was in a plaster cartouche with bookshelves either side, above and below. Inwardly, she was murmuring the last two lines of Mama's riddle.

The key is three and three times three.
The treasure fine is yours and mine.

Whatever the treasure was, they were so close she could almost *feel* it!

Chapter Ten

Three cows grazed in the foreground of the painting. *Three.* Was that significant? The artist's signature was visible on the bottom right. Noris or Norie—not anyone Anna had heard of. There were three lines of books below it and two above. *Three again.*

Gilt numbers were on the shelves. Desperately, her eyes scanned them. 'Three and three times three...' Three and nine... twelve. She gasped, pointing a shaking finger. The digits one and two were clearly visible on the shelf above the painting.

Rose had also worked it out. 'Twelve!' Her voice was shaking.

'The key is three and three times three. Yes!' Izzy's eyes were shining. Stretching, she tried to reach the shelf, then dropped her arm in frustration. 'Mama was not very tall, I think. How did she reach up there?'

'Perhaps I can assist.' Will made for the corner, returning with a set of three steps on tiny metal wheels which he manoeuvred into position.

Three steps. Did that mean anything? *Lord, I am seeing threes everywhere.*

And yet, it was fitting. As triplets, the number three had been their lodestone throughout life.

With a flourish, Will gave way to Anna. He offered a hand

to steady her, and she took it, noticing his warmth and the tingle that went through her at his touch—a connection based on friendship, not a *tendre*, she reminded herself.

With a deep but ragged breath she mounted the steps to explore the section marked with a twelve. Running a hand along the books, she eyed the titles. Gibbon's *The History of the Decline and Fall of the Roman Empire*—in six volumes. Ovid's *Metamorphoses*. Sheridan's *Rivals*... Nothing stood out. She did not even know what she was looking for.

Very well. This would have to be done with method. 'I shall pass you down each book in order. Search it for hidden documents. Be sure to keep the sequence, just in case it is significant.'

Starting at the left, she pulled out the first book—something by Goethe. Eyeing it briefly, she passed it to Will, who in turn gave it to Claudio. Rose, James and Izzy clustered around the large library table, opening the book and searching through it. While tempted to pause and await the results of their search, Anna persisted, knowing logically that would use their time most effectively. Next were volumes by Rousseau, Kant, then Adam Smith, all clustered together by author. Now the section with Gibbon, Ovid and Virgil. *Nothing*. A good deal of the shelf was now empty, with nothing concealed behind. Refusing to be daunted, Anna continued, until it became too far to reach safely.

'Let me move the steps,' Will offered, and Izzy then pounced, announcing it was now her turn to search.

Half an hour later, they had to admit defeat. Having removed all of the books from the section and searched within for hidden notes or letters, they had been sorely disappointed. They had found nothing more than dust, a recipe for arrowroot sauce and a folded note which had initially caused them to exclaim in hope, but which had proved to be nothing more interesting than a list of places taken from the book *Travels through France and Italy* by someone named Tobias Smollett.

'I do not understand it!' complained Izzy, stamping a little foot in frustration as they carefully replaced each book in order, 'It should not be this difficult! It never was in Elgin.'

'Elgin,' offered Rose thoughtfully, 'Was our apprenticeship.

We learned the craft of solving riddles at Mama's knee, but perhaps all the while she was teaching us to master the skill as children so we might decipher the most difficult of riddles if the opportunity came our way as adults.'

Izzy sniffed. 'It is not that difficult. I found "the Lady Blue" and, if she had still been where she was supposed to be, the kine are obvious.'

Will grinned. 'I apologise for moving my grandmother's portrait and almost spoiling the riddle. But do not be disheartened. I have no doubt you—we—shall solve this before long.' He frowned. 'There is a hidden door here. Might that be of significance?'

Smiling at their gasps, he crossed to the fireplace, turning a small wooden handle that had been almost invisible against the shelf. Anna gasped as the entire section opened, revealing another room behind it. 'But I knew this! I vaguely remember it.'

Will grinned. 'You and I often hid in here when we did not wish to be bothered by Izzy and Rose.' He bowed. 'Apologies, ladies.'

'But this is astonishing!' declared Izzy, waving away his apology. 'So clever! May we go inside?'

In they trooped, to exclaim and explore. Unfortunately, the room held nothing more than more books, a small table and a hard chair. 'We believe this was our priest hole, back in the day,' Will shared. 'It may also have served to hide some Scots from the Duke of Cumberland's men.'

'Jacobites!' James laughed. 'I would never have taken you for a rebel, Will.'

'Would you not?' Will answered mildly, and Anna stifled a smile.

Returning to the library, they considered the gilt numbers painted on each section of shelves.

'My grandfather apparently had a desire to systemise and organise his library,' Will explained. 'He intended to keep an index of all his books, organised by category and author, hence the numbers on the shelves. It came to nought, though, as he had underestimated the time necessary to complete such a task.'

Anna studied the numbering. The top section was numbered

from one to twenty in sequence. The middle and lower sections however were punctuated by the door, fireplace and various works of art, so the numbers beneath did not line up mathematically. The neatness and accessibility sought by Will's grandfather did not even extend to the appearance of the numbering, never mind their purpose. Perhaps Mama's plans would be similarly doomed.

'I wonder how Mama thought we might come to be here?' Anna mused. 'She went to great lengths to keep us hidden, it seems to me.' It was only the fact that they had gone to London and mixed with the *ton* that had led them to discoveries—first, Lady Kelgrove and now, ZanZan and Lammermuir House.

'I suspect,' pondered James, 'She worried about you being discovered through some misadventure and hoped that if your identities did become known you would find your way to this place, where you have friends.'

'I think you might be right,' Rose replied, her voice thick with emotion. Anna, too, had a lump in her throat. All these years they had had no notion of the lengths to which Mama had gone for their sake to protect them.

'Right!' declared Claudio briskly, perhaps intervening before his own wife became caught up in the poignancy of the moment. 'Are we continuing with our plans for this morning?'

'Riding lessons?' Anna shuddered. 'Not for me, thank you. I intend to stay here and continue to search the library. But you all may go ahead without me.'

This set off a clamour of debate, which only ended when Will said that he would stay to keep Anna company, while Izzy and Rose would venture out to the stables to what was promised to be a gentle introduction to the art of horse-riding, involving only the quietest of mares.

'Are you frightened of horses?' The door had finally closed behind them, leaving behind a quietness which was causing an unexpected reaction within Anna. Why was her heart suddenly pounding so? And why was she abruptly unable to think?

He was still looking at her, awaiting her answer. Not for him, then, a heart-pounding realisation they were now alone together.

See? He clearly sees me as a friend. It is only my own fool-ish notions that say otherwise.

Conscious of a stab of disappointment, Anna shook herself enough to respond to his question. 'Yes, they terrify me. I do not know why.'

He nodded thoughtfully. 'I believe I know why.'

She caught her breath. 'What? I do not understand.'

His eyes held sympathy and a hint of humour. 'You might say, once I have told you, that it is my fault.' Now the humour brimmed over. 'So perhaps I should not tell you!'

The playfulness in his expression was reflected in his tone. Playful—the taciturn Earl of Garvald? Briefly, she recalled his typical demeanour in the ballrooms and drawing rooms of London, before tilting her head at him. The soul of a rebel hidden beneath an urbane exterior? Perhaps.

'Well, you must tell me now. You cannot tease me so cruelly!'

Sighing dramatically, he took her hand and led her to a settee covered in cherry-coloured satin. 'Very well. Just before you left here, when you were five and I was eight, I let you ride my gelding. You had only ever ridden ponies until then, and you were extremely accomplished.'

'Was I?' The notion was unsettling, contradicting as it did all her beliefs about her relationship with members of the equine family. He had retained her hand, and she allowed it, hoping he would not notice and take it away. He seemed entirely distracted by his tale, and his expression now grew serious.

He nodded. 'You had your very own pony. He was called Tumblethumb.'

She stilled as memories flooded through her. 'Tumblethumb. Lord, how could I have forgotten him? He was so beautiful, and I loved him so much!' Her eyes were now stinging and her throat tight with emotion. *More loss.*

'He is dead, of course.' It was not a question. Tumblethumb had been an elderly pony when she had ridden him sixteen years ago and more. Each new and wonderful discovery she made seemed to be tinged with sadness. Mixed emotions coursed through her—happy memories of her beloved pony, and the knowledge she would never see him again.

Will nodded. 'But he had children and grandchildren. You shall meet them later.'

'Thank you.' Her voice cracked.

With a muffled exclamation, he opened his arms and she went into his embrace gratefully. As her tears flowed he procured a handkerchief from somewhere and passed it to her, and she gave way to the sorrow running through her. This place, Mama's music, the riddle…and now Tumblethumb.

She had adored her pony, and had shed many tears for his sake after they had left. Later, she must somehow have built a wall around those memories to keep them from hurting her. Yet the loss of her beloved pony had stayed with her, unrecognised, all this time.

It is too much. I am only one girl. I cannot endure it!

His arms were soothing, his hands pressed lightly on her back and his heart beating loudly beneath her cheek.

'Thank you,' she mumbled against his coat, suddenly realising she was in the embrace of a man! Will might have comforted her when they were children in this way, but…

'We are not children any more.' Had she really just said that aloud? Their eyes met.

'No.' His voice was tight. 'We are not.' His face was impossibly close. It would take only the slightest of movements for her to press her lips to his. The impulse to do so throbbed within her. It was more than an impulse, it was desire. It was *need*. It was terrifying.

But a lifetime of good sense could not be ignored. Reason asserted itself, and she shuffled away from him, breaking eye contact and dabbing at her cheeks with her handkerchief. 'What you must think of me! I am not normally such a watering pot, I assure you.'

'What I think of you? Only good things, I assure you.' His voice was deep and low, and set her insides trembling.

'You are too kind. But I know that gentlemen do not like it when ladies…' She faltered, for he had raised a quizzical eyebrow. 'When ladies are…'

'Are what? Do pray continue, Anna. I should like to know

what you have divined about all gentlemen, based on your worldly experience.'

She shook her head, managing a tremulous smile. 'You are right, of course. What can I possibly know of such matters? But it is a widely held belief among *ton* ladies that *ton* gentlemen find displays of emotion unseemly.'

Her tone was light, following his lead. Inwardly she was telling herself to be calm. Between remembering the loss of her beloved pony and the unexpected and unlooked-for desire running through her, it was difficult to regain her equilibrium.

Now he shrugged. 'Some men, perhaps.' He thought for a moment. 'But authentic emotion, such as true grief, could never be belittled.'

She swallowed. 'He was a dun bay, Tumblethumb.'

'Yes. A Highland pony, sturdy and gentle.'

Now it was her turn to raise an eyebrow. 'And your gelding?'

'Not so much. But you were determined you wished to ride him, and so I agreed.' He grimaced. 'To my later regret.'

Vague hints of memory were beginning to surface in her mind. 'What happened?'

'All was going well. We were in a clearing in the woods beyond the rose garden. I mounted you on him, and you walked him beautifully in a gentle circle.'

'And then?'

'Something spooked him. A bird in the undergrowth, I think. He reared and you were deposited on the ground. You had been riding astride, and unfortunately your skirts got caught in the stirrup as you fell.'

She gasped. 'I remember! He panicked and ran, dragging me behind him!'

Will nodded grimly. 'Thankfully I had him attached to a leading rope, which I quickly wrapped around a branch before he took off. I knew it was my only chance to stop him, for I would not have had the strength. He did not get far, thank the Lord!'

'Was I injured?' She frowned. 'I seem to remember a lot of blood.'

He closed his eyes for a moment. 'A head wound. It bled profusely, scaring the life out of me. Turned out to be quite small, but at the time all I could see was your face covered in blood.' He shuddered. 'I can see it yet, in my mind's eye. I thought you were going to die.'

He opened his eyes again and Anna saw there pain—pain, sorrow and grief. Like her, he was reopening old wounds, long buried. It had all happened a long, long time ago, yet only now were they able to speak of it.

'I did not die, but then I went away.'

'Yes.' A muscle twitched in his cheek, and Anna realised his jaw was tight. 'The day of your injury, I recall begging you not to die. The day you left, I could say nothing, for it had all been decided already.'

Reaching out, she took his hand. 'I am so sorry, Will. And so glad to have found you again.'

'I, too.' The silence this time was fraught with emotion as well as desire.

Here is where I am supposed to be. Here is my home. The notions flooded through Anna with a sense of rightness.

'Your mother loved it here. She must have had good reason for going away.'

Anna frowned, thinking again of Lady Kelgrove's exchange with the Thaxbys. 'That much is certain. But nothing can be proven, nothing is certain. That is why it is so important we solve this riddle. We must hope that Mama left us more information.'

'Indeed.' He turned his head to look at the painting and she drank in the strength and perfection of his profile before following his gaze. 'Might your mother have hidden something behind the painting itself?'

'Of course! What a great suggestion!'

As one, they made for the painting. Will gently tilted the bottom corner towards him, peering behind. 'I cannot see properly. I shall take it down.'

This he did, carefully loosening the wire from its sturdy nail and laying the large painting directly onto the thick carpet. Judging by the effort evident in his demeanour, the painting in its frame weighed a considerable amount. Kneeling, he then raised it from the top, allowing Anna to crouch down and peer behind it.

'Something is written there!' She made a frustrated sound. 'I cannot make it out.'

'One moment. I shall endeavour to turn the whole thing over.'

Once he had done so they both knelt to read the script etched onto the backing board.

Landscape with Highland Cattle
James Norie 1730

Anna's heart sank.

'I am sorry, Anna.' His eyes held such sympathy it was almost her undoing. Determined not to cry again, she sought refuge in nonchalance. 'We cannot force this.' She managed a smile. 'Now, how are we to restore the cattle to their rightful place?'

He rose, offering a hand to assist her. She took it gratefully, as ever wondering why his touch affected her so.

'I have no intention of even attempting it. I think it will require at least two footmen to raise it to the right height and attach it by its wire. You and I may safely leave it here.' Walking across the room, he rang the bell for the servants.

Anna's mind had returned to her pony, and the incident with Will's horse that had clearly affected her for years. 'Perhaps we should go to the stables after all. Oh, not to ride! I am not ready for that. But I think I must be brave and simply walk among the horses today, in honour of my dear Tumblethumb.'

His eyes blazed with what looked suspiciously like admiration. 'That's my Anna,' he said softly, sending a delicious shiver through her. 'I shall be at your side in every instant. You may rely on me.'

'Thank you.' Now warmth flooded her chest—the warmth of an emotion she was not ready to name. Together, they left the library side by side.

Chapter Eleven

Will was as good as his word, gently guiding Anna through the stable block and out to the paddock. Her heart pounded with fear as the enormous horses moved around her, but she endured, keeping a hand on Will's arm at all times. Knowing that she'd once been a promising rider helped, as did the knowledge of the single incident that had brought terror to her heart.

'I believe,' she mused, 'That, if I had had the opportunity to keep riding after that day, I might have overcome my fear.'

'I do not doubt it,' Will replied, giving her *that* look again—the one that made her feel as though she was special in some way. It made her strong inside, as though she could accomplish anything. Mama had used to make her feel like that, she recalled, and now Will.

'The best thing to do after a fall is keep riding.' He gave a rueful grimace. 'Because of your wound, I took you straight to the house to be tended to, otherwise I would probably have put you straight onto your pony—not my gelding, who would have still been agitated. As it was, our mamas banned you from riding until your wound healed, and by that stage it was time for you all to go.' He shook his head. 'We all knew you were to leave. I recall a sense of confusion from you, and helplessness from me. Neither of us could change it. I was only eight, after all.'

'And I was five. I probably had no real notion what leaving even meant.'

Their eyes met, and once again Anna felt that sense of deep connection to him. Inside this handsome—so handsome!—kind, and thoughtful man, was her dear friend ZanZan. The boy had become a handsome man and she a grown woman, and the feelings swirling inside her were much more complicated than simple friendship.

She was all confusion, and her mind kept circling back to her sisters' insinuation that there could be something between them. For her part, she could admit he was fast becoming something of an obsession with her, but once again her logical mind asserted itself. It had been only a couple of days since her discovery that this had been her childhood home, and that the Earl of Garvald was ZanZan. Naturally, her mind had focused on it. Reason dictated that she hold fast, avoid dramatic assumptions and conclusions and simply wait for the maelstrom of emotion within her to settle. Only then would she have a clear head and would be better able to understand what was happening to her.

He brought her to the ponies then, and she delighted in meeting Tumblethumb's offspring. Although they moved unpredictably around the paddock, they were small enough for her to enjoy the encounter without giving way to fear. She walked beside them, stroked their smooth necks and gave them treats which Will had procured from the kitchen while she had been donning her half-boots.

Afterwards she was in alt, a mix of relief and a sense of accomplishment which she tried to articulate to Will.

'I understand entirely!' he told her. 'And I am proud of you.'

The warmth that rushed through her at these words was like nothing she had ever experienced. Not many people in her life were close enough to claim pride in her actions—her sisters, her guardian, Lady Kelgrove and, now, Lord Garvald and his mother.

However, when he repeated the sentiment later to her sisters and their husbands, she felt only mortified. The men took it in good stead, offering her congratulations and a hope that she would catch up with Izzy and Rose, who by their husbands' account had done remarkably well today. Anna's sisters however exchanged a knowing look which made her momentarily want to pull their hair as she had when they were children. Instead she bunched her hands into fists and offered mild bashfulness, delivered, she hoped, in an unassuming manner.

'You are too kind. I walked through a stable and a paddock, that is all. Now,' she added briskly, 'We should find the other guests, for I fear we are neglecting our social duties.'

At this, Rose simply nodded, while Izzy blatantly rolled her eyes. Determined not to argue, Anna led the way to the drawing room. They were all there—Lady Kelgrove, the Rentons, the Thaxbys and Lady Garvald, who flashed them a look of relief or possibly gratitude when they arrived. Anna felt a pang of guilt. They had truly been neglecting Lady Garvald, who had been left to shepherd and manage the conversation of her more challenging guests for far too long.

The arrival of the three young couples enlivened the conversation, keeping the discourse light and cordial. Anna had no clue what had been discussed before their arrival, but hoped Lady Garvald could now be a little more comfortable.

Mrs Thaxby was in affable mood, with no sign of the distress she had displayed the night before. Was that because the distress had been feigned? Something within Anna felt rather sick at the notion that one could feign distress at the death of a sibling, yet that was the clear impression she had been left with. And was it possible that such an unlikeable character as Mrs Thaxby might be their aunt? Her gaze drifted to Lady Kelgrove, who was currently enjoying a conversation with Prince Claudio. The two seemed to get on particularly well.

Lady Kelgrove knew, or *suspected* she knew, what had happened to Richard, and if George was their father. But their indomitable great-grandmother would tell them what she knew or suspected only when it suited her to do so. Anna clamped down on inner frustration. The game-playing among the *ton* was wearying at times—although in this case it was more likely to be based on Lady Kelgrove's requirement for more proof.

Her mind drifted back to that day in February when Mr Marnoch had told them what he knew of their mother, and had set each of them a task to complete. Rose was to discover their mother's true name and identity, which they had now confirmed. Mama had been Maria Berkeley, granddaughter of Lady Kelgrove.

Izzy's task had been to find the name of their father—a task which was surely about to be completed.

Anna's own quest was in some ways the most challenging. She was to discover the circumstances behind Mama leaving their first home and going to Elgin—although how on earth she was meant to accomplish this she had had no idea. And yet… the story was slowly, gradually, coming to light. Lady Kelgrove knew some of it, and Lady Garvald too.

But they needed more information. That was why it was vital they solve the riddle and find whatever it was Mama had hidden for them. The one letter they had—the letter left with Mr Marnoch for them—had mentioned Lady Garvald with great affection, although not by name.

I hate to leave you now, but I know you are safe with Mr Marnoch—one of the kindest people I have ever known.

Others have been kind to us too, like the Lady we lived with for the first five years of your lives. You may not remember her, but I do, and I can assure you she is as good-hearted and as generous a person as I have ever encountered.

Anna resolved to tell their hostess of Mama's kind words as soon as the opportunity presented itself. But it was Mama's next words that she ruminated over constantly. Once again she repeated them in her mind.

It was hard to leave that place of safety, that haven, that sanctuary, but the old danger had returned, so I had no choice but to flee once again.

The inference was clear: the same danger that had caused Mama to run from her family and hide goodness knew where for the best part of a year before she'd gone to Lammermuir House had reappeared, forcing her to run away again. The Thaxbys were unlikeable, certainly, but were they truly capable of acts so heinous as to make poor Mama afraid for her safety and the safety of her daughters? They were received everywhere, and were surely no worse than tedious? Anna's brain could not take it in.

'What is vexing you?' Will came to sit with her, and she flashed him a smile. 'You are frowning and ruminating. I could sense it from across the room.'

'I was thinking of my mother and wondering about the danger she was running from.' Briefly, she told him about Mama's letter. He was interested, and asked clever questions. Worryingly, his conclusions matched Anna's.

'I do think it possible that the Thaxbys may be the source of that danger. Lady Kelgrove strongly hinted at it. Of course, your great-grandmother is full of guile, and she may well have been indirectly targeting the Rentons, while seeming to focus on the Thaxbys. Who knows? I would urge you to be wary of *all* of them, Anna. Do not confront them or ask questions, for we do not know what these people are capable of.'

He thought for a moment. 'Lady Kelgrove plays a dangerous game, I think.' He shook his head, as if to clear it of dark thoughts. 'Now, tell me, what else did your mother include in her letter? There may be riches not yet discovered there.'

'Oh!' A sudden notion had come to her, triggered by his question. 'There was something about our names. Let me think… yes. Mama said, "Your father loved me very much, as I loved him. There were people who wished him harm, so he sent me away for my own safety, for fear they would harm me too. I wish I could share with you my true name, and his, but I cannot assume you are safe, even now. My belles, my beautiful belles: Annabelle Georgina; Isobel Judith; Rosabella Hemera. By these names you will be known…".'

Saying Mama's words aloud was interesting, for the words were striking her in new ways.

His eyes widened. 'So much information in just a few lines!' He marked them on his fingers. 'First, she is telling you that Maria Lennox is not her true name. Second, that your father sent her away initially. And then I understand he died soon afterwards?'

Anna nodded. 'We believe he had already died when Mama came here.'

'And she arrived here the day you were born?'

'Yes. Lady Garvald took her in that day—Mama had already started her labour. Your mother is all generosity.'

He glanced towards her and Anna glowed at the warmth in his eyes.

There is love in him for his mother—another sign of a good man.

'She is that. They were well met, I think; two good souls. Now,' his tone became brisk, 'Back to your names. I understand why she called you her "belles", for there is Bel and Bella in there. But she also included your middle names. Have you ever wondered why?'

'I was just wondering about it now. And that phrase: "by these names you *will be* known". She might have said "you are known". The words "will be" sound significant. They must mean something, surely?'

'The eldest child in a family is traditionally named after their father, you know.'

She gaped. 'I did know, but I never thought to apply it to me. Georgina. *George.*'

He nodded. 'Yet more evidence that you may unfortunately be closely related to Mrs Thaxby.'

They exchanged a rueful glance, then returned to the puzzle. 'Judith; Hemera—a common name and an uncommon one.' Anna shrugged. 'I would wager they are linked to the Kelgroves or the Fletchers.'

'Let us check in Mr Debrett's book, then. I have a copy in the morning room.'

He indicated the archway at the side of the room, leading to the next chamber. It would be perfectly unexceptional to wander through into there for a few moments. They rose, making polite conversation as they passed the others, who remained engrossed in their own conversations. Once in the morning room, Will took a heavy tome from the bookcase and together they searched through it, quickly discovering that Maria's mother had been called Judith, while George Fletcher's Mama...

'Look! Anne Margaret Hemera Fletcher!'

They eyed one another, smiling at their joint discovery. 'And there it is.' Anna sighed. 'I am Mrs Thaxby's niece. It is practically certain.'

'I am sorry for your trouble.' There was a glint of humour in his eye.

She sent him a wry look, then frowned. 'We should say nothing about this for now in company. I shall tell my sisters and Lady Kelgrove, and you may wish to ensure your mother is fully apprised of everything.'

'I shall. And for now, it is probably better not to pursue it, as you say.' He sighed. 'Lady Kelgrove has some plan; I am certain of it. Let us hope it does not take too long to come off, for the waiting is frustrating for me. I cannot even imagine how it must feel for you!'

She sent him a grateful glance. 'Frustrating, yes, and exciting, and a little frightening, if I am honest. So much has happened since we arrived on Saturday. And it is only Tuesday!'

He laughed. 'Indeed. Who knows what the next three weeks will bring?'

They returned, he to converse with Lord Renton, Anna to find a seat by herself, allowing the conversations to wash over her. Three weeks; three more weeks of being in his company, in this place of her dreams. The two were entirely entwined in her mind and heart.

Three weeks of bliss. And then it would end.

Where would she go? Back to London? To Elgin, to see Mr Marnoch? Both her sisters had invited her to live with them—Rose and James at Ashbourne House, Izzy, Claudio and Lady Kelgrove in Kelgrove Manor. She had so many options. And yet, at moments like this, she felt unsure, confused and quite, quite alone.

Chapter Twelve

Yester Castle was little more than a ruin, aboveground at least, but the excursion was enjoyable nevertheless. Mr Ashman had made it his business to accompany her on the walk through the woods, enlivening the trek with entertaining stories and gallant compliments.

The party had set out after nuncheon, the carriages taking less than an hour to reach the end of the tracks. They had all descended then—Anna and her sisters, their husbands, Will and Mr Ashman. He and his father were staying for dinner again, and Sir Walter and Lady Garvald were currently leading the older members of the house party on a gentle stroll around the Lammermuir grounds, the Renton and Thaxby ladies having proclaimed that the trek to Yester sounded far too energetic. Mrs Thaxby had declared herself to be full of aches, but allowed herself to be persuaded to be part of the gentle excursion.

At Yester, the group paused by a pretty waterfall on Gifford Water, the silvery splash of the water contrasting prettily with the verdant canopy all around them. After that, the paths improved, and they were able to walk three abreast. The combinations changed frequently and, just as they reached the ruins, Anna found herself flanked by Will and Mr Ashman.

There was something a little uncomfortable in the air—she

could not quite say what, but perhaps it was that the gentlemen's comments to each other felt a little barbed. She shrugged. Mr Ashman was a local man, and presumably he and the Earl had known one another for a long time. Who was to say what history might lie between them? For her part, she continued to find Mr Ashman to be perfectly amiable.

'The architecture,' he was saying, 'Was so advanced for its day, that a rumour started locally that Sir Hugo de Gifford had entered into a pact with the devil.'

Her eyes widened. Chuckling, Will took up the tale. 'There is a vast underground hall at the bottom of yon staircase—' he indicated an archway to their left '—and they call it Goblin Ha'.'

'Goblins?'

'Yes.' Mr Ashman waggled his eyebrows theatrically. 'Or Hobgoblin Hall. The space is so vast and well-built for its time that they said no human hands could have constructed it. Ah! Here is my man.'

He walked across to a servant lugging a sack who had just arrived. It proved to contain torches and a tinder box, and before long each of the gentlemen bore a lit torch. Instantly, Prince Claudio feinted with it towards James, who grinned and mimed a counter thrust. At this, their wives rolled their eyes, Izzy murmuring something about men remaining boys for eternity. Play-acting done, they approached the arched entrance to the staircase. The darkness yawned below, maw-like and sinister. Anna shivered.

'You do not have to go down there, you know,' Will murmured to her.

'I know. But I should like to see it.'

'Very well. But take my arm, for the steps are uneven.'

As she did so, Mr Ashman turned from thanking his servant, and she saw his face fall. *Oh, dear!* The young man had gone to quite some effort to organise their excursion, and she wondered if perhaps he might have wished to show her the Goblin Ha' himself.

'Mr Ashman,' she said softly, 'Do please lead the way, for you know so much about this place.'

His face brightening, he moved in front, lifting his torch

aloft as he entered the darkness. Anna and Will followed, and she could hear the others following behind. Within a couple of steps it was clear they would be forced to descend in single file, so narrow was the staircase. With Mr Ashman's torch in front and Will's behind, Anna focused on each step, being careful not to slip on the well-worn stone steps.

'You may place your hand on my shoulder if you need to, Miss Lennox,' Mr Ashman murmured, and she gratefully did so, wondering at the fact that the warmth of his shoulder through his coat did not make her insides flutter, as they would have done had it been Will.

Then they were at the bottom and took a few steps inside the chamber. As the others arrived and the number of torches swelled to four, the hall became fairly well illuminated. Anna looked about her with interest at a vaulted ceiling, sturdy walls and some sort of alcove at the far end. It was a good hall, and an impressive feat of engineering, given it was underground. In its day it must have astounded all who saw it.

'What of the people who lived here?'

Will replied. 'The Gifford line eventually died out, and the castle and lands went to the Hay family, who were next in line through marriage. Both families were ever loyal to Scotland. They say the place was destroyed by Robert the Bruce as he retreated.'

'But why?' Rose asked.

'So it would not be of use to the advancing English.'

This set off some raillery between Garvald and his English friend, which Anna watched with a glad heart. Will was clearly a proud Scot, and she loved that about him.

Catching the direction of her own thoughts, she caught her breath.

Love? No.

Immediately, she reassured herself that there were many things she loved about many people: Izzy's energy; Lady Kelgrove's searing wit; Mr Ashman's earnestness. Well, perhaps not *loved*—not in the case of young Mr Ashman. She *liked* him, but not in the way she...

'Can we go? This place is eerie.' Rose's voice shook a little.

'Of course, my love. Follow me.' This time James led the way, with Izzy and her husband falling in behind Rose, leaving Anna and the two bachelors to take up the rear. Bachelors? Now why would she use that word? It was accurate, certainly, but did it need to be said, even in her head? She was also unmarried, and now had no need for a husband, as both her sisters had made stellar marriages. She would never know the pain of poverty or loneliness in old age, for she would always have the company of her sisters, their husbands and any children they might have. She was quite looking forward to being an aunt.

So why did she feel like sighing now?

The following days fell into something of a pattern. Anna would leave her bed early, write in her journal, then walk in the gardens before breakfast. Will, who was also an early riser, would usually join her, and together they would speak of everything and nothing. Anna had a sense of a single long, bright day when they had played together as children, and another now when they were spending time together as adults.

In between there was a dark night of things not known, and she was determined to fill it by discovering everything that Will had experienced after they had left. He seemed equally curious about her time in Elgin, so they spent hours together talking about their childhood and formative years—the people and places that were important to them. They also talked and debated—sometimes fiercely—about books, music, and politics, and it warmed Anna's heart to discover he had a well-formed mind, along with his good heart. Well, of course he would. He could not have differed so greatly from the child she had known.

On one of their excursions they had ventured into the woods a little, and had been surprised to find Mr Thaxby gathering plants.

'Good morning!' he had greeted them, closing his little sack of botanical samples. 'I had thought to be the only guest abroad so early.' His gaze darted left and right, and it struck Anna that his manner was often furtive, as though he did not like to be the focus of attention. In company, she realised now, his wife did most of the conversing on behalf of them both.

'Oh, we often walk before breakfast,' Will replied.

'Indeed?' Thaxby looked from one to the other, his eyes gleaming at this information, making Anna set her jaw. Why should they not walk early? There was nothing untoward about it. He bowed and left them, and Will turned to watch him go.

'He is a strange little man, is he not?'

Anna shuddered. 'I cannot like him, no matter how much I try. And it is not like me to dislike someone so completely.'

He sent her a warm glance, indicating the path ahead, and they walked on. 'This does not surprise me in the least—neither that you dislike him, nor that it is unusual for you to do so. What I cannot understand however is that you imply you have found something likeable about his wife. And Lady Renton, for that matter!'

She acknowledged this with a rueful grimace. 'Lady Renton and Mrs Thaxby are different in their vulgarity. One seems entirely oblivious, or uncaring, about the impact of her barbs. The other lies and dissembles without a qualm. The former is easier to forgive, for Lady Renton's malice is there in plain sight. Plus, Lady Renton's daughter, Lady Mary, is a darling, and so the mother cannot be all bad, I think.'

'I applaud your logic, and admire your generosity. But Mrs Thaxby…?'

'I know, I know. She thinks only of herself.'

'And money.'

'Yes, wealth, or the appearance of wealth, is everything to her, I think.'

'I suspect she would kill her own husband if paid to do so!' The humour in his eyes made it clear he was jesting, but a shudder went through her. 'Although I believe Mr Thaxby is devoted to her.' There was a brief pause. 'So what redeeming feature can you possibly see in her?' he continued quietly.

Anna thought it through. 'I believe that she is deeply unhappy. Pain radiates from her at times.'

He frowned. 'I have not sensed it. Do you recall the time Lady Kelgrove spoke of George and Richard? My impression was that she feigned emotion in order to leave the room.'

'I thought so too. But her brother died many years ago. Perhaps she has recovered from her grief. And you must admit, Lady Kelgrove was being extremely...'

'Pointed?'

'Yes, pointed. Her implication was shocking, and if false I have no doubt Mrs Thaxby's desire to escape was real. I also...'

'Yes?'

'I feel sorry for her. In London I have heard her speak about her regret at not having children. She was not feigning emotion on those occasions.'

He squeezed her hand. 'You have a kind heart, Anna. Much kinder than mine, for I can find no redeeming qualities in Mrs Thaxby, or her husband. Which reminds me—something curious occurred yesterday, and I should like to know what you make of it.'

She was all attention. 'Something to do with the Thaxbys?'

'Yes. Mr Thaxby's man...'

'John.'

'You know his name? Well, naturally you do, for you are keenly observant. I saw him conversing with Lady Kelgrove.'

Anna thought about this, but could come up with no logical reason why the two might interact. 'Was he assisting her with something? But, no, she is a stickler for etiquette. She would know that while your footmen are at her disposal the servant of another guest should never be approached.'

'Exactly.' He paused. 'I wondered if she was seeking information from him.'

'Information? What manner of information?'

'I know not. But I thought it interesting.' He opened his pocket watch to check the time. 'Shall we turn back?'

There were no answers, only riddles, it seemed. While Anna and Will always had plenty to speak about, she particularly enjoyed trying to unravel the mysteries with him. His mind was good, and they often reached the same conclusions at the same time.

She sighed. Everything else was a muddle. Her sisters were married and she herself was adrift, uncertain of her path. She could dwindle into an aunt, being known for ever as an aunt and sister... There was something different about 'sister' in that context. As the eldest, she was used to leading the others—helping Rose to focus and take action, holding Izzy back from occasional rashness. Now they looked firstly to their husbands, not to her. So where did that leave her? Who exactly was Miss Anna Lennox? Was she more than the sister of Princess Isobel and Lady Ashbourne?

Should she marry, she would gain the status of being a married lady, as well as having her own husband to lean on, to speak to, to hold… Mr Ashman would make someone a very fine husband, but not her. Sadly, Anna's attention was already entirely taken up by another gentleman—a gentleman who was also a dear friend, making it hard to know her own heart or read his.

When he looked at her in *that* way, did he see her as a possible wife, or only his friend? She dared not risk making assumptions. As with the mystery of her parents and the Thaxbys, it would not do to presume. No, she must assume nothing, for to do so in this case risked hurt—a deeper hurt, perhaps, than anything she had ever known.

Returning to the puzzle about Mama, her husband and the Thaxbys, Anna documented everything diligently in her journal, reading over her previous entries at the little desk in her room.

George Fletcher: everything centred around him; she was sure of it. He and Mama's brother Richard had been great friends, and he had spent his summers with the Kelgroves. Was that when he and Maria had come to love one another? Or had that happened following Richard's tragic death, when George had stayed at the Kelgrove country estate for some of his recuperation?

And what should she make of that decision? Had George not felt comfortable in his own home? Or had he simply wished to comfort Richard's family—and take comfort too, from his friend's home, where they had all spent happy times together? George's parents had died when he'd been young, she knew, and the Thaxbys were not warm people. Perhaps Lady Kelgrove had offered him more love than his own family? Anna knew her great-grandmother well enough by now to know that beneath her stiff, blunt demeanour there beat a warm heart.

Her mind moved on, returning to the puzzle involving Thax-by's valet. If John had been with the Thaxbys for a long time it was possible he had known George. Which therefore provided a logical explanation as to why Lady Kelgrove should seek the man out. And a breach of etiquette could be forgiven if the motivation was strong enough.

As to the other riddle, 'the Lady Blue' and the three times three, Anna had at first spent hours staring at the Norie painting, silently begging Mama to show her the answer, to no avail. So they had all agreed to leave it to the back of their minds, hoping that not forcing a solution might be more effective. For ten days now she had stayed away from it, but perhaps her eye would soon be fresh enough for another attempt.

After breakfast the younger members of the party—the triplets and the three young gentlemen—would take to the paddock or the field for riding lessons. Anna, fiercely determined to overcome her fears, was fast catching up with her sisters, and had even ridden a mare around the paddock yesterday. The achievement had delighted her, and of itself would have been enough to ensure that this house party would live long in her memory.

Yet it was the least of the joy she found here—more, the joy of being back in her childhood home, of getting to know Lady Garvald, of spending time with Will.

They were now more than halfway through their stay, and Anna had a sense of time slipping away from her. These were days never to be repeated: walking with Will in the mornings; riding lessons; occasional excursions to beauty spots or simply to visit the shops in Gifford or Haddington; evenings spent enjoying good food and wine, and enjoying the company. The Thaxbys and Rentons were tolerable, Sir Walter and his son were frequent visitors, and of course Will and his mother were a delight.

Anna had taken to spending time with Lady Garvald in the late mornings, when the men would ride out or play their first games of billiards after the daily riding lesson for the ladies. There was to be a full moon in a few days, so Lady Garvald had invited all the local gentry for a soirée.

'Not a ball,' she had assured them firmly, 'For the very notion terrifies me! But we shall have dancing, even if only a dozen couples stand up.'

Anna did not challenge her hostess on this, although privately she felt it would be a ball, if most of those invited decided to attend. There was much to be done, and Lady Garvald was grateful for Anna's assistance with lists, food orders and consultations with Cook, the butler and the housekeeper.

Caterers from Edinburgh who would bring their own footmen had been commissioned, and they would procure fresh fish from Granton and carefully packed elderflower ices from a trader on the Royal Mile on the day. Meanwhile the ballroom was getting a thorough cleaning, along with silverware and crockery. On the day itself, Lady Garvald would cut fresh roses from her garden, and Anna had promised to assist with arranging them.

'Anna, I declare you are a treasure!' Lady Garvald beamed. 'I entertain so infrequently that it is all something of a challenge for me, I must admit.' She grimaced. 'The notion has always filled me with dread.'

'And I have never before assisted with preparations for a soirée. We had a ball in London, but it was my sister Rose who assisted our hostess with the preparations. I declare it is diverting to be involved, and I thank you for including me.'

'Nonsense! Besides, it is a useful skill for any young lady to learn, and so your mother would have said.'

As they worked, Lady Garvald often shared memories of Mama and of the time when they had lived there. Anna had the impression of a strong bond between the two women, and said so.

'Oh, yes! We had much in common, of course, being young mothers and grieving for our husbands. But it was more than that. I believe we should have been firm friends regardless of how similar our situations were. Your mother helped me through some of the darkest times in my life, and I believe I performed the same service for her.' She sighed. 'Of course, I now regret not probing further as to the circumstances that had left her alone and fearful, but at the time I respected her wish not to speak of it.' She smiled. 'But now all is well, for you are returned, and you were always in some sense my daughters.'

She embraced Anna then, and Anna was astounded to find that, while she was naturally delighted that Lady Garvald saw them as her daughters, part of her did not want it at all.

But why?

Was her heart concerned that it might be disrespectful to Mama? But no, for the two ladies had raised their four children together during their years here. Anna had never forgotten the lady who had truly been like a second mother to her. But that would suggest Will was something of a brother. Her mind instantly rejected the notion. He had been a friend, yes; he still was. But she had never seen him as a brother figure, thank goodness. Always as a friend.

Her heart sank as she acknowledged the crux of the matter. Despite having made the assertion that she saw him *only* as a friend, she had slowly come to realise her view of him was entirely different from that of James and Claudio, her actual brothers by marriage, and both now the closest thing she had to male friends. Neither of those gentlemen had ever managed to stir her heart, or her body, in the way that Will did, and so effortlessly. He had only to enter a room for her heart to pound, and when he looked directly at her, or touched her hand, her insides either melted or became infused with pulsating energy.

No, not a friend. Not at all.

Yet he probably saw her as a friend. Apart from a few breathless moments, possibly fuelled by her own imagination, he had been unfailingly and frustratingly friendly towards her, his natural reserve easing in her company in ways more akin to a long-standing friend than a lover. Not that she had ever had a lover. But she saw how James and Claudio looked at their wives, with fire in their eyes. Will had never looked at her like that, not really.

So her sisters, knowing her as they did, had been partly right. They were right about *her*, but not him—and they had seen the truth before Anna was ready to admit it to herself.

She wanted more than friendship. She wanted everything. It had been there all along. She just had not *seen* it before.

Chapter Thirteen

Anna's head was spinning. How could she have been so blind? Why had it taken her so long to realise something so blatantly true that it thrummed through every nerve and sinew of her being? Thrummed through every heartbeat, every thought, every wish, every dream.

Her sisters were wrong about Will, though. He could not possibly view her the way she viewed him. Naturally, they could not read him as they could their own sister. They saw only the neatness of James's best friend—and now, Claudio's bosom bow—marrying the last remaining sister, the spinster.

She shook herself. Such thoughts were unhelpful. Had she not much for which to be grateful? Once more, she listed them in her head: her sisters and their husbands; her great-grandmother; Lady Garvald; Lammermuir House; Will.

He remained ZanZan, her childhood friend, with whom she had been raised for a time. ZanZan had been her best friend. Will did not need to be, for she had met him again only this year, at the age of one-and-twenty. And yet, her instincts told her the man did not love her, for his manner suggested friendly affection, not the passion of a lover.

Could she do anything to change it, to make him see her differently? She ruminated on this, then rejected the notion.

She had no skills in flirtation, no arts with which to attract a gentleman. Having seen young ladies flirt openly all season in London, she shuddered at the very notion. Besides, she could not do anything to risk their friendship. She had only just found him again. She did not wish to lose him.

Suppressing a sigh, she made for the drawing room. The gentlemen had developed the habit of riding out on more adventurous hacks in the afternoon, leaving Anna and her sisters in the company of Lady Garvald, Lady Renton and Mrs Thaxby. Anna now played her part in supporting Lady Garvald, diverting the conversation away from the other two ladies' relentless feud, ably assisted by Izzy and Rose.

Once again, she could not help but wonder why their pleasure had to be spoiled by two ladies who, it seemed, were determined to outdo one another in unpleasantness. There was much talk of Lady Garvald's soirée, the older ladies questioning their hostess on the names and lineage of all those invited to attend.

'And of course,' Lady Garvald concluded, 'Sir Walter and his son, whom you know well.'

'Indeed.' Lady Renton's gaze whipped around to Anna. 'No doubt the son will wish to stand up with you, Miss Lennox.'

'I…' Anna was unsure how to respond, for on the surface Lady Renton's observation was entirely reasonable. She seemed to hint at something more, though, beneath the obvious meaning.

'Mr Ashman will be pleased to dance with many of the young ladies attending,' Lady Garvald assured her firmly. 'For he is a sensible young man, and may be relied upon to not ignore anyone.'

'Humph,' was Lady Renton's response, but Anna sent Lady Garvald a grateful glance.

'They are returned!' Izzy's excited tone revealed that, as ever, being separated from her new husband for anything longer than an hour was a severe trial to her. Anna knew Rose was equally obsessed with her own handsome husband. Anna, having recently listened to her own heart, now understood her sisters as she had not before.

A few moments later the gentlemen entered, having divested

themselves of boots, coats and hats. Unable to help herself, her eyes sought out Will, seeking that thrill of delight that always rippled through her as their eyes met.

There he is! And there it was. Her heart was thumping so loudly she was sure he might hear it from across the room.

His eyes seemed to light up briefly, then he schooled his features into neutrality, greeting the assembly generally and bending to kiss his mother on the cheek. Meanwhile his two friends sat with their wives, while Lord Renton and Mr Thaxby chose a sofa together at quite some distance from their ladies.

'We were just speaking of the soirée tomorrow night,' Lady Renton informed the gentlemen. 'You must all be sure to do your duty by dancing with all of the ladies. All who wish to dance, that is. I myself shall sit it out.' Her air was of one who was expecting to experience *ennui* at an event that was clearly beneath her. Anna bit her lip, hurt on Lady Garvald's behalf.

'Of course!'

'Naturally!'

The gentlemen all agreed with alacrity, and Anna's heart skipped at the thought of dancing with Will. She had done so in London many times, and had always been aware that her heart behaved differently with him. But, now that she knew who he really was and what he meant to her, it would add another layer of wonder to the experience; she had no doubt of it. Yes, she knew his true identity, and more—she knew her own heart.

'Good morning, miss!' Sally entered Anna's bedchamber but, seeing her still seated at the desk, she stopped. 'Oh! Shall I go away again?'

'Not at all, for I am quite finished!' Anna smiled, placing her journal inside one of the many drawers in the pretty desk. 'I shall have a bath this morning, in preparation for the soirée tonight. For now, I need only a simple day dress for my usual walk in the gardens.'

'Yes, miss. And your blue silk is all ready for tonight. What jewellery should you like with it?'

Anna was in the pleasing situation of owning three pieces of jewellery, for the first time in her life. She had a string of tiny pearls from her great-grandmother, a silver cross on a chain from Rose and her husband and a pretty gold-and-amber necklace from Izzy and Claudio. 'The pearls, I think. They will go nicely with the blue gown.'

'Very well, miss. Now, may I quickly dress your hair? Nothing complicated, it is just...'

Anna laughed. 'Yes, you may. Am I so impatient to be outside that you must persuade me to not appear hoydenish?'

The maid blushed. 'Not at all, miss. It is just that since we came here you have been so animated...' She faltered. 'That is to say, I...'

Anna knew ladies could have no secrets from their maids, no matter how hard they tried. 'You may dress my hair, and thank you.' In truth, she *was* impatient. To begin every day by walking with Will was a joy. 'We shall have time for only a quick turn about the gardens this morning, I think.'

She said as much to Will when she met him in their usual spot, suppressing any temptation to behave differently towards him just because she...

'Today I cannot linger, Will, for I am promised to your mother. There is much to do!'

'Indeed! I too shall be busy, checking on both the menservants and the grooms.'

'How many horses do you expect?'

'Dozens! Too many to house in our stables, should it rain.' He glanced skyward. 'We may pray it remains as dry as this all day and night!'

They parted a little later in perfect harmony. Following breakfast and a quick bath, Anna made herself available to Lady Garvald, who gratefully gave her a list of tasks to complete. Dinner was planned for six, with the first of the guests expected to arrive by eight o'clock. Anna had thought she would have plenty of time to see to the matters on her list—including having her bath—but by four o'clock she had only just completed them. Lady Garvald was still in the rose garden accompanied by two of the gardeners, who were cutting the finest blooms to be displayed in large pots and vases throughout the public rooms.

'Oh, Anna, you are an angel! Did Cook find those other tureens?'

'She did, and the scullery maid is even now washing them. And Will has decided which wines are to be served, so I believe we are almost ready!'

'Thank goodness! Yes, those ones as well, please, and some of the yellow ones.' The gardeners set to, carefully cutting the long stems of the most beautiful blooms.

'These are perfect! Would you still like me to arrange them?'

'Oh, yes please, if you would. I have asked for the table in the library to be covered, so they can be done there.'

The library. A familiar tightness made itself known within her. They had not yet managed to solve Mama's riddle, a source of great frustration to her.

Almost twenty minutes later she made her way inside. The gardeners were bringing the flowers to the kitchen door, as was correct, and upstairs maids would be summoned to bring them to the library. Each had their role, and every one of them worked hard.

As she entered the hallway, Anna caught sight of Will, walking away from her.

'Will!'

Before she had even thought about it, she had called his name. The call had not come from her conscious mind. It had come from her heart, the core of herself. She *needed* to be in his company. Always.

He turned instantly and walked towards her, and she fumbled for an excuse. 'Er, do you happen to know if the footmen have brought the vases to the library?'

He took this at face value, seeming not to notice her consternation. Lord, why did she lose all sense of proportionality around him? Also, she should not have been shouting like a fishwife in the market. *What must he think of me?*

'I do not,' he said, 'But let us go there together and find out. Shall we?'

He offered his arm and she took it gratefully, her heart skipping as usual, but still feeling as though he should not be so kind to a hoyden. By the time they reached the library she was a little calmer, yet was glad to see the maids arriving at the same time with the many baskets of blooms. As per Lady Garvald's instructions, the large table had been covered with a thick cloth, and multiple pots and vases containing water had been placed there in readiness.

'What time is it?' she asked Will, assessing the work.

He checked his pocket watch. 'Twenty-past four.'

'I need to get these done by five o'clock, so I can dress for dinner.' She squared her shoulders. 'Very well.'

He was frowning. 'May I be of assistance? Or should we call upon the servants?'

'I actually want to do this myself, for your mother. She has been so kind to me...'

'In that case, I repeat my offer of assistance. Might I do anything to help you in your task?'

'Actually, yes. If you could strip the stems of any lower leaves and thorns, I would be eternally grateful.'

'Would you?' A gleam of humour lit his eye. Picking up a creamy-white rose, he began stripping it briskly. 'Now that is worth the effort, I think. And tell me...' he sent her a wicked glance '...what form will this gratitude take?'

Her jaw dropped. His tone, his words, even that look he had just sent her, all looked a little like flirtation! But, no, it could not be, surely?

He was awaiting a response. 'Oh, I shall have to think about it,' she responded lightly. 'Perhaps I could resist correcting you when you say something that is incorrect.'

'Incorrect?' He feigned outrage. 'Never!'

She laughed and began placing the stripped flowers into the first vessel. 'I think I shall make this one all white, since we have so many of those. Some of the other vases can have mixed colours, including these wonderful boughs.' At her request, the gardeners had provided leaf boughs of different types and lengths. 'Ouch!'

'What?' She pressed her hand to her mouth, and he took it. 'Pierced by a thorn?'

She nodded, mesmerised by the sight of his close study of her fingers. There was a small drop of blood forming on the pad of her forefinger, and as she stood immobile he took it into his mouth, sucking it. She caught her breath. She could feel his teeth against the sensitive pad of her finger, and the pressure of his warm lips as he sucked the tiny drop away.

'There!' he declared in a matter-of-fact way, just as though nothing of note had happened. 'All better! But be careful—there are thorns everywhere.'

'I... Yes,' she managed, bending her head to her task. But her pulse was pounding loudly in her ears, her mouth was dry and her insides were caught up in a sensation so sweet it took her breath away. She dared not look at him, for fear he would see her, see what was going on within her.

Heat. Need. Desire.

This, then, was what her sisters shared with their husbands. Never had she experienced anything like it.

On they worked, in a silence that felt different from their usual companionable pauses. Eventually they spoke again— just small comments about their task, he commenting on the wide range of colours, she asking him to prepare a few pink roses for the next vase. Occasionally, she felt him looking at her, but she would not—*could* not—return his gaze, for she was all confusion.

By the time she was adding the last few stems to the last vase, she felt calm enough to ask him the time and to look at him in a natural way as she did so. 'It lacks nine minutes to five,' he answered. 'We managed it!'

His grin was infectious, with no sign of any hidden layers to it, and she smiled back at him with ease. Behind him was the painting of the cattle.

Nine. Three times three.

Her gaze dropped to the gilt number below the painting, and she gasped.

'What? What is it?'

She pointed. '"The key is three and three times three". Three and nine.'

'Yes, twelve.'

'No, thirty-nine—look!'

It was true. Below the painting was the number thirty-nine,

plain to see. It had been there all along; she just had not *seen* it before. And somehow Anna *knew* that, this time, she was correct. She had solved the riddle.

Chapter Fourteen

Anna was already moving, sinking to her knees on the thick carpet.

'Three shelves.' She counted from top to bottom 'One, two, three.'

Her hand trailed along the books on the lowest shelf, counting aloud until she had reached the ninth. The shelf contained multiple works by Rousseau, but in the ninth position a slim volume stood out. It was not by Rousseau. Her eyes widened as she read the spine: *Lessons for Children* by Mrs Barbauld.

'Mama had a copy of this book in Elgin! She used it for our early reading lessons.' She reached out a trembling hand then paused, fearing disappointment. 'Has this bookshelf remained unchanged in sixteen years?'

Will shrugged. 'Probably. Now, go on.' He had knelt beside her, close enough that she could sense his warmth. Their eyes met, and she was abruptly glad to share this moment with him. 'Take it!'

Holding her breath, she removed the book carefully. Opening it, she flicked through, then more carefully flicked through from beginning to end.

The book was empty.

Her shoulders slumped. 'I was so certain! The numbers, the

fact it was out of place, the very book Mama used to read to us...' She shook her head. 'It should be here!'

'Let me see.' She handed it to him and he turned it over in his hands before opening it. 'How curious!'

'What?' She eyed him in confusion.

'A word here is carefully underlined in pencil. Nothing more, just the one word—see?'

He pointed and she read it.

'Behind.'

He flicked on. 'Again!' He paused near the middle of the book. Once again the word 'behind' had been underlined. Their eyes met, then as one they turned back to the bookshelf, removing the books that had been to the left and right of the riddle's book.

'Something is there!' His voice was tight with excitement.

'I see it! Let me reach...' Slipping her hand into the space they had created, she reached into the area behind, touching cloth. Carefully, he drew it out. It was velvet, carefully folded and surprisingly heavy. Holding her breath, she undid the first fold, brushing away the dust, then the next.

'Paper! A note, perhaps?'

Will was right. As she undid the final fold, a folded note almost fell out. He caught it, but Anna's attention was captured by the beautiful object now revealed, sparkling and twinkling in the light. It was a necklace, but a necklace so wonderful that Anna could scarcely take it in. The chain and setting was gold, the stones a cluster of diamonds surrounding an enormous sapphire.

'Oh, my!' she whispered. 'How beautiful!' Reverently, she held it up to the light, almost blinking at the brilliance of the stones.

'The Fletcher necklace,' he murmured. 'It can be no other.' Unfolding the note, he handed it to her.

Anna gasped. 'Mama's handwriting!'

In a trembling voice, she read it aloud. *'This necklace is the property of Maria Berkeley Lennox Fletcher. Or, if I am gone, it passes to my eldest daughter, Annabelle Georgina Lennox*

Fletcher, and to her heirs. This treasure fine is yours and mine, my darling daughter.'

Mama's signature was below it.

It was too much. His arms enfolded her as she shuddered with emotion. With his arms around her, she felt safe, comforted and cared for.

'Why are you always here when I need you?' she muttered into his handkerchief after a little while. 'I believe I have cried more since coming here than I have in years! I am not normally a watering pot, I swear!'

'So you keep telling me. And I keep replying that you are perfectly entitled to cry in circumstances such as these. As to my being here when you need me, I believe that to be a worthy endeavour, and one which I am happy to take on. Now, if you are feeling a little better, might I suggest you bring this to Lady Kelgrove? For she is our puppeteer, I believe.'

'Yes, indeed! She has our interests at heart, and must know of this immediately!'

Lady Kelgrove was initially cross at being disturbed during her toilette, and made it known in no uncertain terms what she thought of young ladies who called at the *most* inconvenient moments. But once Anna had impressed upon her that she must speak with her privately on a matter of great importance, she sent her maid away.

'Well, what is it, Annabelle?'

For answer, Anna carefully unfolded the cloth. 'Now, that is a necklace I have not seen for many a year,' she murmured. Her tone sharpened. 'Who knows of this?'

'Only Will. We found it together just now, in Mama's hiding place.'

'Good. And is that a note with it?'

'It is.'

On perusing the note, Lady Kelgrove pursed her lips. 'Maria's assertion could not be clearer. She uses the name Fletcher for both of you, and states this necklace is your property. So they must have married.'

Sighing, she refolded the note. 'The difficulty is that I cannot find proof of the wedding, and everything will fall without it. My lawyer and his clerks are searching, but I have had nothing from them as yet to confirm it. I even tried to question one of the former Fletcher servants, to no avail, for he was impressively forgetful.' She lapsed into a reverie, while the clock on her mantel struck half-past five.

I shall be dreadfully late for dinner!

'What can I do with it, Grandmama?'

Lady Kelgrove held up an imperious hand and Anna subsided. She waited, trying not to fidget, while the clock ticked on remorselessly.

Lady Kelgrove looked at her directly. 'What if you were to wear the necklace to dinner tonight?'

Anna gasped at the audacity of it. 'Perhaps Mrs Thaxby or her husband might be surprised into revealing something.'

Lady Kelgrove frowned. 'But, if what I suspect is true, they may be dangerous, and I should not like to put you in any peril.'

'Stuff!' retorted Anna, her eyes dancing. 'What can they do to me at the dinner table?

'Very well. I see no better plan. But tell no one about it beforehand.' She glanced at the clock. 'Not that there will be any opportunity to do so, for you are shockingly tardy, Anna. Be quick, now!'

Anna needed no second bidding. Dashing to her bedchamber, she found Sally in a high state of agitation. 'Oh, there you are, miss!'

'I know. I was with Lady Kelgrove and I am dreadfully late! Do what you can, please.'

By the time she had donned her stays and stockings, undergown, slippers, and the blue silk gown, it lacked only ten minutes to the hour, so Sally dressed her hair in double-quick time.

'Thank goodness you have natural curls for me to work with, miss. If we had to use the curling iron, there would be no chance of me having you ready in time.'

Anna barely heard her, for her mind had been racing the whole time. George Fletcher was her father. There could now be no doubt. And it looked as though her parents had been legally wed. Which meant...

'Sally, tell me, what do you know of Mr Thaxby's man?'
Something about Lady Kelgrove's tone had made Anna wonder
if she believed that John did in fact know something.

'John? A good man, and well-liked among the servants. He
does not deserve the treatment—' She clamped her lips shut.

'Quite. No, I shall not wear the pearls after all.' Rising, Anna
lifted the velvet-covered treasure from her bedside table, where
she had placed it on entering her bedchamber.

Sally's eyes grew wide. 'Miss!'

'Isn't it exquisite? It was my mother's, and now it is apparently mine.' She shook her head. 'I cannot imagine a more
beautiful necklace.'

'Nor I, miss.' Lifting it with great care, she inspected the
clasp, then fastened the jewellery around Anna's neck. 'Ooh,
how beautiful! And sapphires are perfect for your blue eyes,
miss.'

It felt cool, heavy, and decidedly strange. 'And my gown!'
She smiled. 'Now, pass me my gloves and fan, and I shall go.'
She thought for a moment. 'Please do not speak of this with anyone.' She should not have told Sally it was her mother's necklace. That was a detail to be revealed at the right moment—by
Lady Kelgrove, no doubt.

'Of course not, miss!'

Hurrying along the landing, Anna saw a manservant emerge
from one of the other bedchambers, a gentleman's boots in hand.
Normally, this would not have earned any particular attention,
but she had been thinking about this particular servant just now.

As she walked towards him, making for the top of the stairs,
John stood to the side, as was proper.

I must speak with him—but not now. Not when she was already so late. He bowed as she passed, perfectly correctly, but
something about him…

Glancing over her shoulder, she saw that the valet had not resumed his progress. Indeed, he was standing as still as a statue,
his face ashen and his shoulders stiff. Clearly, he had seen and
recognised the necklace. Even now, he would be perhaps recalling Lady Kelgrove's questions, and working out exactly who

Anna was. Still, she need not worry that he would tell his master, for she herself was about to reveal the necklace to everyone.

She could not tarry. Glancing at the tall clock in the hall, a sick feeling went through her. Ten past six! To keep the party late for dinner was an unforgivable insult to her hostess.

Yet that was the least of her anxieties as she stepped through the door.

Chapter Fifteen

~~~~~~~~~~

All eyes turned to Anna and she paused in the doorway, suddenly uncertain. Lady Garvald and Lady Kelgrove had the two chairs beside the fireplace. The Rentons were to the left, the Thaxbys to the right. Her sisters and their husbands were standing by the piano, chatting with Mr Ashman, while Will and Sir Walter were conversing beside the second window.

'Good evening,' she ventured, hearing a tremble in her voice. 'I apologise for keeping you all waiting.'

'Well, since you were assisting me by arranging all of the flowers until very recently, I cannot be critical of you, my dear.' Lady Garvald patted an empty chair beside her and Anna walked forward. 'Both my son and Lady Kelgrove explained that you had left yourself short of time to dress, so I asked Cook to hold dinner for ten minutes.' She nodded to a nearby footman, who bowed and left the room. Dinner would shortly be called.

'What are you wearing around your neck?' Mrs Thaxby's voice was unrecognisable—strangled and strange. Rising from her seat, she advanced towards Anna in an alarming manner. Her eyes were round and almost seemed to protrude, her expression contorted with what looked like rage.

Instinctively, Anna shrank back, one hand going to her throat, then with determination she straightened. Out of the corner of her eye, she saw Will begin to move towards them, then her attention focused back on Mrs Thaxby.

'Mrs Thaxby!' she began, hoping her play-acting was in line with Lady Kelgrove's plans. 'Are you quite well? Why should you want to have my necklace?'

'It belongs to me! Indeed, it was stolen from me twenty-two years ago! I say that necklace is *mine*, and you are a thief!' There was a collective gasp and murmur of disapproval from the assembly.

Anna suspected that Lady Kelgrove's plan was deliberately to shock Mrs Thaxby with the reappearance of the necklace, perhaps in the hope she might say something revealing about Richard or George. So Anna would do her best to play her part.

She managed a light laugh. 'Whatever can you mean? Twenty-two years ago I was not even born! I could not possibly have stolen it!'

Mr Thaxby now came forward, placing a hand on his wife's arm and sending her an intent look.

'My wife is distressed, for that necklace is an heirloom in her family, and was indeed stolen from her twenty-two years ago.'

Will's tone was sharp. 'Mrs Thaxby would do well to control her words. If she were a gentleman, I should call her out for the insult to Miss Lennox!'

Anna's heart warmed at this display of loyalty, and to her gratification she could hear murmurs of agreement from other male voices Both of her sisters' husbands would see it as their duty to protect the honour and reputation of their sister-in-law. Will had done it too. Why? Because he was the host here, or because he cared?

Briefly, Anna met the gazes of Izzy and Rose, trying to send them a message to let her manage this drama in her own way. While Rose looked puzzled, and Izzy outraged, both remained silent.

Anna turned back to Mrs Thaxby. 'Are you certain, Mrs Thaxby, that it is the same necklace?' The woman's eyes flashed with what looked like pure hatred, and Anna recoiled. But Will was beside her, and so she persisted. 'After all, sapphires and diamonds are not uncommon in the *ton*.'

'Of course I am certain. How dare you suggest otherwise? This is the Fletcher necklace. It belonged to my mother, and her mother before it.'

'So was it worn by the wife of the Fletcher heir, then?' A frown of puzzlement appeared on the other woman's brow. 'I mean to say,' Anna persisted, 'It was not passed from mother to daughter, but from each Fletcher man to his bride?'

'Well, yes, but since George died it had to pass to me. As his only living relative, I inherited everything.'

'How did the necklace come to be lost?' Will had decided to join in, and Anna knew he would tread carefully.

'It was not lost, I tell you! It was stolen!' Her tone was fierce. 'After George's death, I went to look for it. It was gone from the safe.'

Will laughed. 'So it may not have been stolen at all! Perhaps your brother sold it. It seems clear it was his property, not yours.'

'He would never have done that, being raised with foolish notions of loyalty and tradition! He was nauseatingly *good*, and so everyone described him.'

'You find it nauseating that your brother was good, Mrs Thaxby?' Lady Kelgrove had decided to enter the fray.

'Of course not! You are twisting what I say.' Visibly struggling, Mrs Thaxby took a breath, then continued in a calmer tone. 'Nevertheless, I say you are wearing stolen goods and, unless you can show you came by the necklace honestly, it should be returned to me. Is that not so, Sir Walter?'

The magistrate stepped forward, just as a gong sounded in the hallway. 'This is all highly irregular, I must say. And just before dinner too!' He eyed Mrs Thaxby. 'Since the loss of the necklace pre-dates Miss Lennox's birth—which you confirmed yourself by saying it disappeared twenty-two years ago—for now I shall leave the necklace with her.' He turned to Anna. 'You are not planning to leave this place?'

'Oh, no! We are fixed here for at least another ten days.'

'Good.' He rubbed his hands together. 'Then I suggest we dine, for we are already late! I shall address this matter in the coming days.'

Lady Garvald assented and led the way on Claudio's arm,

while Will accompanied Izzy—the highest-ranking lady—and
Lord Renton offered his arm to Lady Kelgrove. As the party
paired up in order of rank, James accompanied Lady Renton,
while Sir Walter led Rose to the dining room. That left only
Anna, Mr Ashman, and the Thaxbys. As Mr Ashman offered his
arm to Mrs Thaxby, he threw a reassuring glance towards Anna.

I am among friends, Anna reminded herself as Mr Thaxby
offered his arm with an unctuous smile and a look of pure
venom.

'Miss Lennox.'

She could not speak, nor smile at him. Never until this moment had she resented her usual status as the lowest-ranked
lady in the room. What did such things matter, after all? But it
did matter that she was forced to endure his company as they
walked stiffly to the dining room. Yes, and he was likely to be
seated next to her too. He might wear the social mask, but she
had sensed his anger, seen the fury in his eyes just now.

She was right. Will was of course at the head of the table,
with Izzy, James, Lady Kelgrove, Mr Thaxby, Anna and Lord
Renton to his right, while on Will's left his mother had assigned
Lady Renton, Sir Walter, Mrs Thaxby, Mr Ashman, Rose and
Claudio. That left Anna stuck between Mr Thaxby and Lord
Renton.

Lord Renton was perfectly affable, and made no mention of
the recent confrontation as they conversed lightly during the
first course, allowing Anna's pulse to settle a little. But when
the footmen moved in to serve the second course—beefsteak
and oyster pie, as well as haricot beans *à la bonne femme*—
Lady Garvald turned the table, as was correct, by beginning a
conversation with Prince Claudio. The effect rippled through
the room, everyone now turning to converse with the person
on the other side, and Anna was forced to accept Mr Thaxby's
offer to pass her any dish she would like.

With a neutral expression she requested the stuffed cucumbers and a slice of pie, and he complied, serving her with a
flourish before asking the footman to refill her wine glass. She
drank very little after that, and was relieved when the conversation turned yet again. This time, Lord Renton had less to say,

so she was able to observe Mrs Thaxby attempting to use all her dubious charms on Sir Walter, as well as hearing snatches of the conversation between Mr Thaxby and Lady Kelgrove.

'And did you report it as stolen at the time? Hire a thief-taker, or inform the Bow Street Runners or the constables?'

'Well, no, my lady. We were grieving, you must understand. My wife's brother...'

'Strange. Pass me the cucumbers, Mr Thaxby, if you please.'

A bubble of humour at Lady Kelgrove's audacity threatened to spill out of Anna, and to counter it she asked Lord Renton if he often travelled to Scotland.

'Not as often as I should wish,' was his response, and she laughingly told him he had given exactly the right answer. They then debated why certain among the *ton* despised everything that was not English, and continued in convivial conversation through each subsequent turn. The contrast with Mr Thaxby was noticeable. Anna had seen another side to the Thaxbys tonight—a side that made her shiver. She only hoped she and Lady Kelgrove had made the right decision in provoking such a pair.

Finally, the ordeal was done—at least, the formal dinner part of it. Tonight, instead of the ladies retiring to the drawing room to await the gentlemen, the entire party made their way to the ballroom and hall, where before long Will and his mother began receiving their guests.

Knowing Lady Garvald was entirely occupied, Anna briefly spoke to her sisters, explaining how the necklace had been discovered. They were all excitement, especially given the note, and Mrs Thaxby's confirmation that it was the Fletcher necklace.

'There can be no doubt now as to the identity of our father,' said Izzy. 'I do wish he had not such an unpleasant sister, though.'

On this they all agreed, before the necessities of the soirée separated them. Since Lady Garvald remained occupied with receiving guests, Anna checked all was well with the housekeeper and butler, and helped to solve a last-minute dilemma about whether to place the elaborate silver epergne on the first table or the central one in the supper room. The musicians were already in place on their little dais in the corner of the ballroom, and Anna's flower arrangements had been placed strategically throughout, adding beauty to the already stunning ballroom. While it was still bright outside, hundreds of candles were at the ready, to be lit after sunset.

All is ready.

Before long Will and Lady Garvald came to the ballroom, indicating that all the expected guests had now arrived, and both began making their way around the room, performing more introductions. Apparently everyone invited had attended, and Lady Garvald was at once gratified and worried by it.

'I just hope there are no disasters, Anna!' she confessed. Anna, sensing her disquiet, refrained from telling her that the evening was most definitely more a ball than a soirée, given the numbers of guests. Certainly everyone was dressed for a ball, and once again she was glad of her blue silk gown.

'I am confident that you have planned for every eventuality,' she assured her, and Lady Garvald squeezed her hand.

'Bless you! Now, may I introduce you to…?'

Anna complied, and received with a polite smile the usual astonishment at the fact she and her sisters were identical triplets, and with equanimity various flowery compliments from a number of local gentlemen. Before long, two distinct gatherings had formed—one around Prince Claudio and Princess Isobel, and one around her.

What on earth is going on? She could not account for it. While understanding that she and her sisters were thought of as pretty by the *ton*, never before had she received such attention, and she was not certain she liked it very much.

Thankfully she had already reserved dances for Will, James, Claudio and Mr Ashman, otherwise she might have ended up spending the entire evening dancing with men she had never met before—not a prospect she would have welcomed, for it was so much more comfortable to dance with gentlemen she knew. To her great relief the Thaxbys had taken to a corner of the room and were deep in conversation. Anna shivered just watching them, but just then, during a lull in the general hubbub, she overheard a female voice behind her mention her name.

'Miss Lennox. She is Princess Isobel's sister. My mama has instructed me to make a friend of her, if I can. Imagine! She is related to an *actual* prince and…' The rest was lost as the gentlemen with Anna made some new remark, but suddenly all had become clear. She was not being pursued for her own sake, but for her connection to Prince Claudio. Princes were an uncommon sight here, of course.

With a cynicism that she would not have had a year ago, she understood that even if she had been old, ugly and devoid of teeth, some of those present, men and women, would have tried to court her or befriend her. Turning briefly, she saw the speaker was a dark-haired young lady in a pale pink gown, before her attention was again reclaimed by her sham admirers.

A little later, Lady Garvald introduced her to the dark-haired young lady. She was part of a group—two older ladies, and two younger. The two older ladies were sisters, it seemed, and they each had a daughter. The dark-haired girl was Miss Hughes and her cousin Miss Newton. Anna curtseyed, smiled and said all that was appropriate.

Then Will and Mr Ashman joined them, and the girls' demeanour underwent an abrupt change. Miss Hughes, who had eyes only for the Earl of Garvald, became at once coquettish and flirtatious in a way that Anna could never imagine replicating, while Miss Newton blushed and stammered in the general direction of Mr Ashman.

How interesting!

Abruptly, and with a sense of relief, Anna found herself on surer ground. The mysteries of her parents and of Richard's death could be forgotten for a little time, while she indulged in a habit developed during her *ton* season—that of watching people, and divining them. So she stayed with the two girls and their mamas, much longer than she had with anyone else, and by the end of fifteen minutes was fairly certain that Miss Newton was head over ears in love with Mr Ashman, and that he was entirely oblivious to it.

Regarding the obvious lures being cast by Miss Hughes in the Earl's direction, Will was either ignoring them or was also remarkably oblivious. Anna saw no evidence of any true affection being shared between them, but then, what did she know of the male heart? And gentlemen often chose brides for reasons of alliances and common sense, not love.

She swallowed, suddenly unsure. Once again she was struck by the preposterous notion that she should do *something*—though she was unsure what, exactly. But *something* that might make him see her not as his childhood playmate, but as an eligible young woman.

The dancing was beginning and Will had arrived to claim her hand for the opening quadrille. They had danced together many times in London, but now things were different. First, he was not just the Earl of Garvald, but Will, ZanZan and the man she now knew she loved.

She loved him! Well, naturally she did. Using the word in her head for the first time was novel, but the feeling itself…that had been growing for a very long time. Pausing for a moment to savour this new knowledge, she returned to the differences between dancing with him in London and dancing with him here.

First, she loved him. That made everything different.

Second, they were in Lammermuir House, her childhood home.

Third, she was wearing Mama's necklace.

And fourth, she and Will were opening the ball together. As he led her to the top of the dance floor, and other couples began falling in around them, it struck her that she should not have had this honour, and she said so.

'Why ever not? Who would you have had me dance with?'

'Izzy is highest in rank, and Rose is next tonight.' Lady Renton—who would have ranked higher than Rose—had informed them she would not dance tonight, Anna recalled. Glancing about, Anna noted Lady Renton was engaged with a group of local dames, holding forth masterfully and seemingly enjoying a new audience.

'Very properly, I asked both your sisters—and, well, see for yourself!' He indicated the dance floor. Sure enough, Izzy and Rose were there, taking to the floor with their own husbands, quite in defiance of tradition. 'They were quite determined that I should dance with you first,' he continued, and Anna felt a wave of mortification rising within her as she imagined the knowing smiles and pointed tone her sisters would likely have adopted.

'I see.' And she did. She just hoped that he did not.

'How do you, Anna?' he asked softly. 'The Thaxbys...'

'Let us not speak of it now, for your mother's ball is about to begin, and I am determined to leave mysteries aside for a few hours.'

'Very well—I approve!' He grinned. 'My lady.' He bowed as the musicians began the opening bars, and she mirrored him with a slow curtsey. As they advanced and retreated in the steps of the dance her gaze met his frequently, and their hands clasped regularly.

This is how it should be—he and I together.

Daringly, she spoke to him about the two young ladies.

'How well do you know them?'

He shrugged. 'As well as any man knows his neighbours. Miss Hughes is a similar age to you; Miss Newton, a little younger.'

'And were you close friends with them after—after I left?'

'Not at all. I wanted no other friends.' He took a breath, then continued. 'I spent more than a year trying to punish my mother for something that was not her doing. I was so *angry*. In vain did she host gatherings with the local children, for I remained aloof. Once I went away to school, I began to make friends with some of the other boys, but I never again had female friends like you and your sisters.'

'I see.' And she did. She truly did. Her curiosity about Miss Hughes remained unabated, however, fuelled by something suspiciously akin to jealousy. *Jealousy!* She had never in her life experienced it, and it was astonishing how intense was the feeling. The next time the dance brought them together, she asked, 'What is your opinion of Miss Hughes and Miss Newton?'

Puzzlement crossed his face briefly. 'I have no strong opinions on either of them. They are both pleasant young ladies. Why do you ask?'

She laughed lightly, mostly in relief. 'Miss Hughes has apparently been instructed to make a friend of me, as I am the sister of Princess Isobel.'

His brow cleared. 'Ah. Yes, Mrs Hughes is ambitious for her daughter, I have no doubt. And for her son.'

'Her son?'

'Mr Hughes. Can you have already forgotten him? Is he lost in the throng of your cicisbeos?'

'My *what*?'

'Your admirers.'

She sniffed. 'I understood only married women may have such gallants. And I am unmarried.'

'Yes.' He said. 'Yes, you are.' A strange expression crossed his face. 'But you certainly have admirers. I could barely get close enough to speak to you earlier, and had to ask my mother to extricate you and introduce you to some of the ladies.'

'You...you asked her?'

Why should he intervene in such a manner?

'I did.' He frowned. 'Was that wrong of me? I thought you looked a little uncomfortable.'

'I am perfectly capable of looking after myself, Will! Including fending off *faux* admirers, if needed.'

High-handed. Yes, he had been decidedly high-handed.

Naturally, he focused on one word in particular. '*Faux?* Do you think their admiration of you is not genuine?'

She grimaced. 'I think my most attractive feature tonight is my relationship by marriage with royalty. Or possibly Mama's necklace, which may suggest I am wealthy.'

'If you are the true Fletcher heir, then you are indeed enormously wealthy. And it is true that your sister is now a princess. But it should not change you.' He gave a wry smile. 'Such cynicism in one so young!'

'Yet you do not deny it.'

'I most emphatically do deny it! Yes, being Claudio's sister-in-law will bring you to their notice, but your character and your beauty will keep them with you. I know many of these young men, and they have a healthy dislike for young ladies who are vapid, vulgar or vain, let me tell you! This is Scotland, after all!'

'While I can only admire your skill for alliterative epithets, I am not sure I share your opinion.' She eyed him curiously. 'So have you not found these flaws in me?'

'Not at all, although doubtless you have others yet to be discovered!'

She tossed her head at this, strangely enjoying their verbal fencing, while still remaining cross at his earlier interference.

'A gentleman should not comment on any flaws a lady may have. He should see only her good qualities.'

'I do not think that rule applies to close friends such as you and I.'

Close. She liked that word. *Friends*, not so much.

'And so,' he continued, 'I may say with impunity that you have a tendency to brood, a leaning towards anxiety and a desire to manage everyone around you.' The glint in his eye told her he was being deliberately provocative. 'These may be considered flaws by some.'

'With impunity? I think not!' Impulsively, she threw caution to the wind. 'If we are being frank, as only friends can, in that case dare I say you are excessively reserved to the point of rudeness at times?'

He recoiled. 'Rudeness? *Never* have I been rude! My mother has raised me to know how to behave.'

'Well, if you can caricature me, I must be offered the same privilege!'

'Touché!' He twirled her around, perhaps a little more forcefully than required, then caught her before she should lose her balance. 'But I know you, as those *admirers* never shall!' His expression was grim.

'And I know *you*, Will, better perhaps than anyone save your own mother!'

The anger abruptly went from his eyes, replaced by something thoughtful, rueful. 'And perhaps even better than that.'

The dance had ended. They stood, simply looking at one another, until a hum of conversation around them brought them back to attention. After completing the formal end-bow and curtsey, he asked if she wished him to procure her a glass of wine or ratafia. When she declined, he bowed again and marched off, a stiffness to his gait that she knew denoted vexation.

He talked with Miss Hughes and her mother next. Anna,

conversing with Sir Walter, had to turn away from the sight of their shared smiles and easy conversation. Being at outs with him was disturbing to her equilibrium, yet she remained cross, frustrated and in no mood to reconcile.

What should have been a perfectly wonderful dance together to open the ball had turned into a falling out that, in her mind, seemed enormous.

Chapter Sixteen

Will was entirely confused.

Just when he thought he was making progress, the road had turned sharply and unexpectedly, leaving him feeling as though he was no longer on solid ground. While it was probably inevitable that he and Anna would have a falling out at some point, tonight's disagreement had been unanticipated. Equally unexpected was how affected he was by it. To be out of harmony with her was insupportable. As he watched her talking with Ashman, once more doubts flooded his mind. What was between them, exactly? And how did it compare with the connection between Anna and himself?

The way she looked at him sometimes was so intense, the air seemed to thrum between them. Could she really be confusing such passion for *friendship* still? His friends had strongly urged him to take care, for they said Anna saw him only as ZanZan, not Will. But something within him refused to believe it.

Yet, he reminded himself, she had no experience of such matters, no way of knowing how rare such a connection was. Indeed, Ashman might seem to her a safer option, for Will's passion was too strong ever to be called *safe*. Had she been deliberately provocative earlier, seeking to push him away?

No matter, his challenge now was to observe her with Ash-

man, then workout how the hell to restore the intimacy between them. He stifled a sigh. He still had their shared mission
to uncover the truth, although she had said she did not wish to
speak of it earlier. But Mr Thaxby was clearly angry, and his
lady had spent the evening sending dagger-like glances in the
direction of the Lennox triplets, between copious glasses of
wine. He sighed. He needed to stay alert. If the Thaxbys really had committed murder, then who knew what they might
do to cover it up?

The musicians struck up the opening bars to the Boulanger,
and he recalled he needed to make his way to Princess Isobel.

As Mr Ashman approached to claim her hand for the next
dance, the Boulanger, Anna reflected on Will's description of
her flaws, and reluctantly acknowledged his words, while delivered far too harshly in her opinion, were not strictly unjust.
Ruminating and making herself worried were two of her habits, her pattern of wishing to manage situations as much a response to anxiety as anything else. He probably understood
that. But to hear one's imperfections announced so plainly had
felt…harsh. Too harsh.

Yet she had been equally harsh in return, calling him rude.
A man of such consequence as him would never have been described that way by the *ton*. He was never discourteous, nor
disdainful. He was simply…reserved, aloof, composed.

What was worse, she now understood his reserve and the reasons behind it, and she had been unkind to use the word rude.
Guilt now mingled with her ongoing outrage at his frankness,
both compounded by distress at not being in harmony with him.

Besides, she concluded with a hint of defiance, *it will do him
no harm to think on how he appears to others.*

'Splendid evening, is it not?'

Lord, she was making a habit of being less than attentive to
Mr Ashman. And she had dared to call Will rude! With determination, she smiled at her partner, and before long she was
quizzing him on Miss Hughes and Miss Newton. He knew both
well, naturally, having been playmates with them when they
had all been children.

'Miss Newton was a little younger than the rest of us, and as I recall we used to chase her away when she tried to tag after us!'

'The gentlemen are not chasing her away now,' Anna noted dryly.

'Excuse me? I do not understand your meaning.'

Lord, even clever men could be surprisingly obtuse!

'I mean to say that she is remarkably pretty and, inasmuch as I can judge anyone's character on first meeting, I would say of all the new people I have met tonight she is the one I liked best.'

He smiled broadly, a hint of pride in his tone as he said, 'Well, naturally. Hetty is a great sport altogether! Never any drama from her!'

'I do hope you have managed to secure her hand for a dance, for I fear her card must be almost full.'

At this, he twisted round, his jaw dropping as he observed the throng around her. 'Well, just look at that! Hetty! Who would have thought...and she is in remarkable good looks tonight. I never thought to...'

'Go! Quickly,' she urged, 'For the musicians are nearly ready to start our Boulanger. I shall wait here.'

He needed no further encouragement, and she watched with a satisfied smile as he cut through the group of young gentlemen to speak to Hetty, and how she nodded with a shy smile. They spoke briefly, then he returned, a decided air of relief about him.

'Thank you, Miss Lennox. I got my request in just in the nick of time.' He flushed. 'I have not been to a ball in an age, although we stood up in the Assembly Rooms in Haddington many times last winter. Hetty was away at school,' he added. 'She is different now.'

Stifling a smile, Anna asked him if he needed to reserve dances with any other young ladies. 'Oh, no!' he declared. 'I am quite content to dance only with you and Hetty, for you are quite the prettiest girls in the room!' This last was said with a gallant flourish, and Anna reflected how music, a ballroom and some punch could change the demeanour of even the most reserved of gentlemen.

Apart from Will, of course.

Ever the Earl, he had returned to his mother's side, clearly checking on her contentment, and as Anna watched he made his way to Izzy, whose hand he had clearly secured for the Boulanger.

'Well, by that definition, you must include my sisters, surely?' Anna's tone was teasing.

'Ha!' He acknowledged her hit. 'But they are married, and I prefer to dance with single ladies.' He bowed, as the dance was about to begin, and she responded with a curtsey.

She was still thinking of Hetty. 'And is prettiness the only factor you are considering in unmarried ladies tonight, Mr Ashman? For I think there are other ladies here who may be considered as pretty as Miss Newton.' She paused. 'Miss Hughes, for example.' The dance took her away from him then, but not before she had seen the faintest of frowns mar his brow.

Good. Let him think about why he prefers Hetty.

She was to be disappointed. By the time the dance brought them together again he had an air of resolution about him. 'You are correct, Miss Lennox. I shall ask Miss Hughes to dance as soon as I may. It would not do to slight an old friend by seeming to favour another.'

And so ends my brief career as a matchmaker.

'Very proper, Mr Ashman—although I was not suggesting you were slighting anyone. Miss Hughes is not short of partners, I think, and there are plenty of gentlemen dancing tonight. Lady Garvald need not have worried there would be a shortage of dance partners for the ladies.'

Her meddling had had exactly the opposite effect to what she had intended for, rather than focusing on Hetty, Mr Ashman would now be dancing with both ladies.

But perhaps that might serve to help him see the difference between them.

Still, her probing had reinforced her impression that Miss Hughes was not as likeable as Miss Newton—a notion she found deeply satisfying.

Ha! Let the Earl dance with her all night, then, for I care not!

So she smiled and kept to pleasantries for the remainder of the dance—and for the next four dances, as the young men of the district did their best to flatter her. Thankfully, it was then supper time, and Will came to her as they made their way to the supper room.

'How do you now, Anna?' There was some intent in his voice which left her feeling strange inside.

His question goes deep. It is not superficial.

'I am perfectly fine, my lord.'

He raised an eyebrow. 'I am taking you to mean the exact opposite, Miss Lennox.' His formality matched hers, and she felt a stab of hurt inside at his demeanour—even though she herself had caused it.

His expression turned serious. 'Mrs Thaxby seems certain that your mother's necklace is the Fletcher heirloom.' He had clearly been ruminating himself. Now here was common ground.

'I thought I had indicated I did not wish to speak of these matters tonight!' She arched a brow, letting him know she was half-jesting.

'I apologise.' He bowed. 'It is consuming my attention, I am afraid.'

'Mine too.' This was only half a lie. Both he and the Thaxby mystery were consuming her.

'You are right. She knew the necklace straight away.' She glanced around to make certain no one could overhear them. 'It will not be long, I think, before she realises we may be her nieces.'

He frowned. 'It may take longer than you might expect. Despite her cunning, she is not the cleverest of women, I think. Besides, if she had no notion of George and Maria as a couple, why should she not think the necklace was stolen? There is an old saying: "a thief sees a world full of thieves".'

Anna gasped. 'You think her a thief?'

'I make no accusations, for I cannot be certain. I know only that how people *see* the world reveals much of what they *do* in the world. You, for example, see always good in people. Is it not so?'

She shrugged. 'Does not everyone?'

'No, and that is exactly the point I am making.' He glanced

in her direction again. 'Was Mr Thaxby discourteous towards you during dinner?'

'Not discourteous, no. Stiff, perhaps—on his dignity.' She frowned. 'He is rightly loyal to his wife. It must be difficult for both of them to see me wear the Fletcher necklace.'

'You are much too generous, do you know that? Little wonder, for you were raised by my mother as well as your own, and what I know of Maria tells me she was every bit as kind-hearted as my own mother.'

Her inner glow intensified at this praise of darling Mama, and at the way he was looking at her now—as though she *mattered* to him. She caught the direction of her own thoughts. Well, of course she knew she mattered to him. She was just unsure exactly in which *way* she mattered.

'How is Lady Garvald now?' she managed. 'I have not had the chance to speak with her for the past couple of hours.'

'Yes, your hand has been engaged for every dance.' Was there an edge to his voice? She glanced in his direction, but his face was expressionless. 'My mother is finally beginning to settle,' he continued, 'Understanding that her soirée—which everyone is calling a ball—is going extremely well. Once the supper has been successfully endured, I suspect she might even allow herself to enjoy it a little.'

'I am glad to hear it. And it is a ball, it is clear. But calling it a soirée made it easier for her, I think.'

They had reached the supper room, and Anna's gaze immediately sought out Lady Garvald. 'There she is, talking with that footman. I shall go to her.'

'She is ever anxious about being a hostess—which is why she entertains so infrequently.' His eyes softened. 'Your assistance and kindness has meant the world to her, Anna.'

There it was again, that breathlessness that only he could cause. 'It is the least I can do for her, after everything she has done for us.'

'Garvald!' It was one of the guests, a portly gentleman with a ruddy face. Anna could not recall his name. 'Capital evening, my lord! And I must compliment you on your excellent wines!'

Murmuring an excuse, Anna moved away, reflecting that the

gentleman in question had clearly imbibed copious amounts of said wines.

'Lady Garvald, how do you?'

'Oh, Anna! It is going well, I think, is it not?'

Anna laid a hand on her arm briefly. 'It is going *very* well! Everywhere I go I hear nothing but praise. And just look at the faces of the guests—they are all enjoying the evening, and so should you!'

She gave a wan smile. 'I cannot. I am just so worried that something will go wrong.' Her gaze roved over the food tables. 'Do we have enough pork cutlets? Lord, what if there is not enough meat?'

'There is plenty of meat,' Anna replied firmly. 'I have attended many balls and soirées this season, and if anything your table is more generous than that typically provided in London.'

'Truly? So you believe we have adequate provisions?'

'I know it.'

She exhaled, shaking her head. 'What you must think of me, Anna!' She grimaced. 'The truth is, I have always had a dread of being a hostess. I know it is expected of me—I am, after all, a countess—but there are so many ways to fail tonight!'

'Dare I say your neighbours are universally supportive? If you are subject to any criticism, it would be more likely from certain of your houseguests who make it their business to be perpetually displeased. And you manage them with aplomb!'

'That is true. Although it is difficult, I feel much more sure of myself in my own drawing room, rather than standing in a ballroom as hostess. Oh!'

'What? What is it?'

Lady Garvald was staring at nothing, her face a picture of shock. 'It is you.' Her eyes were suddenly suspiciously bright. 'You are so like her.'

Instantly, Anna knew whom she meant. 'My mother?'

Lady Garvald nodded, swallowing. 'Maria was forever encouraging me, supporting me, taking the extravagance from my fears until they were small enough to manage.' She smiled mistily. 'You have the same gift.'

Anna's heart swelled. They were all thinking of Mama tonight, it seemed—the ball, the Fletcher necklace... 'I am honoured you should think so. But now—' she indicated the merry throng '—you are at a successful ball—yes, a *ball*—and I should like you to enjoy it. Will you take some supper?'

'Perhaps a little something, for my stomach is not as sick as it has been all evening.'

'Good.' Together they joined the queue of people perusing the food tables, asking the footmen to add their favourites to their plates. 'I should warn you,' said Anna, 'That after supper soirées and balls in London sometimes became a little...boisterous.'

'That I do remember.' Lady Garvald gave a wry smile. 'Some of the gentlemen are becoming a little...bosky, are they not?'

'And some of the ladies too, if you look closely.'

'No! Who?'

Anna dimpled at her. 'I shall not tell you, for it is quite entertaining trying to divine who is drunk and who is merely half-sprung.'

Her eyes widened at Anna's daring language. 'Well, I would say that Mrs Hughes may have over-indulged a little, for look at how she is hanging off Sir Walter Ashman. Poor man!'

'I agree. Now, who else?'

Her brow furrowed. 'Mrs Thaxby. I suspect she has a fondness for wine in general, which her husband is well aware of.'

'Have you noticed how he often serves drinks to the ladies? A kind service, but it enables him to disguise the amount his wife is taking, by also serving another lady at the same time. But we are perfectly capable of counting!' she added wryly.

Lady Garvald sighed. 'I have seen it. I think he also tries to manage her pace of drinking, for otherwise she would simply signal the footmen to constantly refill her glass—which is what she does when he is not present.'

They shared a glance, then Anna searched out Mrs Thaxby. 'She is unhappy. And troubled.'

And she may have done a very, very bad thing.

She tilted her head towards Mrs Thaxby's table. 'Look, she is alone. No doubt her husband is procuring food and drink for her.'

'We should sit with her.'

Stifling a sigh, Anna nodded agreement, and together they made their way to a small table near the back of the room. 'Mrs Thaxby! May we join you?'

Raising her eyes to them, eyes dulled by alcohol, Mrs Thaxby nodded and they sat, the footmen bringing Lady Garvald's and Anna's plates and serving all three of them with wine. Mrs Thaxby drank deeply then confirmed in answer to Lady Garvald's query that her husband was indeed reviewing the available dishes on her behalf.

'He knows my preferences, you see,' she informed them, her speech decidedly slurred.

'You are fortunate to have such an attentive husband,' offered Lady Garvald, biting into a morsel of beef.

Mrs Thaxby shrugged. 'Fortunate? On the contrary. I am the most unfortunate soul in England, I have no doubt.'

Oh, dear. The wine is making her maudlin.

'Oh, come now, Mrs Thaxby.' Lady Garvald's tone was brisk. 'You have wealth, security and a devoted husband. There are many who would welcome such blessings.'

'Indeed I am cursed,' muttered Mrs Thaxby, lifting her glass again. 'Cursed from birth.'

'From birth?' Anna was confused. 'Whatever can you mean?'

Mrs Thaxby eyed her malevolently. 'You are young and green, Miss Lennox. You have not yet understood how limited life is for we females.' She shook her head. 'Had I been born a boy, everything would have been different.'

'How? How so?' Anna's bewilderment made her struggle to understand Mrs Thaxby. 'Although we have fewer freedoms than gentlemen, I do love being a woman. Do you not?'

'It is not about being a woman. Naturally I cannot change that, and have no wish to. It is about the *privileges* afforded to men.' Her gaze became unfocused and she murmured, almost to herself, 'Everything I have ever done has been to rectify the injustices I have suffered. Yet still I suffer. Even now, certain people have the arrogance to question, to insinuate... I have often wondered what happened to the girl. If there was a girl.'

She threw a look at Anna—a look so venomous that Anna recoiled a little. 'How came you by my necklace?'

Anna touched it instinctively, while nervousness rose within her.

What should I say?

'I inherited it.'

'From Lady Kelgrove, I presume?' She almost spat as she said the name. 'And where did she come by it? He stayed there, that year. Was it stolen from him then?'

'My dear, I have brought all your favourites.' It was Mr Thaxby, and there was a definite air of disquiet about him.

Had he heard what his wife was saying?

Resisting the urge to exchange a glance with Lady Garvald, Anna pretended to listen as Mr Thaxby expounded in quite some detail about his wife's preferences in food. Mrs Thaxby herself had slunk into sullen silence, and barely picked at it.

Frankly, Anna was relieved when she and her hostess were able to leave the couple, as the next round of dances was shortly to begin. Still, Mrs Thaxby's comment about Lady Kelgrove was reassuring in that she clearly had not yet worked out exactly how Anna had come by the necklace, and why. The comment about a girl was concerning, though. Anna could only imagine the woman's rage when she discovered George and Maria had had three daughters. Shuddering, she realised she could do nothing about it now, so went back to the dancing.

It was after midnight, and the ball was over. Anna stood on the terrace, only half-hearing the bustle behind her as the servants began clearing away empty glasses and scraping at spilled candle wax. Tomorrow the entire ballroom would receive a thorough clean, but for tonight there was a decided air of satisfaction among the staff, who knew the ball had gone well, partly thanks to their contribution.

Anna had been surprised to discover her simple upbringing in Elgin had made her more aware of the needs and aspirations of servants, but she could not regret it, no matter how many times she heard similar transgressions being decried by some members of the *ton* as a 'vulgar' affinity. Even Lady Kelgrove, raised a lady, tended to call all footmen 'John', Anna had noticed. Yet, as far as Anna knew, there was currently only one John in this household—Mr Thaxby's long-suffering valet.

It could never be vulgar to consider the needs of others. So Mama had taught her, and Anna and her sisters had been grateful for every ounce of assistance they'd received from Mr Marnoch's staff as they had been growing up. So she made a point of seeking out both the housekeeper and butler just now, to thank them for all the efforts that they and their fellow servants had made to ensure Lady Garvald's first ball had been a raging success.

Will's mother had retired not five minutes ago, declaring herself exhausted, but Anna had lingered, knowing that if she went to bed now she would not sleep. There was too much going on inside her head, and her heart: the Thaxbys; Lady Kelgrove; the necklace; Mama's note. And, most of all, Will.

A sudden need for silence gripped her. Impulsively, she stepped off the terrace, discarding her evening gloves and leaving them on a nearby table. Moving away from the bustle of activity in the ballroom, she walked slowly and deliberately into the blessed darkness of the garden.

The stars came into view overhead as her eyes adjusted to the gloom. The moon had risen, giving light to the carriages currently on their way home from the Garvald ball, and bathing the gardens in silver-white beauty. She swayed a little, realising that she too was not unaffected by all the wine and punch she had consumed tonight. Even when one did not wish to be half-sprung, it was difficult to avoid a certain degree of boskiness on nights when footmen assiduously refilled one's glass at every turn, and when the exertion of dancing left you thirsty.

There was a stone bench nearby a little to the left, she recalled. Walking carefully, she managed to find it and sat down with a sigh, raising her eyes to the heavens. Somehow, all of her other thoughts and worries had faded in less than a minute, leaving only one person in her mind.

Will. She loved him entirely, completely, with everything she was, and knowing everything he was. Her mind returned to their little falling out earlier, which now seemed meaningless. They truly *knew* each other—surely the perfect recipe for a successful marriage?

Her heart skipped as she acknowledged the direction of her own thoughts.

Marriage?

Yes. She would marry him in an instant if he loved her. But only if he loved her. If he did not, then she would be doomed to a lifetime of unhappiness.

Her mind flicked briefly to Lord and Lady Renton, then to her sisters and their husbands. Yes, a love match was the only way.

Oh, why can he not see?

But it seemed likely he thought of her only as ZanZan's friend, and the three Lennox girls as his long-lost sisters. At least, she had no evidence he thought of her in any other way, and dared not hope too much, for fear her heart would be crushed by disappointment.

If he were to marry—and she had no notion if he was even considering the matter—he would be more likely to choose a woman who knew how to flirt, how to make him notice her in that way. Although he criticised 'vapid' young ladies, she had heard many times how even sensible men might fall foul of a fetching young miss who was entirely unsuitable for them. Recalling Miss Hughes's coquetry earlier, she briefly wondered if she could ape it.

Instantly, her spirit shrank inside with mortification, giving her a clear answer to *that* conundrum. In London, many young ladies had flirted with the eligible gentlemen, much to Anna's bewilderment, who had thought them remarkably silly. Yet now, when she needed to break through the barrier of assumptions Will had made about her, about their friendship, she found she had no way of doing so.

Why can I not flirt with him in the way other young ladies seem to find so easy?

The closest she had come to it was friendly raillery and teasing, such as they had enjoyed earlier when he had asked her what form her gratitude might take. Another young lady might have made more of the opportunity, using coquettish looks and allowing a touch to linger for a little longer than necessary.

But I am me, and can be no one else. But could she try? If given the opportunity, could she be brave? She knew not.

'Are you well, Anna?'

It was Will. Lost in thought, she had not heard him approach. Dumbstruck, she did not answer for a moment, feeling as though she had conjured him up through the sheer force of her love for him.

'Anna?' Now he sounded genuinely uneasy. 'Has something occurred? The Thaxbys…have they said something to upset you?' He sat beside her, and she drank in his beloved features in the dim light. The moon and stars above were painting him in silver, and now that she knew her own heart she wanted only to stay in the moment forever. He was there, just next to her, looking more handsome than any man had the right to, his brow furrowed with concern for her. Her heart swelled in her chest—or, at least, that was how it felt.

'N-no. I am well, thank you.' Her tongue felt sluggish. Was her speech a little slurred? Lord, she hoped not! Briefly recalling her earlier conversation with Lady Garvald regarding the various stages of inebriation of the ladies present, she idly wondered if she herself was full drunk or simply a little bosky.

'My mother's ball was a great success, was it not?' Now there was a hint of humour in his voice, or was she imagining it? Her brain seemed slow, fuzzy.

'It was! Everyone enjoyed it, I think—well, *almost* everyone,' she amended, recalling the Thaxbys and Lady Renton.

'And you enjoyed it, I trust? I know you were concerned about my mother, but you were still able to?'

'Oh, yes.' She breathed. 'It was wonderful. But I may have had too much wine. I declare my head is spinning.' Daringly, she reached out with both hands, resting them on his chest. 'There is only one thing left that would make tonight perfect.'

'And what is that?' His voice was tight, his expression hooded.

She leaned towards him, her voice a whisper. 'Will you not kiss me, my lord?'

Chapter Seventeen

Having seen Anna step into the garden, Will immediately followed. Events from earlier had greatly disturbed him, and he refused to seek his bed until all those in his care had safely retired.

Having the Thaxbys under his roof was not something he welcomed—even more so now that long-held secrets were beginning to emerge. While he still found it difficult to believe that they had murdered George Fletcher—and Richard Berkeley too—he knew he must treat the possibility with seriousness, and that meant remaining alert and doing all he could to keep his loved ones safe.

Lady Kelgrove, while clearly having affection for the Lennox girls, was driven by the desire to know the truth of her grandson's death. And why should she not be? Yet, if the Thaxbys truly were cold-blooded murderers, then provoking them would involve significant risk.

Anna's earlier entrance wearing the Fletcher necklace had caused great consternation yet, even under the shock of discovery, the Thaxbys had said nothing compromising. He was determined to speak with Lady Kelgrove tomorrow. And in the coming days he would need to speak to Sir Walter, too, about the true ownership of the necklace. The last thing he would wish was for any stain on Anna's good name.

He sat beside her, concerned as to why she had gone outside by herself. Had something occurred to distress her? When she replied in the negative, and with a voice thickened by his best wines, he had to suppress a smile. Miss Anna Lennox—the sensible one of the triplets—was decidedly and deliciously foxed.

He deliberately encouraged her to speak further, asking an innocuous question about the ball. Who knew when such an opportunity would come again? For Anna liked having her wits about her, and so usually drank sparingly. Yet he had entirely underestimated the impact on her sensible restraint, for a moment later she placed both hands on him and asked for a kiss.

She followed it up by stretching towards him, pressing her lips to his. Instantly he was lost. His arms slid around her and he kissed her back, thoroughly and expertly.

Finally! It was, naturally, he who came to his senses first. He froze, shock warring with the need to kiss her a hundred times as he had so often dreamed of doing.

Not like this.

He wrenched his mouth from hers then slid back, ensuring there was no contact between them save her hands, which still rested on his chest. Her eyes were closed and she was swaying slightly, sending shame rocketing through him. He should never have taken advantage of her inebriated state. He desperately managed to control the urge to take her in his arms and once again explore every corner of her sweet mouth with his tongue.

No; when he kissed her again he wanted her to be clear-headed and fully aware of her actions. To continue to kiss an inebriated maiden would make him the worst of philanderers, and he was no rake. He should not have done it in the first place! And so, despite every nerve in his body screaming at him to do otherwise, he covered her gloveless hands with his own and gently removed them from his chest.

The sensation of skin on skin was too much for him so, quite without thought, he bent his head and pressed his lips to the inside of her wrist, allowing himself to linger and closing his eyes to better enjoy the moment.

Ah, Anna!

Opening his eyes, his gaze met hers and he caught his breath, for her eyes were filled with slumberous desire. To see her like this was the realisation of a thousand dreams yet frustratingly, as a gentleman, he could not act on them. What if he were to kiss her and more, and she regretted it? He could not risk such an outcome, particularly since it might lose him her friendship too.

'I cannot,' he managed in a gentle tone. 'You are foxed, my Anna, and you do not know what you are doing.'

She frowned in puzzlement, as if he were speaking in a foreign language. Taking advantage of her sluggish brain, he rose, drawing her to her feet. 'The ball is over and it is time to retire. Will you walk with me?'

She nodded, and it crossed his mind to wish for a ring on her finger, and he leading her to his own bedchamber.

Soon, my love.

Tucking her hand into his arm, he accompanied her back to the terrace, through the ballroom and up the wide staircase where they had played together so frequently as children.

'I shall leave you here, Anna. Sleep well.' Raising her hand, he kissed it then turned it over and kissed her palm, daringly touching the sensitive skin for an instant with the tip of his tongue. He was rewarded by a sharp intake of breath, followed by a shaky, 'Goodnight.'

Ah! He knew what it was for one's speech to reveal one's inner turmoil. Anna had no stammer, but the events of the past few minutes had changed everything. Her request for a kiss, the tremble in her voice, the desire in her eyes... A woman did not look at a *friend* with such eyes, after all. Exhilaration rushed through him. Maybe, just maybe, his friends had it wrong. And maybe his dearest wish could be realised after all.

Anna opened her eyes, stretched and turned over. Her head felt heavy, her mouth foul and there was a slight ache when she moved her eyes.

What on earth...?

Memories came flooding back: the ball; the garden; the wonderful kiss; Will's words, when he had refused to keep kissing her.

You are foxed...

Groaning loudly, she rolled onto her stomach, burying her head in her pillow. Mortification such as she had never known flooded through her. Had she really done such a dreadful thing? And had his rejection of her been just as unspeakable as she recalled?

Yes, and yes.

She groaned again. This, surely, had to be the absolute worst day of her entire life. He had taken the kiss she offered, yet on coming to his senses he had rejected her.

Mortification soon turned to distress and she made liberal use of her handkerchief as she cried for her loss: loss of his friendship; loss of that easiness between them... Her foolishness last night had surely ruined everything. The loss of her dearest friend as well as the possibility he might come to love her some day. Loss surrounded her in this place.

Sally came and, like the coward she was, Anna told her to go away. No, she would not be getting up, for she was unwell. Breakfast? *No.* The very thought made her feel sick. Despite knowing she was being self-indulgent, Anna was too unhappy to care. So she cried again and curled up into a ball, until a gentle scratching at the door made her quickly wipe away her tears.

'Come in!' she called, having a fair idea who was there.

'They told me you are ill!' Lady Garvald was all concern, and Anna's heart warmed at Milady's evident affection for her.

'Oh, no!' she denied as Lady Garvald closed the door and walked towards her. 'I believe I am suffering from nothing worse than a surfeit of wine.'

Lady Garvald's brow cleared as she sat on the edge of Anna's bed. 'Oh, dear! Well, at least there is an explanation.' She gave a grin that was half-concern, half-mischief. 'My head felt decidedly muddy when I woke, I must admit. And to think we were busy assessing the other ladies' levels of intoxication at supper!'

Anna had to smile weakly at that, and the next few moments were spent talking about the ball and how successful it had been.

'Such a relief!' declared Lady Garvald. 'And so much easier, knowing you were assisting me.' She pressed her lips together before adding, 'It was quite like having Maria with us, I think.'

Exhaling slowly in a clear attempt not to give way to her emotions, she glanced around Anna's room. 'This was her bedchamber, you know. That is why I asked the housekeeper to put her eldest daughter in here.' Her gaze became distant. 'She always said it was too generous, putting her in a guest room when she was a paid companion. I disagreed, saying that as well as being my highly valued paid companion she was also my dear friend, and this chamber befitted our friendship.'

'Truly?' Anna looked around the room. 'I had not remembered this was her room. She was so often in the nursery…'

'Yes, she insisted on caring for you herself as much as possible. I recall, when you were babies, the wet nurse was astonished by how infrequently she was required. Your mother had a—a *vigour* that made me throw away my own listlessness and truly live again.' Her brow furrowed. 'She had experienced such adversity yet never allowed it to deter her. She was indomitable.'

'Like Lady Kelgrove.'

Lady Garvald nodded. 'And like you and your sisters.'

Anna shook her head as memories of last night washed over her.

How can I ever face him again?

'Not like me. I am weak. I am cowardly. I am nothing like Mama in that regard.'

Lady Garvald took her hand. 'Now, then, what is all this about?' When Anna shook her head, she continued, 'Are you not Miss Annabelle Lennox? Queen's diamond, well-regarded in the *ton*, able to walk into a drawing room wearing a priceless heirloom even though some of those present may wish you harm? Are you not the Miss Lennox who led and cared for her sisters for many years after your mother's death? The Miss Lennox who *notices* and helps and makes it her business to look after others?'

Anna eyed her blankly.

'I shall tell you what your mother told me many times: every failure, every moment of adversity, only serves to strengthen women. We are forged in fire. We are steel. We are iron.' Her gaze grew distant. 'We endure what we must. The pains of our bodies. The vagaries of fate. The slights and humiliations of unhappy people.' Now she focused on Anna again. 'Nothing will break us, for at our heart we *are* the fire. Do you not feel it, burning within you—the fire of hope, of possibility, of powerfulness?'

Anna gasped. Lady Garvald's stirring words were indeed bringing a flame to life within her. 'Yes. Yes! I had not thought of it in such a way before. They call us the weaker sex. They seek to—to manage us, or cosset us. But we are perfectly capable. I mean…' She faltered, lost in her own confusing thoughts.

'We may not be able to heft a heavy weight or control a fiery stallion, yet we are strong in other ways—all of us, including you.'

'Yes.' Anna felt it beneath all the thoughts, all the conflicting emotions. Deep within her was an endless well of herself—of Anna. She dimly felt that connection to other women: the women of her family; her sisters; her mother; her great-grandmother—to all of the other women of her line. And to Lady Garvald.

'You were like a second mother to us,' she said softly. 'We missed you terribly.'

'And I you.' They embraced, then by mutual unspoken agreement began to speak of other things, including the various neighbours Anna had met at the ball. 'I particularly liked Miss Newton,' Anna offered, causing Lady Garvald to beam at her.

'Your discernment is evident, for she is quite my favourite too.' She leaned forward, adding in a confidential tone, 'Until recently, it had occurred to me to wonder if she and my son might make a match of it one day—not because I thought there was any particular attraction between them, you understand. It was more that I wish him to be happy and settled, with the right sort of wife. But it is clear to me now there can be nothing between them. One only has to see someone in the company of the person they *do* prefer to understand that. And I am delighted to say I know now with certainty they would not suit. Not at all.'

Anna did not know what to make of this at all. Was Lady Garvald referring to Mr Ashman or…?

'And what is your opinion of her cousin, Miss Hughes?' There was a knowing look in Lady Garvald's eye.

Anna focused on the question, setting aside all other notions for now. 'I thought her a perfectly amiable young lady,' she replied carefully.

Lady Garvald laughed. 'Ouch! Well said, Anna—faint praise indeed!'

'Oh, but I do not mean to offer her insult. I barely know her.'

'You have divined both of them, I think. But I shall say no more, for I see you are uncomfortable.' Her tone turned brisk. 'Now, I shall send you a tisane, which is even now being prepared by my cook for Mrs Thaxby. She and her husband have a great interest in herbs, you know, and he has recommended this particular tisane for the day after a party.' She gave a mischievous grin. 'I have no doubt it is meant to counter the effects of too much wine, and so may be efficacious for you also.'

She left soon afterwards, exhorting Anna to rest, but Anna could not. While she still felt severe mortification about her dreadful actions the night before, and had no idea how she was ever to face Will again, she had lost the urge to cry about it.

Sally brought the tisane and she drank it, enjoying the warmth and the taste of the fresh herbs within. Restlessness rose within her afterwards, and she knew not what to do with it. *I shall write, then.* Her journal had been of great assistance to her on previous occasions when she had been worrying about something. Writing about her problems or anxieties in her journal often served to reduce them to a manageable size.

This, though, was the most private, most mortifying experience she had ever committed to paper. With determination, she outlined every detail: her shocking forwardness; the divine kiss; his gentleman-like rejection of her advances; her worries about what it might mean for their friendship; her understanding that he clearly did not feel the same way about her as she felt about him. This last was particularly difficult, as it meant the abandonment of long-held dreams.

Finally, it was done, and it truly felt as though some of the awfulness of her mortification had gone out of her body and onto the page. Putting away her pen and closing her journal, she slid open the drawer as usual, then paused. While she had no reason to think anyone might read her honest words, she still wished there was somewhere more private she could stow her journal. Glancing around the desk, a thought occurred to her. Desks often had additional drawers and spaces, not obvious at first glance. Her gaze roved around the expertly crafted bureau-style desk, noticing for the first time a line of beautifully carved flowers on the lower edge of the upper shelves.

Flowers... Mama's chamber...

The hairs on her arms and at the back of her neck abruptly stood to attention and her heart raced furiously. With a shaking hand, she trailed her finger along the line of flowers, then pressed the third flower from the left. Nothing happened. She pressed harder, and this time there was a slight feeling of pressure—a little give that should not be there in a piece of solid wood. Holding her breath, she used her thumb and pressed with great force.

All at once it gave way, as a long-dormant mechanism was sprung. Anna jumped as a hidden drawer popped open on the side of the desk. Mama's secret drawer—she remembered it!

Wasting no time, she pulled it open. It was both deep and wide, and Anna briefly wondered at the craftsmanship that had enabled it to be so well designed that it had not occurred to her to wonder whether the space on the left-hand side of the desk could be accessed.

Inside was a bundle of leather-bound books, as well as a number of loose papers. Ignoring the dust, Anna lifted out the first book and opened it to the first page.

There, in Mama's handwriting, she saw what was clearly a diary entry.

Wednesday, 6 July 1796
The dry weather continues, so the children played all day in the gardens. Anna and Rose dutifully kept their bonnets in place, but my rebellious Izzy made hard work of it. In the end, Anna and Xander cleverly made it part of their game, so she went along with it. I was glad, for I should have hated to bring them inside on such a glorious day. Margaret, meanwhile, is hiding some secret. When I ask her about it, she will only look mischievous and tell me

*she is certain I shall be proud of her. It made me recall
how diffident she was when I first knew her. Together we
have overcome grief and loss, and now we share much
joy in life—particularly through the eyes of our beloved
children.*

That was all but, flicking through the book, she saw that
Mama had made entries almost every day. Most of the book
was empty. Holding her breath, she navigated to the last entry.

Monday, 25 July 1796
*And so I end my habit of near-daily musings, for we de-
part on the morrow. My heart is breaking at the notion
we must leave our home and those we love so dearly, but
I must keep my girls safe. I shall take with us only the
most important items, and so I shall leave behind my little journals. All of it is preserved in my memories anyway, and will not be lost. This house... Margaret and little
Xander... I pray I might return some day, though I cannot
imagine how it would be safe to do so. And I am truly delighted that Margaret is once again making connections
with the* ton. *It is a sign that her healing is complete, I
think. Wrenching the girls away from their ZanZan is the
most heinous thing imaginable, and I am filled with horror at my own cruelty. But it must be done, for those who
killed my husband and my brother have no compunction
and, I believe, no remorse. I only hope I can find another
home where we all might be safe, and where my daughters can grow and thrive.*
Maria Fletcher

Mama had signed it simply, using only her given name and
her surname. Wiping away tears, Anna simply sat for a moment, trying to take it in.

...those who killed my husband and my brother...

That was plain. If both George and Richard had been killed, and by the same evil people, then surely it had to have been the Thaxbys? But why—why would anyone do such a thing?

Turning to the other books and papers, she began flicking through them, realising they covered Mama's entire time at Lammermuir House—the early entries being made on loose sheets before Mama had bought, or perhaps been gifted, her first leather-bound tome.

Anna resisted the temptation to delve more deeply, knowing her sisters had to be here when she did so. So, with a great deal of composure and restraint, she set them aside and rang for Sally, who passed on the message that the princess and the viscountess were to come to Miss Lennox's room as soon as they were able. Sally then dressed her hair and helped her don a simple day dress of white muslin trimmed with embroidered bluebells.

Rose arrived first, a concerned crease on her bow. 'Anna! Whatever is the matter? Are you unwell?'

Anna walked towards her and took both her hands. 'Not at all. Oh, Rose, I have found Mama's journals!'

Rose's eyes widened. 'Her journals? I did not even know she kept a diary!'

'Nor did I. Though she always encouraged us to keep little journals, if you recall. But look—here they are!' Leading Rose to the side table, Anna indicated the books and papers that she had gently dusted with one of her best handkerchiefs after Sally had gone. 'And just look!' Picking up the relevant diary, she turned to the last entry, then waited while Rose read it.

'Oh, poor Mama! How terrible for her!'

'I know.' Anna shook her head slowly. 'She had so many troubles to bear. But she was brave, and strong, and she always did the right thing, even when it was difficult. I can do no less.'

'What troubles do you bear, Anna?' Rose asked gently.

Anna shrugged, dismissing the mortifying memories that once again threatened to consume her. 'I was tasked by our guardian to discover why Mama ran with us to Elgin. We already have most of the answers. The rest, I suspect, are in these pages.'

'How much have you read?'

'Almost nothing. I wanted to wait for you two.'

Thankfully, Izzy arrived soon afterwards, and once she understood what Anna had unearthed she immediately took a journal to Anna's bed, sat down and began to read. Exchanging a knowing glance, Anna and Rose chose a volume each and joined her.

The following hours were a mix of silent reading, exclamation and discussion. Discovery after discovery was exclaimed upon—most of them small details of their quiet life here, but details that were precious in the finding.

Sally brought tea and sweetmeats, but the triplets barely touched them. They uncovered much about themselves, their mother, Milady and ZanZan and their lives as children here in Lammermuir House. There were also multiple references to Mama's dear husband, George, her brother, Richard and her grandparents.

'Mama missed them all, it is clear,' said Anna, thinking about it. 'She lost so much—her closest family either dead or estranged.'

'But she found a new family here,' Rose observed.

'She did. And then lost them too.'

'But she had us!' insisted Izzy fiercely.

'She did. And we had each other.'

'We still do.'

Izzy had been reading on. 'Oh, listen to this!' She read aloud. '"I still find it difficult to understand how George's sister and her husband came to hate him so much. I know he would have happily given them every penny he had to be allowed to live. But, once he began speaking of marrying, they murdered him".'

Anna exhaled. 'So there it is once again, in plain English—Mrs Thaxby and her husband murdered him. She was his only sibling.'

Rose was still thinking about the other aspect of Mama's words. 'She just wanted him to have lived. Unfortunately for our papa, the law does not work in that way. He was still under-age, remember.'

'So he could not gift his estate to his trustees or anyone else.'

'And, if he married, he might have had an heir.'

'So they killed him.'

'Because wealth was more important to them than George's life!' Rising, Izzy paced about the room. 'Oh, if I could I would fight a duel with them—with them both!'

Inwardly, Anna was feeling the same anger. Mr and Mrs Thaxby were received everywhere, and no one knew about their heinous acts other than some of the people here in this house.

'They have killed twice already.' Rose's thoughts seemed to mirror Anna's.

'Yes! We must be careful. If they realise we know, or that we are George's children, they could kill again.'

Just then there was a knock at the door. All three of them hastily closed their books, but it was only Sally, returned once again.

'Beg pardon, Miss, but I've come to dress you for dinner. If you are well again, that is to say.'

'Dinner?' Anna was astonished. 'What is the time?'

Even as she spoke she realised that she had slept late, then spent quite some time feeling sorry for herself before Lady Garvald had called. Then she had been writing, and then...

'Lord, James will be wondering where I am!' Rose scrambled off the bed.

Izzy sniffed. 'I dearly *hope* Claudio is wondering where I am!'

Sally bobbed a curtsey. 'Beg pardon, my ladies, and I do not mean to speak out of turn, but the gentlemen have been riding all afternoon.'

'Thank you, Sally. Please leave us for a few moments.'

Once the maid had gone, Anna carefully placed the papers and books back in the secret drawer. 'We must say nothing of this in public, for I believe there is real danger.' She bit her lip. 'I only wish our great-grandmother could be more discreet. Knowing what we know now, I fear she is putting herself in harm's way.'

'Agreed.' Izzy made for the door. 'I shall tell her after dinner, for it is too late to call with her now. And Anna?'

'Yes?'

'Probably best *not* to wear the Fletcher necklace tonight.'

Chapter Eighteen

Dinner was largely uneventful, mainly because Anna had covered herself in an invisible suit of armour. After the astounding discoveries today, last night's events seemed far away—almost as if they had happened to someone else, or to her, but long ago.

The first time she saw Will, though—when they'd greeted one another in the drawing room just before the gong—she had been unable to hold his gaze and had covered her consternation by crossing the room to speak with Lord Renton.

The evening was warm, and the ladies were making good use of their fans. There was a temptation to drink more through simple thirst, but Anna resisted it. Lady Kelgrove complimented her hostess on the wine, and Mrs Thaxby promptly indicated with a nod to a footman that he should refill her glass. And this after they had only been seated for less than five minutes.

Will, of course, seemed to be completely natural in his manner, showing no sign of uneasiness because of events from the night before. Perhaps, then, he was accustomed to half-sprung ladies making advances to him? Her innards tightened at the very notion. But, no, she would not allow her thoughts to continue to veer in that direction, for that way led to mortification, regret, and utter sadness.

Thankfully, as usual she was not seated near him, being

placed once again with Mr Thaxby. He was polite enough, and the only time she saw anything of the undercurrents was when Lady Kelgrove made a pointed comment about her dear son Richard and how his life had been cut short by what she described as, 'Evil people who will soon, I trust, be brought to justice.'

Oh, dear! was Anna's immediate thought. *My great-grandmother is either deliberately provoking them or is slowly losing patience.*

Either way, there were risks.

Under normal circumstances Anna's gaze would have met Will's, but given the recent happenings between them she dropped her gaze to her plate—which was why, from the corner of her eye, she was able to see the whiteness of Mr Thaxby's knuckles as he gripped his knife and fork tightly in response to Lady Kelgrove's comment. A hit, then! Despite the Thaxbys' seeming nonchalance, Lady Kelgrove's barbs were clearly penetrating whatever armour the Thaxbys had built around themselves.

Afterwards the ladies retired to the drawing room in the traditional manner, leaving the gentlemen to their port. Making a show of hanging her fan on her arm, Anna was careful not to catch anyone's eye as she rose from the table. As they took their seats in the drawing room, Izzy sent Anna a long look before making her way to Lady Kelgrove. Understanding entirely, Anna joined Mrs Thaxby on the satin settee, distracting her with a series of idle questions and comments about last night's soirée.

A brief glance showed that Rose had engaged Lady Renton and Lady Garvald in conversation, allowing Izzy to apprise their great-grandmother of the afternoon's discoveries without being overheard. Sometimes it was good to be a triplet, for they understood one another precisely in such moments.

Their great-grandmother seemed utterly determined to expose the Thaxbys, but had until now only her own conviction that they had killed Richard. Surely Mama's writings formed the proof that Lady Kelgrove sought? Even now, Izzy was apprising her about what they had read today. And, daringly, she was doing so in the same room as the Thaxbys themselves!

'Indeed?' Lady Kelgrove queried sharply at one stage, and Anna hurriedly covered the brief silence with a comment about Mrs Thaxby's tisane. 'I was very grateful for it, for I must admit I felt unwell this morning.'

Mrs Thaxby's eyes lit up. 'Good wine is essential to a happy life, I believe,' she declared, signalling to the footman to bring her yet another glass. 'And having the right tisane to counter its after-effects can help. But there is a better solution.'

'Is there?' Anna looked into her blue eyes, suppressing a shudder at the emptiness she saw there... Emptiness, or maybe just coldness.

She is my aunt. But she murdered my father, and my uncle.

'Yes. I shall tell you what it is, but lean closer, for I do not wish anyone to hear us.'

Anna complied, getting a strong trace of alcohol from Mrs Thaxby's breath. Suppressing an instinct to recoil, it briefly occurred to her that in this moment she was being more judgmental about Mrs Thaxby's drunkenness than the fact that she had committed murder. The latter still felt impossible, even though she knew in her mind that it was true. The former was all too real.

Besides, Mrs Thaxby could say the same of me today, for we both drank with our dinner, and we were both foxed last night.

Anna, however, had had only one glass of wine with her meal this evening as, following last night's events, she was wary of not noticing how much she had.

'More wine!'

'What? More wine? I do not under—'

Mrs Thaxby tutted. 'Must I make myself plain? Wine *before* breakfast. I find it to be the absolute best cure for the morning effects.'

'Oh, I see.' Anna did not, not really, but supposed that remaining perpetually bosky might prevent the symptoms of sobriety.

'Indeed,' Mrs Thaxby continued, 'One might say that more wine is the cure for most of life's ills.' Her gaze became unfocused. 'Lord knows I have suffered, with all manner of sicknesses and aches and ills these long years.'

To Anna's relief, the door opened just then, admitting the gentlemen, who had decided to join the ladies with rather more haste than was usual. The fact that two of the gentlemen were newly married might account for it, but Anna wondered if, having heard from Rose and Izzy confirmation that the Thaxbys were indeed murderers, James and Claudio wished to be by their wives' sides even more than they usually did.

'Leave all to me,' Anna heard Lady Kelgrove order Izzy. Resisting the urge to swing her head towards them, she felt another pang of anxiety. Lady Kelgrove would no doubt be enraged once again, and Anna hoped the new information would not make her reckless.

The gentlemen's arrival triggered the usual adjustments in the seating arrangements. Tonight they were *en famille*, so Sir Walter and his son were not present. Claudio and James sat with Izzy and Rose while, to Anna's astonishment, Lady Kelgrove crossed the room towards Anna's chair—as if she wished to sit with Mrs Thaxby. Lady Kelgrove was clearly up to something, and Anna was helpless to know what to do for the best.

'You may take my armchair, Anna,' Lady Kelgrove instructed regally.

Anna complied—well, there was nothing else for it—rising and making her way to Lady Kelgrove's empty seat. At the same time, Will walked towards the upright chair beside it.

Oh, Lord! I am to converse with him!

Strange to think that conversing with Will had been the high point of every day since their arrival in his home. *But now?* Now all was changed.

'Are you well, Anna?' he began. 'My mother tells me you required a tisane earlier.'

Anna could feel her colour rising. 'Oh, yes, quite well.'

'But you kept to your room all day.'

She eyed him levelly. 'Females need to do so, from time to time.'

Now it was his turn to flush. 'I apologise, Anna! I did not mean to pry. Lord, I am a clumsy fool!'

Anna could not persist in the face of this honest concern. 'It is I who must apologise. For so much—not least the fact that my words just now may have given you a false impression of my reasons for not coming downstairs today.'

Glancing about briefly to ensure no one was watching or listening, she added in a low voice, 'I found my mother's journals in the desk in my chamber. My sisters and I spent quite a few hours reading them.'

'Really? I am delighted to hear it—for many reasons. And what have you learned from the diaries? For, by your manner, I deduce there must be something of significance.'

She nodded. 'The...suspicions we share, about past events, have been confirmed.'

His brow furrowed. 'All of it—George? And Richard?'

She confirmed it, trying to ignore the painful lump in her throat.

Have I lost our friendship through my dreadful behaviour last night?

Having Will as her friend was vital to her happiness, and to lose him again would be unthinkable. They had only just found one another again, and she had risked all by importuning him so dreadfully. She might never have his love, but she hoped she had not lost his affection.

'I must speak with Sir Walter.' Will's brow was furrowed. 'We know them to be ruthless, and you and your sisters may be in danger as soon as they discover your connection to that family. And Lady Kelgrove too, for she has no fear of stirring this hornet's nest.'

'Actually, I suspect the Thaxbys have no idea that Mama married and had children. Until they realise that, then we are just three random young ladies, and no threat to them.'

He raised an eyebrow. 'Young ladies who are now in possession of the Fletcher necklace.'

'Hush!' Glancing about to see who might be listening, she was relieved to see that Mrs Thaxby was currently being distracted by her own husband, who had brought two glasses of wine for his wife and Lady Kelgrove.

He is probably unaware of the three glasses his wife man-

aged to imbibe during the brief period before the gentlemen rejoined us.

She chastised herself inwardly. *Lord, I am becoming obsessed with Mrs Thaxby's drinking!*

They all spoke together and then Lady Kelgrove, normally composed, let her fan slip from her fingers as she looked up at Mr Thaxby.

Oh, dear! What had he said to discompose her? Oh, how she wished Lady Kelgrove would be careful. To be fair to the elderly lady, the Thaxbys had murdered her grandson—something she was perfectly entitled to be angry about.

And my great-grandmother has recently had confirmation of it.

Lady Kelgrove tried to catch the fan but it slipped to the floor, and both Thaxbys retrieved it for her, Mr Thaxby presenting it to her with what was clearly a false smile. Anna shivered. Frowning, she met Izzy's gaze, and instantly Izzy rose, making for Lady Kelgrove and the Thaxbys.

Izzy will not allow them to intimidate her. Not that Lady Kelgrove was prone to being intimidated, but yet…their great-grandmother was only one woman, after all. And, despite her indomitable nature, sometimes her frailty showed through.

Turning back towards Will, Anna was taken aback to see humour in his gaze. He seemed to have kept his eyes on her, and had missed the brief exchange between Lady Kelgrove and the Thaxbys.

'You are telling me to hush? Ah, that is the Anna I remember from all those years ago. You always were something of a managing female—even at five years old!'

He meant to tease. She knew it, yet all she could think about was last night and her inappropriate advances.

A managing female.

This, then, was why her teachers had constantly reminded her to be more self-effacing, more obedient, more ladylike. Because being more self-assured and emphatic led her into situations where she might make an error of judgement—such as last night.

Her thoughts flicked to her sisters. Rose was the most compliant of the three, yet had been seen kissing the viscount in a public park as a debutante—emphatic action indeed. Izzy could be confident to the point of rashness, yet as far as Anna knew she had not done anything as foolish as trying to kiss a gentleman who did not wish to be kissed.

Anna had always seen herself as the leader of the trio—unafraid to be bold when needed, urging caution when needed. Until… Ah, last night's wine had much to answer for!

Realising she was gaping like a fool, she knew she needed to respond. Unfortunately, the words which bubbled out of her were, 'Oh? And you think it a bad thing for a female to have her own opinions, then?'

He flinched—the tiniest of reactions, but she saw it. Then his expression hardened. 'Not at all, and I should have thought you know me better than to ask such a question.'

I have pierced him!

After a full London season, Anna had come to know something about the frailties of male pride, And, of course, Will was correct—she did know him, very well indeed. So this could be more than pride. Might she have hurt him? Abandoning all her inner worries for a moment, she squared her shoulders, declaring, 'Sometimes I am not sure I know you at all!'

The words erupted from her, fuelled by the swirl of confusion inside. What had he been thinking last night when he had rejected her?

He eyed her levelly. 'At all? That seems rather strong.' He frowned. 'There are certainly things you do not know—important things. You did not know me in London, certainly. You did not even recognise me.' Was there a hint of accusation in his eyes? 'But you know me now.' He paused. 'And I know you.'

'Somewhat.' It was almost a whisper. She almost became lost for a moment, drowning in the beauty and power of his gaze and words. Then reality asserted itself. He must not think her actions last night meant anything in particular. 'And we are still friends, I hope?'

Was there a hint of…*something* in his eyes? Something inscrutable and puzzling?

'Why would we not be?' He seemed to hold his breath for an instant. 'You can trust me, you know.'

'Thank you.'

What does he mean by that?

'We must speak more of these matters. We missed our usual walk this morning, but will you be there on the morrow?'

'Er... I shall, yes.' Lord, why had she not thought of some excuse? Mortification mingled with fear of having lost him. Yet the thought that she might have to forgo these walks had felt like bearing a wound deep inside. And he wished to speak about serious matters!

Lord, if he mentions the kiss I shall die of mortification!

'Miss Lennox!' It was Lord Renton. 'Will you play for us?'

She rose instantly, with a polite nod of farewell to Will.

'Naturally! Something gentle, I think, after our lively exertions last night!'

Seating herself at the piano, she found the sheets she wanted and arranged them in front of her. Taking a breath, she paused, then began to play the *andante* from Mozart's *Sonata in A Minor*. Yes, a minor key was right for tonight.

Playing calmed her as nothing else could. Thoughts of her parents, of the evil done by the Thaxbys, even of her mortifying advances towards Will, all evaporated for the moment as she lost herself in the sound of the music and the sensation of her fingers pressing the keys at exactly the right instant, her eyes running ahead on the sheet music.

Someone moved the sheets so she could see the final page properly, which was helpful, for this was not a piece she knew by heart. The movement ended, and her playing was received with acclaim by some, politeness by others.

'Brava!' murmured Will, for of course it was he who had come to assist her. As their eyes met she felt a smile come into hers—for who could not look into Will's warm gaze and not feel her heart swell fit to burst from her chest? *Stop!* She reminded herself such notions had made her behave in a most inappropriate manner. She could not risk such a thing happening again.

No more wine, no more foolish notions!

'But you must play on, my dear!' Lord Renton was insistent.

So she gave them the *menuetto*, then the Turkish *rondo*—as lively a piece as was possible, and one which required the utmost concentration, for the intricacies and speed required could easily be her undoing.

Will turned the pages for her; he could read music, though he had previously confessed to her that a lack of diligence had prevented him from mastering the piano. His preference had been for riding, fencing and, more recently, boxing. But she must not think of him at such a moment, for Mozart demanded all her attention.

Finally done, her shoulders slumped in what felt like exhaustion. Accepting the accolades of the party, including a quiet, 'Well done!' from Will, she waited for a few moments until their attentions quietened, then left the drawing room.

The retiring room used by the ladies was along the same corridor, and on entering she was relieved to find it empty. Sinking down into a soft armchair, she closed her eyes and allowed the remaining peace of the music to wash over her.

Just a moment later the door opened, but somehow she could not find the vigour to look and see who was there.

'Beg pardon, miss. I just need to leave some clean pots and bordaloues here. I shall return with towels,' murmured a serving girl.

Anna lifted her hand but did not open her eyes, and was relieved when the girl left. She would enjoy this blessed peace for a little longer. All too soon, though, she heard the door open again, then close. A swish of skirts told her she was not alone, but something was not quite right. The serving maid's simple linen dress and apron would not rustle so. Opening her eyes, she turned her head to see Mrs Thaxby advancing on her.

'Well, and look at who is here, all alone.' Her eyes glittered, and Anna's insides abruptly clenched in fear. She was suddenly fully alert.

'Ah, Mrs Thaxby.' Using every iota of inner strength, Anna managed to sound self-assured. 'I am afraid I am still feeling the effects of last night's wine.' She knew Mrs Thaxby liked to advise, and wine was clearly her favourite topic. Perhaps that distraction might defuse the rage she now saw in the older woman's eyes. 'A full twenty-four hours since I drank so much, and my brain is still befuddled.'

'Is it? Then perhaps this is a good time for me to pose some questions to you.'

'Questions?' Anna heard the tremor in her own voice. So did Mrs Thaxby, it was clear, for she gave a small smile of satisfaction.

'Your great-grandmother seems remarkably unclear as to how she acquired my necklace.' She tilted her head, as if in sympathy. 'The elderly often become forgetful. But perhaps she told you where she found it, or bought it, perhaps?' Her tone became cajoling. 'You are the eldest, after all, which is why she gave it to you, I conjecture.'

'I am certainly the eldest. But you must ask my great-grandmother, for I cannot say anything on this matter.'

'*Can*not, or *will* not, hmm?' Mrs Thaxby was now uncomfortably close, looming over Anna.

She has murdered twice before. Gathering all her inner strength, Anna rose, as if unaware that Mrs Thaxby was uncomfortably close. Crossing to the mirror, she made a show of checking her side curls. 'It is a beautiful necklace. Did you ever wear it?'

This new diversion seemed to work. Pouting, Mrs Thaxby shook her head. 'Never! The injustice of it rankles with me, as I am sure you can understand.' She sighed mournfully. 'I distinctly recall my mother wearing it before she died.'

'When did you last see it?' Anna asked, genuinely curious.

'Let me think...' She frowned, then her eyes widened. 'George was showing it to his friend Richard the night of...the night they were attacked. Perhaps those brigands took it!' Anger flashed in her eyes. 'I might have known we could not...'She broke off, as if recalling where she was. Her face was pale and she looked genuinely disturbed.

We could not trust them... Was that what she had been going to say? So the brigands who had killed Richard and left George for dead had been hired by the Thaxbys. It had been obvious, but to hear Mrs Thaxby almost say it was shocking.

Suppressing a shudder, Anna made for the door. 'I shall return to the drawing room now. Goodbye, Mrs Thaxby.'

Lost in thought, Mrs Thaxby did not reply, so Anna slipped out, a decided sense of relief running through her. On returning to the drawing room, she saw there had been a further change in the seating arrangements. Lady Kelgrove had reclaimed her usual armchair and was now chatting with Will, while Izzy was now sitting with her husband. Mr Thaxby...

Anna stilled briefly. Something about him was peculiar, and she was not sure why. He seemed agitated, and was currently mopping the back of his neck with a handkerchief, despite the fact that the heat of the day was rapidly cooling. She saw with a quick glance that none of the ladies were using their fans. For a man who was generally implacable and inscrutable, it struck her that Mr Thaxby was behaving in an odd and unexpected way.

'Are you unwell, Mr Thaxby?' she heard Lord Renton ask, even as Lady Kelgrove beckoned her to join them.

'Never better, my lord,' declared Mr Thaxby—a clear falsehood, or so it seemed to Anna.

'Why are you looking at Mr Thaxby so, Anna?' Never one to mince her words, Lady Kelgrove asked the question even as Anna was taking her seat. Thankfully, her volume was low enough that the others had not heard her.

With a nod to Will, Anna thought about it. 'He is acting strangely. Something has disturbed him.' She looked directly at her great-grandmother. 'He heard you—at dinner.'

Lady Kelgrove leaned back in her chair. 'My comment about those who commit evil receiving justice? I hoped he might. How did he react?'

In a low voice, Anna related having observed Mr Thaxby gripping tight his cutlery, and also apprised them of her conversation with Mrs Thaxby in the retiring room.

Lady Kelgrove nodded approvingly. 'Good girl. I believe my barbs have prompted him to take action, but I cannot know for certain.'

'What do you mean? Has he said something?' Will's tone was sharp. 'I will tolerate no risk or discomfort to my guests, my lady.'

She eyed him evenly. 'As to that, none of us can know the lengths they will go to—or may already have gone to. Princess Isobel has told me about Maria's journals. I should like to read them on the morrow, but for tonight I simply continued my current strategy of letting them know in plainer and plainer language that I know them to have murdered my son. What she said to you just now is even further confirmation of two things—that I have the right about it, and that they know, or suspect, that their deadly secret is known—at least by me.'

'But that might place you in danger!' Anna kept her voice low, despite fear for her great-grandmother's safety rising within her. 'If they believe you are the only person who knows, then they might attempt to—to silence you.'

'And that is exactly my plan, child.' Lady Kelgrove remained inscrutable. 'We must bring this to a head—lance this pestilence once and for all.'

Lord, what a foolish plan!

'Even if it costs your life?'

'Even then.' Lady Kelgrove patted her arm. 'I have lived long and achieved much. I shall die satisfied if I can expose the killers of my grandson and his friend.'

Anna exchanged a concerned glance with Will, but Lady Kelgrove was not done.

'They hired the men who attacked the carriage, but George was said to have died of illness, so I suspect they may have done that deed themselves.'

'He was said to have died of some kind of flux, is that correct?'

'Yes.' Lady Kelgrove's tone was clipped.

'Poison? Mr Thaxby is something of a botanist…'

'Precisely.'

Anna was piecing it together. 'When he spoke to you earlier—when you were sitting with his wife—did he threaten you?' She recalled the dropped fan—a highly unusual show of vulnerability from Lady Kelgrove.

Her great-grandmother's eyes danced with merriment. 'Perhaps, perhaps not. But say no more, for here comes his lady.'

Sure enough, Mrs Thaxby had returned. Anna noticed her face remained pale.

It is all coming back to them after twenty-one years of secrecy.

With a brief glance towards Lady Kelgrove, Mrs Thaxby sat with her husband and Lord Renton.

Lady Kelgrove continued, 'All the pieces of this little riddle are beginning to emerge. But one thing we still need is proof of your parents' wedding. All will fall without it, for only a legitimate heir or heirs can disinherit George's sister. Can you and your sisters search for that as you read the journals?'

'Of course. She uses the name Maria Fletcher in them, so I do believe they were properly married.'

Will looked from one to the other, his expression one of admiration. 'I know not why some people insist that females are weaker or less quick-witted than men.' He sent Anna a mischievous glance as he referenced their earlier conversation. 'You two ladies are astonishing.'

At his words, a wave of pride and warmth rushed through Anna. Meeting his eye, she clearly saw there what he had expressed with words: admiration for both of them, an elderly lady and his friend.

Lady Kelgrove sniffed. 'You are only just realising this?'

'Well, no, I believe I have known it for a long time. But I see it now before me.'

'Hrmph. Can you ask Lady Garvald to invite Sir Walter tomorrow? Indeed, I think we may need him to reside here for a little time.'

'Of course. I had already determined to do so, but I shall speak to my mother this instant. One of the grooms can bring a message tonight, for there is still plenty of moonlight.' Rising, he bowed, then made for Lady Garvald, who was currently seated with Lady Renton and Rose.

'A good man, I think,' mused Lady Kelgrove. 'He will do very well.' She nodded firmly. 'It will give me great satisfaction to see you all settled.'

Her meaning could not have been plainer. 'Oh no, but we

are *friends!* I mean, there cannot be anything of...of that nature between us.'

Lady Kelgrove snorted. 'What a foolish statement. Were Lord Garvald to hear it, I suspect he may revise his recently stated opinion with regard to your quick-wittedness.'

'But—'

'Child, listen to me. Friendship is the best foundation for marriage, believe me.'

Anna eyed her dubiously. 'But he only wants friendship.'

Her great-grandmother tutted in exasperation. 'What on earth makes you think so? Have you not seen the admiration in his eyes when he looks at you?'

'Well, yes, but that is simply admiration for his friend. Why, he gave you the same look!'

'Lord save us! If you cannot tell the difference between the way he looked at me and the way he looked at you just now, then I despair for the propagation of the species! Now, hush, before you say anything equally bird-witted, and reflect on what I have told you.'

Chapter Nineteen

Anna hushed and reflected. She reflected until it was time for bed, then tossed and turned for hours, still reflecting. When the birds announced the approach of dawn, she sat in the window seat, reflecting until her head hurt.

In the end she gave up. In truth, she could understand that, if she looked at the situation from the perspective of common sense with a dash of pessimism, then Will saw her only as a friend and wished her to remain that way—his rejection of her advances being a case in point. But then there were the other hints which, if she took them and put them together, created a veritable *symphony* of admiration that was distinct, intent and... and everything she could wish for.

It was safer to believe in friendship, for to hope for more and be disappointed would cause her untold pain. Round and round she went in her mind, until she could no longer think clearly at all.

Finally, it was morning proper, and she rang for Sally.

'Will you be walking in the gardens this morning, miss?' the maid asked, hovering around the various day gowns and walking dresses in Anna's wardrobe.

'I shall, yes,' Anna replied, turning away briefly to hide the heat in her face. 'I shall wear my new gown, please—the one with the lace trim. And the blue silk spencer.'

'Very well, miss. There is, I believe, a pretty silk shawl which will set it off to perfection, if it pleases you? And the bonnet with the blue ribbon, perhaps?'

'Oh, yes! A capital suggestion.'

If I am to walk out with him this morning, and if there is even the possibility that he...that he... I shall try to look my best.

Half an hour later, and with palms decidedly warm inside her thin gloves, Anna made her way downstairs and out to the rose garden. Instead of tying her bonnet under the chin as usual, Sally had tied it to one side, under Anna's right ear. It gave her a rakish look that was decidedly pleasing.

The morning was cool and dry, with only a few puffy white clouds against the cerulean sky. Despite the fact that dozens of roses had been harvested for Lady Garvald's soirée, the garden remained replete with riotous colour and heady scents. Best of all, there was Will, seated on a stone bench, watching her walk towards him. His jacket was blue, his waistcoat gold and white, offset by a perfectly arranged cravat. Buckskins and highly polished boots completed his costume. He looked every inch the gentleman—and the most handsome gentleman she had ever seen.

As she went closer, with each step her dilemma asserted itself. *He likes me. He likes me not. He sees me as a woman. He sees me as a friend.*

One thing was certain—she had to know. Could she be brave and simply ask him? Would it spoil things?

He rose.

'Good morning, my lord.'

Instead of bowing in response to her curtsey, he took her hand. 'Good morning, Miss Lennox. Are we to be very proper this morning?'

Seeing the opening, she took it. *I must know.* 'That I shall leave to you, my lord.'

His brow creased. 'Why so?' Tucking her hand into the crook of his arm, he led her away, down the rose-dappled pathway.

She took a breath. 'While I value our friendship, my mind

keeps returning to my dreadful actions on the night of the soirée. I must apologise for any discomfort I caused you.'

'Well, you did cause me discomfort, that is for certain. Great
d-discomfort.'

Her heart sank.

So I have my answer.

'You see,' he continued, 'I had wanted to k-kiss you for the
longest time, but I had no idea whether you saw me as a man
or simply…'

His voice tailed off, but she knew what he was thinking. 'As
a friend?' Astonishment rippled through her as the rest of his
words sank in. 'You *wished* to kiss me?'

Now there was a glint of humour in his eye. They had come
to the end of the path. Without hesitation, he led her to the
left, towards the woods. Well, why would he not? They often
walked there.

'I did. I do. I have wanted to kiss you since the day I danced
with you in St James's Palace.'

'When we were presented to the Queen—last *March*?' Her
heart was pounding so loudly, she could hardly speak.

He likes me!

'I knew instantly who you were—the Lennox triplets. I knew
Izzy's liveliness, Rose's dreaminess, and you…'

'Yes?' She could hardly breathe.

'You were the Anna I remembered—*my* Anna—except now
you were a beautiful woman. I believe I was lost during that
dance.' He grimaced. 'Yet I was clearly a stranger to you.'

'Oh, Will! I am sincerely sorry. I had no idea who you were.'
Nor what you were feeling. Bewilderment was making it difficult to think clearly.

He gave a rueful smile. 'I came to no harm, I assure you. In
fact, it was a useful lesson. I had been a target for the match-
making mamas ever since my first season. But you treated me
with *friendliness*.' He emphasised the word. 'A lowering experience, but one I doubtless fully deserved. And I knew I had to
tell you who I was, but agonised about how to do so.'

She nodded thoughtfully. 'Hence the house party, for all of us.'

'Yes. Regardless of anything that might develop between you and I, all three of you deserved to know the truth.'

'I shall never forget the moment I realised you were Zan-Zan. It was…overwhelming.' He had held her then, and since, with the affection of…a friend? No, with more; her heart was pounding, her brain struggling to take it all in.

'Yes,' he said simply. 'But by then I had confused matters somewhat by making a friend of you.'

'Then why…?'

'Why did I not continue to kiss you?'

She nodded.

'I told you why at the time.'

'Because I was…' She could not bring herself to say it.

Seeing her consternation, he smiled. 'You were foxed. And you might have regretted it. I told myself that the next time I kissed you, your mind must be clear. But tell me, why did my friends believe you wished only friendship from me?'

She grimaced. 'I did not understand what I was feeling. I thought that I must have half-recognised you all along—my friend ZanZan—and *that* was why…'

'That was why…?'

'That was why I was drawn to you.' She sent him a shy smile. 'But I was—I am—*entirely* drawn to you.'

There! She had said it. Not in so many words, but clearly enough that he must understand she loved him.

'Anna!'

He understood, and the fire in his eyes made a different sort of excitement kindle within her. They were nearly at the woods, and as they took the final few steps Anna had a brief moment to notice everything: how close together they were walking; the warmth of his arm beneath her thin glove; the way they walked in step with each other—just as though this were a dance and they the two most attuned dancers in the world. She noticed the excitement pulsing through her—body, mind and heart entirely focused on him and on the revelations of the past few moments. She deliberately noticed the birdsong, the breeze whispering through the trees and the colours of the woods—greens, browns and yellows.

Now they were among the trees, and, finally, out of sight of the many windows of Lammermuir House.

'Anna,' he said again, and his deep voice reverberated through her. They had stopped, and he turned to face her. 'May I kiss you?'

This is the best moment of my entire life.

'Yes. Please.' She pulled on the ribbon of her bonnet, undoing it, and he made a sound deep in his throat as he watched her.

'Anna,' he said again, lifting both hands to touch her face. He gently stroked the sensitive skin of her cheeks, and she felt as though she might die from the sheer sensation.

And he has not yet even kissed me!

He leaned closer, so close that she could feel the warmth of his breath on her face. His face was a blur this close, so she closed her eyes. An instant later, his lips were on hers—warm, wonderful and moving, moving from side to side—just a little, but it was enough for her to feel as though she had been struck by lightning—small strikes, repeated and giving only pleasure. Now he slanted to fit his lips perfectly on hers, and instinctively she moved too, tilting her head to help the alignment.

When they had kissed before, she'd known that it was wonderful, but she had been unable to clearly remember the details. This time...

Oh, my goodness!

Never had she felt anything like it. Her insides felt as though they had turned to liquid, and the same affliction now affected her bones, for she distinctively felt a weakness at her knees. But there was more to come, for now he parted his lips to explore hers gently with his tongue.

Anna thought she might die from the sensation, so delightful was it. She gasped and instantly his tongue was in her mouth, flicking across her parted lips and leading to a strange moaning sound which she realised she herself was making. She tentatively reciprocated, lifting her tongue to meet his, and his groan of desire was surely the most delicious sound she had ever heard.

After some time, the kiss changed. Now he was demanding, using greater force and more movement, and she met him at every turn, enjoying the new thrill from the passion they were sharing. His hands left her face, sweeping around her back to haul her close, and she gasped at the sensation of his body against hers. Following her instincts, she braced against him and he groaned again, pressing his hips against her midriff even as his hands swept down her back to her bottom. Now he pushed hard against her and she moaned again, not understanding what was happening to her but knowing that she liked it very, very much.

Abruptly he was gone, stepping back and sliding his hands onto her arms to steady her. Opening her eyes, she saw the desire in his and again her insides clenched. Her breathing was disordered, her heart racing, and it occurred to her that surely no one had ever felt like this before? Her body was a pillar of flaming desire, her heart exploding with love for him, and her mind... Her mind soared in the heavens somewhere—absent, but contentedly so.

Their eyes held, and held. As her body's combustion began to cool, the love in her heart seemed to strengthen the longer they held one another's gaze.

'Will...' she managed.

'Anna.' Sliding his hands down her arms, he took both her hands to his mouth and kissed them. Even through her gloves Anna felt the sensation. What would it be like without glove, without any clothing? Little wonder that her sisters spent so much time in their husband's beds. She had had exactly two kisses in her life, but she wanted more. She wanted all of him, all the time—forever.

Bending, he picked up her bonnet and handed it to her. As she carefully re-tied the ribbon next to her right ear, he watched her intently. When she was ready he placed her hand in the crook of his arm again and they walked on—just as though they had not just engaged in passionate love-making in the midst of a Scottish woodland.

They talked then about her advances towards him, and how it had encouraged him to hope. Reassuringly, he had not been put out in the least. 'And I am glad that I did not continue to kiss you then—despite the effort it took not to do so.' He sent her a warm glance. 'Instead, our kiss just now was perfect. We had privacy and sunshine—and neither of us is in any way bosky!'

Happiness bubbled out of her. 'It was indeed perfect. I could not be happier.'

Stopping, he turned to face her again. 'There is but one thing that could complete my happiness, Anna. I—'

'My lord! My lord!'

They turned their heads. A young page was running towards them at full tilt, his little face red from exertion.

'You are to come quickly, my lord!'

Chapter Twenty

❦

Anna's heart sank. Abruptly, all of the realities came rushing back as her mind regained dominance over her body and her heart. Fear coursed through her.

'What has happened?' Will's tone was clipped; he too was concerned.

Is it Lady Kelgrove? My sisters? Have the Thaxbys done something?

The page bowed, still out of breath. 'Her ladyship has sent me to fetch you. I know one of the grooms is being sent for the doctor too, sir.'

A sick feeling rushed through Anna and she exchanged a glance with Will. 'Very well,' he said. 'Tell my mother I shall come directly. Where shall I find her?'

'She was in the breakfast room, sir.'

The page dashed off again, and Anna and Will hurried after him. Neither spoke, but he covered her hand with his, squeezing it gently, and she took some comfort from it. As they neared the house, a horseman passed them, heading towards the gate—the rider one of the grooms whom Anna had met during her riding lessons.

Who is sick? And how bad?

Pausing only to exchange boots for slippers, and for Anna

to hand her bonnet to a maid, they made their way directly to the breakfast room. It was still early, and therefore not unusual for the room to be half-empty. Glancing about, Anna saw Lady Garvald, the Rentons and the Thaxbys, but her sisters and their husbands were absent, as was...

'Oh, my dear Anna.' Lady Garvald rose to greet them. 'Lady Kelgrove's maid says she is dreadfully unwell. She has apparently asked for the doctor to be sent for.'

Without considering why, Anna's gaze immediately flicked to the Thaxbys. Mrs Thaxby seemed unconcerned—but then, other people's troubles rarely seemed to concern her. Mr Thaxby, on the other hand... Anna's eyes widened. He was showing the same restlessness as he had the night before, but was there a hint of satisfaction glinting in his eye?

What has he done?

Oh, Anna knew she was leaping to conclusions. He was no friend to Lady Kelgrove, and news that she was unwell might simply have pleased him. It did not necessarily mean that he...

'Are my sisters still abed?'

Lady Garvald nodded. 'I have sent servants to inform them, so they will be up and dressed before long.' She made a helpless gesture. 'Lady Kelgrove would not allow me into her chamber—her abigail, Hill, was most insistent. She wishes to see only the doctor and her great-granddaughters.'

'I shall go at once.'

With a glance towards Will, and a curtsey to all, Anna hurried out of the breakfast room. As she climbed the stairs, she noticed the sick feeling in her stomach was increasing. Lady Kelgrove was dear to her, and the notion she was unwell was deeply concerning. Worse, the notion that her sickness might not be natural was terrifying.

Knocking on the door, Anna tried to compose herself. It would never do to let Lady Kelgrove know her suspicions. The door opened a crack, then more widely.

'Miss Lennox!' Hill bobbed a curtsey. 'I hope you can help me, for I do not understand what ails my lady!' She lowered her voice. 'She has had a—a *digestive* upset during the night, but is much more affected by it than she should be.' Wringing her hands, she then took a corner of her apron and dabbed at her eyes.

They were already walking towards the large bed. The curtains had been drawn around it and, as she lifted a hand to draw them back, Anna braced herself for what she might see.

Lady Kelgrove looked tiny against her pillows, her long grey hair in a simple braid and a thin linen nightgown exposing her neck and collarbones. Her eyes were closed, her arms lying over the covers, and Anna was struck by how aged and frail she looked. Fully dressed, with her hair dressed and her indomitable spirit, one could easily forget that she was eighty-four. Just now, it was all too apparent.

Anna swallowed, bending over to speak softly to her.

'Great-Grandmother! I am here. It is Anna.'

Her eyes opened and one thin hand clutched at Anna's arm. 'Anna!' Her voice was thready, faint. 'I must speak with you alone.'

'Of course!' Anna glanced towards Hill, who nodded and left the room, quietly weeping. She would be just outside the door, Anna knew, ready to tend to her beloved mistress in whatever way she could.

'Is she gone? Are we alone?' Never had Anna seen the strong, stubborn Lady Kelgrove exhibit such uncertainty, such...was it fear?

'Yes, all alone, I guarantee it.' Anna sat on the edge of the bed. 'Now, what do you need to speak with me about?'

As she gazed anxiously at her great-grandmother's face, a change came over the old lady's expression. The fear in her eyes was replaced with mischief, and she released the hand clutching Anna's arm.

'Ah, good to see my play-acting has fooled even you, Anna, for you and Hill are both quick-witted and discerning—most of the time, leastways.

Anna's jaw dropped. 'Play-acting? Are you not ill?'

'Not a bit of it!' Lady Kelgrove declared cheerfully, just as there was a knock at the door. 'I had nausea and flux during the night, as may happen to anyone from time to time. But I am already recovering.' She gestured in the general direction of the door. 'If that is one of your sisters, bring her in. Anyone else must be sent away.'

What on earth is she up to?

Anna's mind was reeling, but her heart felt only relief that her great-grandmother was not, after all, at death's door.

It was both her sisters. 'We met on the landing just now,' said Rose, her brow furrowed with anxiety. Izzy just looked fierce—which Izzy always did when troubled.

'How is she?'

For answer, Anna waved them in, unsure what she was supposed to say. Sure enough, Lady Kelgrove subjected Izzy and Rose to more of her 'play-acting', then broke into laughter that had more than a hint of a cackle about it.

Bemused, they looked at one another. Anna raised a wry brow. 'Play-acting, apparently. She has been unwell but, she says, is now recovered.'

'What? But why would you do such a thing?' Rose was clearly as bewildered as Anna.

Izzy laughed along. 'Ah, infamous! You fooled us all. I salute you, Great-Grandmother!'

'I used to lead your great-grandfather a merry dance when we were young, you know.' Her black eyes danced with glee. 'He could never tell when I was jesting—a useful deficiency which I fully exploited.'

Anna was determined not to be distracted. 'There is a reason for this, is there not? This is no jest.'

Sobering, Lady Kelgrove looked at Anna. 'Aye.' She sighed. 'Yesterday you told me that we were correct, and that those wicked, wicked people killed Richard.'

'Yes. And George.'

'The first murder,' Lady Kelgrove continued, 'Was simple in its execution—they simply hired ruffians to stage a murder by way of a staged robbery. But the hired men made a mull of it. They killed the wrong man—the intention was to kill George, not Richard.'

She pursed her lips. 'Richard was of no interest to them. Their intention was fratricide, and he was less than nothing to them. But George survived.' She eyed them keenly. 'George's inheritance was their aim. The Fletcher lands and properties are not entailed, so everything passed to the sister, as the closest relative—the closest *known* relative, that is. But I wondered, time and again, how did they kill George?'

Izzy frowned. 'He was said to have died of some sort of flux—not uncommon, even in young and healthy people.'

'Exactly. Yet I know it was murder. And, judging from the Thaxbys' reactions to my barbs, they know it too.'

Anna knew exactly what she was suggesting. 'Mr Thaxby's tisanes! And his interest in all things botanical!'

Lady Kelgrove nodded. 'Precisely.' She took a breath. 'I have reason to believe that yesterday evening Mr Thaxby attempted to poison me.'

There were collective gasps, then the questions began.

'But how?'

'When?'

Anna took a breath. 'You say "attempted"—was he not, then, successful?'

Lady Kelgrove grimaced. 'I hope not, but I cannot be certain. I took a hand in things, and can only pray that I did the right thing.' She looked up at them. 'I must admit, girls, that I did not sleep very well, for even after my physical discomfort eased I was constantly wondering if I would begin to feel ill again at any moment. That was how the idea came to me to pretend to be so.' She grimaced. 'Of course, if he has used something slow-acting, I may yet become ill. But this way I can set my affairs in order before I go.'

'Do not even say that, Great-Grandmother!' Rose took Lady Kelgrove's hand. 'You will be here to keep us in order for a long time yet!'

Lady Kelgrove sniffed. 'Maybe, maybe not. But we must observe them carefully today. And, much as I hate to say it, I must not be left alone with either of them. It would not take much for them to snuff out my life—one of my own pillows would be enough.'

'I did think,' Anna said slowly, 'That Mrs Thaxby seemed untroubled by the news you were unwell. Mr Thaxby, however...'

'Well? Spit it out, girl!'

'He seemed pleased. And also agitated.' She shrugged. 'I may be imagining it, of course, but...'

'Good girl, Anna. Precisely as I imagined! Now, here is what I need you to do...'

They listened carefully. Hill was to be encouraged to go to the servants' hall, where she would undoubtedly reinforce the belief that Lady Kelgrove was deathly ill. Anna was to spread concern among the guests, and also seek Will's assistance, for Lady Kelgrove wished to speak to Mr Thaxby's valet without his master knowing. Rose and Izzy were to bring Maria's journals to Lady Kelgrove's room, where collectively they would assemble the evidence to be shown to Sir Walter. And later, when all was ready, Sir Walter himself was discreetly to be brought to Lady Kelgrove.

'Anna, where is the Fletcher necklace?'

'It is in Will's safe. I thought it best, for Mrs Thaxby is quite fixated on it.'

'Good. Leave it there until all of this is over—unless I need you to incite Mrs Thaxby once again. But, if I am right, all will be clear by the end of the day. Oh, and Anna?'

'Yes?'

'What took place between you and Mrs Thaxby after you played the piano last night?'

Anna shook her head admiringly. 'You miss nothing! I found myself alone in the retiring room with her, and she spoke of the necklace again.' Anna briefly recounted the conversation.

'Hmm. He may be the one to commit the evil deeds, but she is clearly party to it. Now go, Anna. Your sisters will remain with me for now.'

Anna went, firstly sympathetically instructing Hill to go to the housekeeper for tea, and promising to call for her as soon as the doctor came. Hill went—unhappily, it had to be said—and Anna's heart warmed at the abigail's regard for her employer. It struck her that, whether it was soon or a few years in the future, Lady Kelgrove would indeed die one day, and when that happened Hill should be given a safe retirement and a comfortable pension.

As Hill made for the servants' staircase, Anna returned to the breakfast room, where she hoped to find Will and his mother. Bracing herself before going in, she knew that she did not need to play-act, for Lady Kelgrove's words had not been reassuring. If the elderly lady had indeed been given a slow-acting poison, then they might well lose her in the coming days.

All eyes turned to her as she entered, the gentlemen rising from their repast to acknowledge her. Following a round of formal greetings, Anna sat, accepting a cup of tea from the footman and wondering idly how they were all supposed to keep themselves safe from hidden poisons.

'How is Lady Kelgrove, my dear?' Lady Garvald was all sympathy.

Anna answered carefully. 'She has suffered in the night. We must await the doctor's opinion, but I must say I have never known her to take to her bed.'

'That is concerning indeed. Please let me know what I or my staff can do to assist.'

'Of course. My sisters are with her just now, and I shall rejoin them shortly. We plan to take turns for breakfast.'

In reality they could easily have asked for rolls and chocolate to be brought to Lady Kelgrove's bedchamber, but it was important that Anna complete the tasks set for her—including her responsibility to ensure the household genuinely believed Lady Kelgrove to be unwell.

All present asked for their good wishes to be sent to Lady Kelgrove, whether sincerely or just politely. Anna took them all with equanimity, thanking everyone while privately acknowledging that Mr Thaxby looked and sounded entirely genuine. If he had indeed tried to poison Lady Kelgrove, this then represented a level of deception and coldness that Anna could simply not fathom. She shivered.

'It might be this sultry weather,' remarked Mrs Thaxby, setting down her fork to mop her brow. 'I declare it is making me feel decidedly colicky.'

'Perhaps,' Anna murmured, though privately thinking the morning was still pleasantly cool. Mrs Thaxby continually needed to be at the centre of people's attention, which was wearing.

Does she know what her husband has done? Anna could not imagine so.

'The doctor should be here shortly,' said Will, and Anna looked at him properly for the first time. It all came back instantly—the magical kisses and magical words they had shared on this morning's walk. It felt as though a lamp was lit inside her—a lamp that burned with the power of a hundred suns.

He is Will! And he is my *Will!*

'That is good news indeed.' Her words could not have been any more neutral, yet speaking to him, meeting his gaze, made love, hope and passion rise within her. But Lady Garvald gave her a curious look, so she busied herself by taking a sip of tea.

The sound of a carriage outside made all heads turn to the window. 'The doctor, I presume,' observed Lady Renford.

'No! Look, there is a crest!' Mrs Thaxby's tone had a gleeful edge and Anna was wearily reminded of the ongoing battle of wits between the two ladies. They loved to contradict one another—on principle, it seemed.

'It is probably Sir Walter. I invited him for the day. He is impressively early.'

Mrs Thaxby, craning her neck, was moved to pout. 'His handsome son does not accompany him today. What a disappointment that must be for you, Miss Lennox!'

Anna flushed, but could find nothing to say. On her right, Will asked Lord Renton about their planned ride after breakfast, and the moment passed.

The door opened, a footman announcing Sir Walter, who entered with a great deal of bustling and joviality. Despite telling them he had already broken his fast, he accepted Lady Garvald's invitation to join them, and was soon tucking in to beef and eggs, washed down with tea. Claudio arrived shortly afterwards, followed by James, and the gentlemen then dominated the gathering, engaging in a lively conversation about horseflesh and horseracing, to which Anna could contribute exactly nothing. But she did not mind, for it gave her the opportunity to observe the others.

The Rentons, sitting at opposite sides of the table. The Thaxbys, together but saying little. Lady Garvald, gracious and diligent in her care for her guests. Twice Anna saw her beckon the footmen, who would return shortly afterwards with more food, as the gentlemen could clear a board with great efficiency. Claudio and James, with easy jesting and a great deal of wit, were engaging Will and Lord Renton in raillery, and it occurred to Anna once again that both her sisters had chosen well.

This led her thoughts to places where they probably should not go. What had Will been about to say earlier when the page had interrupted them? But *no*, she told herself sternly. Such matters would have to wait, for even now Lady Kelgrove was abed, possibly having been poisoned. And Anna had further tasks to complete—important tasks.

She tried to catch Will's eye discreetly, for she needed to talk to him about Mr Thaxby's valet. Unfortunately, the gentlemen were currently discussing their planned ride immediately after breakfast, following a route of Will's suggestion which he said would guarantee them some fine fences. Sir Walter would go too, Will having offered him what he described as a 'good-hearted' mount. Even Mr Thaxby, who did not join in their levity, could not forgo the enticement of such sport. Anna could almost see in his eyes the moment when he engaged with the idea and agreed to go.

Their meal complete, the gentlemen rose, bidding farewell to the ladies and exiting with a great deal of clatter and noise. Anna could do nothing about it, but she had failed in the final task set for her by Lady Kelgrove—to seek Will's help in discreetly sending Mr Thaxby's valet to Lady Kelgrove. The departure of the gentlemen left a silence, broken by the ticking of the clock and the gentle sound of Lady Renton stirring her tea with a silver spoon.

'Well,' she began, 'Thank goodness for that! Now we shall have some peace.'

Mainly addressing Lady Garvald, she then proceeded to dominate the conversation, filling it with her observations about the weather, her new gown and other such nothings, while Anna became increasingly restless within. Mrs Thaxby concentrated on her wine, with which a footman had helpfully presented her almost as soon as Mr Thaxby had left the room. Anna had not even seen the woman's signal to the servants, but it seemed they were well aware of her habits.

Another carriage arrived soon afterwards—this one plain and crest-free. With a great deal of relief, Anna accompanied Lady Garvald to greet Dr West, a kindly-looking man in his middle years. As they climbed the stairs, he asked for more information about his patient, having been given only the sketchiest of details by the lady's groom, he said.

'Miss Lennox is Lady Kelgrove's great-granddaughter and has been tending to her,' Lady Garvald explained.

'I see.' He turned to Anna as they walked. 'What can you tell me, Miss Lennox?'

What may I tell him?

Lady Kelgrove would likely not wish her speculation about poisoning to be known. Yet, if she had been poisoned, surely the doctor should be informed of it?

'She was sick and also experienced…er…flux during the night.'

'I see. And is she generally in good health?'

Now they were on safer ground. 'Indeed she is—in fact, she is resoundingly healthy for a lady of her age.'

'And…er…' he coughed discreetly '…might I ask how old she is? It is helpful to know in my profession.'

Anna told him, and a moment later they reached Lady Kelgrove's bedchamber. 'This is Dr West,' she said when Izzy opened the door. 'This is my sister, Princess Isobel, and my other sister, Lady Ashbourne.'

Following the greetings, and the usual comment about how alike they were, Dr West proceeded into the room, followed by Lady Garvald. Although their great-grandmother had previously forbidden entry to all but the triplets, Anna hoped she would not mind their kind hostess being present.

As the doctor introduced himself to Lady Kelgrove and began questioning her about her illness, Anna exchanged glances with her sisters. Thankfully they seemed serene, signalling that their great-grandmother had remained in fine spirits since her absence, she hoped.

Now, of course, Lady Kelgrove was play-acting for the doctor—as good a show of weakness and feebleness as Anna had ever witnessed.

She is an absolute wretch!

With her permission, Dr West gently pressed on her stomach and looked inside her mouth, as well as placing his hand on her head to check for fever. His examination complete, he advised bed rest, a tisane of mint leaves and ginger root and an avoidance of rich foods in the coming days. Lady Garvald undertook to ensure everything would be provided for Lady Kelgrove as per his instructions, sending her bedridden guest a look of warm sympathy and concern.

Dr West was just preparing to go when there was an urgent knock at the door. Rose, who was closest, opened it—to reveal a young serving maid who looked extremely agitated.

'My lady!' She curtseyed to Lady Garvald. 'It's Mrs Thaxby. She has just cast up her accounts and is moaning and carrying on like she is in agony! Her abigail has taken her to her chamber and the girls are cleaning the breakfast room, my lady.'

'Oh, dear!' Lady Garvald turned to the doctor. 'It seems you have another patient, Dr West. If you will be so good as to follow me?' With a brisk farewell to Lady Kelgrove and the triplets, Lady Garvald escorted the doctor from the room.

The door closed behind him and Anna took a breath. 'And to think I thought Mrs Thaxby was merely seeking attention when she said she felt unwell earlier. I am chastened, for my thoughts were decidedly uncharitable!'

Lady Kelgrove shuffled into a sitting position. 'You need not feel sorry for either of them, for I believe they both are truly wicked. Now, is the valet coming to speak with me? And what of Sir Walter? Rose saw him arrive nearly an hour ago. Will he stay long enough for us to complete our work here?' She indicated the small pile of journals on her bedside table. One of Anna's sisters must have fetched them. There were no papers, though, and the height of the pile suggested that not all of Mama's diaries and papers had been brought to Lady Kelgrove's chamber.

'Never mind that for a moment,' Anna dismissed firmly. 'Firstly I wish to know how you are. Any further discomfort?'

'Nary a bit! I am well, as I told you earlier.'

'But Mrs Thaxby is unwell,' said Rose with a frown. 'Might she be afflicted by the same illness that struck you in the night? Perhaps it is just a common malady, rather than anything sinister.'

'If it is *not* the same illness then I shall be astonished!' declared Lady Kelgrove. 'But we must be quick, for Sir Walter will wish to speak to you about the necklace, Anna, and we are not yet ready. Bring me the rest of those journals and papers, and be quick about it!'

Izzy came with her, and together they emptied the secret drawer of all its remaining treasures, carefully closing it again.

'What do you think ails Mrs Thaxby?' Izzy asked, her brow furrowed.

Anna shrugged. 'Stomach complaints are not uncommon, and can sometimes spread through a household. We know this.'

'Yes but...' Izzy bit her lip but said nothing further. *Poison.* The unspoken suspicion hung between them. What had Lady Kelgrove meant? And was the possibility now gone, since Mrs Thaxby was also ill? The woman would not have poisoned herself, and Mr Thaxby's devotion to her was indisputable.

As they hurried along the landing back towards Lady Kelgrove's bedchamber, an idea came to Anna. 'Take these!' Handing Izzy her share of Mama's papers, she turned as if to go back. 'I shall join you shortly.'

Why should I wait for Will?

Normally only gentlemen interacted with valets, but the gentlemen were out riding. *All* the gentlemen, including Mr Thaxby. Which meant Anna might be able to speak to his valet without being caught. As she passed Mrs Thaxby's door, she heard agonised wailing from within, and winced. Mrs Thaxby certainly sounded as though she was in severe pain.

The next chamber belonged to Mr Thaxby. Holding her breath, she opened the door without knocking and walked inside. As she had hoped, the valet was there alone. Seeing her, he leapt to his feet, abandoning the garment he seemed to be in the process of mending. He bowed, then stood, waiting. For just a moment Anna stood frozen, sensing the enormity of the moment. If this man knew things, would he tell her? And, despite the abuse he received, was he loyal to his master, as all good servants were trained to be?

'Your name is John, is it not?'

He dipped his head. 'It is.'

'And how long have you been in service to Mr Thaxby?'

A gleam of approval lit his eye. 'More than twenty years, miss. And I served the Fletchers before that.'

This was encouraging. 'Did you?'

'Aye. I was valet to the young master—Mr George, that is. And me only a handful of years older than him.'

Anna's heart was now decidedly faster than it ought to be, and her palms prickled with excitement. *He knew my father!*

'Was Mr Fletcher...that is to say, do you know if he...?' How to word things delicately? Despite his open demeanour, the man might wish her ill as much as his master did. 'Was he good to you?'

'He was the best of gentlemen,' John replied, his eyes softening. He thought for a moment, then added very deliberately, 'And a great favourite with the ladies, despite being so young. But he only ever had eyes for one lady, if I may say so.'

We understand one another.

'Miss Maria Berkeley...' Anna breathed. 'My mother.'

He nodded. 'The very same.' He shook his head. 'I only put it all together very recently when I saw the Fletcher necklace, and then the Lammermuir servants told me that Lady Kelgrove's granddaughter had lived here with her children—you and your sisters, miss. Mr George... We both assumed she was carrying a single baby.'

He knows!

Anna ginned. 'Not Mama! She did not do anything by halves!'

'A formidable young lady, if I may say so, miss.'

'You may certainly say so, and I thank you.' She nodded firmly. 'Lady Kelgrove wishes to speak to you, if it pleases you?'

He straightened his shoulders. 'I always believed this day would come, and I am happy to speak to her again. She asked me some questions before, but I had to feign ignorance. My master…' He grimaced. 'I must warn you, miss, if my master learns the truth…' He swallowed. 'He might seem civilised, but a monster dwells within him.'

Chapter Twenty-One

Nausea roiled through Anna's stomach. Each time she was reminded of the Thaxbys' evil acts, each time there was further confirmation that their suspicions were correct, it made her feel sick, frightened, and perfectly furious.

'I shall do my best to protect you, John,' she said quietly. 'And I believe I can guarantee you a new position, should you need one.' Through Will, James or Claudio, she would make certain of it. Being cast off without a reference was the worst thing that could happen to a servant.

Monster.

She managed a nod. 'Come, now.' Turning, she led the way, allowing him to walk a few paces behind her. Any servants that saw them would hopefully think nothing of it and assume that John was on some legitimate errand. Reaching her great-grandmother's door, she poked her head inside to check who was present. The bed was strewn with papers and journals, her sisters and Lady Kelgrove engrossed in reading. On hearing the door open, they lifted their heads.

'Mr Thaxby's valet is here,' Anna told them softly.

Lady Kelgrove inclined her head regally. 'You may admit him.'

In he came, looking extremely discomfited at finding himself in my lady's bedchamber. He bowed deeply.

Lady Kelgrove came straight to the point. 'Tell me of my granddaughter's relationship with Mr George Fletcher.'

'They loved one another deeply, my lady. It happened after the attack on the heath, when he went to your country estate for his recuperation. I was with him there, and I saw how Miss Maria nursed him, how they came to care for one another.'

'Was his sister aware of their connection?'

'No. Nor her husband. They resented your influence over him, my lady, and at the same time seemed grateful not to have the responsibility of caring for him.'

Lady Kelgrove's eyes grew distant. 'He was like a second grandson to me, particularly after Richard was killed.' She eyed the valet sharply. 'What do you know of that incident?'

'I know very little. As to what I *suspect*, I have not voiced it in a very long time. It would have been dangerous to do so.'

'Will you speak of it now—tell me of your suspicions?'

He squared his shoulders. 'I believe that Mr Thaxby had hired someone to attack the coach that night. I was not there, so I cannot say. But, afterwards, too much seemed strange.'

'The level of violence upon the occupants of a crested coach?'

'Yes. It made no sense, for highwaymen are not normally so ruthless. It was only after the falling out with Mr Fletcher that I began to wonder if there was some connection between the events.'

'Falling out?' Her tone was sharp. 'Due to what cause?'

'His desire to marry, my lady.'

'He told them of it? Lord, his own naivety was his downfall?'

'He was only twenty years old, my lady.' John spoke softly, but it warmed Anna's heart to see how he defended George, even now. 'Thankfully, he had been out and about around town for a short time before he resolved to tell them.'

'Why "thankfully"?'

'He told them only of his desire to marry, without mentioning the name of his lady. They assumed he had developed a sudden *tendre* for one of the young ladies who had lately arrived for the season and, perhaps understandably, were not best pleased with the notion.'

He shrugged. 'At the time it seemed reasonable. He was very

young and if, as they assumed, he had become suddenly enamoured of someone, then as responsible trustees it was right for them to dissuade him.'

'True. Had Maria come to me, I should also have dissuaded her. She was at the time almost eighteen, and with a single season behind her. While I should have been pleased to see her settled, I might have worried that George would eventually stray. Young men can be very volatile, you know.'

'Not my master.' John's tone was firm. 'As steady a young man as ever there was. And he adored Miss Maria.'

'You assisted them to run away?'

'I obeyed my master's orders.' He held her gaze and after a moment she gave the slightest of nods, accepting his perspective.

'Continue.'

He exhaled. 'He did not take me with him, so I had no idea where he was or what he was doing. I only hoped he and his lady were well.'

Anna could hardly breathe. Finally, they were hearing the whole story. *If only Will were here!*

But she would save everything in her memory to recount to him later, for she was certain he would be interested in every detail.

They talked on, Lady Kelgrove asking John to provide more details of the elopement. It had been arranged by letter, John having sent it to Maria's serving maid. 'Young Ellen!' Lady Kelgrove gasped. 'So she knew!'

'What happened to her?' Izzy asked.

Lady Kelgrove shrugged. 'She got a position as a lady's maid in another household. And she never breathed a word, even though she knew I was grieving for my "dead" granddaughter.'

'I suppose,' suggested Rose, 'She could not say anything, since it was Lord Kelgrove himself who put it about that Maria had died.'

Lady Kelgrove pursed her lips. 'True. My husband has much to answer for—and so I shall tell him when I join him after this life is done.'

Anna had to laugh. 'The poor man will be dreading your arrival in heaven, Great-Grandmother!'

This earned a twinkle. 'Poor man nothing! I shall have strong words for him, I assure you! But do continue, John. Where did they go when they eloped?'

'I know not. As I said, Mr George disappeared for many months, and I heard that Miss Maria had died of the smallpox. I assumed him to be distressed at losing her, and was dreadfully worried about him. And then one day he turned up in the Fletchers' country house, bold as brass, and wishing me a good day! To say I was flabbergasted is an understatement.'

'What was his demeanour?' asked Rose.

'He was in alt. "I am a married man," he told me, sending me a wink. "And I mean to inform my sister of it!" So I told him that Miss Maria Berkeley was said to have died, and that sobered him.'

'How had the Thaxbys reacted to his disappearance?'

He sighed. 'They were furious at his disobedience, but at the same time enjoyed the freedom to spend his money as they wished.' He thought for a moment. 'I think his presence had inhibited them to some extent before then.'

He grimaced. 'By that time I had been assigned to the service of Mr Thaxby and came to know him rather better.' He shook his head. 'Doubts had been sown in my mind about the attack on the heath when his friend had been murdered. It seemed a preposterous notion, but I wondered if Mr George had been the one meant to die that night.'

'I came to the same conclusion, but I have no proof.'

'Nor I.'

There was silence, then Lady Kelgrove continued, 'And what of George's death?'

John shook his head. 'That was a bad business, and no mistake. As I say, Mr George had been gone for many months, and came back because he wanted them to approve of his marriage. But after speaking to them he kept saying how he had seen a different side to them, and how they would not approve of his marriage, ever.'

He shrugged. 'I made my own disapproval plain, for I

thought him mistaken—the heat of a fervent mind. Afterwards, though...' He sighed. 'Mr George was right and I was wrong. If I had only seen it earlier, recognised the danger...but I thought it was the eternal tale of young lovers eloping from the justified disapproval of their families.

'I did counsel him to refrain from telling them he was already married, and to whom. I advised him to say only that he *intended* to marry, as he had done previously. "I shall come into my majority in a matter of months anyway, John," he said to me.' John sighed. 'In reality I believe Mr and Mrs Thaxby were already focused on that fact.'

He shook his head. 'For three or four days there were constant arguments, which ended with Mr George warning them that he would shortly be holding the purse strings and that they would do well to remember it.' His lips tightened. 'I happened to be present during that exchange, and I honestly believe that was the moment when Mr Thaxby decided he must be murdered soon.'

'And they clearly did not know it was our mother whom he loved.' Izzy's expression was thoughtful.

'That is correct, Your Highness. Indeed, at one point Mr George hinted to them that he was enamoured of a serving maid. The mistress was filled with rage at the very notion, and made as if to strike him, but Mr Thaxby held her back. "Not like this, my love," he said to her, and something about it made me shudder at the time.' He frowned. 'It still does.'

Anna understood, for his tale was extremely disturbing. Mr Thaxby had coldly planned to murder George and had then carried out his evil plan—presumably, with the full support of his wife.

'What happened then?'

'Mr George got sick...that very night.' He closed his eyes briefly. 'It took three days for him to die.'

Anna found her voice. 'Did he know?' John looked at her. 'That Mr Thaxby had done it?'

John nodded grimly. 'Mr and Mrs Thaxby came to see him when he was sick and, when they left, Mr George was distraught. He told me then that his brother-in-law had admitted to poisoning him, but that it could not be proven, and no one would ever believe him. He wrote to her.'

Rose said, 'Anna,' and something in her voice drew Anna's attention away from John's tale. 'We found this just now, among Mama's papers.' She was holding out a letter.

Anna's eyes roved over it, noting that it was simply signed '*George*'. Taking a breath, she read it.

My Darling Maria,
Our hopes are dashed for ever.

My sister and her husband have poisoned me, and I may have only hours left in this world. They refuse to send for the doctor, and laughed when I suggested it. My love, they believe themselves to be safe and, while I told them I wished to marry, they believe I am enamoured of a serving maid, so they do not suspect the truth. But we cannot be certain they will never find out, for there are more than a few people—including servants—who know about us.

Once I am gone John, my steadfast valet, will deliver this letter, and when you get it, you must not return to our little hideaway. Find somewhere new, somewhere safe. That way, my murderous sister and her evil husband cannot find you, nor our precious child.

They killed Richard too—she admitted it to me today. That was their first attempt to murder me, and your dear brother was accidentally caught in their scheme. I must trust John and believe him when he says he remains loyal to me. He says he will stay in their service and attempt to seek justice for me, and for Richard. He will take care of my inheritance so long as he lives. However, he cannot tell what he does not know, and so I recommend you do not even tell John where you are going.

The money I left you will not last long, but I fear if you return to your family my sister may discover that you are my wife and may try to harm you and our child. Your grandparents, I am sorry to say, have apparently put it about that you died of smallpox. Therefore, I urge you to go where you cannot be found, and where you may be safe.

I am most heartily sorry. I have failed in my duty to pro-
tect you and our child. I know of nowhere in society that
can withstand their enmity and the reach of their wealth.
My wealth, indeed, but their aim all along has been to
take it for themselves.

My eyes grow dim and my hand weak. I must stop soon.
It remains only for me to assure you of my ever-lasting
love and devotion. Some day, my darling wife, we shall be
reunited in heaven. I urge you to be safe, and be happy.
Remarry if it pleases you, and know that my only desire
is—and ever was—your happiness.
George

Lord! Overcome, Anna reached for the back of a nearby chair
for support. Then Rose was there, placing an arm around her
and murmuring words of comfort.

'They *laughed*.' Anna felt a shudder ripple through her. 'I
do not know why that detail in particular is so striking, but it
is sending a chill through me. When he asked for the doctor,
they *laughed*.'

Rose shook her head sadly. 'Yes, they did. And for over
twenty years they have lived off the benefits of their wicked
actions, while our father was dead, and Richard was dead, and
Mama…'

'Mama endured struggles she should never have had to endure,' Izzy finished fiercely, her hands bunched into fists and
her voice tight with emotion. Rounding on John, she asked,
'Why did you never tell anyone? Why did you work for them
all these years?'

He dropped his head.

'Isobel, you forget yourself!' Lady Kelgrove spoke sharply.
'You know his position as a servant means he cannot answer
such demands.'

'You are correct.' Izzy took a breath. 'I am sorry, John. Please
forgive me.'

'Thank you, Your Highness. If I may be permitted to
speak…?'

'Please do.'

'I stayed because of you—all three of you. Course, I did not know there were three, but I knew that Maria lived, that she was with child, and hoped that she was hopefully safe. The last orders I got from Mr George were this: "Deliver the letter into my wife's hand then return and protect my inheritance. Some day Maria will come, or our child will."'

John looked at each of them in turn. 'That day has finally come. And I am pleased to tell you that the old Fletcher servants who remained all worked for *you*, not them. For more than twenty years we hoped. We never stopped hoping.'

'That is laudable indeed. But...' Anna could not understand it. 'What can servants do that would make a difference?'

'You might be surprised, miss. The butler, cook, housekeeper and steward all visited Mr George's sickroom before his death, without Mr and Mrs Thaxby's knowledge. And, for all Mr Thaxby's cunning, he never knew that the steward has been diverting the greater part of the Fletcher wealth into government bonds and gold—to protect it, you understand.

'And Mrs Thaxby could never comprehend just why the chimneys always smoked when she received distinguished guests, nor why we never seemed to have as much silverware as she recalled from her childhood. She had a fondness for expensive jewellery, you see, while he is something of a gamester in secret. So together we have done as our true master requested, awaiting the day when his wife and child came to claim their rightful inheritance.'

Lady Kelgrove chuckled. 'I am glad to hear you were working *for* him and not against him. I should not like to come up against such efficient opposition.'

'And are those servants still in senior positions in the Thaxby household?' Rose asked curiously.

'Mr Baker, the steward, remains, as does the butler and housekeeper. They are currently in the Edinburgh house, for Mr and Mrs Thaxby intend to return there after this house party. There is a new cook, for my mother died some years ago.'

'Your mother? I am sorry, John.' Rose's voice was gentle.

He nodded briskly. 'She would be so happy to know Mr and Mrs Fletcher's children are alive and well.'

They all stilled, for there was a knock on the door. Instantly, John retreated to stand by the wall by the fireplace, his face a mask of impassivity. Rose admitted the callers—Lady Garvald and the doctor. Dr West's expression was grim—a strong contrast to the benign confidence with which he had spoken to Lady Kelgrove earlier.

'My lady,' he began, 'I must inform you that Mrs Thaxby is gravely ill, and that concerns me in respect of your own health.' He approached Lady Kelgrove's canopied bed. 'I know of only two possibilities as to why you have both experienced the same symptoms in the same few hours. One, that there is a gastric infection present in this house, or two, that you have both eaten something disagreeable. I have therefore asked Lady Garvald to review with her cook everything that you both have eaten and to dispose of it instantly.'

'Which of course I shall do,' added Lady Garvald, 'Although Cook is in high dudgeon at the very notion that her cooking may be to blame.'

'Fear not, Lady Garvald. Your cook is entirely innocent.' Lady Kelgrove sent the doctor a keen glance. 'Is there not a third possibility, Dr West?'

He stilled. 'Well, yes, but I discounted it instantly.'

'Why? Because we are of the *ton*? Evil may live among us as much as it does in the meanest hovel.'

'I...see,' he said, his eyes wide. 'I see. And you believe...?'

Lady Garvald was looking from one to the other. 'Surely you cannot be suggesting...?' Her hand flew to her mouth. 'Oh, my lord!'

'Quite,' stated Lady Kelgrove, her tone clipped. 'Yes, Dr West, I do believe it.'

'But how?' Lady Garvald looked horrified.

'When the gentlemen return, I shall speak to Sir Walter. In the meantime, what is my prognosis?'

The doctor looked gravely troubled. 'Given that your symptoms have already eased, I would be hopeful...although there are some substances whose symptoms come back a second time following a brief respite. I urge you to take caution.'

She gave a bark of laughter. 'How, may I ask? My fate is already set, I think.' Her eyes became unfocused. 'As is that of Mrs Thaxby.' She straightened. 'Anna!'

'Yes?'

'Go to Mrs Thaxby. You need to be there when... You understand me, I think.'

When Mr Thaxby realises his wife has somehow taken some of the poison?

'Of course.' She moved towards the door.

'One moment.' The doctor raised a hand and she paused. 'Lady Kelgrove, when do you believe this...event...took place?'

'Last evening.'

'Ah.' He grimaced, then turned to Anna. 'It may be of limited benefit, but you should encourage Mrs Thaxby to empty her stomach. An unpleasant experience, of course, but better out than in!'

Anna nodded, inwardly feeling pessimistic. If Mrs Thaxby had taken the poison yesterday evening and she was only now casting up her accounts, then the substance had had twelve hours and more to work through her body. Lady Kelgrove, on the other hand, genuinely looked well, so had hopefully been purged of whatever noxious substance Mr Thaxby had administered.

As she passed the top of the staircase, a commotion below caught her attention. The gentlemen had lately returned, it seemed, and were currently divesting themselves of cloaks, hats and boots with the assistance of the footmen. Her eyes sought Will, and her heart skipped as she spied his familiar dark hair. As if sensing her presence, he looked up, his face instantly breaking into a wide smile.

Despite her heart lifting, she found she could not return his smile—not with all the talk of murder, and with the scent of death in the house.

I need him by my side.

Without hesitation, she began descending the staircase.

Chapter Twenty-Two

W̶ill had enjoyed riding out—clean air in his lungs, feeling nothing but the thrill of each fence, his mind needing to focus entirely on directing his stallion. If he was honest, it had been the perfect distraction from the sense of menace he had felt earlier. Was it because Lady Kelgrove was ill? No, it was more than that—although, like most of the others, he was deeply concerned about Lady Kelgrove.

Most, but not all of the others. Lady Renton had only a limited ability to consider other people's perspectives and feelings, and the Thaxbys seemed entirely devoid of such sensibilities. As he divested himself of boots and cloak, he fleetingly wondered if that was why Lady Renton and Mrs Thaxby enjoyed their endless verbal battles.

A movement above caught his eye and he raised his eyes. There was Anna, standing at the top of the stairs, and his heart swelled at how divine she looked. Surely no goddess could rival her? His eyes swept over her beautiful face and perfect form, and now his loins recalled their ferocious and tender kisses just hours ago. Had it not been for that interruption by the page, he would already have secured her hand—or so he hoped. A man could never know for certain until his chosen lady had said yes.

Inwardly, he had little doubt, for this was Anna, the other

part of himself. ZanZan had lost her and Will had found her
again. While they disagreed heartily and healthily at times, at
a deeper level he knew that they were destined to be together,
and he sensed that Anna knew it too. As he watched, she began
to descend, but something in her demeanour made the hairs on
the back of his neck stand to attention.

Something is amiss—something more than earlier.

Her expression was serious, her air one of disquiet.

'Anna! What is it?'

The other gentlemen quietened, as if sensing his concern, one
by one turning to look towards her as she descended.

'Lady Kelgrove...?' His breath caught in his throat. The elderly lady was dear to him.

She shook her head, the tiniest of movements. 'She remains
unwell, but now another is also sick.'

Out of the corner of his eye, he saw Mr Thaxby lift his head
sharply.

'Who?'

She had reached the hallway, and now turned to Thaxby. 'It
is Mrs Thaxby. I am sorry to bring you these tidings, sir, but
the doctor says your wife is gravely ill.'

The man crumpled. There was no other word for it. His
hands went to his head, and a strange wailing sound emerged
from him. His knees then buckled, and Will was just in time
to catch him, Sir Walter grabbing him by the other arm. They
exchanged a grim glance above Thaxby's head before leading
him to a nearby bench.

'Now then, Thaxby, rest here a moment.' Will gently pushed
the man's head down between his knees in an attempt to prevent
a full faint. 'You have received a shock.' Looking around, he
caught the eye of the nearest footman and mouthed the word,
'Brandy.'

'Impossible!' Thaxby was muttering. 'But how? I took such
care...'

Will saw that Sir Walter had heard him, for the look he gave
Will was both puzzled and incredulous. Despite wishing it were
otherwise, Will could put only one interpretation on Thaxby's

reaction: that he believed he had somehow inadvertently caused his wife's sickness. Which meant...

'How is Lady Kelgrove?'

'The doctor thinks she is suffering from the same ailment as Mrs Thaxby.' Anna's words were uttered in a neutral fashion, but the look she threw him held reassurance. She glanced at Thaxby, whose head was still buried between his knees, then back at Will, her eyes holding a clear warning.

'I must go to my wife.' Thaxby rose quickly, then reeled a little. 'Where is she?' His eyes were wild, his hands trembling.

'I shall take you,' Anna murmured. 'She is in her bedchamber.'

He set off towards the stairs, and Will rushed to assist him, for he remained unsteady. Together they climbed the stairs, Will vaguely aware of the stunned silence among the gentlemen in the hallway below.

The door opened, and Will's gaze was immediately drawn to the woman in the bed. Mrs Thaxby looked deathly pale, her eyes closed. A serving maid was engaged in wiping her brow with a damp cloth. Her fingertips were blue, Will noticed, and her skin held a strange yellowish tinge. Mr Thaxby ran directly to her, flinging himself upon her chest and wailing incoherent apologies.

'Oh, my dear,' Will made out. 'How could this have occurred...? I am sorry, my love... My dear, my dear...'

Anna exchanged a shocked look with Will, and he responded with a wry grimace. Whatever Thaxby had done, it was clear that he genuinely cared for his wife. Shaking her head, Anna went to the window and opened it wide. The maid sent her a concerned look, and Will was reminded that it was generally recommended to keep closed the windows in a sickroom. But Anna had the right of it, for surely fresh air was better than this stuffiness? It was not as if Mrs Thaxby had caught some airborne disease...

Anna rejoined him and together they stood watching the scene unfold. Mrs Thaxby patted her husband's shoulder, but seemed unable to speak, while he seemed unable to stop crying and muttering. It was mostly unintelligible, but the gist remained clear: there was something about angels too, angels destroying... No, Will could not make sense of it.

'All is lost,' Thaxby said clearly then. 'All is lost.'

He rested his head on the bed, finally silent, and remained that way for a few moments. He then rose wordlessly, walked straight past Will and Anna without so much as glancing in their direction, and left the room.

With an exchanged glance they hurried after him, but he went only as far as his own bedchamber, next to his wife's, entering and firmly shutting the door. A footman hovered on the landing, a bottle of brandy and a glass in his hand. Will nodded in approval.

'Bring it to him,' he instructed the man. 'Tell him I sent it.'

'Very good, sir,' said the footman, and knocked on Thaxby's door. He knocked again, then looked at Will. There had been no reply from within. Walking forward, Will opened the door. Thaxby was simply standing there, in the centre of the empty chamber, his eyes unfocused.

'Here is brandy for you, Thaxby,' Will offered.

'A kindness,' Thaxby said, nodding to the footman who poured him a glass. 'It is not what I deserve, but I shall take it nonetheless, and use it well.'

Taking the glass, he set it on a side table, fumbled briefly with something in his watch pocket, then bent over the glass of brandy. Before Will could even take in what he was observing, Thaxby lifted it and drank.

'No! You must not!' Springing forward, Will tried to knock the glass away, but it was too late. Thaxby had drunk it all.

The man gave a self-satisfied smile. 'My last victory. An unwelcome one, but a victory nonetheless. Now, I shall need the services of my valet in the coming hours and days.' He looked at the footman. 'Can you send him to me?'

Clearly relieved to have an excuse to leave the room, the footman backed out with alacrity. Will's stern glance signalled that he should not speak of this, and the footman nodded.

'Thaxby,' he said, and he heard the emotion in his own voice. He cleared his throat, then tried again. 'Will you speak to Sir Walter?'

'A confession? How quaint!' Thaxby thought for a moment. 'Very well, if only so others may appreciate my cleverness, right to the last.' A flash of anger crossed his face. 'Or almost the last. I still cannot understand how my wife came to be affected.'

Will could bear it no longer. 'I shall fetch Sir Walter.' He did not bow as he left, for such a man did not deserve even a hint of *politesse*.

Anna was still there, on the landing.

'Oh, my love!' Uncaring about any servants who might be passing, he pulled her into his arms, taking solace and comfort from the warmth of her body curved into his. Her arms tightened about him and they stood like that for what seemed like an age, until he felt replenished enough to return to reality. He kissed her then, the briefest moment of his lips brushing hers, and she smoothed his hair back from his brow.

'I am here, Will.' Her voice was soft, and his chest swelled with love and pride at the notion that this woman—this fierce, gentle, steadfast woman—loved him. For she loved him, as he loved her. He knew it as well as he knew his own name.

'Tell me honestly, how is Lady Kelgrove?'

'She is well, and has seemed to recover.'

'Then perhaps Mrs Thaxby might also...?'

She shook her head. 'Mrs Thaxby appears to be suffering from a much more severe version than Lady Kelgrove experienced. Why, my great-grandmother is even now sitting up in bed and directing matters!'

He had to smile at this a little, but he quickly sobered as he recalled Thaxby's latest actions. 'Thaxby took something just now. He added it to his drink.'

She gasped. 'Deliberately? Knowingly?'

'Aye.' He shrugged. 'His choice.' He grimaced. 'He has sent for his valet. Unpleasant tasks lie ahead.'

Anna raised her eyes to heaven. 'Poor John! As if he has not suffered enough!'

He sent her a quizzical look. 'You seem to know a lot about the man.'

'I know more now than I did yesterday, that is for certain. He is with Lady Kelgrove.' Briefly, she apprised him of John's tale.

He whistled. 'Sir Walter will need to hear of this.'

Mischief danced briefly in her eyes. 'Lady Kelgrove has everything in hand, I assure you.' Taking his hand, she led him along the landing towards her great-grandmother's chamber.

'Great-Grandmother? Will is with me, and has news. May we enter?'

A chuckle emerged from the canopied bed. 'Enter, and welcome.' In they went, and Will saw that the doctor was there, with Lady Garvald, Anna's sisters, and John.

My!' Lady Kelgrove declared. 'This bedchamber is as busy as a ballroom today!' She thought for a moment. 'I believe I shall get up. My play-acting has served its purpose, and now I need to be in the midst of events again.'

Anna and Will exchanged a glance.

'What is it? There is something more to be said, is there not?'

Will told them about Mr Thaxby and the brandy, finishing by turning to the doctor. 'He spoke of "destroying angels", if that is of any use?'

'Oh, lord!' exclaimed the doctor. 'That is the colloquial name for a type of toadstool—the Amanita—that grows in these parts. Pure white, looks angelic, but it is, I am afraid, deadly.'

Will felt his innards clench. 'Is there a cure?'

For answer, Dr West turned back to Lady Kelgrove. 'How much did you take? Do you know?'

'Only the tiniest sip. The wine Mr Thaxby gave me tasted strange—I am something of an expert on good wine.'

'And so you dropped your fan, did you not?' Anna had clearly deduced something from the incident the night before.

Lady Kelgrove nodded. 'He saw me take the sip and I was careful not to show anything on my face. I deliberately said something provoking, then pretended to be wounded by his vicious reply. *That* was when I made a show of dropping my fan.'

Izzy's jaw dropped. 'What did you say?'

She shrugged. 'I cannot recall exactly. It was about Richard, and how I remain determined to bring his murderers to justice, I think.'

Rose clapped a hand to her mouth. 'You did not! Oh, Great-Grandmother, you are formidable indeed!'

Will could just imagine it. 'And his reply?' His tone was clipped, reflecting his need to manage the maelstrom of emotion within him.

'It was as clear a threat as he has ever given. He said that some matters are best left in the past, as otherwise they might cause harm in the present.'

There was a collective gasp.

'And he had just handed me a glass of wine containing the poison. I imagine he believes himself to be clever.' She sniffed. 'While they were picking up my fan, I set my glass down and took another... I believed myself to be in deadly danger and it was all I could think to do. She then took mine. It all happened very, very quickly.' She frowned. 'Afterwards I told myself I was perhaps being over-imaginative when that tiny sip had tasted wrong to me. But then I became ill.'

Dr West was still pondering this. 'So you had a sip, but Mrs Thaxby must have taken your glass. If she drank a full glass...' He sighed. 'I shall have to consult my medical texts, but I believe that the Amanita affects the liver and kidneys as well as the heart. Lady Kelgrove, you may become ill again in the coming days, I am sorry to say.'

'I see.' She squared her shoulders. 'But I am well now, and if some pestilence is currently attacking my innards I am not aware of it. So I shall ask you all to go away now, and send Hill to me. I shall see you in the drawing room shortly. Isobel, you may take the books and papers we have selected. I wish you and the prince to assemble them into a logical order, for I mean to speak to Sir Walter next.'

Thus dismissed, they all trooped out. Izzy and Rose hurried to find their husbands, while Dr West and John headed for the Thaxbys' chambers. Lady Garvald, stopping for a moment on the landing with Will and Anna, said, 'I must tell the staff we are about to have another guest afflicted by what Mrs Lowe calls "two-bucket disease".'

She shook her head. 'I know that I ought not to be considering such matters at a time like this, but it pains me to anticipate what the servants are enduring, and will endure in the coming days.' She sent them a keen look. 'It would be most helpful if you could both perhaps smooth things over with Sir Walter and the Rentons. I have sadly abandoned them today.'

Confirming they would, they watched as she hurried off, then turned to one another, Will taking Anna's hands in his. They kissed then—ferociously and passionately, as though to assure themselves that here was love, life and harmony. It was brief, and wonderfully disturbing, but it settled Will to know that, in the midst of hate, loss, and even murder there was love.

By the time they moved on, Hill was bustling towards her mistress's bedchamber, and Will was able to reassure her that Lady Kelgrove seemed much improved.

He frowned as they descended the staircase. 'While I admire and respect Lady Kelgrove's determination, I believe I must now take a hand in matters. I am head of this house, and it is my duty and right to speak to Sir Walter.'

Anna saw the sense in this, and so they parted—Anna to give a brief version of the story to the Rentons, while Will took Sir Walter to his library. When Claudio and Izzy arrived with a smaller pile of books and papers, Will used these to corroborate such parts of the tale as they were able, then left Sir Walter to speak with others of his choosing.

By evening time, Sir Walter was ready to make his pronouncements. They had endured a sober dinner, where no one had eaten very much, and conversation had been minimal. Lady Garvald had rearranged the table, but the absence of the Thaxbys was felt by all. Lady Kelgrove had appeared dressed all in black, and with a fierceness in her expression that Will had only rarely seen.

Afterwards the entire party made their way directly to the drawing room, where Sir Walter stood by the fireplace to address them all at once. Will awaited the magistrate's judgement with a great deal of uneasiness, hoping he had done enough to prove not one but two heinous murders.

Chapter Twenty-Three

The drawing room crackled with tension, akin to the sensation before a thunderstorm. Anna's heart was racing as Sir Walter made his way to the fireplace. What would he say? Had he been convinced? She knew that after speaking with Will in the library the magistrate had spoken to Lady Kelgrove, then John, as well as Mr Thaxby himself. Had the man admitted it?

'As magistrate,' Sir Walter began, his expression serious, 'I could never have anticipated such a to-do in my own vicinity, but this has come to me, and so I have considered the matter carefully. I have spoken to Lord Garvald and Lady Garvald, to Lady Kelgrove, to Mr Thaxby's valet and to Mr Thaxby. His lady is not well enough for questions, but I am satisfied she can have little to add.

'I have also,' he continued, 'been given access to the private diaries and journals of…let us call her Mrs Lennox. These appear to corroborate much of the account I have been given.'

Mrs Lennox? Anna's heart sank. *Why did he not say Mrs Fletcher?*

'I have therefore come to clear conclusions on three of the four matters placed before me. That is to say…' he enunciated on his fingers '…first, the death of the Honourable Richard Berkeley, grandson to Lady Kelgrove. Second, the death of

George Fletcher. Third, the illness affecting Lady Kelgrove, Mrs Thaxby and now Mr Thaxby. And fourth, the matter of the Fletcher estate, as symbolised by the necklace currently in the possession of Miss Lennox. I shall refer to each in turn.

'With regard to the death of Lady Kelgrove's grandson Richard Berkeley, on Hampstead Heath in the year 1789, I find that he was killed by brigands hired by Mr Thaxby. Thaxby has admitted it to me this afternoon, although he states the men were told to murder Mr Fletcher, not Mr Berkeley. Nevertheless, he reports he paid them afterwards, and has never heard from them since.' He bowed to Lady Kelgrove. 'I am sorry for your loss, my lady, and I hope that this information may help you find some peace.'

'I thank you, Sir Walter,' she said, her voice trembling only a little. 'It does.'

Anna felt tears prick her eyes. But Sir Walter was continuing, so she brought her attention back to him. It all seemed like a play suddenly—something that must be happening to someone else.

'Regarding the death of Mr George Fletcher in the year 1790, Mr Thaxby has admitted to poisoning him. When asked why, he stated that Mr Fletcher was making plans to marry, that he was due to reach his majority shortly afterwards and that he had threatened to cut Mrs Thaxby off. Mr Thaxby contends that Mr Fletcher was behaving unreasonably, and that he and his wife were simply being good trustees when they challenged the young man.

'When reminded of the failed previous attempt to murder Mr Fletcher, Mr Thaxby could not then account for it. When asked about Mr Fletcher's marriage, Mr Thaxby was adamant that he had not married, that he could not have legally married as he was underage, and that he had reported being enamoured with a serving girl. He was most clear on this point—that Mr Fletcher was unmarried upon his death.'

'But…' Izzy made as if to speak, but a stern look from Lady Kelgrove silenced her.

Sir Walter continued as though she had not spoken. 'On the third matter—that of the illness affecting three members of this gathering—Mr Thaxby has admitted to having a poisonous toadstool known as Amanita in his possession. He states he attempted to administer this to Lady Kelgrove, as he understood she suspected him of arranging the attack on Hampstead Heath in which the Honourable Richard Berkeley died. He states he cannot account for how his own wife also came to be affected, and swears he never intended to harm her. He also…er… With regard to his own sickness, I shall remain discreet, for regardless of what he may have done I am sure we would all agree the man warrants a proper burial.'

He eyed them all fiercely, and no one contested this. A person who died by their own hand could not be buried in holy ground, and such an event would bring unwelcome scandal to the Garvalds and their guests.

'Under normal circumstances I should be referring this matter for a murder trial—two of 'em, in fact! But if Dr West is correct, and neither Mr Thaxby nor his wife will survive this, then I believe the best outcome for all concerned is to put it down to a virulent illness.

'On the matter of the heirs to the Fletcher estate, I cannot rule, for no clear evidence has been presented to me that George Fletcher and Maria Berkeley were legally married. His trustee Mr Thaxby was adamant on that point, and given his candour on matters carrying more weight and significance I have no reason to doubt him.'

Anna's heart sank. She and her sisters needed no more wealth, but surely Mama's dignity and reputation mattered? Surely George's behaviour towards Mama as a gentleman mattered? For Mama to have been with child meant that they had lived together as man and wife. If Sir Walter believed there was no evidence of a marriage, then all their reputations might be forever sullied. Including Mama's. The magistrate was prepared to use sleight of hand about murder, but not about Mama's marriage. That was so unfair!

But Will was rising, walking towards Sir Walter.

'I thank you, sir,' he said, 'For your diligence and thoroughness. But you must know, after I left the library to prepare for dinner, I continued to search through some of Mrs Fletcher's journals, looking for some hint regarding the marriage—which you had highlighted to me as being unresolved. I know her daughters have not yet had the opportunity to read all of them, but I was searching for some clue as to the marriage, given that was your outstanding concern.'

'And? Did you find something?'

'I did.' Will walked to a side table where he lifted a small book—one of Mama's diaries. A sliver of paper had been tucked inside it as a placemark, so he opened it and began to read.

'Mrs Fletcher writes:

'"How strange it is that I am returned to the vicinity of Haddington, where George and I were so happy! I shall never forget the tiny inn near Ballencrieff where I stayed while the banns were read, while George made all ready in our little cottage. We returned to England once I knew I was with child, in the hope that his sister and her husband would accept our marriage, and so that George could begin to take over the reins of his affairs in preparation for his majority. I was more than six months gone, and George wished for security for our child. So he went to stay with them, while I waited in a nearby inn, praying every day for good news. When his servant came to the inn where I was staying, I opened his letter in great haste and with great hope. Instead, I received the worst news possible. I still have that letter in my possession, and have cried many tears over it.

'"When George bade me run, I ran—and where else should I go but Scotland, where I was so happy? It took a few days, but I managed to book a ticket on the stage to Edinburgh. Unfortunately, the Thaxbys were travelling too, and I was unfortunate enough to see them at the inn in Haddington, so I had to run again, leaving behind my trunk and most of my possessions. But I had my reticule, with his letter, the necklace and the earrings I received from my dear grandmother.

'"I can only assume the Thaxbys left their home before he died in order to distance themselves from any accusations. The Fletcher townhouse in Edinburgh was always George's favourite dwelling, and he had asked me to consider if we might settle there and raise our child in Scotland. But, since the Thaxbys were clearly on their way to Edinburgh, I could not go there. I walked the roads until I found Lammermuir House, and my dear friend Margaret took me in. And so I have seen both good and evil in this life. And I choose always to do good, and to raise my daughters to do the same."'

He lifted his head.

'You will note, Sir Walter, the reference to the banns, and the words she uses—namely "our marriage". It seems clear that they married here in Scotland, where their marriage would have been legitimate, even though she was eighteen and he was not yet one-and-twenty.'

He handed Sir Walter the book and allowed him to see for himself.

'Hrmph!' was his verdict. 'I should need to see a copy of the register, but it does seem possible that this may have been one of the Reverend Buchanan's weddings. I know he would marry runaways, but only if they agreed to have the banns read for four weeks in the regular way.'

Anna's heart was racing. 'They married *here*? Where is the Reverend Buchanan's church?'

Will answered immediately. 'It is the Episcopalian Chapel in Haddington—the Church of the Holy Trinity.'

'Episcopalian… That would make sense, for both George and Maria were raised Anglican.' Lady Kelgrove's expression was thoughtful. 'You girls and your husbands may go to Haddington in the morning to find confirmation of the marriage.'

'May I also go, Great-Grandmother?' Anna asked, her tone teasing. 'I have no husband, but I should dearly like to be part of this.'

Lady Kelgrove waved this away. '*Tsk!* You know I meant to include you and Lord Garvald, although you have not yet made any official announcement. I do wish you would, though, for I think we all deserve some good news today.'

All eyes were on Anna, and she felt a slow flush spreading across her face and neck. 'I… But…'

Will bowed to Lady Kelgrove. 'While I appreciate your frustration, I should much have preferred to m-manage matters in my own way. Nevertheless, I recognise that the moment is upon me.'

At this, Izzy clapped her hands. 'I knew it! Did I not say so, Claudio?'

'You did,' replied the prince indulgently.

Anna's gaze flicked to the others. Rose and James were beaming, as was Lady Garvald. Lady Kelgrove had an air of smugness about her, Sir Walter and Lord Renton looked mildly interested—though not displeased—and even Lady Renton looked as though she approved.

Crossing to where Anna sat on a red satin settee, Will knelt before her. 'Annabelle Georgina Lennox Fletcher—you see, I give you your f-full name—will you do me the great honour of being my wife?'

'Oh, Will! Are you certain?'

'More certain than I have ever been of anything in my life. You and I belong together, and you know it as well as I.'

She did, and any worries about him being bounced into a declaration by Lady Kelgrove dissipated like mist. 'Yes!' she accepted, half-laughing. 'Yes, I shall marry you!'

He kissed her then, in full view of everyone, then drew her to her feet and kissed her again. 'I love you,' he murmured against her mouth as the others applauded. Anna even heard a couple of whistles. *How delightfully undignified!* was her fleeting thought.

'I love you too, Will. And I shall love being your wife.'

Together they turned to receive the congratulations of their family, friends and fellow guests. After a frenzy of hugs from the ladies and kisses on the cheek from the gentlemen, they joined hands and sat together.

The evening lasted at least another two hours, but Anna could not have said afterwards what was discussed. There was sparkling wine, toasts to their future happiness and, eventually, supper. Throughout, Anna remained in an alt, the warmth of his hand in hers anchoring her to the fact that her dearest wish had come true. She was to marry Will, and that was all that mattered.

Chapter Twenty-Four

William Alexander Edward Henderson, Earl of Garvald, married Annabelle Georgina Lennox Fletcher in the pretty chapel in the grounds of Lammermuir House on a warm day in September. The bride was attended by her two sisters, the groom by Prince Claudio and the Viscount Ashbourne.

In attendance was the bride's great-grandmother, who had lately been ill, it was said, but who had made a full recovery. Locals whispered about the dreadful illness that had carried off two of the Lammermuir House guests a few weeks before, and their gratitude that it had not spread more widely.

Also present was the groom's mother—a well-liked lady in the district. Other notables had travelled to be there, including the Dowager Viscountess Ashbourne and a Mr Marnoch from Elgin, said to be the bride's guardian. There was, it was rumoured, even a message of goodwill from the Queen herself!

The bride wore a blue silk gown, a diamond bracelet, and a sapphire-and-diamond necklace said to be worth a king's ransom, while the groom was attired in a Weston jacket, an embroidered waistcoat, and boots by Hoby, and he carried a fine hat said to have been procured from Lock's of London.

Afterwards the newly married couple celebrated with a wedding breakfast at the groom's home, before travelling to the

Fletcher townhouse in Edinburgh, where they would spend their honeymoon. The Lammermuir servants were to have their own celebration at the behest of the groom and his mother, once the breakfast had been cleared away. So it could safely be said that the entire household was guaranteed to have a good day, and that it would live long in the memory.

'We have arrived!' Having spent the journey from Haddington via the coastal road to Edinburgh enjoying the fact that she and her husband were finally alone, Anna had been distracted by the realisation they had now reached Edinburgh. As the coach pulled up outside the Fletcher house, she was acutely conscious of the significance of the moment.

Once the details of her parents' marriage had been confirmed in the wedding register in the Haddington chapel, the lawyers had set to work, and just yesterday Anna and her sisters had received confirmation that they were now the owners of the Fletcher assets. As the eldest, Anna had been awarded both the Fletcher necklace and the various properties, as well as cash in the bank, and the government bonds and gold that had lately been discovered in the ledgers. Izzy and Rose had been given substantial awards as belated dowries, their guardian Mr Marnoch having worked diligently with solicitors from Edinburgh and London these past weeks to ensure all legal processes were completed correctly.

This, though, was the first time Anna and Will had seen the house, Anna having felt strongly that they should not visit until all the legalities had been finalised. From the outside, it was beautiful—warm stone, multiple windows across four storeys and a decided air of elegance.

Will exited the carriage first then handed her out, kissing her hand as he did so. The promise in his eyes left her breathless. With the benefit of the increased privacy afforded to betrothed couples these past weeks, Anna had enjoyed hundreds of kisses from him, and now considered herself quite accomplished in the art. Soon, though, they would be alone, and Anna's entire body thrummed in anticipation of the delights of the marriage bed. Her sisters had told her astonishing things about what would occur, and she was determined to enter the experience with an open mind and a great deal of curiosity.

But first, she had more sober duties to fulfil. As she stepped inside the house and saw the staff lined up to greet their new mistress, Anna could almost sense the presence of her mother in step with her. Maria, as George's wife, should have entered the house as its mistress more than twenty years ago. Anna's heart ached for both of them—their time together cut short, her father's life ended prematurely.

As the butler introduced the senior staff to them, and they in turn introduced footmen, maids, grooms and stableboys, Anna felt the responsibility of it all settle on her shoulders. Just a few short months ago she'd been still at school. Now she was a countess, and responsible for the smooth running of multiple houses and the welfare of the servants working within them. There was a hint of anxiety on some of the faces before her, which she could understand. Mr Thaxby had not treated his servants well and, despite the assurances they might have been given, some might have worried that Lord and Lady Garvald would be equally abusive.

One man knew better.

John had been kept on as some-time valet to Lord Garvald. The Earl had his own man, naturally, but John had been assured he would have work for as long as he wished it, and a comfortable retirement afterwards. And he had earned every moment of it.

'John!' They both greeted him warmly, and his beaming expression displayed his delight.

'Can you please assemble those senior servants you spoke about?' Will asked him. 'We should like to speak to them in private.'

So, before having a tour of the house or even accepting refreshments, the Earl and Countess took the time to thank those who had remained loyal to George Fletcher's memory for more than twenty years, hoping that some day his wife or child might come forward. They listened too, asking sympathetic questions and taking the time to understand how difficult it had been for them all. They were left with a strong sense of the servants' integrity and loyalty, as well as their relief that the matter had now been resolved. The Thaxbys—and their unpleasant demise—were not mentioned by name.

Some hours later, having completed all of their (entirely pleasant) duties, Lord and Lady Garvald retired to their sumptuous suite on the third floor of the house. Darkness was falling, and Sally—who was still reeling from her unanticipated rise in station in becoming personal maid to a countess—had worked with John to make all ready.

The chamber was spotlessly clean, the bed turned down and there were two branches of candles—one on the bedside table, another on the small mirrored table near the window. Suddenly nervous, Anna allowed Sally to remove her gown, undo her stays and unpin her hair—all the while conscious that John was removing Will's boots at the far side of the room. Shaking her head when Sally signalled towards the nightgown she had laid out, she murmured, 'Thank you, Sally, I shall manage the rest.'

'Very good, my lady.' Startled at not being called 'miss', Anna reflected wryly that having a title would take some getting used to. Her sisters had certainly managed. From being simply the three Misses Lennox in Elgin at the beginning of the year, they were now all married—a countess, a princess, and a viscountess. But, much as she held her brothers-in-law in high esteem, Anna knew that she had married the best of men. Surely there was no one more handsome, more generous, more kind-hearted than her own darling Will?

John and Sally went, the valet gently closing the door behind him. As she heard Will walking towards her, Anna held her breath. Keeping her eyes on the gilded mirror before her, she saw him behind her, saw their faces together, and she could not prevent a smile.

'My lady.' Reverentially, he bent and kissed the back of her neck, her ear and her collar bone, sending delicious shivers through her.

'My lord.' She could wait no longer, and turned towards him. Instantly his lips were on hers, their arms moving to hold one another close, closer yet…

* * *

The nightgown proved to be unnecessary, and lay in a heap on the floor along with their clothing until Anna, waking with a start, saw that daylight was peeping through the edges of the curtains. Stirring, she turned in her husband's arms, enjoying the novel sensation of his body against hers and the sight of his handsome face so close to her own in the gentle morning light.

The advice provided by her sisters had proved to be accurate—not least the part where they had tried to tell her how delightful it all was. That part, in fact, they had significantly understated.

How many times they had made love in the night, she could not be sure, for her head was delightfully sleep-lacking, and her mind was wonderfully foggy. Her body knew what it wanted, though, so she stretched a little as she lay beside him. He groaned, moving a little, then opened his eyes.

'Good morning, my love.'

'Good morning, Will.'

His eyes softened. 'Our first morning waking up together. I still can hardly believe it.'

'It does seem improbable that anyone should feel so happy.'

'True.' He kissed the tip of her nose. 'When I recall all those balls and soirées during the season, when you acted like you did not know me... How far we have journeyed, from that to this.'

'And now we are here, safe and married.'

'And in a bed. And naked.'

She moved against him. 'Why, so we are!'

He rolled on top of her. 'Kiss me then, my lady!'

Gladly, she obliged.

* * * * *

The Lady's Bargain With The Rogue

Melissa Oliver

MILLS & BOON

Books by Melissa Oliver

Harlequin Historical

Stranded with Her Forbidden Knight

Brothers and Rivals

The Knight's Substitute Bride

Protectors of the Crown

A Defiant Maiden's Knight
A Stolen Knight's Kiss
Her Unforgettable Knight

Notorious Knights

The Rebel Heiress and the Knight
Her Banished Knight's Redemption
The Return of Her Lost Knight
The Knight's Convenient Alliance

Visit the Author Profile page
at millsandboon.com.au.

Melissa Oliver is from southwest London, where she writes sweeping historical romance. She is the winner of the Romantic Novelists' Association's 2020 Joan Hessayon Award for new writers for her debut, *The Rebel Heiress and the Knight*.

For more information, visit www.melissaoliverauthor.com.

Follow Melissa on social media.
Instagram: @MelissaOliverAuthor
X: @MelissaOAuthor
Facebook: MelissaOliverAuthor

To my three fearless gorgeous girls.
Always be true to who you are.

Chapter One

1882

You're a Bawden-Trebarr, Eliza, never forget that. It courses through your veins, giving you strength, fortitude, resilience and courage. Attributes that are incredibly important, especially for a woman, and something that our forebear, Elowen Bawden-Trebarr, exuded in every way. So never forget that. And never forget who and what you are...

With her mother's words turning around her head, Lady Eliza Carew née Bawden-Trebarr stood in awe of the huge four-storey building that wrapped itself around the corner of Bury Street, in the St. James's area of London. An area littered with many gentlemen's clubs, except this was unlike all the others.

The Trium Impiorum, or Three Wicked Devils, was the most notorious and exclusive gaming hell in the whole of the country, let alone London, as were its scandalous owners, the Marsden Bastards.

Eliza glanced up at the imposing redbrick building with its bay and arched windows, ornate columns and intricate cornices framing the windows on each floor. She took a deep breath and stepped inside the grand entrance, her heart hammering against her ribs, and blinked several times in surprise.

Well, now, this was not what she had imagined when she'd considered the interior of the Trium Impiorum, not that she knew much about such establishments. Heavens, but the gleaming black-and-white mosaic-tiled floor, with the walnut wainscoting in the hallway, was not very different from any palatial town house in Mayfair. Eliza tentatively ambled along to the large open reception hall with a sweeping stairway to the side, towering potted plants on ornamental stands dotted around, her eyes flicking to the many servants busily cleaning and polishing the dark mahogany furniture. This indeed was not what she'd envisioned a villainous lair belonging to the Marsden brothers might look like. Indeed, it could be the entrance to many sumptuous grand houses rather than the interior of one…

'May I enquire as to the nature of your business here, miss?' One of the doors had opened to reveal an older well-dressed man, with a streak of white running through his hair and a matching neatly trimmed grey beard. Not quite what she had expected of one of the proprietors of Trium Impiorum, not that it mattered.

'I have come to see you in person, Mr Marsden, since I haven't received a reply to my many correspondences to you.' Eliza decided to give the man her most winsome smile in the hope that it might charm him. Sadly, it failed to do so. The man gave her an impatient look that one might adopt when dealing with a rather recalcitrant child. 'Again, I must insist in enquiring who you are and why you are here at the Trium Impiorum.'

'I am Lady Elisabeth Bawden-Trebarr and I believe I have already answered you as to the reason why I am here.' Eliza straightened her spine and attempted to look as stiff and starchy as this man. 'Now, would you please do me the courtesy of granting me a moment of your time…in private, Mr Marsden?'

'I am Mr Hendon, the major-domo of the club.' The man looked her up and down before continuing on with a bored, dismissive voice. 'And if you wish to speak with Mr Marsden, I would recommend that you write again and ask for an audience with him. But I should warn you that he is an extremely busy man and therefore cannot guarantee that you will gain any moment of his time…in private or otherwise.'

'But…'

'The Trium Impiorum is no place for a young woman to visit on her own, either. It will not look well on you.'

Oh dear, this was not going quite to plan but then Eliza was not the most forceful of people, despite her exalted Bawden-Trebarr name and the blue blood that coursed through her veins. Perhaps it was more a trickle in her case, nay a drop, because at this moment she did not feel particularly strong nor in any way courageous. In fact, she felt…

'I shall see you out, my lady.' The man ushered her back towards the hallway and the front door that she had taken a long time dithering outside before finally opening. But she was desperate. So very desperate.

'I think not. I have already written many times to Mr Marsden and gained no response.' She twisted back around to face the man and gave him another smile, this one real. 'But I will have my say, Mr Hendon. And I shall cheerfully stay here all day and all night, until I do. Indeed, I will not leave. Please do convey this message to Mr Marsden, if you will.' Eliza sat gracefully down on a handsome wooden barrel chair, which was probably more expensive than everything she owned put together.

The man must have heard something in her words or perhaps because she was not cowed by him, that he finally relented. The major-domo inclined his head before leaving the reception hall, only to return a few minutes later with the message that Mr Marsden would see her briefly, with the caveat that he could only offer the length of time it took for him to drink his morning coffee. And that would be all. How magnanimous of him. Her impression of the man was not favourable in the least, and this just made it sink even lower.

Eliza followed the major-domo up the gleaming wooden staircase, her eyes flicking to the trompe l'oeil paintings running up the length of the walls, which gradually revealed carnal depictions slowly and deliberately. Only once she had reached the first-floor landing could she see the provocative images as they were meant to be seen. Sprites and cherubs engaged in acts that no sprite or cherub should ever be found in. Indecent, scandalous, shameless but strangely beautiful. Strangely alluring. Still, Eliza could feel herself blushing as Mr Hendon caught her staring, making her quickly look away, clutching the handle of her battered leather portmanteau a little tighter. They walked the length of a long, dark hallway and stopped outside a door. The major-domo knocked, which prompted a low, brooding voice from the other side to eventually answer and permit them to enter.

'Lady Elisabeth Bawden-Trebarr is here for you, Mr Marsden,' the man said before leaving the dark and soulless room scattered with strewn foolscap and ledgers all around the large desk. Goodness, if Eliza thought the major-domo was foreboding, he was nothing compared to the man sat on the other side of the mahogany desk hidden in the shadows, deliberately, it seemed. Good grief, how very dramatic. It seemed as though Mr Sebastian Marsden was set on frightening Eliza into fleeing and all before he'd even finished his coffee. Not very chivalrous, but then the Marsden Bastards were not known for their chivalry. The room fairly crackled with tension, which was really ridiculous since Eliza had never even met him before.

'Thank you for seeing me,' she muttered, nervously shifting her weight onto one foot and then the other. And when Sebastian Marsden failed to respond, she continued to fill the silence, which was not always such a good idea. 'You have a beautiful—' _gaming hell, place of vice and debauchery_ '—establishment.'

'Do I?' Heavens, but the man's voice was low and menacing. It fairly sent a shiver through her. 'How so?'

'W-well, the interiors are quite elegantly arranged and the trompe l'oeil wall paintings are...' Good grief, but why did she have to mention those? 'They are quite interesting.'

'Did you take a long, hard look at them before forming your interest, then?'

'Well... I...'

'Yes?'

'Nothing.'

'So, you have come all this way to say nothing?'

'Of course not.'

'Are you trying to make me guess the reason for your visit, then?'

'Are you trying to intimidate me?' she blurted out before she could stop her unruly mouth.

Silence once again filled the room for a long moment before the man spoke again.

'Intimidate you? If I wished to do that, then you would certainly know about it, miss. And I'm not in the habit of intimidating women. This here is me being friendly.'

Friendly, was it? Good Lord, if that were true, then she would never want to be this man's enemy. 'How very obliging of you, sir.'

'Allow me to be frank. I am only being this obliging, this friendly, since you, Miss Bawden, made quite a nuisance of yourself when you threatened to sit at the entrance of my club until I agreed to this meeting. You see, it would not do to have my patrons nor my staff exposed to a witless lone woman entering the Trium Impiorum, seemingly lacking in sense and propriety as she sat in wait for me.'

Witless? Lacking in sense and propriety? Eliza could feel her ire rising but managed to tamp it down. It would serve no purpose to act all missish because of this man's insults. Not when there were far more important matters at hand. Far more at stake.

'Friendly indeed,' she said sweetly, ignoring his provocation. 'And in the spirit of that friendliness may I say how glad I am that you agreed to see me this morning.'

He picked up his cup and took a long sip of coffee. 'The time is ticking away, Miss Bawden, so say whatever it is you have come to say. But be hasty about it.'

Eliza had just about had enough of Mr Marsden's unpardonably rude behaviour. 'It's Lady Elisabeth Bawden-Trebarr and the usual courtesy afforded a woman who enters a room is to stand, before offering her a seat.'

Mr Marsden lifted the small cup once more and took another long sip of his coffee, his whole silhouette shrouded in the shadowy darkness before placing it down slowly. His head moved up and down as though he was studying her intently, probably wondering how it was that a supposed lady was clothed in such shabby apparel, had such a dowdy appearance. 'I see. So, you have come barging into my club to teach me manners, Lady Elisabeth Bawden-Trebarr?' His low voice drawled out her name slowly and with so much scorn, that she almost gasped. Almost.

'Yes, it is a bit of a mouthful, isn't it? Although I do prefer Eliza to Elisabeth…' She prattled on as she often did when her nerves started to show. 'And I'd rather use my maiden name of Bawden-Trebarr than my married one, especially now that my husband is dead, which is rather a relief because he is…that is, he *was* rather awful.'

The man sat on the other side of the desk leant forward, his features finally coming into view and knocked the air from her chest. Why, Sebastian Marsden was so…so very dashing, with a wicked gleam in his dark, almost obsidian-black eyes, impossibly sharp cheekbones and features that sat in perfect symmetry. He was quite simply the most breathtakingly beautiful man she'd ever seen. Eliza gasped; she could hardly help it this time.

'If you have quite finished gaping at me, my lady,' he said with a hint of amusement.

She could feel herself burning with shame. 'I would never gape…'

He raised his brow but didn't contradict her. Not this time, as they both knew that she had.

'In any case, I doubt that you came here to inform me of my shocking lack of manners or that you despised your late husband. Dear me and in private, too.'

'Well, no. That is not it at all.' She pushed her wire-rimmed spectacles back up the bridge of her nose. 'And manners cost nothing, sir.'

'*Mr* Marsden or just plain Marsden would do, my lady. And tell me, have you come here to offer your services?' A choked sound escaped her lips, as he paused momentarily before speaking again. 'To teach me manners?'

'Of course not, you're a…' Oh, dear, but why could she not hold her tongue?

'I'm a…?'

The future Earl of Harbury… Or rather he would have been

had he, along with his brothers, not been declared illegitimate years ago. But none of that was Eliza's concern. She hardly cared who this man was except for what he now held in his hands. Her property.

'A businessman,' she said instead. 'A shrewd one at that, if one is to believe all they say about you.'

'Oh, and what is it that *they* say?'

'Many things, Mr Marsden. But perhaps I should get to the point of my visit.'

'I wish you would.' He steepled his fingers together, his elbows on the table as he made a study of her. 'However, since I have been reminded several times of my manners, would you care to take a seat?'

'Thank you.' She masked her surprise at this sudden pleasantry and sat down on the chair in front of his imposing desk.

'I am in a charitable mood, Lady Eliza, as last night was particularly profitable.' He poured more coffee into his cup. 'May I offer you some?' Eliza declined, watching his large hands complete the task. 'Now, how may I be of service to you, Lady Eliza, bearing in mind that time is still of the essence?'

'It is your business acumen that I hope to appeal to, Mr Marsden. And your sense of fairness.'

'And you believe me to be fair, do you? Is this also something *they* say about me, as well?'

'I hardly know.'

'Ah, so you assume that I am fair?'

She smoothed the creases of her overcoat. 'I do not know what to think. But I hope that I, too, am magnanimous enough not to judge a person from idle gossip.'

He smiled, seemingly enjoying her response. Well, that certainly was a first. 'But you do want something from me, do you not?'

'Yes...yes, I do.'

'Good.' The side of his mouth kicked up. 'Because you can dress it up to appeal to my business acumen, as you put it, but I think it best if you say what it is that you actually want from me.'

'Before I do, may I ask why you would sit in the relative darkness in broad daylight?' Her spectacles had slipped down her nose again, as she gazed at the drawn curtains blocking out all the sunlight; the only source of light in the small room coming from the small oil lamp on his desk and the crackling fire in the hearth. 'It really isn't good for your eyes to attend to those ledgers in such reduced light and I should know.'

Judging from the look on the man's face, Eliza knew that she had gone too far in imparting her observations. Yet, it was something that had bothered her from the moment she had entered this dark, rather sparse and messy room.

'And how is it that you should know?'

'Do you always do that?' Eliza frowned. 'Ask a question after being asked one yourself? In any case, my eyesight has always been poor and deteriorated further after years of reading lurid Gothic tales beneath my blanket.'

He leant forward, his large hands spread on the desk. 'Are you ever going to get to the point of your visit, Lady Eliza?'

'Oh, yes, of course.' She smiled nervously. 'Well, let me see, how best to proceed. You see, I believe that my late husband owed a lot of money to you, Mr Marsden. Indeed, he owed a lot of money to many tradesmen, establishments and creditors, many of whom have since been paid. However, he used something to pay off his debts to you that should never have been used, as it belonged to me.'

'And what exactly was that, my lady?'

'The deeds to my ancestral home, Trebarr Castle.'

The man's brows shot up in surprise. 'Yours? You're Ernest Carew, Viscount Ritton's Countess?'

She nodded. 'I was, Mr Marsden. I am now his widow.'

And thank God for it. However, Eliza did not appreciate Sebastian Marsden looking her up and down again, this time as if to ascertain whether she had once been a countess, something she had largely been in name only, since her late husband, Ernest Carew, had rarely treated her as a wife, much less his countess. After a disappointing wedding night, her late husband had viewed her with barely disguised contempt, disparaging everything about Eliza, from the way she looked, *remarkably plain*, to the clothes she wore, *drab and dowdy*, to her interests and her many causes, *mannish and unnatural*. Purely because Eliza was fascinated by the natural sciences and ancient worlds, as well as her interests in politics, social improvements and suffrage for women. Ernest had raged with indignation at everything she did and everything she said. Eliza was apparently too astute, too clever for a woman, far too opinionated and always had a ready reply. In time, nevertheless, he'd worn her down and those opinions and ready replies had eventually dried on her lips. Along with that, his indifference and revulsion of Eliza threw him into the arms of his many mistresses, not that she'd cared since it meant that he indulged in every licentious pursuit while she was left with her many committees and her books. Yet, it was after his death that Eliza discovered the true extent of his debts. One of which had been settled with the only thing that truly mattered to her—Trebarr Castle and all the land attached to it. And she wanted desperately to get it back. Because she might then get her mother back. Her mother, whom Ernest Carew had sectioned in a women's asylum over two years ago.

'I might not resemble a countess in your eyes, Mr Marsden, and frankly, I don't care either way. All I want are the deeds to Trebarr Castle.'

'In exchange for what, Lady Eliza? What could you possibly give me to settle that debt and buy back the deeds to your crumbling old estate?'

'The only thing that you would naturally accept—money. If you could tell me how much he owed you, then I'll arrange to pay it back to you within an agreed time period. In return, I would like the deeds to my castle and all the land attached to it.'

'As easy as that?' Sebastian Marsden watched her for a moment, before a slow smile curled on his lips. It wasn't a particularly nice smile; indeed it was cold and calculating. 'Without offending your sensibilities, Lady Eliza, I suggest that we dispense with the subterfuge.'

What?

'I do not know what you mean.'

'Don't you?' He raised a brow. 'I think you're bluffing, my lady.'

'I... I would not know how.' What on earth was the blasted

man speaking about? 'Although, this would be the perfect place to hone such skills.'

'Ah, but you are a far cleverer woman than you let on.'

'Am I?'

'Indeed. You come here in this state, wearing clothing that has been mended more times than you'd probably care to remember, antagonise my staff, antagonise me, for the love of God, and offer to pay Ritton's debts in exchange for deeds? While this has all been somewhat amusing, you and I both know that your late husband was not only a desperate gambler and a profligate, but he also did not have two pennies to rub together.'

'Good of you to notice, especially my apparently shabby appearance.'

'I notice everything.'

She tilted her head and studied him. 'I suppose you must when one considers this establishment.'

'Undoubtedly. I gather details about everything and anything that might prove useful to me and mine. I pay attention, and avoid swindlers, charlatans and cheats. At all costs.'

Eliza narrowed her eyes. 'And do you believe that is what I am?'

'I have yet to ascertain that, since I know very little about you.'

'As I do about you, Mr Marsden. What I can tell you is that I would have welcomed avoiding cheats and swindlers but alas, could hardly do so, when I was married to one.'

'A regrettable mistake.'

It had been. But how could she have known what kind of man Ernest was until it was too late? Like her father, who'd pushed hard for the match, Eliza had been taken in by his easy charm and affable manners.

'Oh, yes, but we women rarely get the choices and freedoms that men get.'

'Ah, so you're a radical?'

'And if I am?'

'Nothing.' He shrugged. 'Just another observation.'

Eliza sighed. 'As women, we are even more powerless once we're married, with our person and our possessions given over to our husbands, no matter how proficient we are with the finer details. This needs to change.'

'It does and yet it is also exactly my point, Lady Eliza.' He took another sip of his coffee and set it back on its saucer. 'I may believe you to be far superior to your conniving wastrel of a husband, but I cannot believe that while he sold every earthly possession that had not been entailed to his estate so that he could pay off his debts, you, Lady Eliza Bawden-Trebarr, you have somehow managed to raise ten thousand pounds so that you can buy back your fairy-tale castle? Would you honestly have me entertain such nonsense?'

'It is not nonsense and it is not a fairy-tale castle, Mr Marsden,' she ground out through gritted teeth. 'While it might seem like a crumbling old relic, my ancestral home means everything to me.' Eliza leant forward, gripping the edge of the table with her gloved hands, clinging to the hope that it might give her some semblance of support as she felt the balance of this discussion slowly slipping away under the weight of his derision. 'Trebarr Castle has been in my family for generations and as the last surviving custodian of a castle with such significant historical importance, it is beholden on me to ensure that it's restored to its former glory. To preserve its history and its tradition as a legacy for future generations.'

He started to clap slowly. 'A very impassioned speech, my lady,' he murmured, inclining his head in apparent mock deference. 'However, castles, even those steeped in tradition, afforded some inflated importance because they had once been a part of some revolt or had a king stay under its turrets, are just rock, stone and whatever medieval mortar was used. Nothing more.'

She paled. 'Trebarr Castle is far more than that to me.'

'Is it? Will it put food on your table? Will it clothe you? No, I think not.'

'If this is what you believe then why would you accept it in lieu of the money Ritton owed you?'

'Because I am no fool, my lady. I know precisely how much the land that comes with that pile of crumbling stone and mortar is worth. The Trebarr estate sits on premium Cornish land

and is worth more than ten times what your dearly departed husband owed me.'

'And what exactly would you do with it?'

'Do you really want to know?' No, she did not but sat there waiting for his answer, anyway. 'I could tear it down and flatten it, and build luxury hotels on the cliff instead.'

She felt faint. 'And you would beggar me in the process, rather than allow me to pay back what he actually owed you?'

He gave her a rueful smile, one that she itched to wipe off. 'I am a businessman, Lady Eliza, as you pointed out, and a shrewd one at that. Besides, and I hope you do not take offence, but how could an impoverished widow such as yourself hope to manage to raise such a sum?'

Eliza flushed with embarrassment. God, how lowering. 'All I ask is for you to allow me the opportunity to do so, Mr Marsden. Within an agreed time. I may not have the money yet but I am confident I can raise it.'

'How, my lady? How exactly do you propose to raise ten thousand pounds?'

No, Eliza would not tell him that. Not just for fear of being laughed out of the room but because it was her last trump card. One that even her late husband knew nothing about, otherwise he would have done everything in his power to find it: the Trebarr treasure…

Eliza needed to find the map, decipher the code and go in search of the treasure, the legend of which had been handed down the generations along the female line, since Elowen Bawden-Trebarr herself. Or so the legend claimed. Her mother had filled her head with stories about two star-crossed lovers—the great Simon Trebarr and Lady Elowen Bawden, who overcame their family's enmity and forged their union with a love so strong it transcended time itself. And the treasure they had left their descendants was supposed to be so vastly significant; a princely sum, if it even still existed, that Eliza knew she had to at least try to recover it.

It might seem futile, it might seem insurmountable, but it was all she had. Indeed, it was her only hope. And all she asked for was a chance. A chance to find the treasure, so she could not only win back Trebarr Castle and restore it, but have enough money to get her mother out of Helshem Asylum and make a home for both of them. Yes, it seemed quite impossible, but Eliza was prepared to die trying.

She pushed her spectacles up the length of her nose again, her fingers shaking as she did so. 'I hope you do not take offence either but that, Mr Marsden, is none of your concern.'

'Then in that case I cannot help you.'

Oh dear, this was slowly unravelling. 'Please find it in your heart to help my situation. I am not asking for much.'

'You do not get to determine that, my lady. And frankly, I care not for traditions and preserving legacies of so-called great families of these isles. They are meaningless to me. They are part of the past and I am more interested in the future, in commerce, industry and progress.'

'But, Mr Marsden…'

'I'm afraid I cannot acquiesce to your wishes, Lady Eliza. I am sorry for your situation but it is not of my doing. Nor is it my concern.'

God, the man was insufferable. Eliza stood, her fists clenched to her sides, her nostrils flared. She couldn't remember the last time she was this angry. 'It seems that you are as heartless as they say you are, Mr Marsden. It seems everything they say about you is true after all.'

'Yes, it seems that it is.' He also got up, uncurled his long limbs slowly like a sleek panther and stood towering over her even when he clasped the edge of the table that separated them and leant forward. For the first time since she had stepped into this room, Eliza took in the size, the breadth, the sheer magnitude of the man, with his broad shoulders encased in a tailored single-breasted frock coat, with its matching waistcoat, four-in-hand tie and fitted trousers, and all in the same sombre black. All except his stiff turn-down white shirt. His black eyes glittered as he matched her anger with his, adding even more fuel to the fire. 'And by the by, Lady Eliza Bawden-Trebarr, I sit in the darkness because it soothes me. It's my home. It belongs to me but this is no Gothic tale, it is mine.' He knocked back the remainder of his coffee. 'We're done here.'

Chapter Two

It had been three days since Ritton's countess, *Lady* Eliza Bawden-Trebarr, had come into his domain and shaken Sebastian Frederick Leopold Marsden to his very core. Three days since he had been unsettled by her unexpected visit to the club. Somehow, and this was something Sebastian did not quite understand, he actually felt guilty for turning the woman away after she had come to plead her case, which was not like him at all. He never cared about the wishes of the upper order; what the *haut monde* thought was their due. Not even an impoverished countess.

After all, he'd been publicly ousted as the Earl of Harbury and declared to be illegitimate along with his two brothers after the death of their beloved father many years ago. And that had naturally ensured Sebastian maintained such firmly held beliefs. Indeed, the shame of how it had all come about had given him a focus for all the wrongs that had been done to his family. It had given him a way to direct all of his bitterness and resentment towards the very people who'd scorned him and his brothers, Dominic and Tristan, and their mother.

Yet, he had once been a part of that world; he'd been one of them. Wealthy, handsome, young and a leader among his peers, he'd thought that there was nothing that he could ever have want or need of. Sebastian had been coveted by men and women and been destined for greatness. As the future Earl of Harbury, and head of a powerful dynastic family, he had been born with a silver spoon in his mouth.

But oh, how the mighty had fallen...

He would never forget that terrible time when their whole world came crashing down. It had been during the summer term at Eton, after he'd been informed of his father's sudden death. And soon, after rushing to Harbury Hall, Sebastian had found his uncle presiding over a meeting with his father's solicitors clutching a marriage certificate that had oh, so mysteriously come to light, proving beyond all doubt that their father had been a bigamist. Overnight, everything had changed. He was not even allowed to grieve for their father properly in their home, as Sebastian and his brothers were stripped of everything they'd known; their whole lives altered irrevocably. And with the death of their gentle and loving mother barely a year later, the three boys had been left to fend for themselves and forced into the unknown, their future uncertain.

Yet, after all that bleakness, all that heartache, Sebastian had somehow managed to drag them all out of relative poverty, through sheer will and determination. And eventually, the three brothers had had enough capital to open Trium Impiorum—their home, their reason for being, their whole existence. Out of the ashes of doom and all that. Indeed, the exclusive gaming hell tucked away behind St. James's Place, where the rich, the idle and the powerful came to indulge in vice and sin, meant everything to Sebastian and his brothers. It gave him a huge sense of satisfaction to take from the same men, the same peers and idle fools who had once taken from him. No, the irony of that had never been lost on any of the Marsden Bastards...

Which made his reaction to Lady Eliza Carew née Bawden-Trebarr all the more surprising. The woman's husband had not only been a wastrel but a despicable cheat, swindler and everything he loathed in a peer. His drunken fall from a horse resulting in his early death, being just as pitiful. And though Sebastian had never met the woman until she had come barging into his club, he could not help but feel sorry for the young widow, who had obviously found herself in reduced circumstances. Not enough, however, to acquiesce to her outlandish proposal to regain the deeds of the vast Cornish estate now that it belonged to him. It seemed entirely implausible that the lady could get her hands on that amount of money, in any case. And yet, there had been something more that he'd seen in those pretty hazel eyes of hers, magnified by the strangely endearing round wire-rimmed spectacles, that troubled him. It was her desperation. A desperation that he knew all too well. And it did not sit comfortably with him. Not at all.

'Ah, are you still brooding over Ritton's widow?' His brother Dominic, closest to him in age, leant against the open door, *his open door,* with his arms crossed over his chest and an annoying grin on his face. He must have walked into his office without Sebastian realising.

Damn!

'How were last night's takings?' he muttered, ignoring Dominic's jibe.

'Good. Excellent even.' He rubbed his jaw. 'Although Harbury was here again wanting to discuss certain family matters with us, as he put it.'

'Oh so we're family now?' Sebastian scowled. 'And why was I not informed of this?'

Their cousin Henry Marsden had lately inherited the Harbury Earldom after the death of his father and then years later their uncle. The same uncle who had orchestrated their demise. The same man who'd brought about the claim to prove that Sebastian and his brothers were bastards and therefore not legitimate heirs. All in order to take the Earldom for himself and his heirs; not that Sebastian truly believed their cousin Henry had had any part in it, and not that the claim hadn't been true. That was what had pained Sebastian the most. That their father had indeed been a bigamist. That he had lied to them. That it had all been true. He had caused all of that devastation and the early death of their mother. Whether or not he'd meant it was neither here nor there.

Dominic shrugged. 'I didn't inform you because I didn't want to disturb your meeting with Marrant.'

'But I would still have liked to have been informed.'

'Well, I'm telling you now, Seb.' Dominic slumped into a chair and dragged his fingers through his hair. 'And besides, I've handled it.'

Sebastian sighed, not wanting to get into an argument with his brother. His meeting with his bookkeeper had taken up so much of his time during the night that he could not attend the floors. And although the club was doing well, they still remained financially stretched, with most of their profits ploughed back into the business. However, that did not mean that he shouldn't be informed of important news such as the arrival of their cousin to the Trium Impiorum. 'Well, what did Harbury want?'

'The usual. He wants us to cease buying all the unentailed assets that dear Uncle Jasper was forced to sell.'

Yes, their uncle's mismanagement of the Earldom had been a gift from the gods and one that Sebastian and his brothers had welcomed and used to their own advantage. It had started when a few unentailed properties and parcels of land belonging to the Harbury estate came up for auction. Which neatly fell into the hands of the Marsden Bastards soon after. A transfer of ownership that Sebastian had enjoyed taunting his uncle with before he'd died, after everything he had put them through. Especially his gentle and kind mother, who had never gotten over the disgrace of her husband's bigamy. Their uncle could have chosen to protect her; he could have chosen to look after his nephews. Instead, he'd thrown them out of their home, condemned them all to live in near poverty and shunned them, pretending that they no longer existed.

Oh, yes, Sebastian had welcomed this well-deserved retribution, by taking what he could from the Harbury estate, brick by brick. While Henry may not have been responsible for his father's actions, he was still his damn son. And neither Sebastian nor Dominic nor for that matter, Tristan, owed him any of their loyalty.

'You should have told me earlier, Dominic. I always want to be informed of any possible trouble or otherwise, at the time it actually occurs.'

Yet, for all his conviction in knowing that this was Harbury's due, it still sat uneasily with Sebastian when he knew he was judging Henry for what Jasper Marsden had done. Which, despite it all, was wrong and was unfair to Henry. But then, as he'd explained to Eliza Bawden-Trebarr only a few days ago, he had never claimed to be *fair*.

In any case, none of it was Sebastian's concern. He would waste no further time thinking about Henry, the Harbury estate or this unfamiliar and unexpected feeling of guilt that had gotten hold of him today.

'I'll try and remember that next time Harbury comes here,' which he said he would keep doing until the day you agree to grace him with your presence, as he put it.' His brother grinned. 'Which brings to mind another thing, Seb.'

'Oh, and what is that?' he said on a long sigh.

Sebastian was tired, that was all. It was obviously the meeting with the young widow that had ruffled him far more than he liked to admit.

'A bit of a problem, actually,' Dominic muttered. 'Which needs our attention.'

'Can it wait?'

'I don't think so.'

Sebastian rose and scrubbed a hand across his face irritably. 'Very well.'

The truth was that Eliza Bawden-Trebarr may have presented herself as a dowdy bluestocking despite her relatively young age, but she did have spirit. She might have been desperate in coming here to plead her case, yet she had not cowered before him when doing so. No, the widow had not been afraid of him, even when he had hidden in the dark in an attempt to conclude the meeting as hastily as possible, which he'd failed to do. If anything, it had made her more inquisitive, tilting her head in that strangely endearing way she had, and asking more and more impertinent questions.

May I ask why you would sit in the relative darkness in broad daylight?

Good God, that one had flummoxed him, and for a moment he'd thought about throwing her out. He never allowed anyone to get under his skin or to get too close, especially someone who seemed to be as perceptive as this woman. It had made Sebastian order one of his men to follow her to her residence after she'd left the club—a small town house on the skirts of Chelsea—just to prove that she hadn't been a hoax. An old mistress out to see what she might gain through Sebastian. He had looked into Eliza Carew née Bawden-Trebarr's situation further and confirmed that she was whom she'd said she was and had been living modestly for a woman who'd once been a countess. Meaning there could be no possible way for her to obtain the amount of money required to pay back her late husband's debt. So why come here in the first place? It made little sense.

Charity…that was probably the most likely explanation. Like all members of the haute monde, the *lady* thought to use her wiles to somehow gain the deeds of her estate for nothing. Or perhaps appeal to his sense of honour and fairness. But he'd soon disabused her of that belief. No, he was no longer the man he'd been destined to be. Instead, Sebastian, as well as his brothers, had fashioned new paths for themselves that straddled an ambiguous existence with no need for virtues such as fairness or honour.

Sebastian snapped his head around towards the window as a sudden loud noise of people shouting and chanting from the street below broke through his musings.

'What the hell is that commotion?'

Dominic strolled towards the window, pulling the curtain to the side and peering outside. 'Ah, that's the problem I was referring to.'

Sebastian scowled. 'Which is what, exactly?'

'Possible trouble, or otherwise.' Dominic nodded towards a small crowd that had gathered just outside the entrance of the Trium Impiorum. 'Your friend has returned. Lady Eliza Bawden-Trebarr, and this time she has not come alone.'

What the devil?

'That termagant is no friend of mine.'

'Interesting, as Lady Eliza contradicted that notion when she approached me a moment ago, introduced herself and appealed to me to summon you, her aforementioned *friend*, down.'

'Summon me…?' Good God, she had a nerve. 'This isn't funny, Dominic, and I don't care what she called me! I want to know what the woman wants.'

'The same as before, I should imagine. She mentioned that since her "friendly chat" with you proved unsuccessful, she was resigned to come back here again and try and persuade you. And she would not leave until you agreed.'

Sebastian swore long and low under his breath. 'Well, she will be disappointed once again.'

Dominic smirked, clearly enjoying this. 'You'd best see to her, then.'

'Couldn't you? And while doing so, remove her person from outside the club?'

'I think not as the women she has come with would certainly have something to say about it, and some of them look like they might just bite.'

'What women?'

'Come and see, brother. It seems the lady has brought rein-forcements.' Dominic pulled the curtain back more, allowing a long beam of light to stream into his office. 'Ritton's widow is trouble.'

'That, she is,' Sebastian said through clenched teeth before storming out of the room.

He rushed down the stairwell, bypassing some of his work-ers who must have had the foresight to jump out of his way as he stomped through the reception area and pushed both of the entrance doors with force, making them fly open.

Sebastian scanned the crowd on the pavement and road just outside the club. Two dozen or so women held banners and shouted slogans, while clusters of onlookers stopped in their tracks to see what was going on. His eyes flicked around until he spotted the one woman he'd been looking for. The one respon-sible for whatever the hell this was supposed to be. He tugged the edges of his fitted overcoat irritably as he climbed down the few steps and made his way towards Eliza Bawden-Trebarr.

'What in blazes is this?' he roared as he approached her.

The woman spun around to face him. 'And a good day to you, too, Mr Marsden.'

'This is far from being a good day,' he muttered, dragging his fingers through his hair. 'I would like to know the meaning of this.'

'Oh well, you see, I happened to inform some of my friends from various women's groups of my sad plight. They naturally then decided to lend me their support.'

'Your *sad plight*? Well, that is a misrepresentation if ever I heard one.'

'Oh come now, Mr Marsden, can you not comprehend my situation? Can you not listen to my reasoning?'

'So I am unreasonable because I did not agree to your mad scheme?'

'It is not a mad scheme. It is a desperate attempt to right the wrongs that I believe have been done to me. Surely, you of all people can understand that.'

She was once again saying words that resonated with him; words that made him feel uncomfortable in his own skin. 'And why should I understand that?'

'Because of your past and how you had to overcome it.' The woman shrugged. 'I am trying to do just that, Mr Marsden. Overcome and survive.'

'And by that you mean to take me to task?' He waved his arms towards the various women gathered outside the club. 'By creating all of this?'

'No, I never intended for it to become *this*. It has got rather out of hand. But you see, I mentioned my predicament to a friend and then word must have got around. I had no notion that so many would turn up.'

'Somehow I find that hard to believe,' he muttered through clenched teeth.

'Oh, but it's true.'

'It seems that I underestimated you, Lady Eliza.'

She nodded in apparent agreement. 'Many do.'

But Sebastian was not many. He was a man who prided himself on always being one step ahead of everyone, including an oddity like the woman before him. It was one of the main reasons why the Trium Impiorum was as successful as it was. Because of his attention to detail and always being vigilant. Yet, in Eliza Bawden-Trebarr's case, he had got it spectacularly wrong.

Sebastian looked at the placards the women were holding. One had *Clean London of this pernicious evil* just about fitting it on the placard. Another had *Gambling is evil*. Another that it was *a sin*. As well as *Women resist the wickedness of gambling* in large letters.

If that wasn't bad enough, the women were also shouting slogans. *"No to gambling, no to vice."* And *"Resist this evil from our lives."*

He exhaled through his teeth. 'Who in God's name are these women? And why, for pity's sake, won't they stop this incessant clamour?'

Eliza smiled sweetly and pointed at the small group of disapproving women. 'That group with the placards about the betterment of morals are the Ladies Association of Social Justice and Moral Correction, who I admit are a bit stuffy but are rather vocal and think of themselves as crusaders. I have to say that they invited themselves but were insistent on coming to warn others of the many dangers of gambling.'

Sebastian pinched the bridge of his nose, trying hard to keep his temper in check. 'And the other group, dressed in all that pale froth and lace. The younger women?'

'That group is one that I am part of and is led by my friend over there, Miss Cecily Duddlecott. I can see she is arguing with your brother, whose acquaintance I've just had the pleasure of making,' she said, nodding towards a young dark-haired woman engaged in a heated debate with Dominic. Of course, Eliza Bawden-Trebarr didn't bat an eyelid over anything that was going on. 'Cecily and I formed the TWERM.'

'The what? Dare I ask what that is?'

'The Women's Enlightened Reform Movement.'

God give him strength. 'Well, whoever the hell you all are, I want you to leave now, Eliza,' he snapped.

'I do not believe that I gave you leave to use my given name, Mr Marsden.'

He purposely took a step closer, crowding her. 'And I did not give you leave to create havoc outside my doors, *Eliza*.'

This close, he could see the freckles dusted lightly across her nose and cheeks, as though it formed a map, a language he suddenly wanted to decipher. His eyes took in her appearance, again dressed in greys and unflatteringly modest clothing. Yet, her poise was as impeccable as it was elegant. And her little jaunty hat, fixed to the side of her head, did little to cover her glorious hair, pinned and pulled into a tight, neat bun. Good Lord, but it was the most unusual colour, pale and luminous like spun gold. How had he thought her unremarkable or even ordinary? At first glance perhaps, but a further look made him realise that she was uncommonly lovely. His eyes dropped to her full lips briefly before he looked away, disgusted that he'd noticed all of this about her at that precise moment.

Thankfully, she appeared unaware of his errant thoughts as she raised a brow and crossed her arms. 'I am sorry to create this unrest just outside your hallowed doors. However, I do wonder how a gaggle of women standing outside will affect your business. What will your patrons think? What of the satirists, cartoonists and the newsmen once they get wind of this? It does not bear thinking about, Mr Marsden.'

How had this woman outmanoeuvred him so easily? 'You are enjoying this, aren't you?'

'Not in the least. But as a means to an end, it is quite effective, don't you think?'

Whatever feelings of admiration he'd had dissipated instantly. Eliza Bawden-Trebarr was a harridan. A termagant. A vixen. 'What I think is that you should leave now and take this caterwauling group of shrews with you.'

'Now, now, Mr Marsden, there's no need for such language and besides, you can hardly remove us in person.'

'Shall we put that to the test?'

'Stuff and nonsense. You do not own the roads.'

'Try me.'

She took a step forward so she was standing directly beneath him, pushed her spectacles up her nose and glared at him. 'You wouldn't dare.'

'Wouldn't I?' He bent his head so that his nose was mere inches away from hers, as he clenched his fists tightly and resisted the urge to touch her. Her scent teased him. A scent that was fresh and reminded him of the morning dew in spring. He gave himself a mental shake just to dispel such errant thoughts. 'I can get my men out here right now and instruct them to remove every one of you women from the vicinity of the Trium Impiorum. Drag you all away by any necessary means if need be.'

Her eyes glittered with a sudden blaze of anger that was extinguished just as quickly. How interesting. Eliza seemed to be a woman who kept her emotions on a tight leash. 'You would, however, refrain from doing anything so deplorable.'

'Would I now?'

'Yes, because a gentleman would never do such a thing.'

'And as I told you before, I am no such thing.' He let out an exasperated breath. 'Now go, and take these women's groups and ridiculously named associations with you.'

'I think not. I think I shall stay. Indeed, we shall all stay all day and all night until you finally agree to my terms, Mr Marsden.'

'That is blackmail.'

'I'd imagine that someone like you would be used to something like that.' She tugged on her gloves and shrugged. 'I'd say that for *a lone witless woman seemingly lacking in sense and propriety*, I have rather outdone myself.'

Sebastian marvelled for a moment at the cheek of her as she threw back his asinine insults from their first encounter. But only for a moment. 'Why are you doing this, Eliza?'

She pushed her ill-fitting spectacles along the bridge of her nose and frowned. 'You gave me little choice. And by the by, it's Lady Eliza Bawden-Trebarr to you!'

As she turned to move away, in an obvious attempt to dismiss him, Sebastian caught her by the elbow and stilled. Unable to move, shocked by the contact, the warmth of the touch, even through the layers of clothing, he just stared at the point where his hand wrapped around her arm. It momentarily stunned him. And he, Sebastian Marsden, was not a man who had ever been flummoxed, especially by a bespectacled, delicious-smelling bluestocking partial to ill-fitting apparel. Yet, she was doing just that. This mere slip of a woman.

He dropped his hand, as though he'd been scorched by the touch, and took a step back, needing a little distance from this irritating woman. 'What will it take to make you leave?'

'You know precisely what I am after, Mr Marsden. Allow me the opportunity to pay back my late husband's debt in exchange for the deeds to Trebarr Castle.'

'How? How would you acquire such a vast sum?'

'What does it matter as long as I pay back the debt?' She narrowed her eyes. 'Is it so that you can somehow scupper my progress?'

'And why on earth would I do that?'

'How is one ever to know what is in your head? For instance, I still cannot understand why you continually refuse to allow me the opportunity to pay back Ritton's debts.'

'Because I know there is no way in which you can do it, Eliza.'

A slow, mischievous smile spread on her lips. 'O ye, of little faith.'

'It is more the absurdity of what you're proposing than any lack of faith.'

'Then put it to the test, Mr Marsden. Give me six weeks and if I fail to get your ten thousand pounds then Trebarr Castle and all its land is yours to do with as you wish, and with my blessing.'

Somehow Sebastian did not quite believe her. The woman was certainly trouble. And yet, he needed to get her as well as all these other women away from Trium Impiorum as soon as possible. Away from St James's. In this, she had played a masterful card and had been quite correct when stating how bad the publicity would be for the club. As Eliza had so eloquently put it, the ridicule that this news would garner would spell indefinite disaster if this charade was allowed to continue for much longer. 'If I agree to this, you will leave and take these damn women's groups away from my club.'

'Of course, Mr Marsden.'

He narrowed his eyes. 'I don't trust you, Eliza. There is some mischief here, something shifty at play that I just can't put my finger on.'

Her jaw dropped as she looked indignantly at him. 'There's nothing of the sort. I am just a woman trying to make her way in the world.'

'Somehow I think you are the sort to get on regardless.' Even so, Sebastian knew that he would agree to her terms, and with that decision made, an invisible weight fell away from his shoulders. In any case, in this he had little to lose. 'Very well, if you keep your word and leave now, I shall grant you two weeks to pay back the debt.'

'I need more time than that. Four weeks.'

'Three and that is my final offer, Eliza.'

'But that is still not enough.'

He stuck out his hand. 'That is all I am willing to offer. So will you take it?'

Eliza glanced at his outstretched hand and then at him, before nodding and slipping her gloved hand into his. 'I will, although I still have not given leave for you to call me by my given name.'

A ghost of a smile touched his lips. 'I think we can drop the formalities, don't you?'

She raised a brow as she slipped her hand into his. 'Ah, so you permit me to call you Sebastian, then?'

He gripped her hand and immediately felt the heat from her skin, despite the fact she was wearing leather gloves. This was the second time that this had happened when he'd inadvertently touched her. He swallowed uncomfortably. 'No...no, you may not.'

Sebastian let go of her hand abruptly and clenched and unclenched his own several times in an attempt to rid himself of that damnable warmth. That elusive touch. What the hell was wrong with him? It was her, the woman, standing just before him.

'Three weeks, Eliza, that is all you have. Now, I would like you to leave this area as agreed and take all your women's reformists groups with you.' He spun on his heel and strode away needing not a little distance from Eliza Bawden-Trebarr but quite a lot more.

Chapter Three

It had been one week since Sebastian Marsden had finally agreed to allow Eliza the chance to pay back Ritton's debts. One week, and yet she was still no further along in her quest since that day when Sebastian Marsden had stood in front of her outside Trium Impiorum and glared and glowered at her, surrounded by all the women's groups and associations, until he had finally and surprisingly relented.

It had initially been rather amusing watching him as his panic and frustration grew; so much so that she had thought smoke and fire would billow out of his ears and flared nostrils. God, but she had enjoyed sparring with the man. It was probably churlish of her to do so but he'd tested and challenged her to the point that she'd felt invigorated afterwards. In just the same way as she always did after a brisk walk in Hyde Park. And of course, it didn't hurt that he was far more attractive than she remembered after that first encounter in his office. He was the epitome of a handsome if not doomed hero in one of those lurid novels she'd used to read. Tall, dark, brooding; a little too brooding, perhaps. Actually, if Eliza considered him in the cold light of day, the man scowled at her more than anything else. And his almost obsidian eyes were actually a very dark shade of grey-blue like clouds during the heaviest of thunderstorms.

In any case, it was a good reason not to trust her reaction to him when he was near. He annoyed her despite the sparring, and he was far too dangerous to her peace of mind in a way that Eliza couldn't quite fathom. Besides, how could anyone be that beautiful to look at, with all that chiselled perfection, smell that heavenly of lemons, bergamot and sandalwood, yet be someone whom she would happily throttle? The man was abominably rude and exceedingly vexing but at least he had eventually agreed to her terms and given her time to find the money.

Three weeks...

With seven of those days already gone and only fourteen left! Never mind Sebastian Marsden's panic, hers was starting to make her want to reach for the smelling salts. What on earth was she to do? There had to be something...yes, yes there was...to remain calm and concentrate on the task at hand. Which meant attempting to understand the conundrum that was before her on the wooden table...

Eliza looked at the Bawden-Trebarr heirloom, a beautiful ornate small casket box made from inlays of different wood and decorated with the faded colours of the two Cornish houses— of Bawden in gold, brown and blue, and Trebarr in gold, light blue and verdant green. The casket box, which of course would not open to reveal its secret.

It was tightly closed with a solid metal lock hasp screwed to the lid and fastened to a lock plate, which was attached to the side front. The metal lock plate itself was fashioned to look like the *Morvoren* or the Cornish legend of the Sea Maiden, which had been in some way significant to Eliza's ancestors, Elowen and Simon Bawden-Trebarr. But aside from the exquisiteness of the design, the intriguing aspect to the box was that there was no keyhole and no apparent key to open it with. So yes, it was indeed a conundrum. The only way that Eliza believed it might open was if there was a metal disc of the exact design that would fit on top of the lock plate, and when pressed would release the metal lock.

It was Eliza's mother who had given it to her before being forcibly admitted into Helshem Asylum and warned Eliza to keep it safe and not allow anyone to take it from her, especially not Ritton. And this was something that Eliza had managed to do, keep it hidden away in an old worthless box in the attic of their London home until after his death.

Even now, Eliza could recall her mother's words as she gave the box to her.

It was commissioned by Simon Trebarr for his beloved, Elowen. And within the box itself they placed a secret, which has remained intact for hundreds of years, Eliza, and has only been passed down the generations through the female lines. It is said that the treasure contained inside is only to be used if any of Elowen's ancestors are ever in dire need. If that happens, you must find that which would open the box first. Never forget that, daughter dearest, for it is not so easily found...

Meaning this was going to be far more challenging and difficult than Eliza had first believed. The legend of the Bawden-Trebarr treasure was that it had always been kept as a secret, and was devised by Simon and Elowen on their marriage as a way to protect their daughters and all those who came after them.

Yet, for all Eliza knew, the so-called treasure that was apparently hidden inside the box might have been taken years ago. After all, Simon and Elowen had lived in the fourteenth century, so whatever treasure they'd had hidden away that this box led to, might be long gone by now. And yet, if it had been taken, then why go to all the trouble of having the box sealed again and having the thing that opened it so difficult to find? It was rather like having two treasures to discover—one that she hoped would lead to the other.

It all seemed impossible and showed how desperate Eliza was for her to pin all her hopes on *this* to pay back Ritton's debt. But with no other plan in place, this very risky venture was all she had at present.

Perhaps Sebastian Marsden had been right after all, when he had stated that she was bluffing about being able to pay back his ten thousand pounds. How was she going to find even half of such a sum? The man would think her mad if he knew that *this*...this search for the Bawden-Trebarr treasure was the only solution to her woes. Still, she would not give up—not yet.

Eliza glanced at the table with all her notes, findings and books neatly piled up on one side and the box on the other. The answer to the riddle must be here somewhere but first she had to get the bloody thing open. And she had tried everything, to no avail. The only logical solution was that there was a metal plate somewhere that was made especially to fit the lock plate, cut and soldered in the shape of the Morvoren. However, everywhere she had looked from the British Museum to the Ashmolean in Oxford, there had been nothing in any public collections that looked remotely like it. Aside from rushing to Oxford, Eliza had also spent the past week visiting every pawnshop, antique warehouse and vendor in London as well as a handful in neighbouring counties but was once again left disappointed. It was like searching for a needle in the proverbial haystack.

Of course, Eliza could just take a hammer to the box and break into it and risk destroying whatever was hidden there, which would be quite a pointless exercise. No, she had to find a way.

'Any luck?' Her friend and cofounder of The Women's Enlightened Reform Movement, Cecily Duddlecott, or Cecy as she liked to be called, walked in with one of her footmen, carrying the tea tray.

'No.' Eliza slouched in the chair and sighed. 'Sadly not.'

'Then some restorative tea might be in order.' She directed the tray to be set at a side table before sitting on the small floral settee beside it.

This was Cecy's domain—two adjoining small but pleasant rooms decorated with feminine pinks and blues unlike the rest of the austere dark house that her friend shared with her older unmarried brother, Stephen. The jutting chimney breasts in each room with the matching intricately carved wooden fireplace gave the rooms warmth while plump soft cushions and the Aubusson rugs added a touch of sumptuous comfort. The rooms opened out to pristine gardens at the rear, promoting the necessary need for serenity within the heart of the city. A serenity that was far from how Eliza was presently feeling.

She frowned as she stared at everything on the table. 'I

cannot help thinking that I am missing something vitally important.'

'You have been saying that for some time, Eliza.' Cecy poured the tea and passed the cup and saucer to her. 'Have you thought of the possibility that whatever fits the lock might not be here in London at all? Why, it might not be in England. For all you know it could be lost, damaged—indeed anything could have happened to it.'

'Yes, thank you for that.'

'Oh, I do not mean to be pessimistic in any way. However, it is best to be pragmatic.'

'I know, which is why I have traced the lock plate capturing every detail and took it to a brass founder near St Pancras to have it moulded.'

'Oh, Eliza, you didn't go all the way to St Pancras on your own, did you?'

This was always a point of contention with Cecy, which was rather silly when it was Eliza who was the widow and her friend, whom she had met all those years ago at the Ravendean's School for Young Ladies, who had never married. Cecy had instead been allowed to follow her dream of being one of the first female students to attend Lady Margaret Hall, Oxford, by her forward-thinking parents, something that Eliza would have desired above all else for herself. However, her father had prohibited it and encouraged her to marry Ernest Carew, Viscount Ritton.

You will be a countess, Eliza, just as a young woman of your lineage should be... Her father had repeatedly said that when she had tried to convince him otherwise and yet, the irony of where that got her never failed to amaze her. Being a countess had, in fact, brought nothing but misery and strife. All ending with her situation as it was, and everything to lose if she did not manage to find the money to pay Mr Marsden.

'Of course, I did not go there on my own. I took Willis.'

'Still, you must take care, Eliza, especially when visiting less salubrious parts of London.'

'I am aware, Cecy.' Willis, who was her housekeeper Gertie's son, thankfully lent himself to being the man about the place despite being only sixteen years old, on the account of his height and brawn.

'Even so, I do worry about you traipsing all over London with just a boy for protection.'

'Thank you for your concern but I can look after myself.'

'I know you can, Eliza, but after visiting the Trium Impiorum and taking its enigmatic owner to task, dare I wonder whether you are now taking far too many risks?'

'By that you mean behaving in a manner that is reckless, impulsive or something far worse?' she asked wryly.

'Never that.' Cecy sighed. 'However, I think a little caution will go a long way. After all, I can imagine that a man like Sebastian Marsden could be provoked too far.'

'I have no wish to provoke him in any way,' she said a little too defensively.

'From where I was standing that day, I wasn't sure whether the man wanted to kiss you or throttle you.'

Kiss her?

Eliza was equally appalled and intrigued by such an idea. Not that it was remotely plausible for a woman as unsophisticated as she was to have a man like him want to kiss her. And she certainly didn't need to be reminded of her encounter with Sebastian Marsden. Annoyingly, she had been thinking about him far too often as it was, which would not do.

'Nothing of the sort. He's just a man used to getting his own way. And I'd soon as throttle him myself, for all his imperious and arrogant manner.'

The man might be enigmatic and far too handsome for his own good but he also stood in the way of her getting Trebarr Castle back. Not that Sebastian Marsden believed that she could do it. No, by giving her three weeks to come up with the money he was merely humouring her, assuming she'd fail, anyway and more importantly, using it as a way to get her off his back. The day Eliza could prove him wrong by paying the blasted debt owed to him could not come soon enough! She would then be done with this, all of it. And the only way to achieve that was to get this box open without damaging it.

Eliza peered at the box using her magnifying glass to look

more closely at the smaller details of the lock plate, hoping she had not missed anything. 'In any case, I cannot see how you noticed that when you were engaged in such a heated argument with Sebastian Marsden's own brother.'

Cecy flushed. 'Yes, well, he was nothing but a rude, obnoxious scoundrel.'

Eliza suddenly felt a wave of guilt rush through her, knowing that she had inadvertently allowed her friend to be exposed to such behaviour. If Cecy's brother Stephen got wind of it then he would prohibit further outings. And where would Eliza be then? She had few friends as it was. 'Oh, I'm sorry you had to experience that.'

Cecy shook her head. 'Don't worry. I put the man firmly in his place. Abominable rogue!'

'I'm sure you did.' A faint smile curled at her lips. 'It seems that it runs in the Marsden family.'

'Quite.' She took a sip of tea and placed the cup back on the table. 'But it puts me to mind of another family, Eliza. Your husband's cousin, the new Viscount Ritton, Ronald Carew, came sniffing around here looking for you.'

Eliza grimaced and rubbed her forehead. 'And at my lodgings in Chelsea while I was away according to Gertie.'

'He's convinced that you made away with the Ritton silver, or something that belongs to him. He cannot believe that he's inherited an empty shell of an estate. That there's nothing whatsoever left in the coffers.'

'Well, it has naught to do with me. Indeed, he can believe what he likes. The new, and not much improved, Ritton seems to be just like his predecessor and frankly it means nothing to me.'

'Even so, if he gets to hear about this box or even that there's a possible whiff of treasure attached, I cannot say what he would do.' Her friend sighed impatiently. 'Eliza? Are you even listening to me?'

'Of course, I am.' She sighed. 'Ronald Carew doesn't concern me in any way. This box is mine, given to me by my mother, and it has nothing to do with the Ritton estate.'

'Yet, he could still cause you trouble, which is why taking Willis here and there will simply not do.'

'Surely not,' she teased, raising a brow. 'I cannot recall going anywhere as thrilling as *here and there*.'

'This is no time to jest, Eliza. I do not trust Ronald Carew,' she said, rubbing her forehead with her fingers. 'Perhaps I should speak with Stephen about you using one of our servants.'

'Please, Cecy, that is not necessary.'

It was bad enough that Eliza was all on her own apart from Willis and his mother, the ever-faithful Gertie, who had been with her since she was a young girl, as well as relying on the few friends she had, such as Cecy. But it was quite another to be beholden to Stephen Duddlecott, who just about tolerated Eliza, believing her to be a bad influence on his sister. If only he knew the half of it! Ever since the deaths of their parents over a year ago, Mr Duddlecott had become increasingly protective of his unmarried sister. A little bit too protective, in Eliza's opinion. It was as if those years that Cecy had studied at Oxford had never actually happened, and God knew what her brother would say if he knew about Cecy's involvement in their women's group. Yet, she could not begrudge the man for caring; at least Cecy had someone who looked out for her. Stephen Duddlecott might be a pompous bore but at least he took pains to ensure his sister's comfort. And the man had never questioned the fact that his sister had turned these rooms at the back of his grand Belgravia home into a meeting place once a month for The Women's Enlightened Reform Movement, although in truth he was quite unaware of what went on and believed them to be doing some charitable endeavour or other. Even so, Eliza was happy to come and do her research here from time to time, since her own lodgings in her modest Chelsea town house lacked the library resources as well as the space. But she drew the line at using some of Stephen Duddlecott's servants.

'Come now, Eliza. I'm only concerned for your well-being.'

'I know and I thank you for it.' Eliza sighed, glancing at her friend and offering a weak smile. 'But I simply don't have time to fret. However, I shall promise that I will take care, in particular when I visit the less salubrious parts of London. There, are you satisfied?'

'For now, yes, it will have to do.' Cecily returned her smile. 'So tell me all your findings since I last saw you.'

Which was when they had been together outside the Trium Impiorum with The Women's Enlightened Reform Movement as well as the other groups creating quite a stir. Where Sebastian Marsden had apparently looked as though he might either throttle or kiss her. Heavens. And why on earth was she even pondering on such an absurdity? And at such a time. Cecy must have it all wrong in any case.

Eliza cleared her throat. 'As I mentioned, I've commissioned a mould to be made to fit the lock plate in the hope that it might open the vexing thing. However, that unfortunately is as much as there is to say about any findings.'

'Surely, it can't be as bad as all that.'

'In all honesty, I'm not certain about anything at the moment. All I have done is to have a mould made from a tracing I made of the lock plate. Nothing more.'

'It is an inspired idea,' Cecy said encouragingly. 'Really, it is.'

'It is my *only* idea.' She sighed and shook her head. 'I am starting to worry that I will run out of time.'

'Come now, don't lose heart. Chin up and all that.'

Eliza slumped back in the chair in a very unladylike manner. 'I am trying, I really am, but this is starting to be quite impossible. And the thought of going back to Mr Marsden with empty hands, proving that he was right about me all along, is intolerable, Cecy.'

'Yes, but why would you care about his opinions?'

She sighed. 'I don't know. It's more that I cannot stand the idea of him getting the better of me.' Eliza flicked her gaze to Cecy, who was studying her intently, and looked away. 'Of course, all that matters to me is getting the Trebarr estate back. That was the only reason I approached Mr Marsden in the first place, and where my dealings with the insufferable man begins and ends.'

Cecy smiled, nodding. 'Of course.'

Eliza turned her mind back round to the box, not wanting to linger on anything to do with Sebastian Marsden. 'And to achieve that I need to work this lock out.'

Her friend got up and moved towards her, pulling out another chair and sitting beside Eliza, brushing her fingers over the lock plate. 'It's strange but I can't help thinking that I have seen something that looked just like this before and quite recently, too. Here in London.'

Eliza blinked in surprise. 'You haven't said this before.'

'No, but I've been turning it over my head while you were away.'

'And?' Eliza muttered, hoping not to sound too excited.

'And what?'

'Where do you believe you have seen it?'

'Well, that is just it, Eliza, I cannot recall.'

Her heart sank. Cecy was probably mistaken in her assumption that she'd seen it.

'I know what you're thinking, that I'm probably mistaken, but Eliza, this odd, irregular shape is not something one forgets.'

'It's not an odd, irregular shape, Cecy. It's the shape of a Morvoren.'

'A Morvoren?'

'Yes,' Eliza said. 'Surely, you've heard me talk of it before? The stories my mama used to tell me about the Morvoren, or sea maidens, as well as other myths and legends.'

'How funny. I never realised the lock was in the shape of a sea maiden but yes, now that you mention it, I can see it.'

'Exactly, you can see the long, wavy hair and the long, swirly flick forming her fishlike body. It even has the detail of her scales.'

'It's quite unusual, memorable, really. I just wish I could recall where I saw it.' Cecy rose and ambled over to the small table to retrieve the three-tier cake tray filled with dainty finger cucumber sandwiches, small cakes and fluffy scones.

'Never mind, it might come back to you. In any case, the Morvoren legend has long been associated to the Bawden-Trebarr history and also with this casket box.'

'I hadn't realised.' Cecy sighed and placed a floral porcelain side dish on the table beside Eliza's tea cup and saucer. 'Anyway, allow me to offer you some sandwiches and scones. There's also a pot of clotted cream and some strawberry conserve.'

'Thank you but the tea is quite sufficient.'

'You haven't had a bite to eat since you arrived, Eliza. And you cannot think on an empty stomach. Come, at least have some of the scones, which were baked today. They're Cook's speciality.'

'Very well.' Eliza split the still-warm scone on the plate and spread the thick strawberry jam generously all over before adding a dollop of clotted cream and spreading that evenly on top. Sinking her teeth into the pillowy softness of the warm scone, jam and cream and taking a bite of the sweet concoction was something she hadn't realised she needed until she started eating. Cecy was right; she needed sustenance if she was to be able to think. 'Compliments to your cook, Cecy, this is delicious,' she said, licking the crumbs from her lips. 'As good as any I've had in Cornwall.'

'Cornwall?' Cecy's eyes widened as her fingers touched her forehead suddenly. 'Cornwall...of course, it's Cornwall! That is the connection. That is where I had seen it!'

Eliza wiped her lips with a handkerchief and blinked. 'What on earth are you talking about?'

'Your sea maiden, your Morvoren.' Cecy stood and clapped her hands together excitedly. 'I remember where I saw it, Eliza. I remember it well! It was at a private viewing of the "Cornwall Collection" by an acquaintance of Stephen's, Sir Algernon Bottomley, which we went to see a couple of days ago at the British Museum. He was showing a collection of geological and botanical findings such as fossils, corals, brachiopods as well as artefacts from the local areas of *Cornwall.*'

Eliza also stood facing her, grabbing her friend by the shoulders. 'Are you certain, Cecy?'

'Yes! I am. I remember out of all the bits of stone, limestone and semiprecious bits and pieces, there was a small collection of beautifully carved and moulded sea maidens—one that looked exactly like your Cornish legend of Morvoren and engraved on a metal disc. That could be the piece that might fit onto this lock plate.'

'Yes, it could very well be the thing. Oh, Cecy, you're a marvel!' Eliza hugged her friend. 'A private viewing at the

British Museum, you say? How can I meet this Sir Algernon Bottomley?'

Cecy's smile slipped from her lips and she started to chew on them instead. 'Ah, but there is just one little snag with his collection. You see, what we saw at the museum was a preview of what Sir Algernon is about to take to the Royal Society, with a lecture set for some time this week.'

'When?' Her brows furrowed in the middle. 'When is the lecture happening?'

'I am not certain but I do believe I saw something about it in the newspaper.'

Cecy rushed out of the room only to return with a batch of the week's newspapers, which they started to tear through, trying to find the date for the lecture. Finally, they found it and as Cecy had said it was indeed set for that very week. Two days hence, on Wednesday to be exact, at half past three at the Royal Society.

'Well, that settles it. I shall visit Sir Algernon and try and convince him to...' To do what, exactly? Part with an artefact that was part of his collection? No, that just wouldn't work; the man would never agree and she hardly had anything that might entice him to do so. A more drastic action was needed.

'Oh dear, I do not like that look on your face, Eliza.' Her friend shook her head slowly. 'It's the one that always spells trouble.'

'Oh, not trouble. That is one thing I wish to avoid.' Eliza smiled, her shoulders sagging in relief for the first time in ages. 'Come now, we have only two days and there's a lot to do.'

'I do believe that there's something that you've forgotten.' Cecy looked at her with apprehension. 'The Royal Society and in particular, Sir Algernon, does not permit entrance to women and especially not to his estimable lectures. Heaven forbid that a woman might comprehend his advanced observations. After all, our tiny brains might actually explode from all that knowledge. When I went with Stephen to view his collection at the British Museum, the man was as obsequious towards my brother as he was contemptuous of my presence.'

'Abominable!' Eliza exhaled through her teeth in annoyance

on her friend's behalf. 'In that case, I shan't feel guilty for what I intend to do at his lecture.'

'Oh, dear God, Eliza, dare I ask what that might be?'

She smiled. 'Why, to find the correct Morvoren seal that fits the lock plate and steal it from under his very nose.'

Cecy sighed and shook her head. 'Do be serious, dearest.'

'Oh, I am. But I need your help as there is much to do and little time to do it. Come on, Cecy.'

And so it was that two days later, after the mould that Eliza had commissioned failed to open the lock plate of the box, she put her plan into motion. Her big plan. Thankfully, Eliza did manage to gain entrance to Sir Algernon Bottomley's private viewing at Gresham College as part of the Royal Society with a forged letter of recommendation from Cecy's brother Stephen, and dressed as a young man. Well, maybe a very young man with the austere clothes borrowed from another friend's younger brother. Indeed, this part of the plan had gone exceedingly well. Far better than she had initially thought.

And with this part complete came the far more arduous part of locating and then stealing the Morvoren seal, without any of the other guests noticing. In fact, this was what Eliza dreaded the most as she had to wait and formulate a strategy. Which was challenging enough without the presence of the last person Eliza had expected to find there. And the last thing she'd needed. For there, attending the lecture, was her nemesis, Mr Sebastian Marsden.

Chapter Four

Sebastian could not quite believe his eyes. Perhaps he was imagining it; perhaps he was going mad; but there in the stuffy lecture hall sat... No, it couldn't be *her*, could it?

He had come to the Gresham College with his youngest brother, Tristan, to hear a lecture given by Tristan's old Cambridge tutor, Sir Algernon something or other, when he'd noticed a young man coming inside the lecture hall and taking a seat at the back, closest to the door. Nothing out of the ordinary, except that the chap was the oddest person he'd ever seen in every way.

It was his manner, his gait and the general way he held himself that seemed strange somehow. Apart from constantly fidgeting and sitting in an awkward manner, there was something about him that did not seem quite as it should. Something almost feminine, which wasn't that unusual as there were many such young men. But it was something more. Sebastian couldn't quite put his finger on it but the young chap definitely looked familiar, which made him wonder where he'd seen him. Perhaps he had visited the Trium Impiorum; perhaps he'd been sitting at his gaming tables or had drunk himself into a stupor...but no. He did not believe it was that.

Apart from the tawny moustache and side whiskers and the ill-fitting suit, the young chap looked surprisingly like a certain bluestocking who had plagued him recently. A maddeningly annoying woman who had blackmailed him into giving her three weeks so that she could find ten thousand pounds to pay back her late husband's debt. Perhaps the chap was in some way related to Eliza Bawden-Trebarr, although from Sebastian's research into her he'd found nothing that mentioned any living male relatives.

Strange, but the more Sebastian studied the man the more he realised how much he resembled Eliza. He even had the same round wire spectacles that kept slipping down his nose. And the chap kept pushing them back up his nose just like Eliza did...

Good God, it couldn't actually be her, could it? Sebastian kept his eyes peeled to the *chap*, watching everything he did, hoping to determine whether he was finally going mad or if he was, in fact, staring at a mad woman instead. And just when he was about to look away, convinced that perhaps he'd made a mistake, it happened. Sebastian watched from his seat as the *chap* reached across and unbuttoned his waistcoat, pulling it open and scratching his chest over his shirt. Of course, he wasn't scratching anything but adjusting something and it wasn't really his chest at all, but quite clearly the outline of a taped breast! From where Sebastian sat, slightly to the side of the semicircle arrangement of chairs, and with the beam of light from the window, he could just about make out the tape wrapped around the woman's bosom.

He swore under his breath as he realised that he'd been right all along—it *was* Eliza Bawden-Trebarr who was sitting there at the end of the hall, seemingly without a care in the world. The woman must be as addled as he'd initially believed her to be for her to come all this way so that she could attend a boring lecture dressed as a young man. What the blazes was wrong with her? What on earth was she up to now? Oh, yes, mad, quite mad. He wanted to march over to her and demand answers but knew that he would have to wait. He'd have to bide his time.

The room suddenly erupted into applause, signalling the end of the lecture and an invitation to view some of the collection that Tristan's old tutor had been droning on about.

'You didn't have to come if you found it so boring, Seb,' his brother whispered from beside him.

'I didn't find it boring.'

'Then why the hell have you been staring at the door to the side there instead of at Sir Algernon, who was actually delivering the lecture?'

'A speech that you wrote, Tristan.'

'Which I was happy to write, Seb, but that is neither here nor there.'

'My apologies. I was, or rather I became, quite distracted.'

'With what, exactly?' His brother rose and shook his head. 'I can't imagine anything here that might distract you.'

'Nothing, as it turned out. I thought I saw someone I knew but I was mistaken.' Sebastian stood and clasped his brother on the shoulder as he looked back to where Eliza had been sitting, but the chair was now empty. Damn! The woman must have gone somewhere but where? Sebastian darted his gaze in every direction but could not see her. It was difficult in this sea of black suits, dressed as she was.

'Come, let's go and see the collection itself. Unless you'd rather get back to the club?'

Tristan seemed a little prickly, a little nervous, since this seminar with its lecture and viewing was something he had been closely involved in. It mattered to him, all of this—science, geological discoveries, engineering and technological advancement, the Royal Society…academia—in a way that he did not share. Above all else, Tristan worked hard for it, wanting something outside of the Trium Impiorum much to Sebastian's and Dominic's dismay. Both of them had always known that there would come a time when their youngest brother would outgrow the club and would eventually follow his own path. His interests and his intellect demanded a different pursuit, one which did not involve them. Which was understandable, after all that was what Sebastian had always wanted for his brothers: to be able to be in command of their own destinies. But that did not mean he was happy about it. For now, however, Tristan was still keen to hold on to his duties at the Trium Impiorum even though Sebastian knew that it would not be forever; there was an inevitability about this fleeting time they shared.

'Of course, I want to see this collection of yours, Tris.' He pasted a smile on his face. 'Come, lead the way.'

As soon as they entered the adjoining salon, Sebastian spotted Eliza with her back to the whole assembly, looking at one of the glass cases in the collection.

'Apologies, Seb, but Sir Algernon is summoning me over. Allow me introduce you.'

Tristan's old tutor stood in the middle of the room, surrounded by a group of men, hanging on his every word. Evidently, the stuffy old man wasn't quite finished delivering another speech, but now needed the brilliance of his erudite brother to lend him a little gloss, hoping it might rub off on him.

'You go ahead. I shall join you in a moment.' Sebastian smiled at his brother, who nodded and walked over to stand beside his tutor and field more questions regarding the Cornwall Collection.

But of course, it was *Cornwall*! That was what had brought the woman here... Cornwall. It could be no coincidence that Eliza Bawden-Trebarr was present at Gresham College attending a lecture by the Royal Society about a collection devoted to the same county that her beloved estate was located in. But to what end? And why had she gone to such extremes of dressing as a man just to attend a lecture? Surely, it had nothing to do with her Women's Reform group? No, the more Sebastian thought about it, the more he was convinced that it was not. Which meant that there had to be another reason she was here, dressed as she was. Eliza must have come especially in search of something and it was likely that whatever it was, it was here and part of this very collection. But then again, failing that logic, there was still quite a strong possibility that the woman was completely addled in the head. There was only one way to find out... Sebastian looked over at the back of Eliza and smiled coldly before ambling towards her.

He stood beside the woman as she studied whatever it was in a glass case before her. So intently that she hadn't realised his approach. He stole a quick glance at her, noting that the trousers and jacket she'd donned hardly concealed her shapely feminine bottom. It was quite ridiculous that anyone here could mistake her for a man.

'I am not sure what your game is, Lady Eliza Bawden-Trebarr, but your presence here is unbelievably reckless—even for you,' he whispered.

Sebastian could see from the soft gasp that escaped her lips that he'd surprised her, but not enough to make her give herself away. He could begrudgingly respect the fact that she continued to keep her head low as she looked at the glass case, apparently still studying the artefacts it contained.

'Why are you here, Eliza?' he continued quietly. 'What could possibly have captured your interest that would make you come here dressed as you are?'

'I could ask you the same question, *Sebastian*,' she chided.

'Ah, how lovely. I see you're as quarrelsome and belligerent as I remember.'

'Do you make a point of remembering me?'

God, but the woman had cheek. 'In every detail. You see, I now have a policy of making certain I vet every young woman who enters my club just in case they're the type who believe that they can blackmail me.'

'Very wise, although if I were you, I'd avoid becoming petulant and unscrupulous in your dealings with them. They might then avoid having to blackmail you in the first place.'

'Are you so adamant to poke the lion, Eliza?' he murmured, tapping a tattoo on the glass with his fingers before spreading them wide on it, mere inches away from hers.

'I assume you are the proverbial lion?'

'Did I say that?'

'Not in so many words.' He moved closer to her, his side brushing against hers before she continued to speak. 'Although, I would hope that I'm astute enough not to do something as foolish as that.'

He stared at the glass case looking for clues as to why she might be here but finding nothing of note. 'Apparently not astute enough to know how foolish it is to come here dressed like this.'

'Shoo! Will you not just go away, Mr Marsden? I do not have time for this.'

'Did you…did you just *shoo* me away?' It seemed that even after such short acquaintance, Eliza Bawden-Trebarr never failed to surprise him. And not in a good way. 'Because I would wager that that would be the most foolish thing of all.'

'Well, you would know all about wagering. And for goodness' sake, keep your voice down,' she hissed.

'How you dare to speak so to me.'

He felt her tense beside him. 'As I said, I do not have the time for this…whatever this is, Mr Marsden. And if you won't leave then I shall.'

As Eliza started to move away, Sebastian reached over and stilled her by placing his finger across her hand—her gloveless hand. The moment he touched her the inevitable spark of heat seemed to spread from that singular spot and travel up his arm and disperse throughout his body. What on earth was it about her? It disconcerted him, unnerved him, how something so innocuous could cause such a reaction. In one way it fascinated him; in another this surfeit of feeling horrified him and made him want to pull away. But he didn't. He kept her firmly in place with that one finger and marvelled instead at the graceful slender hand with its neat, short nails, stained with ink. Despite the softness of her skin beneath his, they were bare hands, working hands, used to toil and trouble but nevertheless aristocratic hands. How she could even think that her small, feminine hands could pass as anything other than belonging to a woman, he'd never know.

'I cannot imagine why you keep on making the same mistake, Eliza. Believing that you can do just as you please at any time.'

'I do not know what you mean.'

Was it his imagination or did her voice hold a sudden breathless quality? Was this touch affecting her as much as it was affecting him? But then why would he care? So what if she also felt some sort of strange pull towards him. It mattered not. A woman like Eliza should never rouse an interest in him. And yet, she did. That was what appalled him the most. The fact that he found her attractive despite Eliza being a *lady*. She'd

been a damned countess and was still part of the upper echelons
of society, even if she was now having to live within reduced
means. And that was what was unacceptable to him. For a man
like him should be drawn to a woman like her.

'Can you not guess?' He grazed his finger along her ridiculously soft skin, stroking up the length of her index finger
and down again. Slowly, slowly, wanting to put it to memory.
'First, you come uninvited to my club making demands, then
you blackmail me into an agreement I am still not particularly
happy with. And now I find you here dressed wholly unconvincingly as a young man so you can hear a lecture and view this
frankly uninspiring collection. And for what reason, I wonder?'

'Not uninspiring and not altogether dressed unconvincingly,
either. I gained entrance, did I not? I fooled everyone here.'

'Not quite everyone, Eliza. I saw through this little ruse
immediately and anyone looking closely at you would come
to the same conclusion. So yes, unconvincing. Now, why are
you here?'

'It is not your concern.'

'It has something to do with Cornwall, has it not?' Eliza tried
to pull her hand away, which meant that he must be correct about
her reasons. He wrapped his fingers around hers and clasped
them tightly against the glass case. 'I thought it did. And it has
also got a connection to Trebarr Castle.'

'Let go of my hand, *Sebastian*. People will see.'

'Not until you answer a few questions, Eliza,' he retorted
coldly. 'And yes, people might witness such familiarity between us. From calling each other by our given names to this,
holding hands.'

'People will talk and you know that is not something you invite willingly, Mr Marsden.' The coldness in her tone matched
his. 'Especially since you seem to have forgotten how I am
dressed.'

'As if I could.' He gripped her hand tighter and pulled her
to his side, his head bent low as though he were also studying
all the small artefacts in the glass case. Thank goodness this
case faced the tall bay window so that their backs were to the
gathered men behind them. 'What is it that brought you here,

eh? There's something here in this case, isn't there? Something that has made you once again take such drastic actions without a thought to your safety, your reputation, or your status. Are you always this reckless?'

'Those things matter to me as little as they matter to you. Now, let me go.'

'No, you shall not set the terms here. Not this time, Eliza.'

She did not speak for a long moment as though weighing up the predicament that she'd found herself in. It was obvious that Eliza had not expected to find him here, or for that matter, be caught searching for something in this glass case. Eventually, she spoke. 'Very well, but I cannot speak with you here.'

'Then where?'

'There you are, Seb.' Tristan ambled towards them, making Sebastian remove his hand from Eliza's and take a step away from her. 'Won't you introduce me to your friend?'

'*Edmund* Bawden-Trebarr at your service.' Eliza lowered her voice, which Sebastian had to admit sounded a bit like a young man, possibly an odd-looking one unless Tristan bothered to look closely. She stuck out her hand for his brother to shake.

'Tristan Marsden.' His brother clasped Eliza's hand. 'How did you find the lecture, Mr Bawden-Trebarr?'

'Insightful, sir, insightful. I have a keen interest in Cornwall since I'm from that part of the world, you see.' Eliza had somehow contorted her mouth, making her jaw jut out, and changed the way she stood to more closely resemble a young man. How preposterous, how unbelievably farcical, this was. 'Anyway, I shall bid you gentlemen a good afternoon. I really must be off.'

'Ah, but before you go, *Edmund*.' Sebastian grabbed the woman's arm. 'About that private matter we needed to discuss?'

'Never mind that, old chap. We can see to it another time.'

'No trouble at all. I'd rather conclude our dealings now if you don't mind...*old chap.*'

His brother glanced from one to the other and raised a brow. 'I see that I have interrupted your discussion with er... *Mr Bawden-Trebarr.*'

Ha, so Tristan was starting to pay attention and could see that *Edmund Bawden-Trebarr* wasn't quite as he seemed. That *he* was actually a *she*. The woman by his side seemed to sense this, too, which meant that Sebastian would have to act fast if he wanted to get answers from her in case she bolted out of here. 'Not at all, Tris, but if you wouldn't mind directing us to a small chamber for us to conclude our discussion?'

'Of course. There is a small room that should serve your purpose. Outside the hall, back to the main foyer, the third door on your right. All the other chambers and rooms on the ground floor will otherwise be locked.'

'Good. Thank you, this shouldn't take long.' Sebastian gripped Eliza's elbow, ushering her away. 'Come along, *Edmund*.'

'You're holding on to me too tightly,' she muttered from the corner of her mouth.

'I have to, in case you get ideas about running off, Eliza, or stalling this discussion even further.'

'I wasn't going to do that.'

'Oh, yes, you were. I'd rather not take any chances where you're concerned.'

They did not speak again until they reached the door of the room, off the main vestibule, which he opened with one hand and practically pushed her inside with the other. Sebastian blinked as he flicked his gaze around the room, which was not quite a chamber at all but a small storeroom, with a few tables with strange scientific instruments on them, extra chairs stacked together and some bookshelves packed with ledgers and boxes. Apart from the large window there was no other light and the room was exceedingly cold.

He turned to face the woman who had been causing him far too much trouble lately and frowned. 'Well, are you going to explain yourself, Eliza?'

'I suppose I must since you have made clear your intent to interrogate me to all and sundry.'

'My brother is not all and sundry.' He folded his arms across his chest and glared at her. 'Now, tell me why the hell are you here?'

'As you said yourself, I have a keen interest in the county of my ancestral home. Cornwall and everything Cornish holds a special place in my heart—its unparalleled beauty, its very rugged and wild landscape, the blistering wind along the cliffs, the sea battering against them below.'

'Balderdash, Eliza! Spare me the poetic soliloquy.'

'It's true. This small yet important lecture reminds me of home and of everything I miss about the county. And while I lack the necessary funds to go back to Cornwall at present, this was a rather good alternative.'

He shook his head. 'You expect me to believe this tosh?'

She shrugged. 'I do not care either way, Mr Marsden, but it is the truth nevertheless.'

He stepped in front of her, crowding her as he rubbed his chin. 'You would have me believe that your love for Cornwall propelled you to somehow gain an invitation to this frankly boring lecture that contained nothing remotely of unparalleled beauty, and come here in disguise just to assuage your apparent homesickness?'

She nodded. 'Indeed. I could hardly come as myself since women cannot attend these lectures, ergo the reason for my disguise.'

'It is a terrible disguise.'

'So you have mentioned but it did seem to fool most of the men in that hall, apart from you. Well, and your brother.' She sighed through her teeth. 'And now that we have established everything, I think we've concluded this discussion. Good day to you, Mr Marsden.'

As she made for the door, he made a grab for her. 'Not so fast.'

'Will you stop manhandling me incessantly? I have answered your questions despite finding you exceedingly impertinent.'

'Impertinent, am I?' He started walking towards her, making her step backwards.

'Very much so. Furthermore, you're…' The woman fairly squeaked when her back hit the wall, her feet catching a small desk as she moved and making the box on top of it fall with a clatter of noise, the contents crashing to the floor.

He scowled at her. 'Now, look what you have done. I should imagine that has alerted everyone to our presence here.'

'Good. I've had enough of your insolent, ill-mannered and frankly boorish manner.'

'You have such a way with words, don't you? Not that I agree with being referred to as boorish. The others, though, I'll accept happily.' He stepped closer, placing one hand on the wall above her head, effectively pinning her against it. And with the other he started to peel off her moustache, side whiskers and the other bits and pieces of her terrible disguise.

'Ouch!' she cried, rubbing the side of her face and chin. 'Will you stop it? I still need the whiskers when I leave this blasted place.'

'No, you don't. You fool no one with or without them.'

She narrowed her eyes. 'I know what you're about. You're attempting to intimidate me again.'

'And why would I do that?'

'For some nefarious reason of your own, no doubt. But I shan't fall for it. For I tell you that it won't work, Sebastian.'

His lips quirked into a smile; he couldn't help it. She was highly engaging if not strangely endearing at times. He leant forward, catching her chin between his fingers and tilting it up. 'Do you know you do that, Eliza? Every time you get flustered and annoyed with me, you call me by my given name.'

He watched as a pink hue washed across her face, drawing out the dusting of freckles on her nose and cheeks, and he had a sudden compulsion to brush the tip of his finger across them. Annoyed with his musings he spread his hands against the wall further away from her, just to avoid such a temptation.

'Since you make free of my name, I think it only right that I call you by yours. And I have only ever been flustered and annoyed with you, so that is neither here nor there.'

'Believe me, the feeling is mutual.' He bent his head so that they were now practically nose to nose. 'Now, I shall ask you one last time, why are you here?' When she did not respond, he continued to speak so that he could get some sort of reaction from her. 'You have come looking specifically for something here. Something to do with Cornwall and something that was in that glass case, I believe. I want to know what it is and why you seek it.'

He watched as she sank her teeth into her plump lower lips, her brows furrowed as though she was weighing up whether she should disclose all of it to him or not. She lifted her head and shook it defiantly just as they heard a disturbance in the hall outside the room.

'I say, did one of you hear where that crash came from?' a man's voice boomed from outside.

Damn!

Sebastian groaned inwardly as he screwed his eyes shut for a moment. What dashed bad luck. He opened them again to find Eliza's eyes pleading with him to remain quiet.

Well now...

'You know, Eliza, as far as I'm concerned, an institution such as this should admit women through its hallowed halls, as you call it. But they...' he whispered, pointing to the door. 'They do not.'

'Do you take me for a simpleton?' she hissed. 'Naturally, I wouldn't be dressed like this if I didn't know that.'

'Quite.' His lips curled upwards. 'And if you do not tell me the real reason why you're here, then sadly I'll be forced to tell them that there is a woman in their midst. Imagine what it would do to their delicate sensibilities.'

'You wouldn't dare.'

'Oh, I would.' He grinned, enjoying this far too much. 'You have *five* seconds to tell me...'

'Of all the insufferable, presumptuous men I have ever had the misfortune to meet, you, Sebastian Marsden, are without doubt the...'

'*Four*... You are running out of time. I do hope you don't make a habit of it.'

Her jaw was clenched so tightly, he was worried she might inadvertently break a tooth. 'You annoying, infuriating...rogue. You blackguard... You, you knave... You rantallion fopdoodle.'

'*Three*... My my, you're inventive with your insults. And you don't know what rantallion means.'

'I do since you're standing right in front of me.'

Sebastian had to stop himself from laughing out loud, finding it too much that Eliza had just insulted his manhood without

even knowing it, judging by the confusion on her face. '*Two*...
Oh dear, is that the Gresham men I hear outside these walls?
Do you want such influential men to know of your true identity? Tsk-tsk, it shan't look well for you. What with you being
a *lady* and all.'

'Stop it.'

'Not until you tell me the truth, Eliza.' He raised a brow.
'Well?'

'No, I think not.'

'Alas, you give me no choice... *One*.'

Just as Sebastian opened his mouth to speak, Eliza rose on
her tiptoes and pressed her lips firmly to his, surprising and si-
lencing him at the same time. He was too stunned to move, too
shocked that the woman had resorted to...to this.

Good move, Eliza, he wanted to say, begrudgingly admiring her audacity. Of their own volition Sebastian's arms curled
around her small waist, pulling her tighter towards him as he
heard the muffled shouts and cries from somewhere behind him,
as the door to the room began to open. He no longer cared, even
as he made certain that his much larger body obscured her identity from the men's gazes behind them. Pompous fools the lot
of them. But none of it mattered. The only thing that did matter was that Eliza Bawden-Trebarr was kissing him. And just
as shocking was the fact he was kissing her back...

Chapter Five

Eliza looked from one brother to the other as they sat inside the closed carriage in total silence. They were making the short journey back from Gresham College in the city to The Trium Impiorum in St James's from what she had understood. Not that she had been actually informed of any of it. The two Marsden brothers had acted swiftly and bundled her out of the storage room as fast as they could to avoid any further embarrassment, with all those men from the Royal Society glaring at her as though she was a veritable She-Devil once they realised that a woman had infiltrated their precious male-only institution. And by keeping her head down, her face covered and the two much larger men on either side of her, she had somehow managed to leave Gresham College pretty much unscathed.

She glanced across to Sebastian sitting in the corner with his eyes turned away, looking out the window, and she sighed, quickly dropping her gaze to her hands clasped tightly together in her lap.

Well, perhaps not quite unscathed...

Dear God, but what had she done? She had hurled herself against Mr Sebastian Marsden, pressing her mouth to his just so she could silence the man from uttering her name! Of all the ridiculous schemes that Eliza had ever been a part of, that had to be the worst. What in heaven's name had she been think-ing? The trouble was that she had not been thinking at all; in-deed, she had not given any thought as to where she was or what she was doing. None whatsoever. The only thing that had seemed to matter in that moment was that the blasted man was so impossible she'd felt obliged to prevent any more words from being uttered by those same lips she had kissed. And she had momentarily succeeded. She had shut him up, surprising him as well before he had kissed her back... He'd kissed her, Eliza Bawden-Trebarr, back!

As well as all that, she now knew the feel of his lips on hers; incredibly soft. She now knew the shape of his mouth as it covered hers, slipping and sliding as he'd kissed her. She also knew what it felt like to be held in his strong arms. And what it was to be crushed against him, so that she could feel the ripple of warmth emanating from his skin despite all their layers of clothing.

Good Lord. She could feel herself getting warm just think-ing about it!

Eliza was, however, mortified to recall the look of absolute shock and disgust on his face as Sebastian suddenly came to himself and realised who it was he was kissing against the wall in the back of the storage cupboard with disapproving specta-tors looking on in the hallowed halls of Gresham bloody Col-lege. No wonder the man couldn't even bring himself to look in her direction now. And Eliza was somehow supposed to sit in this carriage and pretend that none of it had happened, as though she was perfectly amenable to returning to his gam-ing club and explaining the reasons for "all of it" to him, even though she had walked out of the Cornwall Collection without being any closer to getting hold of the seal fashioned in the shape of the Morvoren.

It was the excitement of finally locating the thing in the first place that had made her careless. It had made her unaware of Sebastian Marsden's approach as she was staring at the Mor-voren seal until it was too late. And really, she ought to have known better; she ought to have been on her guard when she'd spotted the man in the audience. But Eliza had been complacent, believing that he couldn't possibly see her. Why should he? Her disguise was supposed to have worked; it was supposed to shield her from his notice. But notice her, he had, and at the most inopportune moment. When she'd been quietly jubilant at finally, finally finding what she had been searching for all these months ever since Ritton's death. Eliza ought to have slipped away the moment she had found the seal, so that she could then devise a way to come back and filch it, but instead, she'd continued to stand in front of that glass case, waiting for trouble in the form of Sebastian Marsden to arrive and torment her. So much so that she'd ended up losing her mind! Dear Lord, the man was maddening, and infuriating and arrogant; abominably so. He took particular delight in vexing her again and again. Yet, she was loath to admit it but well, the man could certainly kiss a girl senseless!

Eliza flicked her gaze to the younger Mr Marsden—*Mr Tristan Marsden*, who resembled his older brothers greatly except for his lighter hair and cerulean blue eyes that she detected behind the metal-rimmed spectacles similar to her own. Tristan looked just as furious as his brother but for obviously different reasons. He would naturally blame her and possibly his older brother for embarrassing him in front of his Royal Society peers. From her understanding it seemed that he was in some way connected with the lecture and curating the artefacts from Cornwall. And well, for that, Eliza could hardly blame him. She had caused all that uproar along with the young man's own brother, so his scowl was well placed.

'I wish to convey my deepest apology, Mr Marsden,' she said with a small smile, hoping to coax one out from him in the process.

'While I might at a push accept your apology, Eliza, it does not in any way mean that you can renege on your explanation for all this madness,' Sebastian Marsden muttered coolly.

'Then it is a good thing because my apology was not directed at you but your brother.' Her retort earned her a flash of a grin from Tristan, who then inclined his head at her.

'I thank you, my lady.' The young man regarded her with a

faint smile before continuing. 'And was it really true that you were there because you were desperate to see the collection?'

'Oh, very desperate, Mr Marsden.'

'What? Tristan, you cannot seriously believe any of the nonsense she spouts.'

'*She*, however, is telling you the truth, Mr Marsden,' Eliza said, ignoring the elder Mr Marsden and keeping her eyes fixed on the younger man. 'I was enraptured by Sir Algernon Bottomley's fascinating lecture, and as for the artefacts of my beloved county, all I can say is that they were sublime, truly sublime.'

A surprised laugh slipped from Tristan's lips as he shook his head. 'I had not realised that was the real reason for your presence at the lecture, my lady.'

'I can believe it. Your brother did rather paint me in a very unfavourable light,' she said, softly ignoring Sebastian indignantly huffing and puffing in the corner. 'You see, I have always been particularly taken with everything that hails from my native Cornwall. From the artefacts made from Cornish granite, sandstone and slate to the majestic native flora and fauna and of course the agate gemstone, or the *vicus crystallis* in all the opaque colours that can be found.'

'I am amazed and honoured by your interest, my lady.' Really, Tristan Marsden was rather more mannerly than his brusque and frankly hostile brother. And handsome, too, in a boyish manner with that flop of brown hair over his eyes and that one dimple that popped in his cheek when he spoke so earnestly.

'Oh, it's far more than just merely an interest, Mr Marsden.' She leant forward. 'You see, Cornwall is in my blood. It's made me into the woman I am today.'

Tristan glanced at his older brother uncomfortably at the mention of bloodlines and belonging, which made Eliza feel a stab of regret briefly before he turned his attention back to her.

'Then I can appreciate why you would want to attend the lecture today, my lady.'

'Oh, yes, and please do call me Eliza.' She smiled broadly.

'Very well, Eliza. As long as you call me Tristan.' Dear me, but had Sebastian just growled at them? Irascible man. She would continue to do him the courtesy of pretending he was invisible even though the man took up most of the space in the carriage as he sat back against the plush leather squabs.

'And again I would like to extend my sincerest of apologies to you for causing all that distress at Gresham College, Tristan.'

'Please.' He waved his hand. 'Think nothing of it. I'd like to think that I'm progressive enough, Eliza, to believe that women should have the right to be admitted into such institutions as Gresham College and the Royal Society. I hope that one day soon this will be the case, so that you can come and enjoy the lectures and seminars without having to resort to such extremes as you were forced into.'

Eliza immediately warmed to him. He was so refreshingly honest, so naturally pleasant, so amiable and accommodating…

'Bah, no one can force Eliza Bawden-Trebarr to do anything. She's as obstinate as an ox!'

Unlike his infuriating older brother.

'Take no notice, Tristan,' she muttered, refusing to look in Sebastian's direction despite the obvious provocation. 'I'm afraid that your brother doesn't much approve of women like me.'

'Women like you, eh? Troublesome, meddlesome, infuriating minxes? Is that the type you refer to?' Sebastian snarled.

Eliza gasped loudly and screwed her eyes shut, covering them with her fingers.

Tristan stared at his brother with incredulity and horror. 'Good God, Sebastian! I have never known you to be like this. That is totally uncalled for. I insist that you apologise to Lady Eliza this instant.'

'No, no, that will not be necessary,' she said quickly between sniffling and peering gleefully at Sebastian from beneath her fingers. And found the man was staring right at her, his eyes sparkling with a flare of anger, his brows risen. Oh dear, he was not amused. But did Eliza care? Not one scrap. She needed to get Tristan on her side, especially since he was the one who was connected with Sir Algernon Bottomley's Cornwall Collection.

Of course, that was it! Eliza was suddenly struck by a marvellous idea. What if she could manage in some way to convince Tristan to help her borrow the Morvoren seal, even temporarily, just so she could finally open the Bawden-Trebarr box and find out the secrets it possessed? He could then take it straight back to the collection and no one would be any the wiser. Well, other than Sebastian, who now looked as though he could read everything that was going through her mind, and by the slow shake of his head, he was telling her that he knew exactly what she was up to.

What is your game?

Sebastian had asked her earlier and quite frankly she had not known how to respond. She still didn't. The last thing she wanted to do was to confide in him, as he'd think her even more addled than he already did. Eliza could just see his face now if she explained the truth to him as he expected her to; from the reason why she had been at Gresham College, to the Bawden-Trebarr treasure—the very treasure that she was pinning all her hopes on finding so she could pay back the debt to him and re-cover her estate. If she told him everything, she'd risk not only his ridicule but would also likely never hear the end of his sardonic laughter as he'd mock and pity Eliza for her hare-brained scheme. As well as that he'd probably rescind their agreement to give her time to pay back the money. No, she could not tell him any of it but then she didn't know how she was supposed to avoid doing so. Especially as he was keeping a close eye on her in case she *bolted* as he'd put it.

Of course, Eliza could attempt to trust him and ask for his assistance. After all, the man had protected her when they were caught in the storage room, and he had assisted her out of the college, shielding her from the hostility of the glowering gentlemen. And he had kissed her back as well, which was neither here nor there, since it must have been a lapse in judgement, just as it was for her.

'Either way, my brother's comment was unpardonably rude, my lady... Eliza, so allow me to apologise in his stead.'

'You are too kind, Tristan.' She reached out and placed her hand over his and smiled. 'Your brother has been thoroughly provoked today otherwise I cannot imagine he'd ever mean to be so unthinking and impolite, especially to a gently bred woman.'

Sebastian flashed her a stony glare but did not respond. His temper she sensed was stretched so thin that it might snap at any moment, and despite everything she did not want to aggravate him into doing that. He had helped her after all.

'Even so, he should not have taken out his bad mood on you, Eliza. It was hardly your fault.' They both ignored Sebastian's indignant grunt as he shook his head and turned to look out the window again. 'Anyway, I do hope you managed to see the various agates that were on display before your unfortunate discovery.'

'Yes, I particularly liked the display of the sea maiden artefacts. There were so many fascinating exhibits that I noticed, from the medieval boxwood hair comb, to those little tins. All with the distinctive *Morvoren* design on the pieces.' Eliza bit into her bottom lip knowing that this was her one chance to get Tristan invested in her scheme, while his older brother's attention was diverted elsewhere. 'But there was one in particular that I was studying for a…a pamphlet, an essay, if you will, that I hope to write, in regard to Cornish myths and legends. However, unfortunately, I did not get to take in all the details and intricacies of it, since I was interrupted while I was making my study and putting it to memory. Alas, I attended the lecture with nothing to document it.'

'Oh, I see, that is most unfortunate.'

'Yes, it was rather.' She nodded. 'Very unfortunate.'

Tristan rubbed his jaw in the same way that she'd witnessed his brother do when he was pondering on something. 'They were quite special pieces. Exquisite, really, and I was rather pleased to be able to include them in the collection, much to Sir Algernon's disinterest, who viewed them as historical fripperies.'

She weighed up again how much she ought to say, how much she should disclose and how much she should hold back. Trust, after all, was not something that came easily to Eliza having had it abused by others far too often. And yet, if she said nothing then she was likely to lose whatever sympathetic ground she had gained with Tristan.

'Not everyone can see the value, the true worth of artefacts associated with myth, legend and folklore but those relics, those fragments from a bygone era, are imbued with stories that matter, the stories that give us hope and bind us together collectively. Indeed, they give us a sense of who we are and where we have come from.' She shrugged before continuing. 'I suppose that is why they're so important to me. And why I'm grateful that you had the foresight not to dismiss them as mere historical fripperies, Tristan.'

The moment Eliza lifted her head she knew she had revealed a bit too much about herself as both men were now staring at her intently. Even Sebastian, whose earlier irascible hostility seemed to have been replaced by a strange wistfulness, as though he was recalling now something that he'd forgotten, something perhaps from his own bygone era. A time, possibly, when he might have been free from the worry, obligation and responsibilities that pinned him down as they must do now. A time when he had been cosseted, looked after and cared for. And in that one single moment Eliza perfectly comprehended him, this surly, proud and rather imposing man. She could empathise with the man who'd had little choice in being foisted with the heavy burden of duty and responsibility. After all, she had had a similar experience when her father had encouraged her into accepting a loveless marriage, just because it came with a noble title. None of which she had actually wanted.

Just as swiftly, however, the man turned away, just as she did, annoyed with where her musings had quickly travelled to, and at thinking of anything other than the task at hand—to get the Morvoren seal back.

Tristan coughed and cleared his throat, drawing her attention back to him. 'Yes, that was why I knew I had to find a way to include those pieces. For the er…reasons you so eloquently mentioned.'

He really was a lovely young man, and Eliza hoped that she could somehow encourage him to take pity on her cause and help her. He was, after all, the only person who could.

She sighed deeply in rather a dramatic manner and heard Sebastian snort. Eliza ignored the man. 'But alas now I doubt I would be afforded another chance to capture their likeness.'

'Please do not despair, Eliza. I worked very closely on the collection and can always come up with a scheme for you to have another chance to capture the likeness of those artefacts, as you put it, for your research.'

She raised her brows, genuinely touched at his generosity. 'You can?'

'Yes,' he muttered, covering her hands with his. 'If anyone can, it is I.' He paused to smile almost triumphantly, knowing he was the one to solve Eliza's dilemma before continuing. 'The pieces you're interested in can be brought to you for your attention but only for a short while before I have to return them.'

Eliza gripped his hands in hers and returned his smile. 'Oh, that's wonderful, Tristan, you are such a marvel. I am so indebted to you. Really, I am.'

'I hate to intrude on such glad tidings but I cannot sanction you to help Eliza, Tristan. Not until I have a full understanding of her reasons for being at Gresham College.'

His brother frowned. 'But you heard the lady's reasons.'

'Did I?'

'Yes. They might not be to your liking but Lady Eliza explained herself quite admirably.'

'Well, I am gratified that you are able to bestow such admiration on the lady, Tristan, but I am not so easily convinced.'

Eliza rolled her eyes. 'But that is only because your brother has allowed his dislike of me to govern his judgement.'

'Judgement? Dear me, but you are quite outside of enough, Lady Eliza,' Sebastian said coldly, brushing his hand up and down his face irritably before he leant towards her. 'I cannot believe you would stoop this low to get what you want. But enough of this obvious attempt to beguile and mislead my brother. It is intolerable.'

'How dare you. I am doing nothing of the sort.' She was outraged even though she knew deep down that the man might be a tiny bit correct. But God above, *beguile*? She could never do that, since she knew not how. And all that aside, Eliza was not that unscrupulous.

'You might fool him but you do not fool me, Eliza.'

'Sebastian! What are you about?' Tristan scowled at his brother. 'It's outrageous that you continue to show such unwarranted incivility towards Lady Eliza. I cannot comprehend you.'

She flushed as she placed a hand on Tristan's arm. 'I am certain that your brother has your best interests at heart, but he would have you believe that I am trying to take advantage of your involvement with the Cornwall Collection and that, more than anything else, is rather unfair.'

'It is indeed.' Even in the relatively dim enclosed space of the carriage she sensed the growing tension between the brothers.

Glancing at Sebastian so stiff, so terse, as he sat there almost in disbelief that a mere woman was, heaven forbid, challenging him, Eliza wondered whether he might have suited being a military man instead of a gaming hell owner, barking orders and demanding to be obeyed. And in a sense perhaps that is what he did, anyway, since he was the king of his domain, exuding absolute authority, with his brothers as his lieutenants. So it must gall him that his youngest brother was presently chastising him with his mutinous behaviour.

'Ah, so you're telling me that you believe Eliza managed to cajole me into giving her time to pay back her late husband's debt so that she could regain her precious estate in...yes, Tristan, *Cornwall* of all places. And yet, this has nothing to do with the fact she came dressed as a man to your lecture and take note of the intricacies of some artefact or other because she now has time to write an essay? Come now, you cannot believe this rubbish.'

'Even so, I share the same view about these artefacts as Eliza does.'

The man grimaced. 'Surely, you don't believe all this guff about *fragments from a bygone era*, which are apparently *imbued* with some story or other that somehow matter?'

'I do, yes.' The younger man shrugged.

'Then more fool you. All this nonsense about finding hope... It's nauseating enough to cause indigestion.'

'Surely you're not mocking me, Mr Marsden?'

'No, I am saying that you're a fraud, Eliza.'

'That is not true.' She gasped, taken aback. 'But you, sir, are a cynic. How very unfortunate that you view the world as you do.'

'I prefer to be called a realist. It is far preferable than having some sentimental romantic view of the world. Otherwise, one of these days you might just get your fingers burned unexpectedly.'

'And who says that they haven't already been?'

Sebastian caught her fingers in his hands, lifted them and nodded before dropping them unceremoniously. 'I am.'

'How dare you?' she said in a clipped tone, trying to tamp down her anger. For some reason this annoyed her far more than anything he'd ever said to her in their short acquaintance. 'You make such assumptions about me, about my past, yet you know nothing at all about the life I have lived,' she muttered quietly.

This somehow stunned the man into silence as he locked eyes with her, as though trying to decipher the truth in what she'd just stated. Not that she cared one jot. The man could go to the devil for all she cared but found that in this moment where the air fairly crackled between them, where they were confined in such a small airless space, where they were locked in some sort of battle of wills, it was suddenly impossible to avert her gaze. She drew in a long breath, steadying her heartbeat and allowing a little of the curiosity that she'd always held about Sebastian Marsden to creep in. He was holding himself perfectly still, tempering his emotions, his judgement and rationale to hold on to his steadfast beliefs. Careful, always so very careful not to give himself away. His face was almost inscrutable, all but the glint in his eyes and the twitch in the corner of his mouth.

'No,' he muttered, eventually breaking the strange, awkward silence. 'I would never dream to pretend to know anything about your life, Lady Eliza. However, I can make a fair assumption about you and anyone else who holds on to the past as though it is something that is living and breathing, imbuing it with such a force of feeling and sentiment that it overflows with a surfeit of emotion.'

Eliza was becoming so angry that she could feel herself getting hot. 'You assume far too much.'

'Do I?' he asked coldly.

'Yes, for that surfeit of emotion and feeling that you so evidently abhor goes into creating beauty. It goes into creating art. And if we're really lucky some of that manages to stand the test of time and become fragments from a bygone era, which again binds us to the same surfeit of emotions that initially created them, whether you like it or not. It speaks to us with a voice so that we might understand, that we might better appreciate what it meant, and contrary to what you believe, it's a voice devoid of sentiment.'

He fixed her with an unblinking gaze that made her feel as though she were stripped bare, which was hardly helped by such a rousing passionate speech.

Tristan coughed again, drawing her gaze away from his older brother. 'I, for my part, would be very happy to help you, my lady,' he said, breaking through the tension between them making Eliza blink and look back towards the younger man. For a moment she had forgotten that Tristan Marsden was even there. But he was. Indeed, he was the one who could help her with her predicament, if only she did not need to get around the older brother as well. She should be trying to be far more accommodating and certainly remorseful rather than constantly going toe to toe with the man and aggravating him further. Eliza wouldn't be surprised if she had all but ruined her chances despite Tristan's intentions. None of it could happen if Sebastian prohibited him from helping her. But by God, his condescension, his general dislike of her, was difficult to bear, even though she knew she ought to disregard it. The fact that the man found her so wanting bothered her more than it should, but she knew that was because it felt far too familiar. It was a sentiment shared by most men she came into contact with, except perhaps Tristan, who seemed more of an anomaly.

The carriage suddenly came to a halt, signalling that they'd arrived at the Trium Impiorum. 'You are in luck, Lady Eliza,' Sebastian drawled, the earlier intensity between them all but dissipated. 'It seems that my brother is willing to help you and bring you these fragments of history that you're so keen to observe.' He opened the carriage door and stepped outside and motioned for his brother to follow suit. 'However, you shall come here to do so, under my supervision, where I can in turn understand what you are about, especially since I have been reminded how very little I actually know about you.' He took a step back and addressed the groom. 'Carter, drive Lady Eliza home. Until tomorrow evening at six, I bid you good night.'

Chapter Six

Sebastian could not remember the last time he'd been so thoroughly outmanoeuvred with the aid of his youngest brother, no less, and by a damned infuriating woman bent on creating chaos wherever she went. Eliza Bawden-Trebarr had unequivocally ruffled him from the moment that he'd seen her dressed so ridiculously at Gresham College to having to steal her away for a private chat in the store room, to that surprising kiss, which just for a moment had made him revel in having the woman finally in his arms so he could learn everything about her; from her scent, the taste of her mouth to the feel of her magnificent curves so exposed to his touch in that scandalous attire. And then he'd remembered who it was he was holding, who it was that he was kissing and where they happened to be.

Bloody hell!

He could not recall the last time that he'd felt so unnerved. It had left him visibly shaken and unable to even meet her eyes in that confined carriage as she'd simpered and smiled at Tristan. He was so outraged to be duly dismissed that for one mad moment, he'd wanted to hurl his brother out of the carriage so that he might continue with where they'd left off with that kiss. Madness indeed. The more time he spent with Eliza, the more he wanted to know more about her despite how much she aggravated him. The woman was undisciplined, impulsive, impetuous and impossible. And the fact that he'd acquiesced to her wishes to study those *fragments from a bygone era* that she'd supposedly gone to Gresham College for was astonishing. But even more so was the uncertainty that flickered across her features as she'd attempted to decipher everything about him, as though he was also a puzzle she needed to solve.

And all because he hadn't shared that sentimental nonsense about how relics and artefacts from the past somehow possessed a link to the present. By showing anyone, apparently, who they were and where they were going like some sort of invisible map to a safe and happy destination. He'd never known such wide-eyed naivety and in a woman who should know better after being foisted into a marriage with such a reprehensible chancer. And still, she had not learnt that lesson. Sebastian did not know whether that was a flaw or a strength of her character. That despite everything that life had thrown at her she still viewed it with hope… Still believed in possibilities. Eliza saw the value, the true worth of things, and wanted to discover all its myths, legends and so on.

A surfeit of emotion and feeling might create beauty and art as Eliza had argued so fervently, but when all was said and done, these artefacts were just things—useless things that people who could afford them stuffed into their houses. They did so in the vain hope that all that beauty and art might transcend their existence, giving some meaning to it and yes, link them with another time and another place. But their inflated importance was only a vehicle to exercise their wealth and nothing more. Another way to show the distinction between people who could afford things and those who could not. Besides, what did the poor, the destitute or hungry care about any of that trifling nonsense? What art and beauty could they discern when owning a lot of worthless *stuff*? Unless of course they could get a bob or two for it from people who shared the same views as Eliza. That was what it all amounted to—how much things were worth in cold, hard cash. Nothing more.

When Sebastian, along with his mother and brothers, had their lives turned upside down after the death of his father, they'd scrambled around to take a handful of stuff that reminded them of who they once had been. A link to their old lives. But all it had ever done was to serve as a reminder of everything that they had lost. It had only served to destroy his mother in the end. And the day she was buried, the three brothers got rid of every last remnant of their old lives, either by selling them off or throwing away all those relics from that bygone era. Everything except three jewelled daggers that his father had made, one for each of his sons. And the only reason they'd kept those was because of their usefulness when they were forced to rebuild their lives.

Other than that, Sebastian hadn't needed any reminders of the past. They'd forged a new life and built Trium Impiorum from scratch, knowing for certain that this was what they were always destined to be.

Yet, when Eliza had spoken about old relics and how they could be used almost as a way to unlock the past, he'd felt the pull of her words and suddenly felt himself transported to a different time and place back when he was thirteen during that golden summer when he'd gone fishing with Dominic and their father at a lake in Harbury Hall, their ancestral home. Except, it was no longer that, and it should never have been theirs in the first place.

And that reminder stunned Sebastian into behaving yes, in an unpardonably rude manner to Eliza. She might be difficult but she had not deserved that. His egregious anger was not really meant for her but for another. So he'd thought of the first thing he could do to make it up to her—he'd invited her here to look at the artefacts that Tristan had furtively brought over from Gresham College for her to study at her leisure. Which meant that in a very short time Sebastian would have the pleasure of her company once again. Something he'd wished to avoid, especially since Tristan had been called away by a matter to do with his research paper, and Dominic was organising the main rooms ready for that evening's gambling. Meaning that once again he'd be alone with her.

Sebastian glanced at his desk with the handful of velvet boxes filled with artefacts lined up in a row, which had taken Eliza's interest and frowned. He could not help but think that something about this was still not as it should be. He couldn't quite put his finger on it, but still could not determine what her interest could possibly be in all this stuff. After all, he had agreed to give her three weeks to pay back her husband's debt, yet she still had time for a farce that she'd concocted yesterday, all to take in the beauty of this? No, he was missing something and he promised himself that before she left his office today, he'd be closer to finding out what Eliza was about. But he would do it by employing a different approach. Since thus far, their interactions had been nothing short of a disaster.

A loud, assertive knock on his door brought his attention back to the imminent arrival of his guest.

'Enter.'

Mr Hendon, his major-domo, opened the door to his office and ushered the vexing woman he'd spent far too much time thinking about inside his room. 'Lady Eliza Bawden-Trebarr here to see you, sir.'

'Thank you, Mr Hendon. Could you possibly see to some refreshments?'

'Yes, sir,' the man said as he inclined his head and left, closing the door behind him, leaving him alone with Eliza.

'Good afternoon, Mr Marsden.' For once Eliza was dressed fashionably. Even if it was still a little austere, she had definitely made far more of an effort than before, aside from the Gresham College debacle, which didn't really count.

She was dressed in an elegant dark teal-coloured skirt cut fashionably but without the usual fuss and frivolity so many other women adored, bar a few rows of satin ribbons sewn at the hem. Her fitted jacket buttoned up to the neck was in the same matching colour and was offset with a military-style ribboning on the front bodice with fringing on the epaulettes; seemingly the only extravagance she'd allowed. Her glossy pale blond hair had been pulled into a neat chignon with a small hat trimmed with black netting and ribbons in the same shade as her outfit secured to the side of her head.

Sebastian noted that once again she'd come to his premises with her huge battered old portmanteau as though she was staying for the night. The thought of which made him feel far too warm around the collar.

'Lady Eliza.' He pasted a smile on his face and nodded. 'Please take a seat. I'm glad you could make the appointment.'

She raised a brow before gingerly sitting down on the leather chair in front of his oak desk. 'Thank you. I hardly had any choice in the matter.'

He perched on the edge of his desk and rubbed his chin absently. 'No, I don't suppose I gave you much of a choice in anything. Before we start, I would like to apologise for my behaviour in the carriage yesterday. I was, as it was pointed out to me, unpardonably rude.' He shrugged. 'Forgive me?'

The woman actually looked shocked and slightly bewildered, possibly wondering how a man like him had managed to offer an apology to anyone. This gave him pause waiting for her to realise that he was actually in earnest. That this wasn't some ruse to disparage her in any way. Whether she believed him, however, was another matter altogether. In the end, those good and proper manners that Eliza clung on to for dear life won out. 'Thank you but it's really not necessary. I believe my own behaviour was hardly beyond reproach. In fact, I would like to extend an apology in return.'

'Accepted.' He nodded briskly.

'I am very grateful to Tris…your brother, Mr Marsden, and to you of course for facilitating this…this viewing for me, especially as I caused so much trouble at Gresham yesterday.'

Ah, so they were both attempting to be civil for a change. Well good, even though it did plunge them into the unknown, as they seemed to skirt around one another, not knowing how to go about it.

'Not at all,' he muttered, finding this sudden awareness between them far more awkward than it needed to be.

'In truth, I thought your brother might also be present.'

'Tristan sends his apologies but he had to see to an urgent matter that needed his attention this evening.'

'I see. Well, I'm indebted to you both. Without your approval and agreement to this today, none of it would be possible.'

Sebastian sat back against his chair and contemplated the

woman sitting in front of him. He looked to see whether it was rancour or sarcasm that she was attempting but found nothing in her manner to suggest that. Was this some new strategy of hers? This apparent demureness, which was wholly at odds with whom he believed her to be. He wasn't certain and she must have realised this as she pushed her spectacles up the length of her nose before explaining. 'I can see that I've surprised you but I hope you know that my gratitude is sincere.'

'I do now.' He smiled faintly before clearing his throat. With the pleasantries behind them he wanted to get this over and done with. And as quickly as possible.

'Shall we commence?'

'Yes.' She nodded excitedly as Sebastian stood and opened the four velvet boxes one by one to reveal the sea maiden artefacts that had taken Eliza's fancy.

He heard her gasp as each one came into view, making her stand as well.

He watched her in fascination as her eyes glittered with excitement just as a child might when receiving a gift on Christmas Day morn.

'What is it about these particular knickknacks that has you in such rapture?'

She raised her head and blinked behind those spectacles of hers. 'You wouldn't understand.'

He chuckled dryly. 'I suppose after yesterday, I can't blame you for thinking that but I am actually intrigued.'

Eliza worried her bottom lip before shrugging, evidently coming to a decision. 'The truth is that I have always been interested in folklore and mythology, especially...' Eliza suddenly looked a little uncomfortable, seemingly catching herself before she revealed more.

'Especially?' he said, encouraging her on.

'Especially myths, legends and fables that capture the inner workings of the heart. Stories such as Tristan and Isolde, Hades and Persephone, Leyla and Majnun, Radha and Krishna, and of course, Romeo and Juliet.'

'Ah, so happy tales?' he asked sardonically.

'I suppose at their very core they all share the same notion of the tragic love story. Stories that explore the intensity of emotional connections that nevertheless are destined to doom.' She paused for a moment as she studied something that looked like an elaborate comb, frowning before placing it back on his desk. 'Ultimately, though, these stories serve as a warning about the perils of forming such…such dangerous and misguided attachments.'

So he was not the only cynic when it came to matters of the heart. But perhaps for different reasons. Sebastian did not believe in marriage, let alone love, after the disastrous example of his own parents and the terrible consequences of their ill-fated union. And he was in no hurry to make the same mistakes as they had. After all, there were very few people he trusted and depended on; never mind allowing himself to be foolish enough to give his heart to a woman, someone faithless and capricious. It was not something he'd ever wanted for himself. Besides, he was content with his life as it was, and there was no reason to complicate it unnecessarily with a wife… It was not as though he didn't have the same healthy appetite as any other red-blooded male, but sex and marriage were not mutually exclusive. Not for him, anyway…

That, however, did not seem to be what Eliza's aversion to—what was it again?—ah yes, *emotional connections* was all about. For her, it clearly stemmed from her unhappy marriage to Ritton and not for the first time, Sebastian pondered on the nature of that marriage. Had the blackguard broken her heart? Had he even cared for her? Evidently not.

'So how do those items fit into your interest of mythological tragedies?' He nodded at the various artefacts depicting sea maidens and mermen.

'Mythological tragic love stories,' Eliza corrected before continuing. 'These knickknacks as you call them are part of a Cornish folklore that, yes, end just as tragically as the others. This beauty is Morvoren, a sea maiden, and is part of a story called the *Mermaid of Zennor*,' she murmured, tracing her fingers up and down an irregularly shaped metal disc with an engraving of a maid with long, flowing hair and a tail that swirled and formed part of the shape of the seal. 'Legend has it that a beautiful strange maiden with long white flaxen hair arrived in the village of Zennor, near the Cornish coast, and settled her sights on a handsome young man by the name of Matthew Trewella. Morvoren opened her mouth and sang to him with a voice as beautiful as a songbird and enticed him, pulling him more and more under her spell.'

'So, it was love at first sight?' he mused.

'Does such a thing exist?' She shrugged. 'In any case, Matthew followed Morvoren out of the village and towards the cliffs overlooking the sea. Needless to say, after he left to follow Morvoren, he was never seen or heard from again. But according to legend if you visit the coastline near Zennor on a stormy day, you might just hear Morvoren and Matthew singing an ode to one another. The wind carrying their voices into the air.'

'Very touching.'

'Or possibly it's more of a cautionary tale.'

Sebastian reached out and cupped her gloved hand gently and heard a small gasp escape from her lips as he lifted it to inspect the seal she was holding. It was an impulsive thing to do and he wasn't certain why he had. Only that he couldn't help touching her when she spoke like this. So wistful, so pensive, as though these relics and the made-up tales woven around them were somehow more interesting and more important than her own life, her own experiences. That they were more real to her than anything else in her life.

But as always, a visceral burning heat bloomed and spread from where they touched innocuously to every part of his body. And all from a chaste touch. Sebastian didn't have a name for this or why it happened but it was incredibly disconcerting. It must be that being this close to her reminded him of the previous day in that storeroom when he'd held Eliza, kissed Eliza, wanted more from Eliza, preferably for her to be naked in his bed.

Sebastian could not understand his reaction to her and had wondered over and over about this odd visceral attraction to her. It did not make any sense; she was someone he'd never normally find attractive and yet he did. He very much did…

He bent his head to take a little closer look at the seal before dropping her hand, clenching and opening his own hand several times, trying to get rid of the strange residual heat. 'And the caution that was gained from this tale?'

'Not to trust a stranger.'

'Of course.' Well, he could certainly agree with that.

And knowing that they had this in common, this inability to trust, inability to rely on others, this self-sufficiency that meant there was little room for anyone else in their lives apart from a select few, his brothers in Sebastian's case, made him suddenly inexplicably uncomfortable. He didn't want to have this connection to this woman and he certainly did not want to feel any heat from a mere touch on a gloved hand.

He cleared his throat and scowled, watching her with her face bent low towards the artefacts she so revered lined up on his table. 'Is there anything I can assist you with?'

She lifted her head and gave him a small, awkward smile. 'As a matter of fact, yes. I don't suppose you have a pot of ink and a quill I can borrow. I seem to have left mine at home.'

He fetched a pot from his desk drawer and rose to sharpen a blunt quill for her, placing them both on the table, gratified to be doing something other than having these damned disagreeable musings.

'Thank you.' She unclasped her portmanteau and peered inside and groaned. 'Drat, I seem to have also mislaid a sheet of foolscap. It's so unlike me to be this absent-minded.'

'Not to worry. I think I can spare a sheet,' he said, moving to the small wooden chest of drawers at the side of the room. 'Ah, it seems that I don't have any in here. Would a small unused notebook suffice?'

'I thank you but I cannot accept a whole notebook from you. A single sheet would suit my needs far more.' She rose. 'I shall return after visiting a local stationer.'

'Sit, Eliza. You do not need to go anywhere. I shall go and enquire about finding you what you need. Please, I insist.'

'I am putting you at an inconvenience again, Mr Marsden, but thank you.'

'It's quite all right, and in any case, I should also enquire about where the refreshments have got to. If you'll excuse me for a moment.'

'Of course.' She stood as well and gave him another winsome smile.

'Oh, and Eliza, while I have made free of your name as have you with mine once or twice, I think you should call me just Sebastian from now on, don't you?'

He noted the colour rise in her cheeks as she nodded. 'Thank you, I shall… Sebastian.'

Chapter Seven

Eliza blew out a breath she hadn't realised she'd been holding and absently rubbed her fingers against the back of her gloved hand as though it might erase the feeling of Sebastian's touch from just a few moments ago. Feeling a little dazed, she slumped back in her chair and pushed these unwanted feelings away as she didn't have time to ponder on any of it now. Not when she only had a few precious minutes with the Morvoren seal before the man would return. It irritated her that she was considering something wholly unrelated, when the excitement of finally having the seal in her grasp should be all that mattered. Especially after she had deliberately managed to get Sebastian to leave his office so that she might attempt to open her box with the metal engraved seal on the table as expediently as possible. Even so, she still felt that sting of guilt pierce through her for deceiving Sebastian and just when he'd unexpectantly begun to behave with civility towards her. But it could not be helped.

Lifting the box out of her portmanteau, she grabbed the Morvoren seal from the table and slid it into place in the lock plate. She felt her excitement bubble inside and took one deep breath before pushing the seal down and hearing the distinctive click as it slotted into place before releasing the metal lock.

'Eureka,' she muttered with a little laugh, 'it worked!'

Behind her she heard the sound of a slow clap and knew instinctively who it was. She swallowed uncomfortably, waiting for his acerbic retort.

'May I offer my felicitations, my lady,' Sebastian drawled, making her title sound almost like an accusation. 'Because we now come to the real reason for your interest in all that *stuff* that you so eloquently described earlier, do you not think?'

She shut her eyes momentarily and shook her head. 'The explanation I offered for my interest in the Morvoren was just as I said, Sebastian.'

He walked around and perched on the edge of the desk to face her. 'Perhaps, perhaps not.'

'Yet, it's nevertheless the truth.'

'What? Even the part about the *surfeit of emotion* that you insisted needed to be injected to create art? That, too?'

'Yes, even that.'

He gave a short, hard laugh. 'But you also decided to keep vital information from me for whatever reason. However, I would like to know everything, if you please, Lady Eliza.'

The presumption of the man in believing he had a right to know everything about her situation was galling and yet, Eliza instinctively knew that he was due some explanation. Her sense of fairness demanded that he did after everything he had done for her, even if it had been begrudgingly granted.

She rubbed her forehead and sighed deeply. 'How to explain.'

'In the usual manner, I'd expect.'

Eliza felt his eyes on her and found that for once she couldn't meet them. She didn't want to see the usual glare of disapproval and censure with an added wariness that she could hardly blame the man for.

'Well?' he said. 'I am waiting.'

She gripped her hands together tightly to prevent them from shaking. 'I realise that and hope that you might understand once I tell you everything.'

Could he, though? Could Sebastian Marsden be able to appreciate that she had never meant to misguide him intentionally? After gaining three weeks to pay back the debt, she'd never wanted him to know how she had planned to do it, knowing full well what his response might be. Ridicule and disbelief. But now, being caught in this unfortunate manner, she was forced to tell him, anyway.

'No, Eliza, you do not get to request any understanding from me. I shall judge for myself and make my own decision.'

'I expect you would.'

'I would, yes. So, would you like to explain now or do you need a little more time to consider your answer?' he said, raising a brow. 'Shall I help? For instance, you can begin by explaining whether you meant to filch this seal yesterday from under the noses of all those stuffy academics? Was that the intention of your ruse?'

'Yes,' she said quietly. 'I had to. There was no other choice.'

'Ah, *choice* is an interesting word, Eliza, do you not think? For instance, I could choose to be as accommodating to you as I have been from the first time you entered this room, making outrageous demands of me. Or I can choose to take that box that you're clutching so tightly and have you thrown out of here. I can even choose to terminate the agreement we made regarding the payment of Ritton's debt so you could gain your precious estate back.'

She paled, her heart beating so fast as she lifted her gaze to finally meet his cold stare. 'Very well. The truth is that I have been looking for this seal ever since Ritton's death, never wanting him to suspect what this box might mean to me.'

'Which is what, exactly?'

'Something rather special and personal.' She took a deep breath before continuing. 'But he…he took such a perverse enjoyment from tormenting me, much to my shame, and took anything and everything away from me if he believed it to be of some importance to me.' From people to possessions, it had mattered not to the late viscount. 'Which is why I had to hide this box, with the search of this seal beginning in secret the day after his burial and in earnest after my imposed mourning period was over. However, until recently, I had no luck in locating it.'

'I see.' His eyes had filled with such bleak fury that she wondered at the cause of it. Wondered whether it could possibly be what she had said about Ritton's behaviour towards her that had put that blaze of anger in his eyes. After a long moment, Sebastian addressed her again. 'How did you know it would be part of the Cornwall Collection?'

'My friend, Miss Cecily Duddlecott, remembered seeing something like it at a preview of the collection at the British Museum.'

'And did your friend also see fit to attend the collection in disguise as you did?' he asked sardonically.

'No, Sebastian, she didn't have to because she attended with her brother, who provided her with an escort. I, however, had no such thing, and with the presentation to Royal Society at Gresham College predictably prohibiting women, there was little else I could feasibly do if I wanted to see for myself whether the seal was the one I had been looking for or not.'

'I see. And it must have been a surprise to have encountered me there.'

'It was.' She nodded, swallowing uncomfortably. 'I did not know that you would also be in attendance or that your brother was involved with the collection.'

After a long moment, Sebastian spoke again but his earlier asperity seemed to have faded. 'So, you thought to come in disguise to somehow take this seal.'

'Yes.'

'To what purpose?'

'To open this box, as nothing else would, and believe me I have considered many possibilities. For it to open, however, it had to be the original seal.'

'I see.' He crossed his arms over his chest and studied her for a moment. 'And what is so unique about this particular box?'

'As I said, it's a family heirloom.'

'Indeed.' He sighed in apparent frustration. 'You have explained all that well enough, Eliza. But I cannot help thinking that there's more to this than merely keeping your family heirloom from Ritton's grasping hands.'

'Yes,' she said quietly.

'And will you not tell me? Can you not explain the reason that you needed to have this box opened?'

This was the part that Eliza was dreading. The part that would confirm what Sebastian already believed about her; that she was quite mad, foolish or whatever else he'd think about this outrageous scheme. For if she disclosed why the box needed to open, she would also have to explain what she hoped to gain from what she might find inside it.

'You would think me addled...' Eliza looked up and caught a bemused gaze before adding, 'perhaps even more so than usual.'

'Ah yes, I forgot, you must know me so well through our... handful of exchanges.' He raised a brow. 'And no, I don't actually think you're addled, Eliza. I think you're a clever woman bent on getting your way by any means—and if you need to lie and cheat to accomplish that, then so be it.'

'That's not true.'

'Then tell me everything, so I might understand.'

'I... I...' How could she explain all the ugly sordidness of her marriage to Ritton.

'Does any of this have to do with paying back the debt you owe me?' Her eyes snapped to Sebastian's. She felt herself flush as she scrambled to think of what to say, which was unnecessary since he responded instead. 'I shall take that as an affirmative answer.'

Eliza took a deep breath before continuing. 'The truth is that this box was given to me by my mother before Ritton condemned her to an asylum, Sebastian.'

'Did you just say that Ritton put your mother in an...an asylum?'

She nodded. 'As I explained earlier, he liked to torment me by taking away anything that he...he deemed important to me. That, unfortunately, included people. And my poor, powerless mother was one such person who became a pawn to his schemes and when he found her unbiddable, when he believed her to be interfering in our marriage because she challenged his treatment of me, he had her locked away. Indeed, it was remarkably easy to do as no one dared question a viscount.'

'Dear God, Eliza.' He leant forward and placed his large hand on hers, giving it a gentle squeeze. 'It's a good thing that Ritton is dead. Otherwise, I'd kill the bastard for thinking that he could bully women in the way that he did you and your mother. It is something that I cannot abide...not ever.'

Eliza was stunned, unable to take in Sebastian's sudden gesture of support for the situation that had been foisted on her. And after his earlier antipathy this was far more surprising than she could ever have imagined. Her gaze dropped to his hand covering her gloved one. She could once again feel a warmth bloom in every part of her body from this one contact, this one touch, and yet what made Eliza unwittingly grateful was that Sebastian seemed concerned...for *her*. Genuinely, possibly, surprisingly, without doubt. She realised then that this gruff man was far more than he appeared. He cared deeply for people and things; from how he behaved towards his own brothers to this sympathy he offered her now—given to a woman who'd constantly frustrated and exasperated him. It somehow made her want to weep, especially since no one, save her mother, had ever cared that much for her before.

'Thank you,' she whispered, feeling a little moved.

'There are many things that people assume about me, my character and the life I choose to live, but one thing I will not accept is a man who'd exert his power over a woman. So, please do not thank me, Eliza. I'm sorry that you were forced into such an unpleasant situation. I'm sorry you were forced to endure him.'

'As am I,' she muttered, feeling a little exposed, a little vulnerable, knowing that this protectiveness had caught him unexpectedly on the raw just as it had her.

'And your mother, she is...she is still alive?'

'Yes, she is still there even now after Ritton's death.' She swallowed uncomfortably. 'So, you see, what I am trying to do here is as much for her as it is for me.'

He nodded and removed his hand from hers. 'Will you tell me the rest?'

And just then Eliza understood implicitly that Sebastian Marsden deserved to know everything about the legend of the treasure and what she hoped to do with it. Perhaps it had been the manner in which he'd given her his unequivocal support and comfort by something as innocent as holding her hand. Perhaps it was his understanding and empathy, telling her that he could not *accept a man who'd exert his power over a woman*, while he must still have been annoyed with her deception, that made Eliza realise that he should know all of it. Indeed, it would be a relief to finally get it off her chest.

If he then took the decision that she was absurdly foolish in pinning all her hopes on this then so be it, but at least he'd know the truth. At least he would know the reasons for it and why she wanted to find the treasure, pay back the debt and get the Trebarr estate redeemed. And far more importantly, free her mother.

'The box contains secrets that indicate the whereabouts of the Bawden-Trebarr treasure—a legend within my family that my ancestors have hidden for over four hundred years.'

'I beg your pardon?' he muttered, his jaw dropping. 'Did you just say the Bawden-Trebarr...*treasure*?'

She smiled and nodded. 'Yes...yes, I did.'

Sebastian stared at Eliza for a long time, allowing the moment to stretch, unable to quite believe what he had just heard. After so many revelations this afternoon...this was her apparent explanation? A lost treasure! No wonder she hadn't wanted to tell him any of it.

'Allow me to comprehend this. Your whole scheme of paying back the money Ritton owed me has rested on...hunting for treasure?'

'A legendary treasure, yes,' she said quietly as though admitting a terrible confession. 'A four-hundred-year-old treasure, to be precise.'

Sebastian laughed in disbelief; he couldn't help himself. Of all the hare-brained schemes he'd ever heard, this had to top them all. It was breathtakingly absurd in its naivety. Like one of the long-ago games he'd devised with his brothers as rapscallion boys causing havoc in Marsden Manor, playing pirates on the hunt for looted treasure.

'I know it's difficult to understand. I know it might seem like madness but it is what I have been planning for a long time.'

Sebastian's eyes lingered on her face before dropping to the box she'd been holding. After everything that Eliza had disclosed, he didn't have the heart to deny her this. He could not bear to deride her dream. Her determination and the patience that she must have had in willing it all to come together was not only commendable but also unbelievably incredible.

Hell, it was all incredible but dash it all, a treasure? She was hunting for bloody treasure, of all things?

Sebastian had been prepared to act accordingly when he'd encountered her in this office not half an hour ago when he'd found her furtively hovering over that box of hers with the seal in her hand pushing it into something. He knew then that she had wanted to get him out of this room to do whatever she needed to do. But this? He could never have expected any of this.

'Let me understand you, Eliza.' He dragged his hand through his hair. 'You seek a four-hundred-year-old family treasure?'

'Yes.'

'All to pay back Ritton's debt?'

'Yes,' she said again.

'But how can you be certain that it still exists, if it ever did?'

'I don't.'

'And even if does, why was it not found years, decades or even centuries ago?'

'I do not actually…know that it wasn't.' She shook her head slowly. 'The legend of the treasure has only ever passed down through the female line. And according to my mother, my ancestors intended for the treasure to be sought only when their female descendants have an actual urgent need for it.'

'Which you do.'

'Yes,' she whispered, before lifting her head and squaring her shoulders. 'I must try.'

Sebastian laced his fingers with the fingers of her pristine kidskin-gloved hand and frowned. She must be desperate as well as determined to go through with such a scheme. But it showed him Eliza's resilience, fortitude and courage, that even after she'd been knocked back time and time again by her reprobate of a husband, she was still willing to find a way to gain back her dignity and family honour. Virtues that were evidently very important to her.

Even her attire seemed to have been purposely chosen to appeal to his vanity. It was as though she was seeking affirmation and to appease his opinion of her should he find out about this treasure. Or perhaps to prove that she was sane despite her desperation.

The truth was that he'd anticipated one outcome, confident that he knew how to handle the situation, but then had been handed quite another. And it had left him feeling curiously bereft, as though he'd been knocked off his normal axis. More than anything, he felt furious that a woman, and one like Eliza Bawden-Trebarr, had felt she'd need to resort to this to regain her standing in the world. And he'd had the nerve to lecture her about having choices, when in reality she'd had very little choice over the situation she'd been forced into. The injustice of it all made him angry, with himself just as much as with everyone else.

Sebastian almost wanted to give her the damn deeds to her estate and wish her well with it. But no, he strongly doubted she would accept it and it wasn't what they had agreed, in any case. If he simply gave back her castle, Eliza would naturally believe that he'd want something from her in return and that would never do.

'I know that it seems like madness,' she muttered again. 'But this...plan is the only one that I have.'

Meaning it was all she could do. Sebastian suddenly felt jaded knowing full well how the world treated a woman like Eliza, who was not quite the same as the usual accepted notions of femininity, of what she should be and how she ought to behave. And he could see quite clearly how someone as quick-witted and intelligent as Eliza would threaten the masculine pride of a man like Viscount Ritton. No wonder he'd resented her. No wonder she'd hated him.

It made him burn with anger that Eliza had to resort to this subterfuge to gain the peace that she craved. Had she not said that at their first encounter here in this very room? And hadn't he, a man who prided himself on his sense of fairness and justice, dismissed her, possibly like every other man in her life had done? God, but he felt heartily ashamed of himself.

Nevertheless, he would help her in getting her mother out

of whatever asylum Ritton had stuck her in. The utter bastard. Everything she'd said about her late husband only confirmed what he knew of him, but Sebastian could never have imagined that the man would be as bad as this. To take enjoyment from belittling and bullying not just any woman but a woman who should have had his care, his protection and his respect if not love, was as cruel as it was unforgivable. He was glad that she was well rid of that monster. Which made him ponder on what she would have done had he not perished. Good God, what if the man hadn't died unexpectedly? Would Eliza have waited indefinitely as she worried about her mother withering away in an asylum and powerless to do anything about it? And to think only half an hour or so ago, Sebastian had been ready to throttle Eliza, believing that she was determined to deceive him yet again when he'd come back into his office to find her furtively fixing the seal to her heirloom of a box... Which apparently led to treasure. It was ludicrous. Truly ludicrous.

'Knowing your tenacity, I can well believe that you have been planning this for a long time, Eliza. In fact, your patience is admirable. However...'

He watched as her shoulders slumped. 'You wish to rescind the agreement we made?'

'No, Eliza, that is not what I was going to say.'

She looked a little bewildered. 'Then what?' She sighed deeply. 'Forgive me, but I don't understand.'

'I would like to help you in any manner I can.'

He watched Eliza's bewilderment, as she blinked repeatedly behind those ill-fitting spectacles, give way to a slow smile that curled around her lips but without the usual cynicism and doubt. It made her look so young, so damn guileless and innocent, that it almost took his breath away. He wondered whether he deserved this smile. It spoke of hope and faith—virtues that he didn't know he could accept from her. And they weren't something he could easily give in return, either, despite his sudden impulse to help her, which was not like him at all. Sebastian stared down at their entwined fingers and frowned, realising that he should not have touched her, even if he still wanted to take her into his arms and press her close. Hold her, so that he might be able to erase the difficulties that she'd been forced to shoulder on her own. But that would not do. No, he did not need a complication like that in his orderly life, and holding Eliza, kissing Eliza, or doing anything other than keeping matters cordial between them would lead them down a path that he had no inclination to travel along. This pull of attraction, for that was what was simmering between them, had to be quashed now for both their sakes.

Sebastian released Eliza's hand and crossed his arms over his chest to stop himself from touching her again.

'You would like to help…me?' Her brows furrowed in the middle. 'May I ask how?'

He shrugged. 'First, if you would allow me to know the details then I would be happy to help you with your mother, Eliza. I can make enquiries on your behalf.'

'You would do that for us?'

'I would.' He watched as she looked at him in surprise.

'Why?'

'Because I cannot accept the injustice of it all. I cannot stand the fact that a powerful man chose to inflict so much pain and suffering on women in his care, just because he could. It was cruel of Ritton to do so.' It also reminded Sebastian about his own mother, who had been plunged into an untenable situation, forced to accept the ignominy of her husband's deceit after his death, stripping her of everything she knew and sending her to an early death. 'Believe me, Eliza, I understand what you went through more than you can possibly know.'

Eliza's gaze lingered on him for a long moment before she nodded her thanks. 'It was cruel, yes. And…and your offer is very generous,' she muttered awkwardly. 'I'd be very much obliged to you, Sebastian.'

He gave her a small smile, hiding the fact that he, too, was feeling a little uncomfortable with this newly found accord between them. 'It would be my pleasure. Although I cannot promise anything at present, I shall try my best to start the process of getting her out. I may be a gaming hell owner but I do have some influence as well as a few influential men who owe me a favour or two.'

'Thank you.' She reached across and placed her hand over one of his, which were still crossed over his chest.

He dropped his gaze to where her small gloved hand lay over his for a long moment before having to pull his attention away. He cleared his throat. 'As for the rest, we can discuss that tomorrow afternoon at your convenience.'

'The rest?' She frowned. 'To what are you referring?'

Sebastian's eyes flicked to the box in her hand and then back to her face for what seemed the hundredth time since she had explained her outrageous plan, and the absurdity of it suddenly struck him again.

This was how she had thought to pay back Ritton's debt, and to get her castle back... This, a treasure. She thought to find it within the three weeks she'd negotiated—an ancient treasure from hundreds of years ago that had probably already been found. Had already been squandered. Yet, Eliza was pinning all her hopes on finding it. It was all so highly improbable.

And that she would go to such lengths to try to gain her inheritance back, and use some of the funds to ensure her mother's release from an asylum, was impressive if somewhat foolhardy. Indeed, it all came down to a box...a box that would magically solve the predicament she was in. When in truth, it was Sebastian who had the power to solve it. It was he who could make all of her problems go away. But how to help her without denting that pride of hers? How to help her when this was never part of their agreement?

'You do not have to do this, Eliza,' he murmured. 'You do not have to go in search of treasure as a way to pay back the debt.'

'Oh, and how am I supposed to pay it back?'

'I do not know but as I said we can discuss this further tomorrow at your house. We can come up with a plan, a proper one.' One that would not lead to possible danger and certain disappointment, he thought to himself.

'I realise that the plan I have devised must seem very lacking to someone of your estimable intelligence,' she said tartly. 'However, it is the only one that could gain such a large sum of money in under three weeks. Besides, I do believe that there is something in this box. Legend has it that the Bawden-Trebarr treasure is so vast it's actually priceless.'

'Then I shall ask again why it hasn't been found before?'

She leant forward, and her face was so close to his that he could easily count the freckles dusted on her nose and cheeks. 'Because the box is actually a conundrum, Sebastian. It serves to guide us to the source of the treasure through a cipher or a puzzle. And this is only after it has been opened, which, as you know, I have managed to do just now.'

'Even so, perhaps we can come to some other agreement.' Eliza's brows shot up behind those round spectacles of hers, her brown doe eyes looking even larger as she stared at him in astonishment. Quite frankly, he didn't blame her for it. She could easily interpret what he conveyed to mean another agreement, one that might take advantage of her reduced circumstances. 'Whatever you're thinking please do refrain from doing so, as I didn't mean anything that might be construed as taking advantage of your situation.'

'Oh, and what might that be?'

'I am not proposing that you pay back the debt by agreeing to any indecent arrangement. I would never propose *that*, Eliza.'

Sebastian watched as she flushed, her face suffused with a dark pink hue. 'No, I can't imagine I am the type of woman who'd ever inspire that particular proposal from a man.'

Good God, was the woman *disappointed* that he hadn't suggested she become his...mistress as a way to pay back the debt? She couldn't be; it was too damn ridiculous if she was. 'Would you like me to propose that to you?'

'Did I say that?' she murmured, leaning forward as did he, her eyes dropping to his lips. 'I only mean that whatever this other agreement of yours might be, the last thing it could ever be is something as outrageous as you proposing I become your... your...'

'Mistress?'

'Yes,' she whispered.

'Well, I hope it's because you believe me to be a principled man who would never demean a woman in your situation in that manner.'

She shook her head. 'As I said, it's because I would never be a woman who might inspire such a scandalous proposal in the first place.'

He raised a brow. 'Ah, so you believe yourself to be undesirable?'

'Perhaps but it is of no matter.'

'No matter?' He was leaning forward so far now that her lips were mere inches away from his own. He cupped her jaw, his thumb tracing her lower lip back and forth, back and forth. 'I beg to differ. And just so you know, I find you very, very desirable, Eliza Bawden-Trebarr.'

Sebastian pulled her the final tiny distance towards him, and watched in rapt fascination as she closed her eyes, her long lashes fanning against her skin, her lips opening a little just to take a small steadying breath in a tantalising wait for his kiss. A very welcome and wanted kiss.

And just when his lips were about to touch hers, just when he could feel her hot breath whisper against his skin, there was an abrupt knock at the door.

Eliza jerked back suddenly as his brother Dominic walked into his office and stopped midstride.

'Ah, my apologies, Sebastian. I didn't know you had…er… company. Good afternoon, Lady Eliza.'

'Good afternoon, Mr Marsden.' Always the possessor of good manners, Eliza rose and curtsied gracefully as Dominic bowed. She placed the box back inside her portmanteau and closed it before looking up again. 'And now that matters have concluded quite satisfactorily between us with our agreement still intact, Sebastian, I would leave you in peace.'

God, the woman was stubborn. 'Wait, Eliza. Before you go, can I ask you not to do anything about the casket box? Not even to open it until we discuss everything again tomorrow?' Sebastian knew that if he let her go now without securing her word, she would jump headlong into the unknown in pursuit of finding this supposed treasure. And for some reason he wanted to be there for her, just in case she needed him.

Eliza frowned and leant forward and spoke so only he would

hear. 'Why? What possible reason could there be for you to help me in this?'

'Because I would like to assist you where I can and because I want you to know that you're not alone, Eliza.'

She gasped softly and stared at him for a long moment as though she were trying to ascertain his sincerity. 'Very well. Until tomorrow.' She nodded before taking her leave. 'Sebastian. Mr Marsden.'

'Until tomorrow.'

Not for one minute did Sebastian trust that she'd be able to keep to their agreement. Even so, he would protect her; he would still look out for her. Sebastian didn't know why he felt this fierce need to protect her, but he did. Perhaps it was, as he'd said, because she was all alone in the world, save a friend or two, but whatever the reason, he felt compelled to do it. He knew he had to.

Chapter Eight

Eliza glanced down at the box on the table in the front parlour of her Chelsea town house the following day and frowned. She had managed to resist the temptation to look inside the now opened box and had gone about her day, seeing to errands, selling off a few more valuables at a pawnshop and even meeting with her father's solicitor. She had certainly not pondered on the meeting that she'd agreed to have later that afternoon in her home with Sebastian Marsden. Well, perhaps that wasn't quite true.

Eliza wanted to keep to the agreement she'd made with him just as much as she wanted to forget that strange interlude when Sebastian had almost kissed her in his office. But when she considered how desperately she had wanted him to and would have succumbed to him so very willingly had his brother not interrupted them when he did, she burned with shame. And all because she had taken offence that she was not the sort of woman who'd inspire a man to propose a dalliance with. To have as a *mistress*. But no, shockingly, she was just such a woman in Sebastian's eyes, not that he would ever suggest such a demeaning thing. And she liked him all the better for it. Since it spoke of an unwavering respect that he held for women, not that she'd ever done much to earn his respect.

And just so you know, I find you very, very desirable, Eliza...

It was simply the most outrageous thing anyone had ever said to her. To *her*, Eliza Bawden-Trebarr. She was definitely not the kind of woman who'd ever arouse such ardent declarations in anyone, especially from a supposed rogue like Sebastian. Yet, he apparently found her *very, very desirable*!

Heavens...the man had shocked himself with that outburst and it had been reluctantly uttered, in any case. But quite apart from that, he had stunned her again and again with his care and protectiveness of her. And it was this along with being so dazed after their almost-kiss that explained why she'd agreed to discuss matters to do with the debt and the box itself the following day.

Yet, as the day progressed, it was becoming increasingly difficult not to be curious and drawn to it like a veritable Pandora's box waiting for her to look inside. Especially after the length of the time it had taken to get the blasted thing open as well. So just after lunch, when she had entered the room in search of the book she'd left in the parlour, the box beckoned, making her eventually sit down on the wooden chair and tap a tattoo on the round table before reaching for it.

Surely, it would do no harm if she just had a peek. After all, even though he'd asked her not to, she had never actually promised Sebastian that she would not look inside. Yes, there was nothing wrong with a quick glance and it was her box, after all. Holding her breath, Eliza lifted the metal lock hasp, which would open the lid that finally revealed the inside of the Bawden-Trebarr box.

Just like the outside, the inside, too, was beautiful and ornately finished with the same inlays of different wood and decorated with the same colours of the two Cornish houses.

'Ah, I see you've started without me, Lady Eliza?' Sebastian stood in her door frame swallowing up all the available space with his size and sheer presence. 'Well, there's a surprise.'

Her maid Gertie walked up behind Sebastian. 'A Mr Marsden is here to see you, my lady.'

'Thank you, Gertie. I can see that,' Eliza said with a little breathless quality in her voice as she found Sebastian in her home, albeit earlier than she had expected him.

'Eliza,' he murmured, bowing in front of her.

'Mr Marsden. Good to see you again.' She smiled up at him and gave him a nod. 'Gertie, can you bring in some tea please?'

'Yes, my lady.' Her housekeeper come maid bobbed a curtsy before shutting the door behind her.

'So...' he murmured, his gaze darting around the room.

'So?'

'You just couldn't stop yourself from taking a peek, could you?' His eyes fixed on hers as he shook his head.

'I think we both can agree that I have done jolly well to last this long.'

'Indeed.' He moved to stand beside her. 'Well, what have you found? May I take a look?'

'Believe it or not, I had only just opened it when you er... announced yourself, so we can inspect it together, if you wish.'

'I do wish it.' He took off his black woollen top hat and placed it on the table. 'The possibility of there being a Bawden-Trebarr treasure has certainly piqued my interest as well as my curiosity.'

Eliza gingerly opened the box again and took a closer look. Around the inside edges of the wooden casket box the standards of house Trebarr with a lion and house Bawden featuring an eagle, both with gold bezants in their respective colours, were displayed in each of the four corners. The interior was divided into four compartments of various sizes made from the same wood and decorated in the same elaborate manner. In one, there was an old metal box that fit snuggly inside. Eliza carefully lifted it out and opened it to find medieval hairpins and a long strip of old faded cloth.

'This could be a ribbon or a token. One that possibly my ancestor Elowen Bawden gave her husband, Simon Trebarr. Look, some of the embroidery has remained and in the Bawden colours of gold, brown and blue, and the Trebarr ones in gold, light blue and green, even if it is faded.'

'It seems so.'

Eliza nodded before placing it back and brushing her fingers inside the box. 'Other than that, there doesn't seem to be anything else, apart from this—a battered, empty leather case. How disappointing.'

'Surely, your ancestors would have employed a far more ingenious way to hide clues for their hidden treasure, otherwise it would be far too easy.' He glanced across at her. 'And what exactly are we looking for, anyway?'

As much as Eliza hated to admit it, she rather liked the way Sebastian had said *we* as it spoke of a comradery that she hadn't ever dreamed could exist between them. 'I do not quite know but something that might contain some sort of clue. An instruction of sorts as to how to go about finding it. Not a handful of rusty hairpins and a faded bit of cloth.'

'Don't forget the old leather case.'

'As if I could.' She sighed deeply. 'Do you think there might be any hidden compartments in the box?'

'Possibly, but the whole thing looks to be made out of a single piece of wood, so I don't think that the casket box itself has any hidden compartments. If it does, then it could be somewhere here on the inside.'

Eliza slid her hand inside, brushing her fingers along and into every corner, trying to feel for anything unusual, as Sebastian tapped against the surface to see if there were any hollow spaces. But no, again, there was nothing out of the ordinary. Her heart sank.

'Let me look at that leather case again,' she muttered and Sebastian passed the small square case to her.

Eliza turned over the case that like the box was decorated with the Bawden and Trebarr colours and motifs. And going down its length were the indented marks of whatever had been kept inside the case. How curious. The very shape and design of it seemed familiar to her, making her wonder where she could possibly have seen something like it before.

Sebastian bent his head towards hers as he studied it. 'What do you suppose used to be kept inside the case?'

'I'm not certain but whatever it was must have made those long vertical marks.'

'True enough. The compact little shape reminds me of something you'd find as part of a gentleman's grooming set. I have a similar one that I keep my hair comb inside.'

'Of course, a hair comb! I could kiss you, Sebastian! Those indentations could very well have been made by the comb teeth. And wait...' she exclaimed excitedly as she lifted her gaze to his. 'I saw a beautiful boxwood comb in your office yesterday, which also came from the Cornwall Collection. It intrigued me both when I was viewing it at Gresham College and yesterday as well, because the Morvoren motif was so familiar as were the Bawden and Trebarr colours painted into the wood.'

Sebastian had raised a brow, a slow smile curling around his lips. 'You could kiss me, eh?'

'Oh, I'm terribly sorry. I didn't mean...as in I shouldn't have said that.' She flushed as she took a step back.

'Nonsense. There's no need to apologise. I know how you like to throw yourself at me.' He winked as he placed his hat back on top of his head. 'I'll take my leave, Eliza, and see if I can locate this hair comb at the Trium Impiorum.'

'That's very good of you...but one moment, if you please,' she said, following him outside the room. 'What do you mean, I like to throw myself at you?'

Sebastian had made his way to the front door, his long strides eating up the short distance. 'Never say that you've forgotten how you initiated our first kiss, Eliza. Tut tut.' He grinned as he murmured over his shoulder. 'I'll send word if I locate it.'

'Thank you...and I never initiated anything,' she retorted as he strode out the front door. But of course, she had. She'd thrown herself at Sebastian and surprised both of them with that kiss in the supply cupboard at Gresham College. And had thought of it every single day since. She sighed, giving herself a mental shake before ambling back to the parlour.

Eliza had better things to do than ponder on a silly kiss that only came about because she'd needed to silence Sebastian. And after that, a near kiss yesterday evening in his office. It was best to forget kissing him altogether and put her mind to good use by continuing her search of a possible secret compartment inside the box until she heard back from the blasted man.

However, it was a few hours later when Sebastian finally

contacted her. His brief note informed her that he'd been too late as Tristan had already returned all the artefacts from the Cornwall Collection to the museums, collections and private owners who had lent the items, including the boxwood medieval hair comb. The owner of the comb was one Sir Horace Middleton from Green Street, Mayfair, who also happened to be a regular at his club and had been surprised by Sebastian's interest in his beautiful medieval comb.

Drat...

Eliza continued to read Sebastian's missive, which stated that Sir Horace would be happy for him to view the comb, but it would have to be at his home that evening as he was hosting a soiree, which he would be delighted if Sebastian could attend. Sebastian had accepted the invitation on behalf of himself and Eliza, the Countess of Ritton, and asked Eliza if he could escort her there.

So it looked as though she was attending a soiree that evening, one of those affairs that she'd always dreaded when she'd been married. However, Ritton was no longer alive to cause her embarrassment as he'd used to when he openly flirted with any one of his many mistresses in front of her.

Yet, she couldn't quite accept Sebastian's escort, either. Oh, she was naturally grateful for his help that day, knowing that without him, she would never have thought of the case being used for a comb or have so promptly tracked down its owner. But to have him escort her to the soiree? It somehow felt too friendly; certainly too intimate, and after their recent truce and attempts at cordial civility, she felt this might be a step too far.

At times, Sebastian's innate arrogance made her want to hit him over the head, and yet he was also kind and unexpectedly caring, which surprised her more than she could ever say. Especially since those were not virtues she had ever known in a man before. And certainly not in a man like Sebastian Marsden.

And quite apart from Sebastian's inherent kindness were the times in their short acquaintance when he looked at her; when he actually saw her, and made her feel as though she were not invisible, that her views and opinions mattered, even if he didn't agree with them. He made her chest tighten as though she could scarcely breathe. As though it was her heart that ached. Even so, she could never get involved with Sebastian. It was certainly not the sort of thing that she would ever do. Eliza just wasn't that kind of woman—one who'd get into tangles with brooding, handsome gaming hell owners. And she could certainly not encourage anything beyond a friendly acquaintanceship by allowing the man to escort her anywhere.

With that in mind, she sent word to Cecy and asked her whether she was attending the soiree with her brother and if so, whether she could attend with them. To which she received a reply to say that they were going and that they'd be happy to escort her.

With that arranged, Eliza wrote Sebastian a short yet polite note, explaining that she would meet him at the soiree that evening. And then pushed all thoughts regarding him to one side, setting about getting ready for that evening before leaving to go to Stephen Duddlecott's house so that they could all attend the soiree together.

Her evening dress was not what one would consider to be in the height of fashion, but she looked well enough in a simple pale duck egg satin silk with a fitted bodice, sitting just off the shoulder with a draped neckline, and a skirt of contrasting striped silk and a pleated underskirt that poked from beneath the scooped hemline. She wore small flowers in her hair along with crystal pins and had her hair arranged in the new French style, having one lock of her pale fair hair curled and placed over one shoulder. She decided to forego her spectacles in the hope that it might render her a little more feminine than usual, although it did make it difficult to see all around her with clarity, so she placed them in her mother's small evening purse to use later when needed. Along with her white gloves and a single black ribbon at her neck with her mother's locket dangling from it, Eliza had completed her toilette and had then dashed to Cecy's wearing her black velvet evening coat. It was a good thing that she didn't attend many evenings such as this soiree since this was one of only two evening outfits that she still owned; the rest having been sold to pay off Ritton's other markers all over town.

Eliza arrived at Sir Horace's house in Green Street some-
time later, along with the Duddlecotts. They were ushered into
the main reception salon where she was introduced to Sir Horace by his sister, Mrs Linden-Brown, who then took Cecy by
the arm to discuss something of great import. With Sir Horace
and Stephen Duddlecott taking their leave briefly, Eliza stood
alone at the furthest corner of the room, watching the many
guests arriving and mingling together, the low hum of chat-
ter filling the salon. She grabbed a flute of champagne from a
passing servant and took a long sip to steady her nerves before
tapping her toes to the rhythm of the music played by a string
quartet. She could do this; she could wait in this room, mingle
and chat to the crème de la crème of what society had to offer
before having to meet Sebastian Marsden. Eliza knocked back
the remainder of her champagne before taking another flute
from yet another servant. God above, but this was not going to
be as easy as she had initially thought. It had been such a long
time since she'd attended a society event such as this and she'd
hated it just as much then as she did now.

'Ah, here you are, Eliza.' Of course, there was only one man
who spoke to her in that informal manner and that was Sebastian.

He had appeared beside her from out of nowhere without
her noticing. But then again, most things were a little hazy and
not because she'd consumed too many glasses of champagne
but because she wasn't wearing her spectacles. Even so, how
did the man constantly do that? It was astonishing that such a
large, tall man was able to prowl around like a lithe panther, so
effortlessly without gaining notice. It was quite a skill indeed.

'Good evening, Sebastian.'

'And a good evening to you, too, my lady,' he drawled, shifting a little so that he now stood in front of her, bowing and keeping his eyes trained on hers.

Her heart gave a jolt as she took in the way he looked, dressed
in his fine evening attire of a fitted fine wool black tailcoat,
with black waistcoat and tailored trousers and a pristine white
shirt and bow tie. His dark hair was slicked back, making his
chiselled features even more prominent, even more striking.

And for Eliza to notice this without her spectacles was quite remarkable. But then, she had never thought to see him dressed so, packing all that masculine brawn and sinew into such elegant finery. God, he was so impossibly handsome it made her inhale softly. No wonder the man caught the attention of every woman in the room. He was that magnificent. Indeed, Sebastian Marsden looked every inch the earl that he had been born to be. But no, another man filled those illustrious shoes now. She gathered herself together before speaking again.

'I am glad to see you here.'

'I'm very happy to hear that, although I must confess,' he said, dropping his voice to a low murmur. 'I was surprised that you declined my escort here tonight, Eliza. May I ask whether it's because of who I am? One of the notorious Marsden Bastards?'

Sebastian might have delivered this quip in his usual detached manner, but Eliza would never dream of hurting his feelings, even inadvertently. It wasn't in her nature to do so.

She snapped her eyes to meet his. 'Of course not. That would never have entered my head.'

'Then it was because of my notoriously amoral club?' His mouth turned upwards at one corner but she somehow sensed a tension emanating from him. Did he think that she felt he was somehow beneath her?

'If you must know, Sebastian, I was nervous about coming here tonight. I haven't been out in society much since Ritton's death and well, even when he was alive, I never particularly enjoyed evenings such as this.' She took a deep breath. 'So, I thought it more prudent if I came with my friends then draw any unwanted attention if…if I came…'

'With me?'

'Yes.'

He inhaled before speaking. 'And if *you* must know, I do not usually attend society events such as this, either. They make me come out in a rash and I avoid them at all costs.'

She turned to face him. 'So how is it that you agreed to come to this soiree, Sebastian? Especially since social gatherings are, as you say, not to your taste.'

'And now you know all about my tastes? But then again, perhaps you do,' he murmured in a low voice, making her feel a little warm and a little breathless in her fitted dress, which suddenly felt too tight. He sipped the champagne from his flute, watching her before continuing. 'Sir Horace frequents the club regularly and like many men of his ilk extends invitations to me and my brothers, hoping to get into our good graces so that we might extend his credit in the process. Poor Sir Horace. I cannot imagine his sister is too thrilled about my presence here.'

Eliza was suddenly annoyed on Sebastian's behalf for the injustice that society matrons like Sir Horace's sister directed at him. How dare they when they knew nothing about him, other than the fact he was declared illegitimate after his father's death and that he'd had to make his own way in the world. If anything, there was much to admire in a man like Sebastian Marsden. Resilient, brave and honourable. 'Oh, hang the sister. Women like her love to look down their noses at anyone who they deem beneath them. But you are never that, Sebastian.'

'I never took you to be such a fierce protector.' His brows shot up. 'And of someone like *me*. Whatever happened to those famous good manners of yours?'

'Having the night off.'

He chuckled, shaking his head. 'You need not worry as I don't care for the opinions of old tabbies such as Sir Horace's sister. Besides, this is the first society event with mixed company that I've had the pleasure of attending,' he remarked sardonically.

'Riveting, isn't it?'

'Indeed,' he said, taking another sip of champagne. 'But still, I also hate the idea of becoming an object of curiosity. Like you, I would rather avoid that unwanted attention.'

She smiled up at him, understanding his meaning, knowing that he had done this for her. So that she could get another chance to study the medieval comb at the earliest convenience. 'Then I thank you for coming tonight, Sebastian, when you really didn't have to. When you could have asked for a private viewing another day. When you could have avoided this evening.'

'But then that would have taken more time and knowing you a little as I do, I expect that you might have done something impulsive to get hold of the comb again, since you seem to have an uncanny ability to get yourself into all sorts of trouble. And frankly, I could not afford that risk, since I have a vested interest in you finding the treasure.'

'You do?'

'Certainly. I am a man of my word, after all.' He flicked his gaze around the room before glancing back in her direction. 'But if you continue to smile up at me in that way, Eliza, we are going to get far more of that unwanted attention that we're both trying to avoid.'

'Oh, yes, of course... I'm sorry,' she said, flustered and looking away. 'Well observed.'

How mortifying to be found admiring Sebastian so openly that it had to be pointed out to her by said man.

'It's one of my many...er...talents.' He coughed, clearing his throat. 'And yours, too, I should imagine, to be able to see without your spectacles. May I ask why you have forgone them this evening?'

No, Eliza did not want to explain her vanity, knowing that it was quite laughable for her to want to appear far more than she was.

'No reason,' she muttered, feeling a little exposed to Sebastian's scrutiny. And just like that she wished in part that she was doing this on her own, without Sebastian's help. For one thing, she was finding it difficult to be around him, with this unwelcome attraction simmering between them and bubbling up to the surface constantly. It made her forget herself when she had more important things to consider. And second, she didn't want to explain, nor reveal, more about herself to him. It wouldn't look well on her.

Eliza took a step away, wanting a little distance just for a moment, but did not see a servant carrying a tray of champagne flutes by her side and collided into him, making the poor man stumble back. He would also have fallen over had Sebastian not helped to steady him. The flutes of champagne, however, did fall, crashing to the ground.

*Oh dear…*so much for not wanting to draw attention to herself!

Sebastian bent down to the floor to help the servant, seemingly finding it difficult to stop himself from laughing.

'Do you mind?' she huffed, lowering herself to help him with clearing up the broken pieces of glass.

'Not at all.' He chuckled. 'I do not know how it is that you manage to go on when you stumble from one scrape to another.'

'Oh, very easily. I live to be the source of your entertainment, especially since I *stumble from one scrape to another*,' Eliza muttered, smiling apologetically at the servant who was trying to get both of them to leave it to him. Sebastian held out his hand to help her rise back to her feet.

'Thank you,' she said as she ran her hands down her dress, smoothing any creases and smiling inanely at some of the guests whose attention they had roused with the unfortunate accident.

'Apologies, Eliza, I shouldn't have laughed,' he said from the side of his mouth.

'Oh, do not worry. I'm quite used to making a complete fool of myself.'

'I wouldn't say that,' he said softly. 'You just have a knack for it. Besides, you wouldn't have collided with that poor fellow if you hadn't forgot your spectacles this evening. Where the devil are they?'

'I didn't forget them,' she said through gritted teeth as she stepped back behind a huge potted plant, hoping it might hide her. 'I chose not to wear them.'

'And why would you do that?'

She grimaced. 'It seemed far more fitting at a society event, and without them I also look more inconspicuous.' As well as looking more feminine, something she wouldn't dream of disclosing to Sebastian.

'Fitting?' Sebastian stepped back as well, to stand beside her once again, and inclined his head in greeting at a few of the guests who caught his eye. 'It isn't very fitting to stumble about into poor, unsuspecting servants, when you can barely see. Or is it the large quantity of champagne you've guzzled down that has you so unsteady?' he teased.

'Must you plague me like a bad smell?' she whispered.

'Bad smell, eh?' he murmured, his brows furrowed in the middle. 'That's not what you said before. I believe you quite liked my...er...smell.'

Oh, God, she did. Sebastian's usual delicious scent of sandalwood, bergamot and lemon had been enticing her as it wrapped around her senses, making her feel a little light-headed, or perhaps that was indeed the champagne? Either way, she didn't have time for it.

'I did.' She grabbed another flute of champagne and after giving Sebastian a defiant look, swigged the whole lot in one gulp. 'But now I find it a bit cloying.'

'Is that so? Well, in any case, I feel it best to keep a close eye on you, just so you don't tumble into any other unsuspecting guests or servants.'

'So that I don't make an idiot of myself, you mean?'

'Indeed.'

'What would I do without you?' she muttered sardonically as she tried to place her flute on the side table and missed. Had it not been for Sebastian's quick hands catching it before it fell down, it would have crashed to the floor.

'I simply don't know,' he said, placing the flute carefully on the table before looking her up and down. 'Besides, you don't need to forgo your spectacles, Eliza. I find that they add a certain charm to your person that I must admit I rather like.' The backs of his fingers touched her gloved hand accidentally as they stood side by side.

Eliza swallowed, feeling a little breathless. This was the way it was with Sebastian Marsden. One moment she was grateful to him for his kindness, the next he was exasperating her with his annoying habit of watching her intently and constantly challenging her, and then finally he had to say something wonderful that stunned her completely.

He thinks I have a certain charm? And he rather...likes me?

Well, she could quite easily wrap herself in the warmth and tenderness of such words. Ones that made her feel like she was cocooned against the harshness of the world around her. She smiled up at Sebastian, wanting to be held in those muscular arms of his.

'Although it would also help in your endeavours if you could actually see where the devil you're going as well,' he added.

Or perhaps not…

God, the man was infuriating when he pulled and pushed her emotions this way and that; she had no time for any of this.

'Well, as I said, I wouldn't know what I'd do if you weren't here, Sebastian. I'd probably fall flat on my face.'

'Very probably,' Sebastian agreed. 'By the by, I'm not the only one here tonight who has been watching your every move.'

She frowned. 'What do you mean?'

'There on the other side of the salon. But I suppose if you'd not forgone wearing your charmingly practical spectacles, you might be able to recognise the blighter who's been giving you daggers from a distance,' he said. 'I must say, he looks remarkably like your late husband.'

'Ronald Carew…' she growled in irritation. 'The new Viscount of Ritton.' And a major pain in her backside. The man had persistently attempted to see her in the past few weeks but Eliza had no interest in being accused, yet again, of stealing from the Ritton estate. Of all the bad luck to encounter him here, however. This night was beginning to go from bad to worse!

'Has he been giving you trouble, Eliza?' Sebastian said in a clipped tone as she looked up to find that all prior amusement had been replaced by an implacable coldness in his eyes that made her shiver.

'Nothing that I cannot handle,' she said, trying to placate the large, suddenly outraged man beside her. She felt strangely humbled that he felt this protective of her and could not think of the last time anyone had acted that way on her behalf. Still, she didn't need to drag anyone else into her battles. 'Please, Sebastian, there's nothing you need to worry about.'

'Very well, but do let me know if the man causes you any discomfort.'

'Thank you.' She sighed deeply. 'For now, I would rather not have to encounter him.'

'Understood.' Sebastian nodded. 'What ho, Sir Horace, old chum. How are you? Lovely evening.'

Sir Horace raised his pink-hued pudgy face from a short distance away and ambled towards them.

'What in the blazes are you doing?' she uttered from the side of her mouth.

'I believe I'm killing two birds with one stone. Keeping away unwanted men and getting you the chance to view your medieval comb, Eliza,' he said, winking at her.

How was it that she'd almost forgotten about the real reason she'd come to this soiree? Most likely because of the man who stood beside her, who made her feel all kinds of emotions that befuddled her senses. Well, no more. Eliza could not afford to become diverted from her endeavours. Especially not by Sebastian Marsden, even if the man meant well.

Chapter Nine

Sebastian felt Eliza's nervousness as she stood beside him. And as well as that, he had sensed her unease at the possibility of coming face-to-face with the new Viscount Ritton, which was quite surprising. It was not something that he had expected from her and he decided to get one of his men to enquire into that situation at a later time. Still, he'd be damned if he allowed anyone to believe they could cause Eliza more distress. The woman had had enough of that from her late husband.

'Try to smile, my lady. Sir Horace is about to reach us.'

'I am smiling,' she insisted through a fixed grimace.

'Really? Is that what you call it?'

'Yes!'

'Try and recall that beguiling smile you gave me a moment ago. The one where you looked so enthralled with me.'

'I was never enthralled with you!' she denied in a heated whisper.

'Were you not? My mistake. It must have been something else entirely that made you blush in that endearing way.' He nodded at Sir Horace. 'Ah, Middleton, good to see you again. May I introduce the Countess Ritton to you?'

'Her ladyship and I were already introduced earlier, Marsden.' Sir Horace sketched a formal bow and smiled pleasantly from one to the other.

'Indeed, Sir Horace, I'm delighted to be invited to your soiree and to have had this opportunity to meet you in person.'

'And I, you, my lady. I'm glad that you are out in society again after the premature demise of your husband after falling off his horse. Terrible accident.'

'Thank you,' she murmured.

The man turned to Sebastian. 'I must say I'm very glad that you accepted my invitation, Marsden. There's a small matter that I would like to speak to you about in private. At your convenience, of course.'

And there it was. The trade-off that Sir Horace was seeking in exchange for allowing them access to his precious comb. It was always the way with these men who frequented his club. Why else would the man have insisted Sebastian attend this frankly boring soiree? They sensed a bargain could be made in gaining more credit, or for markers to be written off, and thought a glass or two of champagne would seal the deal. In this case, however, Sebastian was prepared to acquiesce to the man's demands as he wanted Eliza to ascertain whether the comb was important to her search or not.

'Certainly, Sir Horace. You can come by the club tomorrow afternoon and we can discuss your…er. small matter then.' He gave Horace Middleton a speaking look, warning him not to mention any of it to Eliza.

'Capital.' He beamed. 'Capital.'

'And as to the other matter we spoke of, Middleton?'

'The other matter?'

'Yes. I was telling Lady Eliza of your vast collection of Devon and Cornwall-related artefacts.'

'Oh, yes, I have a bit of soft spot when it comes to Cornwall as my old mother was from that part of the world.'

'What a happy coincidence eh, my lady?' Sebastian slid his gaze briefly to Eliza's in feigned surprise before addressing Middleton again. 'For Lady Eliza is also keen on old medieval relics and artefacts.'

Eliza smiled. 'Yes, I suppose I am.'

'It must be because Lady Eliza hails from the county itself just like your dear mother, Middleton, and as a Bawden-Trebarr, my lady is naturally drawn to all things Cornish. Do I have the right of it, my lady?'

Sebastian gave his head a tiny shake when he saw a slight look of panic enter her eyes. She turned her head and smiled again at Sir Horace. 'Yes, yes, of course. For that very reason, Mr Marsden.'

'Bawden-Trebarr?' Sir Horace's red face screwed into a scowl. 'Did you say Bawden-Trebarr?'

'It was my maiden name, Sir Horace. I am, in fact, the last of the Bawden-Trebarrs.'

'Are you indeed?' Sir Horace suddenly beamed at Eliza. 'By Jupiter, but of course! That must be the reason for your interest in my boxwood hair comb. Allow me to show it to you. Please come this way. You, too, Marsden.'

Sebastian fell into step beside Eliza as they followed Sir Horace out of the main salon in silence and strode along the hallway and down the sweeping staircase, entering a room on the ground floor.

They followed him inside a plush, well-stocked library filled with many leather armchairs and rows upon rows of bookcases groaning with first editions and huge dusty old tomes. The roaring fire in the grate along with the oil lamps dotted around the room gave the impressively huge space a snug warm glow.

'There,' Sir Horace said, steering them towards a glass cabinet set against the furthest wall in the room. 'This is what I believe you were seeking, my lady. A comb that is believed to have been gifted to Elowen Bawden by Simon Trebarr when they were bound in marriage, bringing your ancestors together, my lady.'

'Thank you, Sir Horace.' Eliza smiled, putting her hand to her chest as she looked at the beautifully crafted medieval comb that had brought them to this soiree. 'It is indeed very thrilling to see something so precious.'

'Yes, it is.' He chuckled. 'Hasn't this turned out well?'

'Very well. But it seems you have rather overwhelmed Lady Eliza, Middleton.'

'I have, I have,' he said, putting his hands on either side of his hips, evidently very pleased with himself. 'It is like rolling back the hands of time when one looks at something like this.'

'I believe so, Sir Horace, thank you.'

'My pleasure, my lady.'

Just then the door of the library opened and a servant came in and glanced around until he saw them together at the far wall. 'I'm sorry to intrude, Sir Horace, but you're wanted in the main salon by the mistress.'

Meaning the man's sister, whose idea this evening's soiree probably was, wanted Sir Horace to be beside her attending to his hosting duties rather than showing them his treasured artefacts.

'Go ahead, Sir Horace, but if you'd allow Lady Eliza just a little more time to appreciate the comb, we shall follow you in a moment or two,' Sebastian said with an implacable smile.

The man nodded as he turned to leave. 'Take all the time you need, my lady. Marsden.'

The door shut, leaving Sebastian and Eliza in the library alone. For a long moment she just continued to stare at the hair comb—such an innocuous everyday item—and wondered how this could in any way shed light on the whereabouts of the Bawden-Trebarr treasure. If it even existed.

Eliza sighed deeply. 'It certainly seems to be the one we've been seeking.'

The only noise in the room that could be heard was the occasional crackle of the fire spitting and hissing in the fireplace.

'I believe it is.' He frowned, looking across at her. 'However, I did think you might be more excited to find it again.'

'Oh, I am, thanks to you and of course, Sir Horace.' She turned slowly towards him. 'But what I want to know is what you negotiated with him to facilitate this viewing, Sebastian. And before you deny you did such a thing, remember that I was once married to a man who used similar stratagems in his dealings to get around bargaining away markers that he owed. Not that Ritton was very good at it.'

Of course, Eliza would see through his ruse with Middleton. The woman was whip-smart, but she was also impulsive, chaotic and disorderly, which strangely enough he also liked about her. It somehow made her far more interesting.

'I know you must think that I am interfering, Eliza, but I believe I was thinking of you and finding a solution to the problem at hand—namely getting hold of the comb and finding more clues to your quest.'

'And I thank you for it but I would still like to know the terms you set with Sir Horace.'

'I believe that is between Middleton and myself.'

'You understand then that it puts me in a very difficult situation, Sebastian. I cannot have you negotiating such terms without my knowledge.'

He sighed irritably. 'Eliza, the debt that Ritton left you, which you're hoping to repay, is already a considerable amount. I thought to lessen it by making my arrangement with Horace Middleton privately. It was in no way meant to put you in a difficult situation, as you put it.'

'That is indeed very thoughtful of you. However, it would also make me even more beholden to you than I already am.' She shook her head. 'And I cannot allow that. If this...this collaboration between us is to work, then we need to be honest in our dealings.'

The truth was that he couldn't help coming to the woman's aid like some knight in shining armour. Yet, Sebastian could not understand why he wanted to. Aside from the visceral attraction that he felt for her, which still confounded him, he couldn't comprehend this need to help, assist and to protect. It was damned inconvenient!

'Very well,' he ground out. 'Our dealings will henceforth be honest and transparent.'

'Thank you. And the amount you negotiated with Sir Horace for us to have access to the comb?'

'Eliza...'

'The amount, Sebastian, if you would be so kind to tell me.'

'Five hundred pounds.'

She gasped. 'That is...quite a steep sum for a private viewing, if you do not mind me saying.'

'It is not just for a viewing. Sir Horace has agreed to sell us the comb, and will therefore bring it with him to our appointment tomorrow.'

'I see. Well, again, I must thank you for your foresight, Sebastian, although I am at a loss to understand why you'd undertake such an agreement with the man and think to keep it from me.'

It was a good question. Why did he care? He came back to this question again and again and he still did not know the reason. Yet, he did care. The very fact that he had even attended an evening such as this, that made him feel exceptionally uncomfortable in his own skin, especially since he was forced to be amongst the very society that he always despised, even though Eliza had surprised him earlier by coming to his defence against anyone who might look down at him, made him realise the extent to which he did indeed care about Eliza Bawden-Trebarr's situation.

'What with your appreciation of old relics and artefacts, I thought you'd want to have the comb tucked back in its rightful place in its case inside the casket box. And I told you, I have a vested interest in you finding this treasure, if it exists. As I can get the debt paid and you can have your castle and estate back.'

'Very true. I'm grateful for your intervention, but you will add the five hundred pounds to Ritton's debt.'

'It is not necessary, Eliza.'

'On the contrary, it most certainly is.' She choked out an unsteady laugh. 'I don't have much left, Sebastian, but I still have my pride.'

'And you know what they say about pride?'

'That it comes before a fall?' she scoffed. 'Oh, I know. I have fallen many times and am prepared to fall and fail again, if it means that I can hold my head up while I attempt it. So, you will add the sum to the tally of what I owe you, if you please.'

'Very well.' He exhaled in resignation.

'Thank you,' she said, her shoulders sagging in relief as she slipped her hand in his, 'for making this all possible.'

'My pleasure.'

He swallowed uncomfortably, realising then how important it was for this woman to have this one hold on determining her own future when she'd been powerless to stop everything and anyone from being taken away from her before. Something he knew that she had in common with his own mother after his father's death. Was that why he found it imperative to help and protect Eliza when he himself had been powerless to do so for his own mother? In truth, it was likely the reason why he went out of his way to help Eliza, even if she wasn't always the easiest to deal with. But then, neither was he.

They descended into a silence but unlike before, the tension from the room seemed to drain away. In fact, the silence was now more companionable than anything else.

'Is that some kind of writing on it?' Sebastian asked as he picked up a magnifying glass left on top of the glass cabinet and passed it to Eliza. 'Just there.' He pointed at one of the intricate carvings on the hair comb.

Eliza nodded, squinting behind the magnifying glass. 'Yes, they're engravings with each of the family mottos on them. The one on the left is from house Bawden, with its motto of *karensa a vynsa cevatys ny vynsa.*'

The way she pronounced the words as they softly rolled from her lips sent a bolt of lust through his blood. He gave himself a mental shake. 'What does it mean?'

'It's Cornish for *love would, greed would not.*'

'And the Trebarr motto?'

'It's *Franc ha leal atho ve.*'

'In Cornish as well?'

'Indeed, it means *Free and loyal am I.*'

The two mottos couldn't be more different.

'Of course, they are quite…different from each other.'

'That's just what I was thinking.' He frowned. 'They seem to contrast one another, greatly.'

'I suppose that's true. Yet, perhaps complement each other, too.'

'Ever the optimist.'

'Not always. However, I like to think that the Trebarr ambition for greatness was tied to their honour and loyalty to one another. That it was this that actually made them great, especially when it was given freely.'

'And what of the Bawden motto?' Sebastian asked. 'Do you

believe that love can conquer all while eliminating greed? Whatever that means.'

'No, I admit the Bawden motto has always stumped me. If anything, it's far more open to interpretation.'

'You've obviously had more time to ponder on it. However, its very vagueness is what makes it open to how you want to define it. For instance, it's unclear whether the motto is referring to courtly love, family and kin love or even love of one's country.'

'True.' She nodded. 'But that is the beauty of both mottos. On their own they're fine and estimable, I suppose, but together they're strong, remarkable, powerful and complete one another in every sense.'

He glanced over at her and noted her wistful expression. 'I can imagine how you took delight in having all the family stories passed down from your mother.'

She nodded and smiled absently. 'And my father, who was also a Bawden-Trebarr but from a different, more distant, branch of the family. Their marriage was to preserve the family name, and continue the longevity of future generations. Much good it did them with me as their only surviving child.' Sebastian had not known this. Indeed, when Eliza had said earlier that she was the last of the Bawdens and Trebarrs, she had meant it literally. 'In any case, as far as Elowen and Simon and their two great houses go, I believe they must also have completed one another for here is yet another example of their love for one another,' she said, lifting her eyes to his.

'Behold, a comb.'

'Not just any comb but one that was commissioned specifically to be given as a token of love.'

'A happy story, then?'

She shook her head. 'Not quite. There was a time before the union of Elowen Bawden and Simon Trebarr when the two families contrasted in every sense. They were essentially mortal enemies.'

'Mortal enemies, eh? You have a furtive imagination, Eliza.'

'It is true. The hatred that the Bawdens and the Trebarrs bore for one another was the stuff of legend.'

'So, you're saying that Elowen and Simon were star-crossed lovers?'

'They were. They married against the wishes of Elowen's father. Against the wishes of their clan, their kin,' Eliza revealed with a faraway smile on her face. 'My mother did used to fill my head with stories about their love, which was wondrous, overcoming all of adversity. In fact, I think that was the real legend of the Bawden-Trebarrs—the everlasting love between Elowen and Simon. A love for all time.'

'Very Romeo and Juliet.'

'With the exception being that their union did not end in tragedy but a long and gloriously happy life together.'

'Ah, so not a cautionary tale like you mentioned before.'

'No, not for them.'

'So they did have their happily-ever-after,' he murmured.

'Yes. Although they had to go through much strife and difficulty before they did.' She sighed and shook her head. 'In any case, all that tosh about finding one's all-consuming, everlasting true love like Elowen and Simon did built up in my head, and I admit it was something that I longed for myself when I was younger. I truly believed in it. But after my marriage to Ritton I realised it was not for me, after all. That what made Elowen and Simon's story unique was that they were exceedingly lucky to have found one another. Not every person has the same fortune in finding it. As it happens, very few do. A very lucky few.'

'I must say that for the life of me, I can't imagine a woman like you with a man like Ritton,' Sebastian said with a frown. 'Why did you marry the blighter?'

He wondered whether she was going to ignore that impertinent question but eventually she answered, with resignation and dismay.

'It seems very shallow of me but it was because he was a viscount, because my parents—in particular, my father—wanted me to. Because Ritton showered me with so much attention and could be, believe it or not, very persuasive and charming. Oh, when we courted, in those early days, he was attentive, charismatic and amiable. But it was all an act. The moment we married and he got his hands on my dowry, he changed overnight. He was hostile, aggressive and cruel. And he enjoyed nothing more than humiliating me as he often did in society, by his mockery of me, or by parading his paramours about town, lavishing them with expensive gifts and making my life as miserable as possible. At first, I believed it was my fault for being unfeminine, as he accused me of being, so I would try to please him. I tried to be a good wife to him but nothing I did was ever enough.'

God, but Ritton was fortunate that he was dead and did not have to face Sebastian now. Justice would certainly have been meted out to the man if he had been. In truth, the viscount had been nothing but a pathetic bully. Even so, it was now the second time tonight that Eliza had referred to herself in such unflattering terms. A terrible thought nagged at him.

'Tell me, was it Ritton who insisted on the removal of your spectacles at functions such as this?'

She raised a brow in obvious surprise. 'How did you know?'

'A lucky conjecture.' He took her hand in his. 'But know this, with or without your spectacles, you're beautiful.'

'Oh, you jest, Sebastian.'

'I speak in earnest, Eliza,' he murmured, lifting her hand to his lips. 'You are indeed a uniquely beautiful woman.'

'Thank you,' she said as colour flushed into her cheeks and down her neck.

'Perhaps it's a bit forward of me to say so. However, it is the truth.' He shrugged, feeling that he might have overstepped again. He had to keep reminding himself that he mustn't get too close to this woman, as that would undoubtedly complicate their arrangement. 'And you never know, Eliza. You might marry again.'

'Marriage? Oh, I think not.' She shook her head. 'I think I have had my share of that. And besides, I am not the sort of woman who should have ever wed, Sebastian. In truth, I believe that I would've been far happier had I remained a spinster.'

'You cannot think that just because you were once wed to Ritton, Eliza. The man was never worthy of you.'

'No, he wasn't. I do believe that there are some people who

are lucky enough to find that elusive happiness when they meet another person who completes them. But mostly they don't.'

'I thought you believed in that cautionary tale between star-crossed lovers but it seems that you're a romantic, Eliza.'

She gave a short laugh. 'Don't say it as though you have a bad taste in your mouth.'

He shrugged. 'It might be because I don't think that notions of love have anything to do with marriage per se.'

Mutual respect in one's alliance would have been sufficient had he been getting leg-shackled, as he would have once been expected to as the heir to the Harbury Earldom. But no longer. Besides, love was not an emotion that had ever held much sway with him since it left one far too exposed, far too vulnerable. He doubted he was even capable of truly loving another now, as the harshness of his life had shaped him to be quite a different man—one who'd had to learn to be ruthless in order to survive.

'Yes, that's true. I don't mean that love is a necessary component for a successful and happy marriage. Only that for me, after all the years that I had to endure living with Ritton, nothing now would entice me back to the altar. So you see, I am resigned and know that marriage is not something that is destined for me, as it was for my ancestors.'

Sebastian exhaled heavily and wondered how it was that they were here on this evening, at this soiree, in this room, staring at a medieval comb, confessing such intimate and personal things to one another. 'It is not fated for me, either. Perhaps once it was, when I was destined for…for another life. A boy who would grow to be someone else with a name so powerful, revered and commanding. One that would have made me into a very different man to who I am today.'

'But why would that difference in who you are now make you believe that you are fated to be alone?'

'I never said anything about being alone, Eliza,' he said wryly. 'Only that I do not believe in the institution of marriage itself. It's not for me.'

And never will be. Sebastian had vowed after the death of his mother that he would never be part of something that could cause the suffering and destruction of a helpless woman. And for what? His father's belief that he was above the law, that he could be so reckless and stupid as to forget something as important as a drunken night that had ended with a clandestine marriage to a young tavern maid at Oxford? A careless act that would later wreak havoc on his family, his wife of twenty years, his heirs.

'But what if you wanted to start a family? You would not want your children to suffer the ignominy of…of…'

'Being born as bastards?'

She caught her lip between her teeth and looked up at him. 'Yes, I suppose. Not that I would ever think of you as such,' she added quickly.

That made him want to smile; this woman who was so always forthright about everything she said and did, caring not a jot for the opinions of others and what they thought of her after her treatment at the hands of her worthless husband, which had undoubtedly made her stronger. Yet, she felt the need to shield him from the unpleasantness and shame of his birth. It touched him more than he could say. That she said this without even a trace of pity humbled him far more than she would ever know.

'That is what I am, in the eyes of the law,' he said, gently reaching out and running a finger across her cheek. 'And all because my father forgot that he had married another woman before marrying my mother.' He shrugged, dropping his hand and wondering why this conversation had suddenly turned to topics that made him so intensely uncomfortable. Still, he felt compelled to explain. 'I cannot ever begin to comprehend how someone could forget something as important as that and yet my father did. The folly of youth, I suppose, and believing that he was in some way invincible, that his actions would not come back one day to haunt us all.'

'I'm so sorry,' she murmured, placing her small gloved hand on his arm.

He swallowed uncomfortably. 'I doubt my father intended for his family to pay for his misdemeanours in the cruellest of all possible ways and yet it did. It left many scars. My mother, for one, never got over the shame of it.'

Sebastian's gaze dropped to her hand as he felt her squeezing his arm gently. 'Your poor mother.'

'Indeed,' he said, giving her a weak smile. 'And yours, Eliza.'

'Yes, they both seemed to have paid heavily for the misdemeanours and sins of their husbands. In my case, my father was far too dazzled by the prestige and supposed honour of Ritton's ancestry. Yet, he failed to see the man behind the title. He failed to see how venal, cruel and ultimately pathetic the man he'd bound me to was.'

'And as your father, he should've protected you.'

'As yours should have protected you—all of you.'

Sebastian nodded. 'So, you see, I, too, am resigned to what fate threw at me.'

Eliza lifted her hand from his arm and slowly peeled off both of her gloves, before cupping his jaw with her bare hand. A jolt of heat coursed through him, pooling in his groin. He looked down at her large eyes filled with concern and tenderness, wanting to touch her but knowing that if he did, he would not stop from wanting more from her. 'Yet, even with all that adversity, Sebastian Marsden, you still made a huge success of your life and those of your younger brothers. You rose to the challenge of rebuilding your life, which you did so...so very admirably.'

'Is that a compliment, Eliza Bawden-Trebarr?' he said, unable to keep a slow smile from curling around his lips.

'What if it is, Sebastian Marsden?'

'What if...' he murmured softly, dipping his head and touching his lips to hers, gently, reverently, as though he was testing the softness of her mouth, reminding himself again of the feel of her. Blast and damnation, but ever since that first time he'd kissed Eliza in the store cupboard at Gresham College he had wanted to do it again. And again. And again. Sliding his arm around her he pulled her closer as he deepened the kiss.

Chapter Ten

Eliza felt as though she was falling down, down, melting into Sebastian's kiss, as he slanted his mouth across hers over and over again. He wrapped his hand around her head, cradling it lightly, as all her senses heightened and she felt every little touch, every caress. Her whole body seemed to be ablaze, her clothes so tight, so constricting. She wanted to rip them all off. And then tear off his clothing as well, so that she could press herself close to the man, feel the pounding of his heart next to hers. Good Lord, but Eliza must be losing her mind. She did not believe that she was but heavens, she couldn't think very clearly at that moment.

His other arm drew her even closer and she went willingly. Eliza realised that she was trembling a little.

'Are you cold?' he asked as he nipped the shell of her ear.

'No,' she moaned, tipping her head back, giving him greater access to her flesh. 'But oh, yes.'

'Which is it?' His fingers traced a trail down her neck and across her bodice, his mouth following the same path. 'Yes or no?'

'Must you ask questions at this time?'

She felt his smile against her skin before he answered her. 'Yes. With you always, yes.'

Eliza wound her arms around his neck and drew him down as she went up on her tiptoes. 'How can I be cold, when you make me burn as much as you do?'

She pressed her lips against his and kissed Sebastian Marsden with all her being, as she threaded her fingers through his hair. It seemed that was all the encouragement he needed. He touched his tongue to the seam of her lips before deepening the kiss more by sliding it inside her mouth, devouring her. She matched every move, every flick, slide, nip of his lips, mouth, tongue and teeth and heard him growl in his throat. It was devastating, shocking, delicious and unlike anything she had ever experienced before. As though neither of them could get enough of one another. His one hand in her hair, loosening her tresses, with tendrils tumbling around her face, her pins falling out and scattering all over the floor.

'Burn?' he whispered. 'I make you burn?'

'Yes, oh, yes.'

He kissed her mouth again but this time taking his time; slower, gentler, far more languid as though there was no urgency, and time simply stood still, which of course it hadn't. They were in the library of Sir Horace Middleton's house. In the middle of his awful soiree.

She pulled away slightly and sucked on her swollen lower lip as she stared up at him.

'What is it?' he asked.

'Nothing, I just... I cannot... I mean I...'

'There you are, Eliza.' Cecy's voice sounded from across the other side of the library. 'I've been looking for you everywhere. And here you are... Oh, my goodness.'

Eliza screwed her eyes shut and pulled away abruptly, knowing that it was too late. Cecy had obviously seen her in Sebastian's arms, in such a shocking and scandalous manner. How awful must it look to her friend, as though they were engaged in a sordid *affaire*. But then they had been devouring each other's mouths only moments ago so Cecy had every right to be shocked. And although Eliza was a widow and was therefore allowed certain freedoms that were usually denied a young unmarried debutante such as Cecy, it was still unbecoming to be caught in this manner. She turned and gave her friend a weak smile and felt her cheeks burn with embarrassment.

'Oh, Cecy, how fortuitous,' Eliza said lamely but, in all honesty, she still felt so dazed from those earlier melting kisses that she couldn't think of anything else to say.

'Yes, very fortuitous,' Cecy said from across the room, with her hands behind her back, looking at her feet. Thank goodness Cecy had found them on her own and had not come with a gaggle of guests. That was the last thing she needed. 'I came looking for you, Eliza, because Stephen is desirous to leave, if that…that is amenable to you?'

'Yes,' she practically squeaked, wanting to be far away from this awkwardly difficult situation that she'd been discovered in. God, how mortifying. She half turned and curtsied at Sebastian before striding as fast as she could towards Cecy. 'Good evening, Mr Marsden.'

'Before you leave, my lady, you might want to take these.' His voice hoarse and raspy. Good, at least he was just as affected as she was by all that had transpired between them.

Eliza stilled, took a deep breath and turned back towards the man who was holding her gloves in one hand and a couple of her silver-and-diamante hairpins in the other. She felt herself flush profusely, even more than before. Rushing back, she went to take the items from his outstretched hand. But when Eliza reached out and touched his much larger hand, it closed around hers so briefly that if her senses hadn't been so heightened already, she might have missed it. Her eyes shot to his for just a fleeting moment and she saw the smallest of smiles, lopsided and frankly boyish, playing around his lips. His eyes glittered with unbanked passion and bemusement before he let her hand go and bowed in front of her. Eliza turned and dashed back to her friend, knowing that this evening had not gone the way she'd imagined. Not at all…

The following day, Eliza kept on reliving that kiss, or rather those hot and passionate kisses, she'd shared with Sebastian Marsden in Sir Horace's library. It had come about so unexpectedly after they had shared such intimate and personal stories about their pasts and after discussing the Bawden and Trebarr mottos for goodness' sake. How did it go from that to Eliza throwing herself at him so ardently, so eagerly, and practically pawing at the man? Yet, Sebastian had seemed to be just as affected by her, too. And that was something that Eliza could not comprehend. That she could have such an effect on a man like Sebastian Marsden was frankly extraordinary. Yet, it appeared to be true. After all, had he not declared that he found her desirable? That he thought her…beautiful?

But what now? Where did it leave her with paying back what she owed him so that she could regain her estate? In very murky and uncharted waters. Eliza did not know where she stood on these important matters with him. It confused her beyond measure with her own feelings about him in total disarray. Lord knew that she was attracted to him but what woman would not be? He was the epitome of powerful, handsome masculinity. And with that confident air of self-assurance he had, oozing with natural charm and intelligence, Sebastian Marsden was the most fascinating man she'd ever met.

Still, Eliza could never forget that she had once trusted another handsome, amiable young man. And that had not ended well. While Sebastian was a vastly different man to Ritton, could she believe that he'd be true to his word and assist in getting her mother out of the asylum and continue to help her as he had been doing? Indeed, she was not even certain why he was helping her—apart from having a *vested interest* in Eliza finding the treasure to pay back the debt. He'd even arranged to pay Sir Horace Middleton for the medieval comb behind her back so that she wouldn't need to worry about owing more to him. Why would he do that? It humbled her that he would care but it also made her uncertain and unsure how to proceed with him.

She lifted her head at the sound of a commotion outside in the hall. What on earth…?

Eliza raised her brows and shot up to her feet, having been staring out the French doors and into the small lawned garden for the past few minutes. The sounds of raised voices got louder before the door violently swung open and Ronald Carew stormed in with Gertie following behind him, wringing her hands. 'I am so sorry, my lady, but his lordship would not accept that you were not receiving visitors today.'

The young viscount swung around to face her. 'I'll be damned if you think that I will not be received by you, Lady Elisabeth. After weeks of turning me away as though I were nothing but dirt underneath your shoes.'

'Thank you, Gertie, it's quite all right. His lordship will not be staying long. You may go but leave the door open, if you will,' she said with a smile, before turning her attention back to the viscount. 'How dare you presume to think that you can just storm into my home and terrorise my servants?'

'Had you the decency to receive me earlier, then we would have avoided this, madam.'

'Decency, you say? After this behaviour, I cannot and will not account for any unpleasantness that you have caused.'

'You forget yourself. I am now the head of the family, Lady Elisabeth.'

'And you appear to have forgotten that I am no longer a part of it.'

'You are still the Countess of Ritton, Lady Elisabeth, and as such you will behave accordingly.' He moved close to her, crowding her, his foul breath upon her. 'I want to know more about my cousin's debts, which I have inherited. I cannot believe that you would've been blind to them.'

'I care little for what you believe. And as for Ernest's debts you'd best meet with the estate lawyers and Ritton stewards instead of harassing me.'

'And yet, I cannot help but think you've been hiding something,' he said pointedly, his lips curling into a sneer.

She swallowed uncomfortably, wondering how in heaven she was going to get the man out of her house. Just as she was about to come back with another rejoinder, she heard a voice near the vicinity of the door.

'Am I interrupting?'

Thank God Sebastian was standing by in the door frame, his features schooled in steely, implacable composure. But she had never, however, seen him like this…as though he was holding on to his anger with a tight leash.

'How good to see you, Mr Marsden,' she said in a shaky voice. 'My late husband's cousin, Viscount Ritton here, was just about to leave.'

'Ritton,' Sebastian said with barely concealed coldness, his indignation emanating from his powerful frame. 'Move away from Lady Eliza, if you will.'

Ronald Carew pulled back but kept his eyes fixed to Eliza's. 'I cannot believe that you would entertain a man who beggared the estate of the viscountcy. Yet, once again, I find you in such familiarity with this...this scoundrel, just as I happened to witness at the Middleton soiree. It is utterly shameful.'

'Get out.' Eliza had had enough of the entire Ritton family, wanting nothing more to do with any of them.

'This is not over, Lady Elisabeth,' Carew muttered as he made his way towards the door.

'Oh, I think it is,' Sebastian retorted, brushing a bit of lint from his coat as he blocked the door with his frame. 'I will not hear of you pestering Lady Eliza again, Ritton. Do you understand?'

'Are you threatening me?'

'No, it's just a friendly reminder.' Sebastian glared coldly at the man before moving aside for him to pass through. 'But you would do well to remember it, Ritton.' The much smaller man must have recognised the intent in Sebastian's voice as he gulped before nodding, unable to say more. 'Good, I am so glad we understand each other.'

They were left in silence, Eliza reeling from the dreadful man's departure.

Sebastian looked soberly at her. His eyes now far more guarded and cautious than the last time she had seen him. 'Are you all right, my lady?'

'Yes, thank you.' She pasted a bland smile on her face as she addressed her maid, who was now hovering by the door, clearly still in shock from everything that had transpired. 'If you can bring the tea through, Gertie, thank you.'

'Certainly, my lady,' she muttered before bobbing a quick curtsy and leaving the room, closing the door behind her.

Eliza turned slowly to face him, rubbing her now throbbing

forehead. 'I am glad that you're here, Sebastian. It seems that I'm always in debt to you in more ways than one.'

'It's nothing, I assure you. But if that bastard comes here again, especially when you're alone, then I want you to send for me.'

'I shall, thank you.'

'You know I cannot bear men who believe they can bully and abuse women into submission.'

Eliza blinked up at him and tilted her head, wondering whether he was referring to his mother. After all, only last night he had mentioned that his mother had not been well protected after his father's death. Did Sebastian believe that he'd failed to do so when he'd been nothing but a boy himself? Was that why he had continually wanted to help and protect her? Because somehow Eliza's situation resonated with what had happened to his own mother? Possibly...

But oh, her heart went to him, this proud, gruff, honourable man, who was nothing like the scoundrel that men like the new and not improved Viscount Ritton wanted to paint him as.

'No, neither can I, Sebastian. They are all cowards—as is Ronald Carew. And I would prefer not to think of the Ritton name any longer.'

It was a relief to have Sebastian arrive at her house when he did, even if it was awkward seeing him again so soon after the intimate kisses they had shared yesterday evening. At least after Ronald's outburst, she would be spared from discussing what happened between them.

'They seem to be rotten to the core in that family. Every other male worse than the one preceding them,' he said irritably as he dragged his fingers through his hair. 'I'm glad that you're no longer part of them.'

'As am I.' She nodded, her shoulders sagging a little as she turned to face him. 'Please, do take a seat. I am happy to see you, Sebastian, but I did not expect to see you so soon after... last night.'

She felt a blush creep up her chest and flood her cheeks as she waited for the man to speak. And yet, he didn't. For a long moment he stared at her and then without preamble, Sebastian took out a small velvet box from the pocket of his grey woollen overcoat and held it out to her. Eliza tentatively stepped forward and had to stop herself from leaning into the gorgeous lemon-and-sandalwood scent of his that always managed to wrap itself around her as though it were casting some indefinable spell on her.

Frowning, she took the velvet box from him and placed it on the table before opening it up. Taking a small surprised breath, she stared at the medieval boxwood hair comb.

'I see that your meeting with Sir Horace went well.' She flicked her gaze back to Sebastian's and smiled. 'What would I do without you?'

'I only did what most men would do, when they are in the position to help a lady.' He shrugged, looking a bit sheepish.

'Oh, I am not certain there are many men who would.' But then there were not many men quite like Sebastian Marsden. 'Thank you…again.'

That he'd done this for her made Eliza feel a lick of warm gratitude trickle through her and something else, something far more intimate and tender.

'You're quite welcome.' He seemed a little uncomfortable as he nodded towards the medieval comb and the Bawden-Trebarr casket box that she'd left on the table. 'Well? Are you going to inspect the comb?'

'Of course,' she replied as Gertie opened the door and brought over the tea tray laden with a steaming teapot, cups and saucers and a few lavender-spiced biscuits that she'd baked earlier that morning. 'Thank you, Gertie. How do you take your tea, Sebastian?'

'A drop of milk and no sugar please.' He took the cup that she passed to him, their fingers brushing briefly, sending a frisson of awareness up her arm. 'So, is there anything you can decipher from the comb, Eliza?'

She turned the comb around in her hand as she looked closely at it from behind her magnifying glass that she'd picked up from the table. 'No, not really. It is just a comb albeit a beautifully crafted one. I cannot make anything else out, apart from the front being slightly different in design than the back.'

'May I take a look?' he asked as Eliza passed the comb to him, their fingers skimming against each other again.

Goodness, but the way her pulse skittered whenever they touched was outside of enough! She really had to get a hold of herself around Sebastian as this would not do at all.

'Oh, yes, you're right. The two sides are very subtly different in design. I wonder why?'

'It is curious because the craftsmen certainly went to the trouble of making both sides of the comb look exactly the same.' She glanced up at him and pushed her spectacles up her nose. 'But other than this, I cannot see anything else out of the ordinary.'

'What about if you put the comb back in the original case and then inside the casket box. Perhaps something might present itself then?'

Eliza did as Sebastian suggested but sadly still, she could think of nothing. In fact, there was seemingly nothing more to it. She slumped indecorously on the chair beside the table and rubbed her brow for a moment. 'It seems that there's nothing about the comb that indicates how we should proceed.'

'No, it doesn't seem so.' Sebastian stood as he ran his fingers through his hair. 'Perhaps it was one of the other empty compartments that would have contained the clues needed.' He crouched over her, and lifted the leather case out of the box before removing the comb to inspect it once again.

'Perhaps.' Eliza shrugged before straightening in her chair as she suddenly pondered a far more intriguing possibility. 'Or perhaps not. May I have the comb, Sebastian? I would like another look at the differing designs on either side of it.'

Wanting to avoid yet another touch of his hand against hers, Eliza somehow managed to miss the comb as he passed it to her. She watched motionless as it fell and hit the side of the metal magnifying glass on the table.

'Apologies, Eliza,' Sebastian murmured.

'No, no, it was my fault.' She frowned, annoyed with her clumsiness. 'But no harm done. It's still in one piece.'

'Not quite.' He prised the comb from her fingers and turned it backwards and forwards. 'Look, there is now the smallest of gaps between the two sides. It must have come away when it hit the magnifying glass.'

'Yes…but wait, of course!' she exclaimed. 'That's the reason why the two sides have a slight difference in design.'

He nodded, understanding her. 'Because they are two different pieces stuck together to make it look as though it was made from one solid piece of wood.'

'Which means that this very small space in the middle, where you have all the intricate work, with the Bawden and Trebarr mottos engraved, is actually…hollow.'

'Brilliant.' Sebastian grinned. 'And it raises the question of why your ancestors wanted this beautiful comb to have a hollowed-out bit in the middle.'

'Are you thinking along the same lines as me?'

'I would say yes, if you're thinking along the same lines as me.'

She nodded excitedly. 'They wanted to hide something in the hollowed-out part.'

'Precisely.'

Her smile slipped from her face. 'However, to find out what that may be, we'd need to fully prise the comb open. And we cannot do that, as it would damage the comb, Sebastian. After all, it is an important piece of my heritage that you paid a considerable amount of money for.'

'Ah, but who said anything about damaging it? With any luck we'll open it and see if there's anything inside the comb. Afterwards, a craftsman can carefully restore it, as long as the two sides remain in one piece and don't break off. The difficulty will be the delicate comb teeth.'

'And how exactly are we to do that?'

'Watch. Like this.' He started to feel his way around the edges before fetching a small, jewelled dagger from a sheath strapped to the inside of his trouser leg. When he glanced up and caught Eliza's quizzical stare, he shrugged. 'It's an old habit from being a gaming hell owner. I never leave the club without it.'

'Yes, one never knows what dangers one might find in the sleepy streets of Chelsea.'

'True,' he said as he continued to feel his way forward, running his fingers and the tip of the blade around all the edges of the comb. 'The sleepy ones are always the worst.'

She chuckled softly. 'Any luck?'

'Just one moment. I think that there's something right here and...' Sebastian ran the small dagger over the edges again, hoping it might loosen the wood before placing it back in its sheath. 'It is slowly coming apart. Here, give me your hand.' He grabbed her hand in his absently and drew her fingers along the edge. 'Can you feel it?'

Eliza did feel it. She felt the warmth of his large hand covering hers. She felt the same spark of attraction, as she did every time they touched. And it was just the same as always; as it was last night at the soiree. With that came the flood of memories of being in his arms, being pressed against him and having his mouth on hers. Just the thought of it and Sebastian's nearness was beginning to make her feel too warm and breathless. But judging from his eager reaction to show her the opening of the comb, he was clearly unaffected by touching her. But then why would he be? Sebastian Marsden could have any woman he wanted, as a lover, a mistress or for a short dalliance. Had he not already explained that he would not remain alone despite vowing never to marry? There would certainly be no shortage of women vying for his attention. Even at the soiree, Eliza had noticed women young and old trying to garner his attention or catch his eye. And why did that thought give her such misgivings? Why did the thought of the man being with another woman make her feel so desolate...so jealous?

Because in a matter of time, that would be precisely what he'd do. He would be with another. Indeed, there would soon be no reason for them to continue to spend any time in each other's company. Which was just as it should be. After all, Eliza had come to him so that she could try to get her estate back, so that she could help secure her mother's release. And she would do well to remember that.

'Yes, it is the smallest of narrow gaps,' she muttered. 'But it is coming away, Sebastian. Do we need any other tools? I can ask Willis, my housekeeper's son, if he has anything that might work better than a mere dagger.'

'A mere dagger, you say.' He gave her a swift shake of the head before resuming. 'It's a beautiful piece studded with jewels on the hilt and the finest sharpest blade. I tell you that it is more than up to the task of prising this small sliver of wood open.'

She smiled. 'Ah, so you are not so immune to such artefacts from a bygone era, after all. Where did you get it from?'

He didn't answer. Instead, a muscle jumped in the corner of Sebastian's eye as he continued to work with his dagger against the wood, carefully so as not to break anything off. After a long moment he answered her. 'My father. He had three individually handcrafted daggers made for each of his precious sons,' he said bitterly. 'And in truth, it's the only thing we have left from him. That we managed to keep as they were legally ours and did not belong to the Harbury estate. So, yes, this dagger is definitely from a bygone era.'

Eliza stilled his hand by placing her own on top and giving it a squeeze. 'I can see why you would choose to take it everywhere you go.'

'Can you?' he asked.

'Yes,' she said, pulling out her mother's locket from around her neck. 'As it's the same reason I carry this with me everywhere I go.'

Sebastian paused and looked up at her. 'What is it that you're trying to say, Eliza?'

'That by always carrying your dagger, it's as though you're carrying a small piece of your father with you.'

Sebastian stared at her, his gaze penetrating, unfathomable as it flashed with some unknown emotion before being masked over, barring her from seeing any more. He turned away and continued to work in silence as Eliza watched him, mesmerised by the dextrous and efficient way he worked methodically but relentlessly to loosen and prise the comb open.

She hadn't known this about Sebastian Marsden. That he carried the one thing he had left from his father. The very man who had lived so recklessly, so carelessly, that he hadn't realised that he'd been a bigamist and had plunged his whole family into absolute disaster after his death. This was what Sebastian carried about with him. A gift. Yet, he'd claimed that he hated the idea of relics and artefacts from the past. He'd even mocked her for doing so…yet he carried this. Why?

'Don't get any ridiculous notions in your head.'

'I cannot know to what you are referring.'

He sighed before turning his head around. 'Do not get any sentimental hogwash into your head because I can tell that is exactly what you're doing, Eliza Bawden-Trebarr.'

'I wouldn't call it sentimental hogwash per se.'

'Oh, but I would.' He took a long moment as though weighing up how much he was willing to say, and how much he wanted to conceal. 'The truth is that there is no real reason why I carry this dagger wherever I go, other than I like it. Apart from being exquisitely made, the dagger is versatile. Note what I am currently using it for. And it's practical. But other than that, it holds no value to me.'

'Despite your father gifting it to you?'

'Despite that.'

Eliza didn't know why but she didn't quite believe him. There were plenty of daggers that he could own that were just as versatile, just as practical, but it was this one that he was attached to. And although he might not want to admit it, she couldn't help thinking that it was precisely for sentimental reasons that he carried it wherever he went. Because it reminded him of a man whom he'd loved but had been ultimately disappointed by. He'd left Sebastian not only to fend for himself after the death of his mother, but caring for his younger brothers as well.

Sebastian made one last flick of the wrist before placing the comb on the table.

Carefully, he used the tips of his fingers to prise the wood open very slowly and as he lifted his dark gaze to Eliza, he smiled. 'Well, can you see anything between the two?'

'I am not completely certain yet but yes, I think there's something there.' Eliza grabbed a small teaspoon from the tray and using the round tip of the spoon placed within the opening, she started to carefully drag out whatever was there.

She paused then glanced up at Sebastian for a long moment before taking a deep breath and pulling out the edge of what looked like a folded piece of vellum. She exhaled long and slow as she teased the remainder out and held it gingerly in her hands.

Very carefully, she unfolded the old vellum in case it crumpled and disintegrated before they'd even had a chance to see what was written on it. Taking another deep breath to steady the butterflies in her belly, she placed it on the table and raised a brow. For there, on the decayed piece of vellum, were faded, strange markings all over it. Whatever could they mean?

'It looks like a parchment with some sort of message inscribed on it.'

'I believe so.' She nodded. 'Or possibly clues to direct one to the Bawden-Trebarr treasure.'

Sebastian smiled. 'Then it seems as though the legend was true after all.'

'Yes.' She lifted her eyes to meet his. 'It seems that it was.'

Chapter Eleven

Sebastian paced back and forth under the great pillars at the entrance of the British Museum, waiting for Eliza to finally arrive. They had agreed to meet at the museum after finding the folded parchment hidden inside the comb the previous day, but she was more than half an hour late. Where on earth was she? He knew how impulsive and single-minded Eliza could be once she had the bit between her teeth, and she certainly had that now with this new discovery. What if the woman reneged on their meeting and decided to continue on her own? What if she had got into another difficulty just as she'd done yesterday, when he'd walked into her parlour to find Ritton attempting to intimidate her? The man had been lucky that Sebastian had not tossed him out on his backside, as he'd wanted to. But he'd certainly got a rude awakening last night when Sebastian had entered the viscount's venerated home and gave him another friendly warning that if he ever spoke to Eliza again, let alone came within a hundred yards of her, his life wouldn't be worth living. As usual with bullies, the man had spluttered and whimpered but eventually agreed. Good. Sebastian would not allow Ritton or anyone else, for that matter, to hurt her. He paused midstep.

When had Eliza become so…so precious…so vital to him?

Even thinking about the woman in such terms knocked the air out of his lungs. The truth was that Sebastian liked her…he liked her a lot, even if that surprised him more than he could say. And as he'd admitted to her himself, he found her desirable and was finding being in close proximity to her increasingly difficult. Especially now that he knew the feel and taste of her mouth. She had somehow gotten under his skin and lingered there. And he could not help any of it just as he could not help the sun from rising.

However, that did not mean that he was no longer frustrated by her. How in the name of all that was holy had she not got into trouble before he'd met her, he would never know—even when she decided to wear her spectacles, as she should. And yet, he just couldn't help himself; he liked Eliza…very much indeed.

'Good morning, Sebastian,' she uttered from behind him. 'Are you going to continue to pace in that inordinate manner? For I must say it is making me feel quite giddy.'

'It doesn't take much to make you giddy, especially if there are any poor, unsuspecting servants around.' He turned to face her, removing his hat and inclining his head in greeting. 'I hope you're well on this fine morning, Eliza?'

'Thank you, I am, and I hope it finds you in good spirits as well.'

'It does,' he murmured as he tucked her hand into the crook of his arm and started for the door to the entrance of the museum. 'I do hope you do not make a habit of being late for appointments, however, as we continue to work together.'

'Try as I might, it is one of my many flaws.'

'I can hardly believe it.'

They walked together through the huge wooden door and into the black-and-white marble-floored foyer with tall ceiling, arches and pillars in the classical Grecian design.

'I must admit that what I am intrigued by is why you'd want to work with me, why you'd want to help. I know that you have said something about having a vested interest in me finding the treasure. Yet, in doing so, you would lose my Cornish estate that you had designs on building a few hotels on. It's something that

I have been wondering about, Sebastian, as I cannot understand why you would choose to lose all that.'

It was something that he could not understand, either. But then by helping Eliza, he would still have a reason to be close at hand, should she need him.

'That is exactly the point, Eliza,' he said gently. 'I'm now in the enviable position of being able to choose, to be able to do as I please. And yet, through no fault of your own, you do not have that same choice.'

'Few women do, Sebastian. Of any station.'

'I realise that. Which is why I want to redress the balance, I suppose. I… I cannot stand the injustice of it.'

'Very noble of you.' She looked up sharply at him, pushing back her spectacles as she realised her mistake in using that damned word. She quickly added, 'In the truest sense you are indeed very noble and honourable. Indeed, the most noble and honourable man of my acquaintance.'

He shrugged. 'Not bad for a bastard gaming hell owner.'

'But you are far more than that, Sebastian.'

Was he? Is that how Eliza saw him? More than the mere parts that made him who he was? He strangely liked to be valued by her.

'Cease your praise, my lady, or you might put me to the blush.' He grinned. 'Besides, you'll make me forget the news I bring you, regarding your mother.'

'My mother?' Eliza halted and glanced up at him eagerly. 'What? Oh, what has happened? Please tell me, what news?'

'It's nothing of note yet, but I've managed to ask the asylum she's at to review her case.'

She blinked several times at him before a slow smile spread on her lips. 'Oh, Sebastian, you have my eternal gratitude. Thank you.'

'There's a long way to go. However, I'm hopeful that this is the first step in getting her out of there.'

She grabbed both his gloved hands in hers and squeezed them. 'How can I ever repay you?'

This was something that Sebastian could not and would not think about. Not at this moment in time when everything between them was as tenuous as it was. He preferred to worry about that at another time, when they both might know where they stood with each other.

'I believe that parchment we discovered yesterday might hold the answer to that,' he said flippantly as they walked inside the main entrance hall and into the huge galleried rooms.

'Touché.' She laughed as they began to stroll side by side again, stopping occasionally to look at some of the exhibits. 'And thank you again. It's most welcome news.'

He shrugged. 'I did promise to help, if I could.'

'You did. And in return I wish to honour my promises just as well.'

'I am certain you shall do your utmost to.'

She raised a brow. 'You make it sound as though you doubt my sincerity.'

He gave her a pointed look. 'Quite the contrary. I don't doubt it but you do realise that you're pinning all your hopes on what you might find on that vellum inside your portmanteau.'

'It is all I have, Sebastian. That and my wretched pride.'

'I know it. It's the same pride that refused to allow me to gift you the hair comb that I bought from Sir Horace, and the same pride that would also refuse me, should I choose to give you back your ancestral estate, which I have the power to do.'

'Of course not. I could never accept that.'

'Indeed. So, you see, I have to help you find the treasure. I have to help you get back your crumbling old castle. There's no other way,' he drawled. 'Now, where to, my scholarly blue-stocking? I still do not know why we are here.'

She paused midstep before lifting her head. 'We're here to decipher the inscription on the vellum. But oh, Sebastian, look... look around you and take this wondrous place in. It really is the most magical of places.'

'If you say so. You know my opinions well on the subject of knickknacks from bygone eras.'

She sighed. 'It is a shame that I cannot convince you of the splendour of some of the exhibits here.' She pointed at a huge familiar stone. 'Take for instance the Rosetta Stone there. It looks like an ordinary slab of stone but look closer and what do you see?'

'Strange inscriptions, and if memory serves from those days at Eton, one column that looks vastly similar to some of the Greek we used to learn.'

'Exactly. The significance of this stone is that because of our understanding of both the Greek and Demotic inscriptions on either side there, scholars were then able to decipher the Egyptians' hieroglyphs. Those strange markings there.'

'Fascinating.' It genuinely was. Sebastian could admit to being impressed with the large stone, especially the Egyptian hieroglyphs that had Eliza in raptures. Not that he wanted to dwell on other things that had the woman in raptures, namely their heated, intimate kisses and those soft moans that escaped her lips. He gave himself a mental shake. 'So, you're interested in this unusual Egyptian language, then?'

'Yes, aren't you?'

'Well, I cannot say that I have given it much thought.'

She stopped to address him. 'Don't you see that with the Rosetta Stone, scholars were able to unlock the hieroglyphs and understand so much about this ancient civilisation that would otherwise have been closed off to us? It is this that interests me. The fact that this unremarkable-looking stone manages to link us to the past. It tells us about how these people lived thousands and thousands of years ago.'

'While I can comprehend how thrilling such a thing is, I fear that I will never be interested in anything that links us to the past. I rather prefer to live in the present and firmly believe that the past belongs in the past.'

'Ah, but without it how can one learn and move forward?'

'Like many things, one step at a time, Eliza.'

She frowned. 'You and I are never going to agree on this, are we?'

'I don't suppose that we shall.' He flicked his gaze around the place. 'No, sadly, this dusty old place does little for me, interesting as the Rosetta Stone is. Indeed, I cannot recall ever coming here unless I was forced to.'

'Which you were not on this occasion. You need not have accompanied me, Sebastian.'

No, he did not need to have come here. There were a million and one things that needed his attention, and traipsing all over London, following Eliza on her quest, was certainly not one of them. It amused his brothers, especially Dominic, immensely. The jibes he'd had to listen to the past few days regarding following his bluestocking around apparently like a lost puppy was outside of enough. But cool and collected, he never rose to it, knowing it would only confirm their beliefs regarding Eliza. And in truth, Sebastian could have got one of his men to keep a close eye on her but had wanted to do it himself.

'True.' He raised a brow. 'But I insisted on coming.'

'Yes, you did.' She nodded. 'And I could hardly forget your opinions on this *stuff*, with the exception of your practical and versatile dagger. Why it practically makes you come out in a rash.'

He gave a short laugh and shook his head. 'How well you seem to know me.'

'I do.' They stared at one another for a moment before Eliza coughed, clearing her throat. 'Anyway, we haven't come to look at the many wonderful exhibits but to look at some old Celtic and Cornish inscriptions that I need to check against the markings made on the vellum.'

'Yes, and I assume it's well protected somewhere in that overly large portmanteau?'

'Yes, it is. And what is wrong with my practical and versatile portmanteau?'

'Nothing except you always seem to carry the whole world and everything you own in there.'

His jest was met with a small smile. 'That's possibly because everything I own can fit quite neatly inside it, Sebastian.'

Implying that her worldly possessions consisted of so few items. He could kick himself for his thoughtlessness. Damn it, but it didn't seem right that a woman like Eliza should be reduced to this. It did not seem right at all. Even when there were many women and children littered all over the city in far worse circumstances than Eliza. And while his natural instinct was to help many of those in need, it was this one woman who presently seemed to matter to him. And for reasons he could still not fathom.

'Eliza, I did not mean...'

'I know.' She nodded. 'Come, we need to get to the first floor, and by the by, Sebastian, were you aware that you just called me *your* scholarly bluestocking? That you used such words?'

Naturally, Eliza would notice his mistake and rather than pretend that she'd misheard him, insist on finding out more.

'I had not noticed.' He turned to her and gave her a bland smile. 'It must have been a slip of the tongue. Come along, then. Let's see about these Celtic and Cornish inscriptions of yours.'

They continued to the side hallway that led to the stairwell and ascended the stairs in silence. On reaching the first floor, they moved from room to room until they eventually reached the one space that housed the exhibits dedicated to Celtic, Brittonic and Cornish artefacts dating back over a thousand years. Eliza then moved into the next smaller antechamber just off the room.

'Where are you going?' Sebastian asked. 'I thought we'd come to look especially at the Celtic and Cornish room?'

'Not quite,' she said as she moved towards the lone man, evidently a steward working at the museum. The smaller antechamber housed many rows of desks, with oil lamps over each one and chairs beneath each desk. 'We've come here for something very specific.'

They reached the steward, who was standing beside a small desk with an opened tome on top. He gave them a curt bow before speaking. 'My lady, you have only one hour before I come back for it. Please take care and keep the oil lamp away from the book.'

'I shall, thank you.'

Eliza waited until the steward left and lowered herself onto one chair as Sebastian sat beside her. 'So, would you like to explain why we are here and what we are doing?'

'Certainly. This—' she pointed at the huge book '—is the *Vocabularium Cornicum*, a twelfth-century Latin-to-Kernewek or rather, Cornish, glossary. It will help us decipher the transcript of the message in the vellum.'

'Wait one moment, Eliza.' He turned to her. 'Last time we looked at the vellum together, there was no message that I could see. Just a load of faded jumbled-up words that made little sense. Please do not say that it was this...this Kernewek, or Cornish language?'

'Well, yes, it is all in Cornish but no, that's not what any of the jumbled-up words were.'

Eliza took the vellum from her portmanteau and smoothed it out flat on the desk and then got out her large magnifying glass and a sheet of foolscap. She started to read from the glossary and make notes on the foolscap using the inkwell and quill that had already been provided.

He frowned. 'I don't comprehend.'

'The jumbled-up words—that is exactly what they were, Sebastian.'

'Were?'

'Yes, and now they're not.' Eliza had her head down as she continued to look through the glossary and then make more notes on the foolscap. 'I managed to decipher the message into legible Cornish. All I need to do now is translate it into English—hence the need for this glossary.'

'Allow me to understand you, Eliza. You have already deciphered the vellum? When did you do this and...how?'

'I did it yesterday evening after you left, knowing it was a good use of my time to decipher the message before coming here.' She lifted her head and glanced at him. 'And as for the how...it was really quite simple once I realised that the first and last letter of each word had been replaced by one letter sequentially before the actual one. So, any word starting with the letter *b* for example in the text was actually starting with the letter *a*. And so on.'

'That's brilliant, Eliza,' he said, smiling at her and shaking his head in amazement. 'Absolutely brilliant.'

'Thank you,' she said, giving him a bashful smile. 'It's something I quite enjoy doing, actually. Deciphering and decoding manuscripts.'

'I'm impressed.'

'Easily so, it seems.' She chuckled, dismissing his compliment at hand, which bemused him slightly.

Eliza did not seemingly know how take flattery, which once again showed the extent that she had been spurned and overlooked by those who were supposed to cherish her so. He hoped that at least her friends, such as Miss Cecily Duddlecott, did. She seemed to be just as uniquely different as Eliza.

'So, are you going to tell me what the translation says?'

She nodded. 'Look through the magnifying glass, Sebastian. The first line is *Rag karrow Bawden ha Trebarr.*'

'And that means…?'

'"For the love of Bawden and Trebarr,"' she said, pointing at the second line. 'You can see that I have deciphered the second line into Cornish, too. *Ny dal keles man an pyth a thue gvelis veyth.*'

'Yes, I see that,' he said, looking at both the original vellum through the magnifying glass and the line that Eliza had written out after it had been decoded. 'And have you worked out what it means yet?'

'Yes, it says, "it must not be hidden at all. What shall come shall be seen."'

'Very cryptic and vague as that could refer to anything.'

'True, but if we manage to work out more of the translation then perhaps we have a better chance of making sense of the message.'

Sebastian rose and took off his hat and his grey superfine coat before sitting back down beside her, pulling the chair closer to hers. 'Tell me what you would like me to do to help, Eliza.'

She smiled at him, covering his hand with hers. 'Are you certain that you want to spend your time in this dusty old place when you have far more important matters needing your attention?'

He returned her smile and nodded. 'I am.'

'Very well,' she murmured, holding his gaze for a long moment before glancing back down at the vellum. 'In that case, let's both look for the words in the glossary so that we can translate them together.'

Together… Now there was a word he'd never been comfortable hearing about himself in connection with another. And yet, this time it did… It made him feel like a part of something. Something that stirred deep inside his chest, unequivocally different and unknown.

He swallowed uncomfortably, unable to say more, pushing away those unwanted feelings and pulling his focus back to the task at hand. 'So, where do we start?'

'From the beginning,' she said, catching her bottom lip between her teeth, as she did whenever she was excited by something or other.

They worked tirelessly and in silence, trying to piece together the message bit by bit, translating the Cornish painstakingly into English, so that finally they had the message written out.

'There, I think we have it.'

'I believe we do,' she said, nodding absently. 'And so, *nyns yw. Dh'aga gemmeres dh evos own rag y dhewgh wir yn pub redya*, means…'

'"Lest you go astray from where you should always be."' He frowned. 'What do you think it's saying here?'

'That perhaps when you're in need and are far from home, which in my ancestors' case would be…'

'Trebarr Castle.'

'Exactly, and then the next line, *gwrewgh fowt ow owr y'ma*, means…'

'"Seek my heart." Or in this case, perhaps it means to seek the treasure?'

'I believe it might.' She nodded. 'And then *ha teuth yn-mes*.'

'"And go abroad"—from Trebarr, one would assume.'

'Yes. And the next line seems to elaborate on it. *Mes an kribow Trebarr dell dy grendrevethoryon gol in dhe voyowgh*.'

'Which means, "from the coastline of Trebarr into your neighbour's palms."'

'And, *gweres ha pwegh dodh mos theni ow splaneth warlergh an gwarri dheag*.'

Sebastian read the next translated line. '"Seek and you shall find my heart beneath the sacred oak tree." So again, I would surmise that the heart in this case must be a reference to the Bawden-Trebarr treasure.'

'As would I and it's evidently buried beneath a great oak, in a neighbouring land near Trebarr—possibly their ancient enemy's. The Bawden land became part of their estate after Simon and Elowen's union.'

'That sounds plausible. And the next line is?'

'Tragyas bys yn fy unn y dhewlangterdhe Elowen bys Bawden.'

'Which means, "forever in my heart, oh, daughter of Elowen of Bawden." That is directed solely at you, Eliza…'

'Indeed. I have goose bumps just reading it,' she said softly. 'It's incredibly touching. Exceptionally moving.'

He smiled. 'As you should. And finally it ends with *Rag karrow Bawden ha Trebarr*, just as it did at the beginning.'

'"For the love of Bawden and Trebarr…"'

They both sat in silence for a long moment, pondering on everything that they had uncovered together. Sebastian read through the message again and again. It was all quite astonishing—this voice from over four hundred years ago, speaking to them as though they were right there in this room. It sent a shiver down his spine. He glanced sideways at Eliza, who had tears in her eyes, staring at the words, knowing that it was her this message was for—to the daughters of Elowen of Bawden…

And though Sebastian would like to believe that he had been of some help in uncovering the hidden faded words on the vellum, it had mainly been Eliza who had instigated the search. She had been the one driving it. It finally made sense to him now why she admired artefacts such as the Rosetta Stone, since they allowed her to appreciate how, in some way, everyone was linked to one another. How the knowledge of a language could break through the veil of misunderstanding and the unknown, allowing us to make sense of it all. This was what she wanted to be able to uncover and learn. And it was this that she had tried to make him understand; tried to reason with him to see the importance of being able to unlock the secrets of the past because by doing so one could gain perspective, knowledge and insight.

And suddenly, Sebastian understood Eliza's fascination with the past was because of moments like this. Moments that made her comprehend who she was and where she came from. Moments that must now vindicate all she had believed about herself. And to think he had once mocked her for her overzealous interest and diligence regarding this quest, questioning her reasoning. It made him feel ashamed. But it also made him experience an ache somewhere deep inside his chest.

'You should feel very proud of yourself, Eliza.'

'Thank you.' She turned to him and smiled as she wiped the tears now streaming down her face with the back of her hand. 'But I could not have done any of this without you, Sebastian.'

'Oh, I rather think you could,' he murmured as he reached out and cupped her cheek. 'You, Eliza Bawden-Trebarr, are capable of anything.'

They locked eyes with one another and slowly, very slowly, moved closer until their foreheads touched.

'So what now?' he asked.

'Now?' she said, gently rubbing her forehead against his, skin to skin, back and forth. 'Now we make plans. We need to start the search for this tree in Cornwall, at Trebarr Castle itself...'

She pulled away slightly and lifted her gaze to his, frowning a little. 'Not that I have any expectation that you would accompany...'

Sebastian silenced her by reaching over and placing one finger on her lips and shaking his head. 'I want to... I want to accompany you.'

He watched, riveted, as she took a small shaky breath before nodding. 'Yes.'

'Yes...' He lifted her chin up with his finger and moved closer to her, his lips touching hers. He covered her mouth with his but just as he was about to deepen the kiss, wanting to taste her again, the steward came back into the room, making them pull away from one another abruptly.

'Are we finished here, my lady?' the man asked Eliza as she dropped her head and looked away.

'Yes... Yes, I suppose we are.'

Which could not be further from the truth, for Sebastian knew with alacrity that they were not finished at all. If anything, this was just the beginning.

And God help him with that...

Chapter Twelve

Eliza stood on a platform at Paddington the following morning, with her leather trunk as well as her trusty battered old portmanteau. Wearing her fitted military-style jacket, matching long skirt and a smart buttoned-up shirt with lacing at the neck, her mother's onyx brooch at the neckline and a long cloak to keep out the cold, she felt ready to undertake this journey that would effectively take her back to her ancestral home. A figure pierced through the fog of steam from the locomotive engine of the train from the Paddington to Exeter leg of the journey and stepped closer towards her.

Tipping his hat, Sebastian inclined his head in greeting and walked in front of the porter carrying his trunks.

'Good morning, Eliza.'

'Good morning,' she said, staring up at him, taking in his handsome appearance, as well as his impeccable attire.

'I hope you are well,' he murmured, throwing one of his dazzling smiles in her direction resulting, as it always did when he looked at her like that, in her feeling like she'd been struck by a jolt of lightning.

She nodded, unable to say more.

Oh dear, how on earth was she going to cope? The awkwardness of travelling with Sebastian alone, after she'd decided to leave Gertie and Willis at her house in Chelsea, so that no one would think that she was travelling to Cornwall, made her feel uncertain of herself. Again. And while she felt grateful to have Sebastian's protection as he accompanied her on this journey, Eliza had never travelled alone with a man who wasn't her father or husband. Until now. It might be scandalous, even for a widow, but that wasn't the real reason for her awkwardness. No, it was the fact that she would be travelling together in such close proximity with a man whom she was constantly aware of and to whom she was ridiculously attracted.

It was bad enough that Eliza thought about Sebastian constantly. Bad enough that she had to continually push away any lingering thoughts about that night in Sir Horace's library. Bad enough that he tormented her endlessly in those vivid dreams of hers as she tossed and turned at night reliving every touch, kiss and caress. Bad enough that she'd agreed to have him help her at the British Museum of all places. To top it all, Eliza must be addled in the head to have agreed for him to accompany her to Cornwall. Alone. Being with him day and night, night and day, as they travelled to Trebarr Castle. And yet, she had agreed, knowing that his mere presence was comforting, even though her constant awareness of him was frankly exhausting, let alone unbecoming.

Eliza should certainly not be having such lascivious thoughts about him. Indeed, Sebastian made her feel breathless, made her heartbeat quicken and made her pulse hitch whenever he was near. And that was before he'd even lifted his dark, smoky eyes to meet hers, or threw her one of those laconic smiles that transformed his hard, angled features into something so much softer—boyish, even. It sent a tumult of emotion racing through her. That blasted surfeit of emotion, which she'd once mocked him about, was now something that she didn't know what to do with.

How on earth was she to endure being close to the man with the hum of all this unfettered desire between them? She exhaled before retuning his smile. Eliza would just have to keep herself in check around him and refrain from doing anything that might embarrass either of them.

'Well, shall we?' he said, raising a brow as he ushered her to their train carriage.

'Yes.'

They boarded the train and walked down the long, narrow aisle until they found their first-class carriage, as though they were on their way to embark on an elicit *affaire* rather than being on the hunt for Eliza's family treasure. And after Sebastian tipped the porter who'd carried their trunks and put them in the luggage holdalls, they took their comfortable plush seats opposite one another, with a table separating them. After ordering a pot of coffee, they both descended into what appeared to be a comfortable silence, and yet it was anything but. It seemed wholly ungracious to be resentful of the elegant luxury that was afforded her in the first-class carriages, but Eliza would never have been able to sit here had she been on her own. She glanced at the man who sat across from her and knew to whom she should be thankful for this unexpected indulgence and sighed.

Dash it all, she was not as green as all that to believe that Sebastian might want more from her despite all this simmering attraction between them. If anything, Eliza was probably placing too much importance on his attraction to her despite everything he'd said, since a handful of heated kisses was all that had ever transpired between them—which for an experienced, worldly man such as Sebastian Marsden amounted to very little, compared to her. Besides, it was not as if she wanted anything more from him, anyway.

Still, she couldn't help but feel vulnerable and confused. Despite having once being married, Eliza realised that she actually knew very little about men. Not that she'd cared one jot that she didn't. Until meeting Sebastian Marsden. Now all her thoughts were in disarray. All her beliefs about herself shattered and unclear. She was not certain of anything anymore, especially of the man sat across from her, seemingly without a care in the world, reading his newspaper.

But in truth, Eliza owed him so much already. From allowing her extra time to repay Ritton's debt, to purchasing the comb from Sir Horace, to assisting her at every turn—albeit begrudgingly at first after he'd encountered her unexpectedly at Gresham College—to dealing ruthlessly with the dreadful Ronald Carew. And then there was the manner in which he'd insisted on helping her at the British Museum as they'd worked together to uncover the secrets of the vellum efficiently and expediently. It had surprised her. Indeed, they'd made a good team. Eliza had found those quiet moments together at the museum some of the most intimate and riveting moments in her entire life. Especially as Sebastian had shared her joy at finding the four-hundred-year-old message from her ancestors in the vellum. The sheer relief at this discovery had made her feel so emotional that she had not been able to stop the tears from streaming down her face. And when she'd looked up, it was Sebastian who had been there for her. It had been Sebastian who wiped away those embarrassing tears. It was Sebastian who had eventually congratulated her and who had then kissed her. And it was Sebastian who was now accompanying her to Cornwall, wanting to see this quest to the end, as he'd put it. Eliza did not dare hope for more but this uncertainty made her feel uneasy as well as putting her on edge.

'May I ask you a question, Sebastian?' she said, leaning forward.

'Mmm?' he muttered from behind the newspaper.

'I am, as you know, grateful for your escort but will you not be missed? Do you not have matters to see to at your busy club?'

'Would you rather I wasn't here?' He folded back his paper and gave her a shrewd look. 'With you?'

'No, of course not.' She took a sip from her coffee cup before returning it to its saucer. 'It's only that I do not know how the Trium Impiorum will get on without you.'

'Be easy, Eliza, the club is in good hands. Dominic, Tristan and my major-domo are overseeing everything while I am away.' He sighed. 'But that's not what you are asking, is it?'

She swallowed uncomfortably. 'You must admit that…that travelling alone together is highly irregular. It's really not the done thing.'

'No, I don't suppose it is. Indeed, I was mildly surprised that you decided to travel without your maid.' Sebastian raised a brow. 'But do you care? Do you truly care what anyone might think about us?'

'No,' she said, shaking her head. 'Not at all… Well, actually, perhaps a little.'

'What is it that worries you?'

'What if someone should recognise me or you, travelling together…alone?'

'That's highly doubtful,' he drawled as he resumed reading his newspaper.

'Or perhaps recognise our names?'

'What has suddenly got you into this state?' He pushed down his paper and frowned. 'Our names? Well, then, from this moment forth we shall be known as Mr and Mrs Weston—a boring and sedate married couple. Does that suffice?'

She flushed at the idea of being *Mr and Mrs* anything with Sebastian.

'No, it does not… Mr and Mrs Weston—of all the nonsensical ideas.' She lifted her head to find him grinning at her. 'Oh, you were jesting.'

'I was.' He nodded. 'Do not worry yourself unnecessarily, Eliza. Be easy, take in the passing scenery, take a nap but whatever you do, try not to fret.'

She sighed. 'Yes, I suppose you're right.'

They fell back into silence as Eliza looked out the window, taking in the beautiful countryside and rolling hills as the train had left the dirt and grime of the city. And apart from a few short exchanges, they remained in quiet contemplation as the steam train continued its journey southwest to the coastal city of Exeter. As dusk settled, and the rain thrashed against the window with the wind howling outside, her eyes closed gradually with the monotony of the train travel lulling her to sleep.

It seemed as though it was only a moment later when Eliza woke with a jolt as a soft caress grazed across her cheek. 'Wake up, sleepyhead. We have arrived in Exeter.'

'Oh,' she said, stifling a yawn behind her gloved hand. 'We arrived far sooner than I thought.'

'Oh, yes, very swiftly done,' he muttered sardonically. 'It's only taken a mere eight hours to get to Exeter. With many hours to go until we venture further west.'

Eliza rose but could not contain another yawn, making Sebastian smile at her, shaking his head. 'Come along, Eliza, before you start dozing off again.'

They disembarked and collected their trunks but after discovering that all further trains were suspended from departing that evening, Sebastian and Eliza knew that they would need to secure overnight lodgings in Exeter.

Heavens above.

This was precisely what Eliza had been concerned about, not that she didn't trust Sebastian. It was more that she did not quite trust herself around the man than anything else. She followed him out of Exeter St David's station and waited to hail a carriage before driving through the city trying to find a hotel or inn. Yet, each and every one they stopped at had no rooms to accommodate their needs until they drove to the Half Moon Inn on the corner of High Street and Bedford Street in the centre of the city. But even here, they were full to the rafters. The only availability the Half Moon had was just one bedchamber, which Sebastian and Eliza agreed to take, otherwise even this would soon be taken by someone else as well. Which meant of course that Eliza's earlier apprehension rose to the surface again. And before Sebastian could answer the innkeeper when he asked for their names, she blurted out: 'We're Mr and Mrs Weston.'

Sebastian turned slowly towards her, his face incredulous.

'What is it?' she whispered from the side of her mouth. 'This was your idea in the first place.'

'I was jesting,' he hissed back.

'Well, I could hardly share a room with you as a single, unmarried widow! What would the innkeeper think?'

'He would think exactly the same as he does now that we're Mr and Mrs bloody Weston.'

'Well, try to be more convincing. Otherwise, I'll die of shame.'

'I'll see what I can do, *Mrs Weston*.'

'I'm glad to hear it, *Mr Weston*.'

The innkeeper showed them to their room as a young lad brought up their trunks behind them.

'I hope the room is to your satisfaction… Mr Weston?'

'Indeed it is. I thank you, and spotless, too, which is a relief as lint and dust play havoc with my wife's incessant snoring.'

Eliza raised a brow. *Oh, it was to be like this, was it?* 'Aha, what a jester you are, Mr Weston, when you know you're a veritable window-rattler yourself.'

The innkeeper looked from Sebastian to Eliza, unsure what to say. 'Well, we do pride ourselves on our rooms bein' as you say, spotless.'

'And it is, my good man. Can you please bring up a tub and some hot water for my wife to be able to bathe and a maid to help?'

'Yes, sir.' The man nodded after Sebastian placed a few more coins in his callused hands. 'And would you be wantin' an excellent dinner that ma missus of the Half Moon prepared earlier? Steak n' kidney pie and gravy with treacle puddin' n' custard for afters.'

Her stomach made a noise as Sebastian nodded at the man. 'That sounds delightful and with a bottle or two of your finest claret. On second thought, perhaps one.' He looked pointedly towards Eliza. 'Mrs Weston has been known to guzzle the claret as though it's mother's milk. And then she'll have all your patrons complaining with her warbling. Can't have that now, can we?'

The innkeeper looked down at his feet. 'Righto, sir.'

'Oh, and just before you leave,' Eliza said, smiling, 'perhaps a bath for Mr Weston, also? It would be so soothing for my husband's terrible gout.'

The innkeeper couldn't get out of the room fast enough, and he left, hastily shutting the door behind him and leaving the two of them alone in the well-appointed room, with a blazing fire in the hearth adding a welcome warmth, a large four-poster bed taking up most of the room and an armchair beside it. Sebastian leant against the small dining table with his arms crossed over his chest.

'Gout?' he muttered.

She shrugged. 'Seemed like a fair exchange since I guzzle claret like—what was it again? Oh, yes...mother's milk. So charmingly put. And apparently, I snore, too.'

'No, Mrs Weston does. I don't know whether you snore.'

'And I hardly know whether you do, either.'

But soon, they'd both find out, since they were sharing this room. And of course, they both came to that realisation at the same time as they looked away in different directions, unable to meet each other's eyes.

Eliza slumped in the armchair and started to absently tap a tattoo against the side of it.

'May I ask if there is anything wrong?' Sebastian said, watching her from under a hooded gaze.

'Wrong?' She stopped tapping and frowned. 'Of course, there is something wrong. For one, we are now stuck here in Exeter instead of being on a train heading west toward Penwith.'

He pulled away from the dining table and ambled towards her in that easy way of his before starting to remove his overcoat.

'What...what on earth are you doing?'

'Getting comfortable,' he murmured, moving past her to hang it on the coat stand. 'Any objections?'

Yes! she wanted to scream as he returned to sit on one of the dining chairs, spreading out his long legs in front of him and then crossing them at the ankles as he got *comfortable*. Well, at least one of them was.

'Not at all,' she said instead, failing to keep the irritation from her voice. 'Do as you must.'

'I hope that I'm not making you feel nervous, by any chance, Eliza.'

Again, her unadulterated response would be yes, yes, yes but she schooled her features to being as unconcerned as possible. 'Should I be?'

'Not at all.' He got up at the sound of a knock at the door. 'We are married, after all.' He raised his voice a little. 'Not now, Mrs Weston, but certainly later, unless my gout is playing up...'

Sometimes Eliza could happily throttle the man, he was that annoying. And as if he had an inkling of what was passing through her head, Sebastian winked at her before opening the door, admitting the innkeeper, who came inside the chamber along with a few servants carrying trays of food, setting them on the table. Steaming dishes of steak and kidney pie, bowls of cooked carrots, greens and mashed potatoes, as well as the promised treacle tart and custard, all of which made her tummy rumble from the delicious aromas wafting in the room. Rolls of freshly baked breads with a few knobs of butter were also placed on the table, along with not one, but two bottles of claret. Ha! And after everything Sebastian had said about her being a claret guzzler!

Sebastian declined the offers of serving them, stating that they'd see to themselves, meaning the servants left with a promise to come back later with the hot water and tub as well as a maid to help Eliza. They descended into another long silence. And were once again alone. Eliza used the time to busy herself with taking off her cloak and military-style jacket, hanging both up on the coat stand, while Sebastian removed the lids from the dishes. She sat down opposite him as he dished out food onto both their plates.

'I hope you're hungry,' he said, passing her plate back to her.

'Famished.' She placed her napkin on her lap before picking up her cutlery.

'Good. Tuck in.'

But Eliza suddenly couldn't eat even though she was holding the cutlery in her hands. Despite the fact that she hadn't eaten all day and was very hungry, she just couldn't do it. Instead, she pushed the plate away and drank the claret, enjoying the dark, fruity warmth of the drink slipping down her throat.

Sebastian lifted his head and frowned. 'What is it? I thought you said you were famished but you seem to be drinking your wine instead.'

'I don't know why I'm not able to eat,' she said.

Sebastian sighed before also putting his cutlery down as well. 'You need not worry yourself about any of these… arrangements, Eliza. Just because we're sharing this chamber doesn't mean that…anything needs to change between us. And if it puts your mind at rest, I'll sleep on the armchair while you can take the bed.'

'Thank you,' she muttered lamely, wanting to say that quite the opposite was true. That she trusted him far more than she did herself. That she would much rather he slept on the bed beside her.

'You honestly didn't expect me to insist that we share the bed, did you?'

She shook her head. 'It is fair to say that my expectations in a situation such as this are very limited indeed.'

How could she say in words that she found her attraction to him to be a highly inappropriate distraction and one that she could hardly afford?

'I wouldn't doubt it but you have nothing to fear from me.'

'I do know that, Sebastian,' she muttered, taking another sip of the delicious claret and holding out her glass for another measure. 'And by the same token, you have nothing to fear from me, either.'

Sebastian let out a bark of surprised laughter before drinking his claret and pouring some more for Eliza. 'My fear has always stemmed from your unpredictability. Otherwise, I believe I'm safe with you. Now eat.'

He thought that she was jesting with him when she was being in earnest. Eliza might be safe from him but she wasn't quite certain that he was safe from her clutches. Not when she wanted desperately to press her nose to his neck. When she wanted to kiss him again. When she itched to touch his hair, his skin...everywhere. Heavens, but where had these scandalous thoughts come from?

'That is good to know. But in all honesty, Sebastian, when I ventured to the Trium Impiorum all those weeks ago I would never have thought it within the realms of possibility that you would willingly come to the British Museum to help translate the deciphered message, let alone leave London to come to Cornwall with me.'

'Neither did I.' He shrugged as he took another bite of the pie and mash smothered in thick gravy. 'But it is perhaps time that I visited the estate that was given to me in order to settle a debt.'

'Ah, so you do not come for only my benefit but for your own as well.'

'Did I give you the impression that it was purely for yours alone?' he teased. 'After all, I do possess some curiosity about an estate that has inspired so much time and effort to claim it back. And if I like it very much and if I were the unscrupulous sort, then who knows, I might even renege on an agreement made in good faith.'

She laughed. 'Abominable behaviour if that were true, which I rather doubt, as you are not the unscrupulous sort.'

'I'm very glad you think so.' He chewed slowly before swallowing and wiping his lips with the napkin. 'And since you know that I am not to be feared, nor the unscrupulous sort, you should be at ease and eat your dinner, since you're clearly hungry.'

She did as she was told and finally started to eat the hearty food with good appetite. They descended into a comfortable, companionable silence as they devoured every last morsel. And after taking the final bite, Eliza placed her cutlery down and wiped her lips delicately before reaching for the second bottle of claret.

'I hope you're satisfied that my hunger has been satiated?'

It was clearly the wrong thing to say, as Sebastian, who was about to take another sip of claret, stilled, his eyes catching hers, clearly taken aback. His eyes seemed to smoulder then and catch a blaze momentarily as he stared at her intently before he appeared to snap out of whatever it was that had him transfixed. Eliza was not quite certain what had happened but at least she was no longer as nervous of being in this chamber with the man. It all seemed so silly now to have been apprehensive of being alone with Sebastian, when all she had to do was to resist his charms. Which she was convinced she could do, with a snap of her fingers. Eliza licked her lips and reached out for the now practically empty bottle.

'Except perhaps for this empty bottle of claret.'

'Because we have guzzled it all. I did tell the innkeeper what Mrs Weston was like.'

'You did.' She leant forward and gave him a saucy wink. 'Only because Mrs Weston hopes that by guzzling all this claret, she might not hear Mr Weston's terrible snoring.'

He smiled. 'A veritable window-rattler, I hear.'

'Indeed.' She chuckled.

'In any case, I would like to open the second bottle so that I can gain more courage, but I think I've had enough.'

'I don't quite follow.' He frowned as he lifted his eyes to hers. 'Why would you need to gain more courage? Is this still about you feeling uneasy about us sharing this chamber?'

'No, no, no,' she said dismissively, waving her hand about. It was more because she wanted to pounce on him, which of course she would not do. The thought did make her giggle a little, though, as she envisaged throwing off all caution to the wind as well as her spectacles before leaping into his arms. 'Poor Sebastian. Always so sensible, so honourable, so steadfast, so dependable. And always thinking of others.'

'You make me sound like a bore.'

'No, that would be Mr and Mrs Weston,' she said, shaking her head. 'I doubt one could ever describe you as a bore, Sebastian.'

'What a relief,' he said wryly.

'Yes. But maybe I could do with a spot more claret or perhaps we can get a bottle of brandy instead?' she mumbled. 'I'll have to ask the maid to slip some by when she comes here later. After all, Mrs Weston does have a bit of a problem.'

'It seems Mrs Weston might have something else on her mind?'

'No, no,' she muttered dismissively.

Sebastian caught her hands in his. 'What is this really about? You have been in quite a peculiar mood ever since we arrived at the Half Moon.'

'Must there be something?' she said, pulling away. 'It's not as though I can't stop thinking about kissing you again or stop thinking about what happened in Sir Horace's library that night. Because I can tell you that I haven't given any of it a second thought. And anyway, you know quite well that I am peculiar, Sebastian.'

His eyebrows shot up. 'You haven't given any of it a second thought?'

'Didn't I say so?'

'You did. But now I do feel rather guilty, Eliza.'

'Why so?'

He leant forward as though he were imparting something of great import. 'Because I on the other hand have thought about that night in Sir Horace's library many, many times.'

'Oh.' Eliza opened and closed her mouth several times before finally speaking. 'Very well, then. I've thought about that night quite often, too, if you must know.'

'You have?' He gave her a look of feigned surprise, the vexatious man. 'Quite often, eh?'

'Yes, well done, for making a bluestocking widow feel so marvellously wanted and valued from all your prodigious attentions.'

Sebastian smiled as he reached out and cupped her jaw. 'Oh, Eliza.'

'No.' She stepped back and shook her head. 'No, Sebastian, I do not need your pity just because I cannot stop thinking about that night, about kissing you and about ravishing you.'

A slow smile curled around his lips. 'You wish to ravish me?'

Oh, God, what was she doing being so indiscreet and disclosing all her secret thoughts to this man? Still, it was always better to let out the truth than to keep it all hidden, wasn't it? Taking a deep breath, Eliza held her head high. 'Did I not say so?'

'Yes.' Sebastian crossed his arms over his chest and pressed his lips together as though trying not to laugh. 'Indeed, you did but I am trying to understand all that you have said. Trying to make sense of what you are about.'

'Have I not made myself quite clear, Sebastian?'

'Yes, but allow me to understand you,' he murmured, prowling towards her with that slightly lopsided grin of his. 'You wish to seduce me?'

'Yes. No.' Her shoulders sagged as she sighed deeply. 'I'm not sophisticated enough to do that, Sebastian. Which was probably the reason I had hoped to gain a little courage with the claret.'

He raised a brow. 'I see. And what did you wish to do with that courage exactly?'

She took a shaky breath just to steady her nerves. 'There's a spot just beneath your ear that I have been wanting to press my lips against since we sat together at the British Museum. I would also like to press my nose to that spot and inhale.'

'You wish to inhale me?' he teased.

'Among other things.' She threw her arms in the air. 'I want to kiss you again and touch you all over and do so many other things that no proper lady should ever know anything about, let alone dream of doing.'

For a long moment he just stared at her, before shaking his head and swallowing. 'Well, this is all rather unexpected, to say the least.'

She exhaled. 'I think I'm a bit overcome at being alone together in the same room as you, Sebastian. I'm not very experienced at such things. You see, I find you equally if not more. A lot more...' She took a deep breath. 'I find you very desirable. But this is not good, Sebastian. You're far too much of a distraction.'

'Because you can't resist me?'

'Of course, I can resist you. I have done so the last couple of days, haven't I?'

'You do surprise me.' He raised a brow. 'And your intent on seduction has been made very clear, Eliza.'

'Oh dear, has it? Please know that I would not necessarily act on any of it. You really are quite safe from me, Sebastian.'

'Am I? You have, after all, made this extraordinary revelation on the very first night we have got to Exeter after forcing us to dissemble as the hapless Mr and Mrs Weston.' He sighed deeply, shaking his head. 'I acknowledge that I have thought about our...indiscretions in the past but now that we're alone in this bedchamber, you spring this on me? How do I know you won't just pounce on me especially since you're bent on seduction?'

She paled as she slouched in the armchair. 'Oh dear, perhaps you are right. Perhaps I'm the unscrupulous sort after all.'

Sebastian chuckled and shook his head 'Wait, wait, I'm... I'm only jesting with you, Eliza.'

Sebastian threw her a smug smile, the fiend, as he leant against the table and watched her from over the rim of his glass. 'I must say, however, that your revelation is rather enlightening. Albeit delivered in your usual blunt fashion.'

Eliza's head dropped forward and she closed her eyes. 'I didn't mean to disclose so much. It's been a heady few days, what with finding the vellum, and then translating it together at the British Museum.'

'Ah, yes, when you wanted to press your nose to that spot beneath my ear and inhale.'

'Will you stop teasing me?'

'Yes, of course, I'm sorry.'

'As am I.'

'No need.' His smile felt suddenly like an intimate caress. 'It's perfectly normal and natural to have such feelings.'

'It is?' she whispered.

'Yes,' he said softy, the teasing glint in his eyes replaced by something far more potent. Far more enigmatic. 'What if I told you that I feel exactly the same as you?'

'You do?'

His eyes raked her up and down as Eliza suddenly realised that Sebastian was also finding it difficult to keep this desire, this want and need, contained.

'Yes.' His smile turned wolfish. 'Come here, Eliza.'

'Why?'

Every scrap of his jesting and teasing had evaporated now. 'Because you cannot seduce me from the other side of the chamber. Although we shall limit this seduction to that kiss you've been thinking so much about.'

Without even realising it, Eliza had risen from the armchair and was moving towards Sebastian, still leaning against the edge of the table. 'I had no idea there could be a limit on seduction.'

Good Lord, had she actually uttered those sultry words?

'What kind of a man would I be if I were to take advantage of you, when you're still not completely sure?'

'An ordinary one.' She tilted her head to the side as she studied him. 'However, I do believe you're anything but ordinary, Sebastian.'

'Thank you,' he muttered wryly, before inclining his head. 'I do try.'

'A little too honourable, perhaps.' She shrugged.

'Is there such a thing?' He cradled the nape of her neck and started to caress her spine with the pad of his thumb in round, circular motions. 'The truth is that I want you, Eliza, very, very badly, but you need to be certain—and not require a couple of glasses of claret for courage—before you come to me.'

Oh, heavens…she took in a small intake of air before leaning into his caress. 'I… I am.'

'Are you?' he said hoarsely.

'Yes,' she murmured, trying to catch her breath.

His eyes darkened as he dipped his head and lifted her chin with his finger. 'Good, because it seems that I'm the unscrupulous sort, after all.'

And with that his lips were on hers, devouring her mouth.

Chapter Thirteen

The knock at the door made Sebastian lift his head and pull away from the woman in his arms, eliciting a groan from her. He'd forgotten about the request of a bathtub, hot water and a maid to help Eliza with her ablutions. He was tempted to tell them to go to the devil but knew that would be unfair to these hardworking souls. So with a reluctant sigh he gently removed Eliza's arms from around his neck and moved away, noting her eyes fluttering open, dazed and slightly confused.

'No, don't go,' she whispered.

He smiled before letting in the maid along with a handful of servants carrying the large basins of hot water and the bathtub. 'I shall see you after you have readied yourself for bed, my darling…er… Mrs Weston,' he murmured with that playful curve of his lips for the benefit of the servants and a heated gaze for Eliza before closing the door behind him.

He exhaled slowly through his teeth and marvelled at how this night had transpired. God, but it was an impossible situation and one that he now wanted to grasp onto with both hands, even though he knew it was best to avoid taking Eliza to his bed tonight. For despite all his assertions, it would change everything between them irrevocably. And yet, it felt as difficult to resist as it would denying himself his next lungful of air. He ran his shaky fingers through his hair as he thought of returning to the chamber. But for now, he would go to the taproom and while away his time.

Sebastian made his way back to the chamber an hour or so later after mulling everything over in his head, knowing full well that he would have to reluctantly withstand Eliza's clumsy attempts to seduce him tonight, thanks to her rather enthusiastic imbibing of the claret. Even so, he had to admit that she was vastly more endearing and adorable than if she'd been a skilled temptress. It flattered and charmed him more than he could say that she would just come out and tell him about her attraction to him. And this was what he loved about her, this innate honesty and forthrightness. She might be peculiar, as she put it, but he was endlessly amused by this quality to her character as it made her unique and interesting.

Sebastian stilled midstep.

What he loved about her...?

Damn but what an unfortunate slip. It was obviously a mistake, after a long day of travelling and the frustration of sharing only a kiss when his body still throbbed for more.

Sebastian clicked the latch of the wooden door open and walked in, closing it behind him. He glanced around the room, astounded at what was before him. For the chamber was now a perfect solace of tranquillity and serenity with the oil lamps dimmed and the fire crackling in the hearth. But far more compelling was the tableau before him of Eliza in her prim and proper night-rail, evidently asleep on the huge four-poster bed.

He stepped quietly towards her and watched for a moment as she slept, making little snoring noises, which made him smile. God, the woman was an enigma. One moment she wanted him so fiercely she was fairly shaking with need, the next she'd obviously collapsed into bed from sheer exhaustion.

With a sigh, Sebastian disrobed, peeling off all the layers of his clothing, washed and used his tooth powder and brush before changing into a loose-fitting cambric sleeping suit. He wore the shirt part as well, despite usually discarding this when he was in his own bed. The last thing he needed was to give Eliza a fit of the vapours from his nakedness, although from his experience of her so far, one never knew how the woman would actually react!

Sebastian got into bed and closed his eyes. As long as he could pretend that Eliza was not in the same bed, then perhaps he might have a small chance of getting some much-needed sleep. Which, of course, proved rather futile as it seemed only a short while later that a small, narrow beam of light poured through the small gap between the curtains, causing Sebastian to wake and feel a solid body pressed against his back and a woman's arm loosely slipped over his waist. Eliza had obviously moved in her sleep and nestled herself against his back, which meant of course that he was suddenly very aware of her soft curves, with only a handful of scant clothing, rather than the many usual layers, separating them. A bolt of lust coursed through him.

He exhaled a shaky breath as he felt himself harden. What on earth was the woman trying to do to him? Kill him on the spot? He was just a red-blooded male, not a saint. Very carefully, he removed Eliza's arm from his person and shuffled along until he reached the edge of the bed, so that his back was no longer touching her front. But just as quickly as he'd untangled himself from her, she moved in small increments until she was once again pressed right up against him.

Dear God, what new hell was this? Sebastian could either endure this ordeal and make sure he kept his hands firmly to himself, or he could try to move her back to her side of the bed and likely wake Eliza in the process. Or he could quietly remove himself from the bed altogether and still possibly wake Eliza! He could feel her soft, breathy snores against his back, making him smile despite this awkward predicament. *How very like Mrs Weston...*

In the end he elected to stay put and live through it, hoping that Eliza might eventually roll back to her side of the bed, instead of attaching herself to him.

And yet, she did not move again, remaining stuck to Sebastian like glue as he closed his eyes for a short time only, knowing it wouldn't be long until he'd need to get up.

He woke up again some hours later when he felt Eliza stirring behind him.

'Oh,' she eventually said in a rather muffled voice. 'Oh... oh dear, I seem to have moved across the bed so much that I've grossly invaded your privacy, Sebastian.'

'And a good morning to you, Eliza.' He smiled inwardly as he slowly turned around to lie on his back. 'And yes, it seems that you have.'

'Yes, good morning.' She shot upright into a sitting position next to him, pulling the coverlet up to conceal her form, despite the fact she was wearing that hideous night-rail, which covered every inch of her. 'Oh, Lord, and after I promised that you'd be safe from me...'

'Just as I promised that I'd sleep on the armchair.'

'Which was never necessary as this bed is big enough for the both of us. That is, if I'd remembered to behave with more decorum. I am sorry, Sebastian.'

'For what, exactly?'

'For everything,' she muttered, rubbing her fingertips against her forehead in that familiar way of hers. 'For my indiscretions last night, for practically throwing myself at you and for using you as a human coverlet. I have never behaved in such a brazen and wanton manner before.'

'Yes, you did rather paste yourself to me.' He couldn't help but tease her a little. 'Perhaps you were on the hunt for the sweet spot beneath my ear.'

'Oh, God, I forgot about *that*.' Eliza covered her face in her hands. 'I'm dying of shame. How utterly mortifying.'

'Again, I'm jesting, Eliza. And evidently doing it quite poorly.' He reached out and prised her fingers away from her face and dropped a kiss to the top of each hand. 'Besides, I'm rather fond of your newly acquired brazen and wanton manner.'

'Oh, stop. I embarrassed myself terribly last night.'

'Did you?' he drawled. 'I had not noticed.'

'How can you be so understanding?'

'Easily.' He put one hand behind his head. 'You forget the many things that I also disclosed to you last night.'

She flushed pink in the small area of exposed skin at the top of the frilly collar of her night-rail, the colour spreading up her neck and into her face. 'No, I haven't forgotten.'

'And neither have I, Eliza.' Sebastian laced his fingers together with hers. 'Let's not worry about any of that.'

'What should we worry about, then?'

'At this moment, I cannot think of a single thing.' He caressed the soft skin of her wrist before pressing his thumb across her vein and feeling her pulse quicken. He took a deep breath. 'Instead, we could consider carrying on where we left off?'

This close he could see her take a small intake of breath. 'And where...where is that?'

'That is up to you to decide, Eliza.' He bent his elbow and placed his other hand beneath his head as well. 'You see, I have had ample time to consider your forthright declaration about all the many things you'd like to do to me and find that I am amenable to them all.'

'I see.'

'So, you may continue your pursuit to seduce and ravish me at your leisure.'

'Well, this is an interesting development,' she said breathlessly. 'Especially since I had thought to stop being so brazen and wanton.'

'I'd rather you didn't.' He grinned up at her. 'But the choice is entirely yours, Eliza.'

She stared down at him for a long moment as she deliberated over all that he had said, while he did not move an inch. Eventually, Eliza reached over and brushed her thumb across his lower lip, backwards and forwards and still he did not move, knowing that he would stay true to his word. It was Eliza's decision in terms of what would happen next. As he'd said last night, Sebastian wanted her desperately but it was meaningless if she did not fully embrace the desire she felt for him as well. In that, Eliza had to claim it for herself without being swayed either way by him.

She bent her head and pressed a quick, hard tentative kiss to his lips before swiftly sitting up again, as though she was testing the shape of his lips. She did it again, her eyes dropping to his mouth, taking a big gulp of air into her lungs. She kissed him once more but this time lingered longer, her breath warm as she licked into the corner of his mouth. And still, Sebastian did not move, his hands clasped tightly together beneath his head.

Eliza moved closer and tangled her tongue with his. He groaned as she slanted her mouth across his and kissed him again and again, getting bolder and more demanding. This was what he'd hoped that she would do. Unleash the passion that had always been there, but that she'd locked up inside herself. He'd tasted it before and knew her to be a far more sensual creature then she believed. But this was something she needed to discover for herself. She had to realise that desire was not shameful or embarrassing but natural and wondrous. Or rather it could be...

Sebastian buried his hands into the pillow beneath his head, so that he might refrain from touching her. Not yet, not yet... even though it was killing him that he wasn't allowing himself to take her into his arms.

Eliza pulled away from his mouth and dropped kisses slowly and assiduously all over his face, jaw and down his neck.

'Is that the spot that you've been searching for?' he murmured. 'Is that where you'd like to inhale me?'

'Yes, yes, yes,' she whispered as she rubbed the tip of her nose on that spot beneath his ear before licking and nipping his skin. She moved her way down his neck again, making him exhale through his teeth. 'Your scent here makes me weak at the knees.'

God, she was killing him...

Eliza pulled away to sit up and started to undo the buttons of his shirt, her eyes glazed, her pale blond hair mussed. Had she ever looked more alluring, more beautiful, more enticing? No...not to him. He thought at that moment that she was the most beautiful woman he'd ever known. And once she had undone the last button, her eyes snapped to his. Taking a shaky breath, Eliza drew aside the opening of the shirt to reveal his naked form. She grazed her fingers and nails across his chest and abdomen, so slowly as though she were putting to memory the shape of him. Sebastian hissed as Eliza lowered her head and kissed, licked and nipped his exposed skin, following the trail that her fingers left as she explored him so excruciatingly slowly, he thought he might howl from both excitement and frustration.

He panted as Eliza then lowered herself to lie across him, her face just inches away from his own, and smiled. 'Do you not want to touch me now?'

'More than anything,' he rasped. 'But knowing how you're such a stickler for good manners, I thought to preserve the right of courtesy for ladies going first.'

'Very commendable as well as thoughtful of you, Sebastian.'

'I'd like to think so,' he drawled as he finally pulled his hands free from beneath his head and slipped an arm around her waist, letting his hand move up and down her spine. He needed this damn thick cotton night-rail gone but once again, that would be Eliza's decision.

As if she were reading his mind, Eliza sat back on her knees, keeping her eyes locked on to his. She took a few shaky breaths, her chest rising and falling rapidly as she unbuttoned the mother of pearl buttons that ran from her neckline all the way down to the lace-front yoke. Sebastian's eyes dropped to the exposed skin where the material gaped open, and before he knew what she would do next, Eliza pulled each arm free from the long, billowing sleeves of the night-rail and pulled the garment over her head before throwing it on the floor.

He stared at her, his jaw dropping as he took in Eliza sitting beside him in bed, with just a sheer cotton chemise and a half corset, all of which left very little to the imagination. The woman was all lush curves, long, shapely limbs and soft, soft skin. She was the most sensual creature he'd ever encountered and she was his. At least for now…

She helped Sebastian remove his shirt altogether before climbing over him and straddling him, making him feel every part of her glorious body.

Dear God…

Sebastian cradled her head and pulled her down for a fierce hungry kiss with his free hand as Eliza threaded her fingers into his hair, gripping him tightly and kissing him back with just as much intensity and fervour. She seemed to want and need him with the same fierce desperation as he did her.

He kissed her slowly, tasting her deeply, before holding on to her waist and swiftly flipping them both around so that he was now on top and he had her beneath him. Damn, but he could no longer resist the woman. His fingers skimmed down her front, undoing the laces of the half corset quickly and discarding it. He cupped her small, pert breast in his hand through the sheer cotton chemise and bent his head to lick the underside of her breast, before taking her erect nipple into his mouth and sucking it, making her moan and arch her back. Eliza pushed to sit up and gently swatted his hands away, giving him a coy look before pulling her chemise over her head and throwing it on the floor to join the rest of their garments.

He took in a shaky breath as he looked his fill of Eliza in her glorious nakedness. Damn but she was so adorable if not a little vulnerable as she held her head up and held his gaze, his captivating bluestocking.

'You're beautiful,' he murmured, sinking his fingers into the pale golden hair tumbling down her back.

'As are you, Sebastian,' she said softly, leaning forward to cup his jaw. 'I have never known anyone quite like you.'

He turned his head and kissed the palm of her hand. 'And I have never known anyone quite like you, either.'

They were simple words, honest and true, but in that single moment in time they encapsulated something momentous and significant, something far more powerful than Sebastian could hope to understand…but he would reflect on it later. For now was the time for something else altogether. It was time to feel, to explore, to cherish and to worship…all that surfeit of emotion that they had once spoken of.

He lifted her over him so that she now sat on his lap and smiled at her, kissing her neck, catching her earlobe between his teeth. As his hands roamed over her shoulders and back through the thick strands of her hair.

'Mmm, I want to see whether I can also find the spot, the very spot that had you in raptures.' He nipped and sucked on the long, pulsating vein that ran down her throat.

'But that spot may be quite...quite different to yours.'

'True.' He pulled away and gave her a wicked smile, marvelling at how Eliza could make such an incredibly brazen comment quite unknowingly. She seemed to have no idea of the double entendre she'd made, which delighted him more than he could say. 'Perhaps I should go in search of it.'

'Oh, but that's not what I meant.'

'I know,' he murmured, gently pushing her back down so that she was lying on the bed again. 'I have become quite good at unravelling your clues and trying to decipher their meanings.'

'Is that so?' she hissed as he ran his hand from the base of her neck all the way down, taking in every curve and dip of her body, skimming her breast and alighting on to the softness of her stomach.

'Yes,' he whispered. 'I have it on good authority that if I were to find what I am looking for then it might unlock many secrets that I have been seeking.'

'Then you should certainly proceed with your search.'

'I intend to.' He lifted her arm and dropped kisses on each finger moving to the palm of her hand, and the delicate soft spot on her wrist. 'No, not quite here.'

He grazed his teeth along her arm, across her shoulders and chest and moved lower, nuzzling his way to her breast, kissing, nipping and licking her. 'Let me see... Could this be the spot?'

'I cannot... I cannot tell.' Her voice was barely audible.

'Then I must ascertain it myself.' He smiled against her skin, before continuing to kiss his way down her body, kissing her stomach, swirling his tongue inside her belly button. 'Mmm, it is not here, either.'

His fingers caressed her body with his mouth, teeth and tongue following the trail left by his hands, before taking hold of her leg, and kissing his way down to the arches of her feet, her ankles, and then moving back up again. He licked into the delicate skin behind her knee and watched as Eliza moaned, thrashing her head from side to side.

'Almost but not quite here, either.'

He flicked his eyes to hers, watching them glitter and darken as he pressed a kiss on the inside of her thigh. 'I feel I am getting close now.'

He turned his head and pressed his face between her thighs, kissing and nipping that sensitive skin there as she arched her back.

'I believe I have found the spot,' he murmured as he gently pulled her legs apart even more and buried his head between her thighs before worshipping her there, making Eliza buckle and scream his name.

Sebastian wanted Eliza to lose herself to this desire. He'd known all along that she possessed a wild intensity and wanted to unleash the passion that he doubted she was even aware of and yet was there, hidden deep inside her very soul. And he wanted it. He wanted it desperately for himself.

Chapter Fourteen

Eliza could not quite comprehend what was happening. What in heavens was Sebastian doing to her? It was as though she had no control over her body as he elicited the most extraordinary sensations again and again and again from her. Every touch, every kiss, every caress, was felt deeply in every part of her. And now he was kissing her, using his mouth, teeth and tongue in the most scandalous way.

Heavens above…

She had no notion that it could ever feel like this and thought she might die if he stopped doing all the clever things he was doing. It was all becoming too much to bear. Far too much…

Eliza moaned and whimpered as she lost herself more and more to this…this forbidden pleasure. It built to a crescendo inside her, before she suddenly screamed, thrashing her head from side to side as she came completely undone.

Her breathing was rasping and coming in spurts as her eyes fluttered open, to find Sebastian now above her, his lips curling into a wide smile. Eliza reached out and placed her hand on his jaw, caressing his face.

'Oh my, that was…incredible.' She took a moment to exhale. 'But I want you. I want all of you, Sebastian.'

She watched as his eyes darkened. 'Are you certain?'

'More than anything.'

Sebastian got off the bed and disrobed completely before returning to bed and moving back into Eliza's waiting arms. His gorgeously strong and agile body covered hers as he placed himself in between her legs. He dipped his head and caught her mouth with his, kissing her hard as he supported himself on those huge arms bent on either side of her. He lifted his head and pinned her with his glittering gaze, making her feel breathless before he entered her body in one long thrust.

Eliza gasped loud as he filled her completely, making her clench tightly around him and closing her eyes as she arched her back instinctively.

'Open your eyes, Eliza,' he demanded. 'Look at me, sweetheart. I want to see you. I want to see every little thing in your eyes.'

She opened her eyes but was unable to utter a word, never taking her eyes off him as his movements became relentless, quickening the pace with his thrusts. Eliza melted into him with the heady push and pull of their bodies coming together as one. Sebastian rolled them both to one side before flipping them over so that once again he was beneath Eliza and she was straddling him on top. He continued to move inside her as she whimpered and embraced this new perspective from above, liking being in control. She smiled at him—this beautiful man who had desired her, liked her and wanted her as much as she desired, liked and wanted him. They seemed to be two halves of the same coin completing one another in a way she'd never thought possible before—not like this. Not for her... Even in this, he was saying wordlessly that together they were equally matched. It made her feel adored; it made her feel empowered. And it made her feel so much for him that she could burst into joy at this exquisite moment that was theirs.

He had wanted her to come to him with a clarity, so that she was certain she knew what she was embarking on. And now... Now Eliza finally understood what he had meant. Because this was no quick fumble in the dark. This was something else entirely. Something far more potent that needed her to go into it with her eyes wide open.

Sebastian sat up, wrapped his arms around her and held on to her tightly, taking her mouth in another long, drugging kiss. He increased the pace, penetrating her so deeply that she knew she could not hang on for much longer.

Eliza screamed his name over and over again as she shattered into a thousand tiny pieces, just before Sebastian pulled away from her body and found his release on the bed.

The peace she'd found as she lay in Sebastian's arms was unlike anything Eliza had ever felt before. In truth, nothing that morning was quite like anything she'd ever experienced. It was as though everything that she had once believed and accepted could be possible in a relationship between a man and woman was now replaced by this unfettered newness. Which was something far better, stronger, meaningful and beautiful. Something quite unquantifiable, that she could not put a name to. A word that she could not yet ascribe to this feeling, which nevertheless made her head spin. And it was all because of *him*... Sebastian Marsden. The last man she'd ever have believed she could have such feelings for. And yet, she did...

'Are you well, Eliza?'

'Perfectly so,' she said on a yawn. 'And you?'

'Never better. Go back to sleep,' he murmured. 'It's still quite early.'

'But what of catching the next train? What of getting to Penwith?'

'There's no rush. We can get the next one.' He bent down to kiss her forehead. 'Sleep, love.'

Love?

But of course. That was the elusive word that she sought. The one that matched how she felt about Sebastian Marsden. It was love...she was in love with him. But how could it be true? Could she trust her own judgement when she had erred so badly before with Ritton, when she had also believed herself to care for him? Was it all too soon in any case, to believe that this feeling was actually that profound emotion rather than a momentary sensation of gratification after what had just occurred in this bed? A glorious sensation that would soon pass, in any case. Only time would tell and with these uneasy thoughts running through her head, Eliza drifted off to sleep cocooned in Sebastian's arms.

The next time Eliza opened her eyes, it was to find Sebastian with a towel wrapped around the lower half of his body, secured around his hips. The sight of him with wet hair, evidently after he'd bathed, and peering out the window, made her heart clench tightly. God, he was a magnificent-looking man. In the daylight she could feast her eyes on his taut, rugged body, all sinewy muscle and long, powerful limbs. And to think this was the man with whom she had lain, who had given her the most unimaginably exquisite pleasure. And to whom she had given herself so completely—Sebastian Marsden. A man who was a contradiction in every sense. One who was scandalous and apparently ruthless and hard but just as equally kind, generous and thoughtful, even though he found it difficult to trust or allow anyone to get close to him. Just as she did. This made him flawed in a way that made him real and human. And it was this that she was drawn to. This human and very real side to the man.

Sebastian turned away from the window and caught her staring at him. Their gazes locked and for a long moment all she could do was just stare into those fathomless dark grey eyes. Even from a short distance the intensity and smoulder felt like it could engulf her whole. He pushed away from the wall that he was leaning against and prowled towards her with a smile that promised all manner of scandalous pursuits. A smile that was nevertheless achingly tender, making her feel breathless and a little dazed.

The soft mattress sank down as he sat on the edge of the bed, pressing his lips to hers softly in a long, lingering kiss.

'Good morning,' he murmured, running his fingers through her hair. 'Again.'

'Good morning.' She pulled the coverlet up, concealing herself, suddenly feeling a little shy. 'Again.'

'I hope you're hungry as I have ordered a hearty breakfast to be brought up.'

'I am, thank you.' She frowned a little. 'But should we not make haste to get to the next train heading west?'

'I have already made enquiries, Eliza,' he said, playing absently with a lock of her hair, curling it around his finger. 'The trains have been cancelled this morning due to the inclement weather so there is really no need to rush anywhere. We can get the next train later on in the day.'

'Oh, I see.' She raised a brow and gave him a small smile from beneath her lashes. 'But what will we do to amuse ourselves?'

'I can think of a few things.' He winked before bending down and catching her lips with his, devouring her mouth. Eliza slipped her arms around his neck and pulled him down on the bed with her, as someone knocked on the door.

Sebastian lifted his head and threw her an impish grin. 'Do not go anywhere. I shall be back in just a moment.'

'Make sure that you are.'

Goodness, who was this wanton, sultry woman that she had become? Eliza barely recognised herself anymore. She watched as Sebastian rose, threw on his shirt and long robe, and ambled across the room to open the door to a couple of servants carrying trays of food and tea for them to break their fast. They set the trays on the table before leaving the room, just as Eliza got out of bed and walked towards the veritable feast.

'Did I not ask you to stay abed, Eliza?'

She shrugged. 'You're familiar with what I'm like, Sebastian, and know that I'm not very good at taking instruction or doing as I'm told.'

'Quite. I'm exceedingly familiar with you, love.' He smirked as he approached her from behind and wrapped his arms around her waist. 'And I have never met with a more exasperating woman than you, Mrs Weston.'

'You...you wretch, Mr Weston.' She feigned mock outrage at his not so loverlike words as he laughed, pressing a kiss to the side of her neck. 'Here I thought you were the most wonderful man in every possible manner, yet you disparage me so abominably.'

'Shocking behaviour,' he murmured as he kissed her along

the length of her neck. 'It's just as well, then, that I like you as much as I do.'

Her breath hitched at his admission. One that Eliza was certain he hadn't especially wanted to make, judging by how he'd just stilled behind her, his arms that held her to him, slackening. Sebastian had also once again called her *love*. Had he realised this, too? What did it all mean? Eliza stepped out of his embrace and poured tea into two cups before turning around and offering one to Sebastian.

'I like you very much, too.' She smiled, hoping that this would dispel the sudden tension in the room. 'Very well indeed. In fact I... I.'

I feel an emotion far greater than mere like.

'In fact you...?' he repeated.

I love you... Eliza had already realised the truth of her errant feelings but before she embarrassed herself more, she tried to think of something else to say.

'In fact, I am enjoying our time together greatly, Sebastian,' she said lamely, knowing that it was as though she were describing a society function rather than their far more scandalous diversion. 'I'm glad you came with me to Cornwall.'

'As am I,' he said. 'But you make it sound as though there is a limit to our time together.'

'Ah, but you said yourself that there was a limit to seduction.'

'Indeed, but perhaps I was wrong.'

She shrugged. 'If you say so.'

'Oh, believe me.' He gave her a heated look. 'I do.'

Eliza gave him a small smile, which he returned before they sat down and filled their plates with eggs, slices of ham, toasted bread and local Devon butter. The silence between them stretched as they ate and pondered on everything that had occurred between them since they had arrived at the Half Moon. It was not easy being in such close proximity with him in this chamber with all of this tumult of emotion that she had to prise apart and decipher, hoping to understand it all. Eliza could do with being alone, even for a short moment or two just to think about her feelings for Sebastian and all the implications. Yet, at the same time, she could not bear to be anywhere but in this room…with Sebastian.

'You're doing it again, Eliza.'

She lifted her head and frowned. 'Doing what?'

'Pushing your food around when you're clearly hungry. You seem to do that whenever you're agitated, or thinking of something or other.'

'It does seem that I cannot do more than one thing at a time,' she admitted wryly.

'May I ask if anything is the matter?'

Yes. What do I do when all of this is over? When we get back from this visit to Trebarr Castle? What happens to this newly found attachment between us? But more importantly, what do I do with all of these feelings that I have for you when you have said in the past that you do not believe in love?

Eliza had always been so vigilant to shield herself from hurt, building walls to protect her bruised and battered heart only to have those walls smashed to pieces with her heart now belonging to Sebastian, anyway. And without the man even knowing…unless she told him now. Yet, she felt exposed, vulnerable, unwilling to put herself in a position that might end in heartache and disappointment. She couldn't do it…not yet, anyway. And might he not think that she was trying to manipulate him and use this tentative attachment between them as a way to get around the debt that she owed him? God, it made her feel wretched contemplating all of that.

'I wondered what would happen if I…if I were unable to pay back Ritton's debt?'

Eliza had always had a terrible knack for blurting things out without always thinking them through. It was something that had always managed to get her into so much trouble in the past. And with that one question she'd suddenly made everything that she had shared in this room with Sebastian feel a little sordid and wrong…when in truth it was quite the opposite.

He gave her an implacable look. 'Is that what has really been worrying you, Eliza?'

'No, yes… I do not know.' She sighed, shaking her head. 'I just do not know what to do with any of it.'

'Any of what?'

'These feelings that I have for you.' She made herself look up and meet his implacable gaze. 'This surfeit of emotion between us.'

Sebastian did not say anything for a long moment, watching her from over his cup of tea before he sighed, his eyes softening. 'Must you do something about it? Now?'

'I would like to know...' She took in a deep breath before continuing. 'I would just like to know how things stand between us, after everything we have shared. After last night and also this morning.'

'I do not know the answer to that myself, Eliza, except to say that my feelings for you are unlike anything I've ever known before. I have nothing to compare to it.'

Her heart made an erratic beat. 'You don't?'

He smiled and shook his head. 'No. And it scares me as much as it clearly scares you. But I want to see what happens and where it takes us.'

'As do I.' She realised then that this would be enough. It was enough that Sebastian felt this much for her. She would follow him anywhere and see where it would take them. Eliza would rather have this honesty from him than any declarations that were untrue. But dear God, it scared her as it evidently did him. Something that neither of them had ever expected.

He reached for her, cupping her jaw and brushing the pad of his thumb along her cheek. 'Even so, I want you to know that I care deeply for you and would have no more talk of the debt that Ritton owed me. You, Eliza, have never truly owed me anything. Now eat.'

Sebastian might believe that now but would he always think that? Because in truth she owed him far more then he could ever know. And because of that Eliza knew that she had to find the treasure. Otherwise, the Bawden-Trebarr estate and Ritton's debt would always come between them.

Sebastian had been on the brink of telling Eliza what he truly felt—that not only did he feel deeply for her but that he was falling in love, an emotion that only a few weeks ago he would have laughed at and dismissed. How had everything changed so much in such a short time? It seemed so improbable, inexplicable and frankly unbelievable and yet it was true.

And yes, it made his head spin, scaring the hell out of him. He did not know what to do about any of it…not yet. All he knew was that he wanted Eliza. He wanted her ardently and with a passion that he could not quite comprehend himself. But he would… He would find a way through this so that he could keep her in his life somehow.

Eliza rose and held out her hand to him before taking him wordlessly back to bed where once again they made love. This time it was achingly slow and languid and tender as every exploration, every touch, every kiss, was heightened before they succumbed to the heady insatiable desire burning between them. Afterwards, when they were sated and replete, their bodies tangled together, they just held each other. Held each other in the quiet solitude while the rain thrashed against the windowpane outside.

Sebastian pulled the edge of the coverlet over them and tucked his hand beneath his head and wondered whether he'd ever felt this sanguine…this content.

No, never.

'What are you thinking?' Eliza turned her head and pressed a quick kiss on his chest before nestling against his shoulder.

'Ah, so now you wish to know my every thought as well?' he teased.

'No, keep them. I was just being curious as always.'

'But I like your curiosity and how you're intrigued by the world around you.'

'Do you now, Mr Weston? It seems that you are quite captivated by me.'

'It seems that I am.' He smiled as he dropped a kiss on top of her head. 'Have you always been so curious, then, about everything around you?'

'You mean, have I always been a bluestocking?' she murmured. 'Yes, I suppose I have. As a child I was always in a rush to learn more, to discover and to read as much as I could and I never changed the older I got. I always wanted to find out about anything that I did not quite understand, even in areas of academia that were deemed unsuitable for a young and impressionable woman, much to my father's dismay.'

'He did not approve?'

'No, he was incandescent with his censure and disapproval of me. That was why he forbade me from attending Oxford, even though I managed to pass the entrance examination. It had been a dream of both Cecy's and mine, ever since we met at Ravendean's School for Young Ladies many, many years ago as girls. But my father had other plans for me, and pushed for an alliance between Viscount Ritton and myself while Cecy... Cecy attended Oxford without me.'

'I'm sorry, Eliza. That must have been very disheartening.'

'It was.' She shrugged. 'But there was no point clinging onto the past and what could have been, so I made the best of what I had, which in fairness was very little.'

'I'm sure that was difficult,' Sebastian said as he absently threaded his fingers through her hair. 'You must have had regrets.'

'Too many but to no avail,' she said sadly. 'We must do what we can to move forward in life and live with what fate throws at us.'

This was something that Sebastian knew he did frequently—cling onto the past until it became fetid, seeping into his very soul. 'I know but with the best will in the world, however, it's not always easy.'

'No, it's not.' She paused a moment before continuing. 'Just as it must have been difficult for you when your life changed irrevocably.'

No, it had never been easy and at times Sebastian felt the darkness would consume him, but eventually he'd learned to let go of so much that once had him shackled to his past. Yet, some of it would always remain. Always...

'My father's death changed everything irrevocably, as you said, and for so long it was difficult to accept the truth of that.'

'I can understand that you did something far greater, Sebastian. You survived and made something of yourself despite it all.'

'I had no choice in the matter. And after my mother's death, my brothers and I were completely on our own.'

'That could not have been easy.'

'It wasn't,' he said bitterly. 'She was a gentle, kind-hearted soul and she was crushed after my father's death.'

This was not quite what Sebastian had thought they would be discussing in the aftermath of intimacies with Eliza, and yet, he was doing so, anyway. There was a rightness about sharing his feelings with her about that terrible time, when he'd never acknowledged them to himself let alone anyone else. But then Eliza Bawden-Trebarr was not just anyone.

'I'm so sorry.' She cupped his jaw, caressing his face. 'Was it long afterwards that you started the Trium Impiorum?'

'Not exactly. The money that we had ran out soon after my mother died, so I did all manner of jobs to keep us from ending up in the workhouse. From working in a Thames shipping yard, to working as a tosher, just to put food on the table and be able to pay for the roof over our heads. Eventually, I found a job as a clerk in a solicitor's firm, which brought in a steady income. But it was all a million miles away from what I had been destined for—becoming an earl,' he said with a shake of his head. 'Dominic and Tristan also worked once they were old enough, although, I made sure to get tutors for Tristan when funds allowed since he showed an interest in more scholarly pursuits, and he eventually went to Cambridge.'

'Oh, Sebastian, you really are the very best of brothers.'

'Tell that to Dom and Tristan.' He snorted. 'Anyway, it was hard, it was gruelling, actually, but we did it.'

'And so, you eventually saved the funds to be able to buy the gaming club?'

'Not quite. My father had made provisions for my mother and my two younger brothers, should anything happen to him. Provisions that were unentailed from the Harbury estate. However, my uncle Jasper, who became the Earl of Harbury after my father's death, contested this, too, and it took years to resolve. By then my mother had been dead for a number of years and we had all but forgotten our old lives. So, you can imagine our surprise when we found that we were actually due the unentailed portion after all, despite everything my uncle had done to prevent that eventuality. And with the money safely in our pockets we stuck up the proverbial two fingers at him and all the rest of the aristocracy by opening the Trium Impiorum.'

'And thank God for it.'

'Indeed. It's still going from strength to strength.'

Eliza turned her head and pressed a kiss to his chest. 'You should be rightly proud of your achievements.'

'I am but I can never forget the way it all came about. I can never forget that it was from that moment after my father died. And try as I might, I cannot get away from how it has made me feel so damn resentful.'

'I understand, Sebastian, but how could you resent the life that had been yours for the taking, when it was not your fault that you were forced to make it into something else?'

'Because it had all been a lie,' he said on a sigh. 'Everything to do with my father and his lofty Harbury title had been a lie. Everything. It was as though my brothers and I were given the key to the kingdom and told that all its riches were ours to take, and just when we reached out to claim it, it was all snatched away. And then to make matters worse, we had to endure the shame and disgrace of my father's sins—most of all my mother, who gave up on life altogether after her whole world shattered. And I was too young to do anything about it.'

'I'm so sorry,' she muttered, lifting her head and supporting it with her bent arm. 'But your father's sins, although terrible and painful, were, I dare say, never intentional. I doubt he ever meant for any of you to suffer in the way you did.'

'What difference does that make, Eliza? We suffered, anyway,' he said bitterly.

'It makes all the difference,' she said, gently laying her hand on his chest, over his beating heart. 'Don't you see that your father was a man who unintentionally hurt his family with a terrible mistake that he'd made? I doubt he'd ever wanted that to happen.'

'No, of course he didn't.'

'Because he must have loved you all so much,' she murmured, brushing her fingers across his chest. 'And somewhere deep down inside you have always known that, Sebastian.'

'What?' His brows furrowed in the middle as he flicked his gaze at her. 'What do you mean?'

'Think on it, Sebastian. Why else would you keep on your person a jewelled dagger that your father once gifted you, which, while practical, could have fetched you a pretty penny when you were so desperate for funds?' Before he could respond she continued with her bold assessment. 'And why would you use the sums from the money he left you and your brothers to create The Trium Impiorum, even if you believed he might have disapproved of it—which you have really no idea of knowing, by the by. Your father might even have approved of what you and your brothers did, after the manner in which you lost the Harbury estate and were made to accept the ignominy of being declared illegitimate.'

Sebastian blinked in surprise. How could this woman know any of this when she had no prior knowledge of who his father was? And yet... And yet, what Eliza had said somehow resonated with him, and was far closer to the type of man his father had been than the one Sebastian had inadvertently fabricated in his head so that he could throw all his frustration and his resentment at it. It was as though he had forgotten. Or perhaps chosen to forget who his father was because he couldn't bear thinking about the past. Because in truth, his father *had* loved them, all of them, and would never knowingly have subjected his wife and his sons to the pain and hardship that they had endured after his death.

He suddenly remembered more as memories of that time came flooding back. His mother's complete devotion to his father's memory even after the revelation that he'd been a bigamist had been astounding. As well as how she would never allow Sebastian or his brothers to disparage their father in front of her. Perhaps Eliza, with her usual astuteness, had been right. Perhaps his mother had died of a broken heart. Perhaps his mother would have given up on life, anyway, because she missed her husband terribly after his death. In the aftermath of their spectacular fall from grace, she had been subdued, and Sebastian had always thought it was because of the shame she had felt. But their mother had been made of hardier stuff than that. She wouldn't have cared what people said; she would have held her head up and behaved with her usual grace. It must have been that she was suffering from the unbearable pain of losing her husband, someone she'd loved so desperately. And when she'd caught a fever in that terrible winter, she had just faded away…

Sebastian turned and kissed Eliza on her head. 'How is it that you can see things in such a singular manner?'

She looked surprised. 'I cannot say.'

'I can. You're simply a marvel, Eliza.'

Perhaps that was one of the many things he loved about the woman. She constantly surprised him with her forthright and passionate manner. Indeed, Sebastian had realised this about Eliza from their first encounter—that she was unlike anyone he'd ever met before. Perhaps he'd sensed it from all the letters she'd bombarded him with before demanding that he meet her, and why he'd sat purposely in such darkness the first time she had come to the club unannounced. To try to intimidate her, to try to scare her into leaving him alone. But she'd seen through all of that in her no-nonsense manner. She'd seen through his darkness and she had seen…*him*. And it was this that had intrigued Sebastian. He had been drawn to the light she seemed to carry in her very soul. And as he lay next to her, he realised with unease that he always would.

Chapter Fifteen

By nightfall, Sebastian and Eliza had caught the later train to Penwith, in Cornwall, and had hired a carriage from the station that would take them to the Trebarr estate. With the journey from the station eventually taking them off the main roads to pathways that gained them access into the rugged and wild terrain of this part of Cornwall. As the carriage trundled along, Eliza sat at the edge of the seat waiting for that first glimpse of the incredible ruins of Trebarr Castle with bated breath, unable to contain her excitement.

And then suddenly, as they turned a corner and drove past a wooded thicket, the clearing opened up to reveal the beautiful old ruins bathed by the moonlight casting shadows and light all around it. Eliza sucked in her breath and asked to stop the carriage. She climbed down and raced across to the castle ruins with Sebastian following in pursuit behind, calling her name.

God above, but she had been waiting so long to set eyes on this place again. It had been too long. Far too long since she had been here as a little girl clutching onto her parents' hands as they explained the importance of it to her.

'It's just as magnificent as I remember,' she murmured once Sebastian caught up with her. 'Perhaps even more so.'

Sebastian looked around the huge area and nodded, catching her hands into his. 'Yes...yes, it is.'

'Over there is the main castle keep where they would have had the main solar chambers and where the lord and lady—Simon and Elowen—had their living quarters.' She pointed at the large building made from local stone. 'And that there on the raised plinth would have been the Great Hall where they would have enjoyed many banquets and celebrations. It's actually very well preserved if you would like to have a look?'

'Shall we not return in the morning when we might see everything better? I would hate for you to slip on one of those cracked steps and fall and hurt yourself, Eliza.'

It was far more prudent to come back in the morning light but Eliza just could not wait to have a look around. 'I will be fine, I promise.'

'Very well, then, in that case, wait right here while I go and fetch the oil lamps from the carriage to help light the way.'

Sebastian climbed over the boulder and back onto the pathway to the carriage before returning with a couple of hand-held oil lamps in bevelled glass from the carriage, pressing one into Eliza's hand, who had for once done as she was requested and waited for him with a huge smile.

'Show the way, my lady.'

They walked hand in hand, holding up their respective oil lamps as they climbed the stairs leading to the Great Hall. Eliza pushed the ancient wooden door open with a creak and they were plunged into further darkness apart from the light provided by the oil lamps, which they shone around the chamber trying to see the old hall.

'Incredibly, the roof stands but it looks as though it would need some repair.' Sebastian nodded up above while holding out the oil lamp.

'The repairs should certainly be made on what is otherwise an excellent example of a hammerbeam roof, which is actually older than the one at Hampton Court Palace.'

'Interesting.'

'As the current owner of this estate I'm glad you think so.'

She moved towards the faded muralled wall. 'Beautiful… Look, Sebastian, can you see what is on this wall? The Bawden-Trebarr standards in their respective colours.'

'It seems to be a replica of what we found inside the box.'

'It is,' she said softly, wanting to take in all the finer detail and intricacies of the design. 'With both the Bawden and Trebarr mottos entwined. *Karensa a vynsa covatys ny vynsa.* "Love would, greed would not…"'

'And the Trebarr motto of *Franc ha leal atho ve.* "Free and loyal am I."'

Eliza spun around to face Sebastian. 'You remembered the motto and in Cornish as well?'

'I did.' He smiled sheepishly as she approached him. 'Since it was important to *you*.'

'Oh, Sebastian.' Eliza placed her gloved hand on his gorgeous face. 'I… I…'

She loved him. More than anything in the world Eliza wanted to tell him at that moment and in this place—this hallowed place, the very hall where her ancestors came together. She wanted to make him see everything that she held in her heart. And tell him that she cared for him, that she loved him, but the words felt as though they were stuck in the back of her throat. She opened her mouth to try again…

'Oho…who goes there?' A man's voice boomed from the other side of the hall.

Sebastian moved in front of Eliza to stand tall in a protective stance. 'I am Sebastian Marsden, current owner of this estate. And this is Lady Eliza Bawden-Trebarr, who I have accompanied here. Who are you?'

The short and rather rotund man came forth and looked up at Sebastian and frowned in surprise. 'Bawden-Trebarr? Did you say Bawden-Trebarr, my good sir?'

'I did.'

'Bless my soul, a Bawden-Trebarr has come here at last.' He clapped his hands together and bowed to them. 'Yer very welcome here, my lady. And yer, too, sir. Come please. Yer must come to the Sailor's Mermaid, the local pub in these 'ere parts where yer'll both be the guests of honour, so yer will.'

* * *

Eliza and Sebastian followed the man, Silas Brunde, a steward of the estate, in the carriage that carried their trunks back onto the main path and to the nearby hamlet of Trebarr, which consisted of a handful of small stone-terraced cottages with just one detached building—The Sailor's Mermaid—along with a smithy and a row of shops overlooking a small village green. They could hear the raucous revelry inside the pub, and when they entered, following Silas inside, it seemed the whole pub turned to look in the direction of the newcomers. Yet, the moment Silas Brunde announced who they were, there was a hushed silence before the pub suddenly erupted into cheering.

The pub was filled to the rafters with people who shook their hands as they were ushered to a small central table. Tankards of beer and ale were brought over to the table forthwith, and a couple of musicians playing the flute and fiddle resumed making their merry music, while the revellers stamped their feet, danced and sang along.

'I had not expected such a welcome as this,' Eliza muttered to Sebastian over the din; the first words she'd spoken to him since that stupendous moment in the Great Hall when she'd wanted so desperately to tell him of her feelings. The moment had obviously passed but she hoped to get another opportunity to tell him later.

'Yes, I believe they are exceptionally glad to have you among them, Eliza.'

'Me?' she said in surprise. 'Don't you mean you? After all, you are the owner of all this.'

'Who knows, by tomorrow when we start digging for your treasure, there might be a new owner. Or rather the rightful owner of the Bawden-Trebarr estate.' Sebastian held out his tankard of ale to her, which she clicked hers to in a toast.

'I'll drink to that.'

'Then here's another toast, Eliza,' he said, holding out his tankard. 'For tomorrow and everything it brings.'

'For tomorrow,' she murmured as she slammed her tankard against his.

* * *

But the following day did not quite turn out exactly as either Eliza or Sebastian had hoped. When Eliza had woken up in the bedroom of one of the widowed Trebarr tenants who had insisted on having Eliza stay at her house, unlike Sebastian, who'd made do with one of the rooms at the pub, she had been filled with so much optimism for what that day might bring. But she could not have known then how badly it would turn out.

After breaking her fast at dawn and meeting Sebastian along with a few farmhands who'd volunteered to help them dig near the largest and most magnificent oak trees and woodland that the deciphered and translated vellum had mentioned, it soon became clear that they did not know exactly what they were doing. Each dig proved fruitless and soon the excitement and heady anticipation of finding the Bawden-Trebarr treasure that the vellum alluded to fizzled into a damp squib. All that they had achieved was lots of unsightly deep holes in the ground everywhere.

Eliza, however, could not stop even when the day was almost ending and she was tired and exhausted in every way because of their failures. She would not and could not give up as it would mean giving up on so much more than just losing the estate.

'I believe we should stop for today, Eliza.' Sebastian came upon her wearing work clothes, his shirtsleeves rolled up to reveal those hard-working arms of his. 'The light is starting to fade and many of the farmhands have decided to stop, too, as they need to get up early for their work tomorrow morning.'

Eliza wiped the sweat from her brow and looked up in dismay at the area around them. 'I understand but it must be here. It must.'

'The treasure, if it is still buried, could be anywhere, though,' he said gently. 'It was always going to be a huge challenge to find it, even if it was still here.'

Sebastian was right, of course. This had always been a fool's errand, and the proposal she had presented to him had always smacked of desperation. It had been a mad scheme but she had followed it blindly, willing it to happen as she pushed for it relentlessly and refusing to listen to the voices of reason around her. God, and she believed herself to have a scholarly mind—a bluestocking, who was analytical and rational in her findings, yet she could not even see what was before her eyes at how ridiculous this all was. That this whole search was hopeless. And despite all their findings, it had always been so.

'I think I've found summat, my lady.'

Sebastian and Eliza exchanged a surprised look before quickly making their way toward the young farmhand who had called out to them. They crouched down on the grass beside him as he dragged out a large wooden box.

'Well done, Sam,' she said as she studied the box, trying to tamp down her excitement, knowing full well that this could be yet another false hope.

'Well?' Sebastian murmured. 'Shall we open it?'

Eliza nodded as he brought a crowbar to break through the wooden box. Once the lid broke open, they looked inside to find it filled with earth and old straw, but something else was hidden in its depths. Something that was wrapped in very old material. They set it on the ground and began to untie the knotted ends, letting the material slide down to reveal yet another box—a box identical to the one that Eliza had. The Bawden-Trebarr box.

'It exists.' She sat back on her feet and exhaled slowly through pursed lips. 'I cannot believe it actually exists.'

Sebastian smiled at her and nodded. 'Yes, it seems that it does. And it seems that just like yours, it needs the correct seal to open it.'

Eliza nodded before fetching the seal that Tristan Marsden had surreptitiously allowed her to bring on this expedition, so long as she brought it back in one piece. Taking a deep breath, she placed the metal seal in the centre of the box and pressed, listening to the familiar click as it slotted into place before releasing the metal lock. She opened the lid of the box but unlike the one in her possession, this one was completely empty. Whatever had once been there was now gone. Lost through the annals of time.

They both stared at the box for a long moment, neither wanting to admit defeat.

'I'm sorry, Eliza.' She heard Sebastian murmur from beside

her as he reached over and covered her hand with his, giving it a squeeze.

But her mouth was too dry to respond other than to nod lamely, and being filled with a huge sense of disappointment as it all came crashing down around her.

'It doesn't matter, Eliza. Not now,' Sebastian said as her eyes filled with tears.

Was he mad to think that? Annoyed with herself, Eliza wordlessly gathered the seal and stuffed it back inside her portmanteau irritably as she rose and threw the empty box aside. Sebastian moved to follow her. 'Did you hear me, Eliza? I said it matters not that we were unable to find the Bawden-Trebarr treasure. Not to me.'

'That speaks well of you, Sebastian, but it matters very much to me,' She said bitterly as she continued to march away from this clearing with Sebastian following behind her. 'And this does change everything.'

He was upon her so quickly, stilling her by her elbow. 'How so? I fail to understand you, Eliza.'

She spun on her heels to face him. 'Can't you see that this failure, this disappointing loss, will change everything? Including what we have between us. Don't you see that this failure would always come between us?'

'No, Eliza. I don't,' he said as he laced his fingers with hers. 'What I believe… In fact, what I know is that I love you.'

What…?

She nearly stumbled backwards with that unexpected declaration. Dear God, but Sebastian's feelings mirrored her own. Oh, she knew he desired her and had said he liked her very well but…*love*? No, she never would have believed it. And declared at such a time as this with the failure of the find still ringing in her head. Oh, what a mess. Sebastian had said that they should see where this…this liaison would take them just over a day and a half ago—heavens, but it felt like a lifetime ago now— and yet it had already taken them here—to precisely nowhere.

She slipped her hand free of his and dropped her arms to her sides. 'I love you, too, Sebastian. More than you will ever know.' Sebastian smiled and stepped forward to reach for her, just as she took a step back and held up her hand.

'But I wish now that I had told you the truth of my feelings back in the Half Moon Inn or when we were standing in the Great Hall of Trebarr Castle yesterday evening, instead of now, in this moment...this moment when everything that I tried to achieve has all been for naught.'

'Come now, does it matter, after we have told each other our innermost feelings? I love you and you say you love me—which, by the by, is the most wonderful thing I have ever heard. Surely, that is all that matters?'

Eliza hugged her arms around herself, suddenly feeling very cold. 'I wish that were true but it cannot be.'

He frowned. 'I don't comprehend you, Eliza.'

'Don't you see that the failure of today changes everything between us?' she murmured softly. 'That my inability to regain this estate by paying back Ritton's debt will now and forever cast a doubt over everything between us? We can never come together in whatever this is between us, as equals, which for me was of the utmost importance.'

He moved towards her. 'I don't give a damn about the Bawden-Trebarr estate—it's yours with my compliments,' he ground out through clenched teeth. 'And I don't care about the debt. All I care about is you, Eliza. *You*, for the love of God.'

Eliza reached out and cupped his jaw as he turned his face and pressed his lips in the centre of her palm. 'But don't you see, Sebastian, that you will one day wonder about the timing of this disclosure? You will wonder whether my love for you had been an attempt to manipulate you in some way just to gain back this estate.'

'You would think so little of me?'

'Of course not.'

'Good, but let's for the sake of argument address your rather arbitrary assumption. Allow me to ask you whether you are trying to manipulate me in gaining the estate that I'm freely giving you, anyway. So, are you, Eliza?'

'No, Sebastian, I am not.'

'Then what is all of this about, sweetheart?' he said on a frustrated sigh.

'All I know is that perhaps not now, not even tomorrow, but someday that niggle of doubt would surface, Sebastian, and I cannot bear to lose your good opinion of me, your respect and even your love.'

He had once had those very doubts when he'd asked what her game was. Would his concerns not resurface again in the future? Eliza had no way of knowing but knew it would destroy her if she were to lose his trust. In any case, what could she bring with her into this union? Nothing. Which meant that they were set to be unequal from the very start. It raised the very important question—what kind of future would they have, then?

'Eliza, I...'

She silenced him by placing her finger against his lips and shook her head. 'I want to come to you. I want to be with you, but on an equal footing, even if our laws and our society do not quite accept that yet. This is who and what I am, Sebastian—a woman who believes in what Cecy and I set up in The Women's Enlightened Reform Movement.' He smiled briefly at that. 'But how can I come to you if this...inequality, this disparity, stands between us? How?'

Eliza gave him a small, sad smile before turning on her heel and leaving him to ponder on everything that she had said, striding quickly to get away from this place.

Chapter Sixteen

It had been the most arduous journey back from Cornwall early the following morning accompanied by Sebastian. Eliza had spent the night shut inside the old widow's cottage, needing time and space with all her thoughts running around her head, not knowing if she was making the greatest mistake of her life in stepping away from a future with Sebastian Marsden. Neither had spoken very much outside of the usual pleasantries as they travelled back to London via Exeter, but this time without the overnight stop. Thank goodness as Eliza would have found that an impossible intimacy. It was unbearably awkward as it was to travel in such close proximity to Sebastian when what they could both do with was having some time apart. And yet, Eliza felt that her heart was shattering into tiny little pieces, anyway, especially the closer they got to London.

By nightfall they had reached Paddington and after Sebastian had dealt with a message that had been waiting for him on arrival, they hired a carriage to take them to her town house in Chelsea. Strange but it seemed after everything that she had been through she was right back where she'd started from.

'I want to thank you for everything that you have done for me, Sebastian,' she said as the carriage came to a stop outside her house, and she swallowed uncomfortably as she held out her hand.

He took her proffered hand and pressed a chaste kiss on the back of it. 'You might want to thank me for something else, Eliza.'

'What do you mean?'

'Go inside and find out,' he murmured before tugging her back by her fingers. 'But know that this, Eliza Bawden-Trebarr, is by no means over.'

He gave her a quick, hard kiss on the mouth before jumping out of the carriage and helping her down, walking her to her door. After her trunk was also delivered, he made a curt bow and got back inside the carriage, leaving her bewildered. Good Lord, what had he meant about this not being over? And what did Sebastian mean when he told her that there might be something she'd want to find inside the house?

As if to answer her question, the front door swung open and Eliza's mother stepped out onto the porch and ran towards her, enveloping her in a tight embrace.

Oh, God, this was what he'd obviously meant. Sebastian had told her that he would help her with her mother's plight and he had not let her down. It made her want to weep when she considered everything that he'd done for her, time and again.

Oh, Sebastian...what am I going to do about you?

It was over two weeks since Eliza had seen him. Two weeks since she had looked on that beloved face and spoken to him. Oh, she had sent several missives to him, thanking him effusively for the safe return of her mother, which she later found out was partly due to Sebastian's reaching out to his cousin, Henry Marsden, the new Earl of Harbury, which she knew in her heart he would never have done if it hadn't been for her. And wanting to do this one service for her.

And then to add more fuel to these feelings of being beholden to Sebastian, he had reverted all ownership of the Bawden-Trebarr estate back to her, just as he'd said he would. She had tried to return it to him, but it came back yet again with his solicitor's letter including the landowner's registry seal on it. It was now

Eliza's legally and there was little she could do to change that. All of which made it difficult to know what to do about Sebastian Marsden and her feelings for him. She could not go to him as she desperately wanted to because of all the things she had said to him in Trebarr that night. The reservations she'd had about the inequality of their alliance, as well as these feelings of inadequacy over her failure to find her own way out of her problems, had not diminished. Not by any stretch.

But dear Lord, how she ached to be near him, to talk to him, to touch him. She was heartsick and nothing, it seemed, would mend it.

'Are you even listening to me, Eliza?' Her mother's words broke through her musings.

Eliza blinked and took a sip of tea before returning the cup to the saucer. 'Pardon, Mama, I was not attending.'

'No, you were not, dearest.' Her mother frowned as she set her teacup on the small table in Eliza's back parlour and watched her for a long moment. 'Is this still about your Mr Sebastian Marsden?'

'He is not my Mr Sebastian Marsden.'

But he should be, he should...

'You and I both know that is a lie, Eliza,' her mother said quietly. 'Do you love him?'

'Yes, Mama.'

'And he loves you?'

'Yes, I believe so.'

'Then why have you been moping about the place for two weeks? Why have you kept away from him since you parted?'

'Because I wanted to be with you, Mama. You cannot know how much I have worried for you. How much I missed you. It's my greatest joy to have you back with me, safe and sound.'

'And mine, too, dearest. And yet it would never have been possible had it not been for your young's man intervention.'

'I know,' she uttered bleakly. 'I know.'

Her mother reached out and slipped her hand over hers. 'Eliza, do not mistake strength for being prideful.'

Prideful? Is that what she was being?

'It is far more complicated than that, Mama. I am indebted

to Sebastian in a manner that would always come between us. It would always cast a shadow on how we came to be together as a man and a woman and it would compromise my values and beliefs in the suffrage of women.'

'Very admirable, Eliza, but consider that Mr Marsden has not asked you to compromise your values and beliefs, as far as I'm aware.'

'No, of course he hasn't.'

'And yet, you seem to believe in the notion of coming together as a man and woman, as you rather vulgarly put it, in terms of a monetary equality when you should be thinking of equal minds, equal values and equal hearts, which from my understanding seems to have been the case between you and Mr Marsden.'

Eliza covered her face with her hands and shook her head. 'I wish it were as simple as that.'

'Tell me, Eliza, is this more to do with being afraid to commit to Mr Marsden because of what happened with Ritton?' *Yes, no, she was no longer certain.* 'Because if it is then you need to find your courage and fight for this love of yours. For it is a rare thing and not something that comes along too often in life.'

'Perhaps I don't have the conviction left to fight for anything.'

That was certainly true. Eliza herself had never believed that she would one day find someone and be loved by him in return. After Ritton, she'd thought any chance would be elusive, practically out of reach for someone like her. And yet, she had found it in Sebastian.

'You are scared, Eliza, and I can understand why. However, that is not the woman you are, especially as the descendant of all those women who came before us, namely Elowen Bawden-Trebarr.'

'I know that, Mama, but I'm not certain whether love can be enough, as there are too many challenges, too many obstacles in the way for me and Sebastian.'

'Then find a way, dearest.'

'I thought I had,' she said sadly. 'I thought that if I'd found the Bawden-Trebarr treasure when we went looking for it then at the very least, it would have been something.'

'May I see the vellum that you and your Mr Marsden discovered together?' She smiled up at her daughter. 'I still haven't seen it despite the exciting story you regaled me with about finding it.'

'Yes, of course. I'll fetch it now.' Eliza rose, leaving the room momentarily before returning with both the vellum and the transcribed translations, and held it out for her mother.

'Thank you,' the older woman said as she scanned her eyes over the vellum and the translation. 'Well, it seems that you have both done a thorough job here.'

'Yes, we…we worked well together,' Eliza muttered as she slouched back on the chair. 'But it all came to nothing when we went looking for the blasted oak tree that the vellum refers to on the Trebarr estate.'

'What did you say?' Her mother froze and lifted her eyes to hers. 'You looked for it by an oak tree on the Trebarr estate? In Cornwall?'

'We did, but to no avail.'

'Oh, my sweet girl, I don't think the Bawden-Trebarr treasure was ever in Cornwall, but in Devon,' she said earnestly. 'For it was in Devon where Simon and Elowen pledged to be together, so therefore that's where the treasure, if it's still buried, would be.'

'I don't understand—why Devon?'

'Because that was where Elowen Bawden was escorted to by Simon Trebarr no less, as she was promised to another man. But just before he left, Simon told Elowen of his love and begged her not to marry the rather odious Sir Roger Prevnar and that he would be waiting by an old oak tree in a small woodland on the edge of Dartmouth, if she would choose him instead. And so he waited and waited. And on the morning of Elowen's wedding to Sir Roger, she absconded from his castle and met Simon underneath the old oak tree that I'm certain the vellum refers to. That is where they pledged their love to one another. So you see, the tree was…'

'In Devon and not Cornwall.' Eliza stood abruptly, shaking her head. 'Oh, Mama, do you know what this means?'

Her mother frowned. 'No, dear.'

'It means that I must be away to Devon on the very next train,' she said excitedly.

'But dearest, please wait...'

Eliza, however, had already left the room, needing to quickly stuff a few things together in her handy portmanteau. Her mother's explanation of the whereabouts of the treasure propelled Eliza into action, and once again, she soon found herself boarding the next train from Paddington heading to the southwest in search of the Bawden-Trebarr treasure, praying it hadn't been ransacked already...

Sebastian had been brooding for over two weeks now, ever since he'd returned from Cornwall in a dark mood, flitting from a bleak cloud of despair to anger to an ache deep within his chest. He couldn't quite believe the turn of events that had led to his estrangement from Eliza and all because of her pigheadedness in needing to pay back Ritton's debt. God, as if he cared about that!

However, in quiet contemplation, Sebastian recognised that with everything that had transpired between them ending in the disappointment of finding nothing in Cornwall, Eliza needed time. Time to come to terms with her feelings for him. And time to know what it was that she wanted. But what if she truly believed that they had no future despite their confessions of love for one another? What if she was adamant that he had no place in her life? Good God, he would have to convince her, woo her, anything to make her realise that he wouldn't give her up without a fight. He'd meant every word when he told her that he meant to keep her... And yet, if she had truly decided against a future with him then wouldn't he have to accept that, let her go and get on with his life without her?

Damn it, apart from those very proper letters filled with gratitude for everything he'd done, he'd not heard from or seen her in over two weeks. How the hell was he supposed to get on without her? How? She had barged into his life in a whirl, upending everything in it and then she'd left it in exactly the same way. Exasperating woman. If only she would burst into his office and demand something outrageous again from him.

Sebastian rubbed his brow, knowing the truth of it was that he missed her terribly. He missed her so much it actually hurt. A knock at the door snapped him out of his reverie.

'Come in.'

His major-domo opened the door and walked in. 'Lady Bawden-Trebarr is here to see you urgently, Mr Marsden. Shall I see her in?'

Eliza? Here?

'Of course!' He stood and started to pace the room before turning around to see that it was not Eliza but her mother who had been ushered into his office.

Tamping down his disappointment, Sebastian bowed. 'My lady, it is a pleasure to see you. How may I be of service?'

'Good day, Mr Marsden, I am sorry to come here unannounced but I thought you might want to know that my daughter has once again left London in search of the Bawden-Trebarr treasure, if it is even still there. On account of what I told her.'

What the hell has she done now?

'What did you tell her, my lady?'

'That the treasure had likely never been buried in Cornwall but Devon, a woodland on the edge of Dartmouth, to be exact. And oh, Mr Marsden, she left so soon afterwards and all alone. I cannot help but feel concerned for her well-being.'

'But why would Eliza do that?' he thundered, unable to keep the anger from his voice, even in the presence of Eliza's mother. 'Why would she not ask for my help?'

'Perhaps because she believes she has already asked too much of you. Because she has something to prove to you. With Eliza, it could be anything.'

'Yes, it could.' He exhaled irritably. 'And I presume you would have me follow her, my lady, despite Eliza's rejection of my suit?'

'I would, yes.' The older woman's sad smile was so reminiscent of her daughter's it made his heart clench. 'My daughter loves you, Mr Marsden, but after her marriage to her late husband, she lost who she was for a long while. Until she met you. But I also believe she is also unsure as to whether she is truly worthy of you.'

Sebastian felt as though all the air had been knocked out of his chest. 'Unworthy of me? But I'm... I'm the one who is...'

'Illegitimate?'

'Exactly.'

'That is not something that would make one jot of difference to Eliza, Mr Marsden. You must know that about her by now.'

'I do.' There was never any question of whether Sebastian would follow Eliza Bawden-Trebarr. 'I shall go on the next train, my lady. And I shall find her. Of that, you can be assured.'

'Thank you. That would ease my worry.' She smiled. 'I do not like to think of her being alone. And you know Eliza has always been so alone, especially during her marriage to Ritton. My husband never should have pushed for the match.'

He nodded, unable to say more. Sebastian sprang into action and after assuring Eliza's mother that he would find her and bring her back home, he rushed to get the next train from Paddington, knowing that she was probably one train ahead of him.

Thank goodness that the journey to Dartmouth in Devon had not taken as long as when she had travelled to Cornwall a fortnight ago, but it had still taken the better part of the day by the time she'd arrived. Eliza had, however, decided to wait to venture to the small woodland that her mother had described lying northwest between Dartmouth, near Bayard's cove, and the old remains of Stromley Castle, until the following morning, which was quite unlike her. So after organising the hiring of a vehicle and a man to help her with the dig, she set off after breaking her fast, eager to find out whether the Bawden-Trebarr treasure was still buried where her mother had believed it could be. Devon...it had always been in Devon that the Bawden-Trebarr treasure had been hidden and specifically under an old oak tree on the edge of Dartmouth—if indeed it was still there.

A little while later they entered the small wooded area and Eliza began to search for the largest, oldest oak tree, as a dense fog wrapped itself around her legs, making visibility a little harder. Pushing her spectacles up her nose, she looked and felt her way along so many trees that did not quite fit the description her mother had given, dismissing them all until she encountered an old majestic-looking oak. She let out a shaky breath as she felt her way down the gnarly bark of the ancient trunk, knowing that it must be this one.

With the decision made and with the assistance of the hired help, she started to dig close to the tree but not too close that they'd damage its ancient roots. They hopefully wouldn't need to dig around the perimeter of the tree as her mother had been adamant that the site would most likely be north of the tree itself, away from Dartmouth and facing the clearing closest to the remains of Stromley Castle.

'I think we might need another spade, Mr Jenkins,' Eliza muttered, wiping her brow.'

'Very well, miss, I shall return with one from the cart.'

Eliza continued to dig before she heard Mr Jenkins return. Crouching on the ground she started to pull out a long, spindly weed with her bare hands. 'I shall take that,' she muttered, holding out her hand without bothering to look back and grabbing hold of the smaller spade that the old man had fetched for her. 'Thank you.'

But then she heard a vastly different voice to the kindly old man behind her. 'You're welcome.'

Eliza dropped the spade and spun around to find Sebastian Marsden crouching low behind her.

'Hullo, Eliza,' he drawled. 'Fancy finding you here.'

She stared at him for a long time, drinking in the sight of this beloved man. 'What... What are you doing here, Sebastian?'

'Looking for you.' Even his voice made her pulse quicken.

'You were?'

'Yes.'

For a long moment Sebastian and Eliza were rooted to the spot, neither of them saying anything.

'Are you... Are you well, Eliza?' He eventually broke the silence.

'Yes.' She noticed the dark circles underneath his eyes and the thin white lines at the corners of his mouth. He looked so tired and weary as he rose and stepped closer. 'I am well.'

'Good.' He exhaled an irritated breath before turning around to look at her with an irate gaze. 'Because perhaps now you might like to explain what the hell you're doing all the way out here, on your own?'

Oh dear...

'I assume you must know that since you're also here, Sebastian.'

'But why, Eliza? Why would you not ask me to accompany you?'

'Surely, you must know that I had to do this on my own.'

'Do I? You and your pride, Eliza Bawden-Trebarr,' he said, shaking his head as he turned his back on her.

'I'm truly sorry, Sebastian,' she said, moving to stand behind him and placing her hand on his back.

'What for, exactly?'

'For doubting you. For doubting myself.' She sighed as she gently pulled him around to meet her gaze. 'And I'm sorry for causing you pain. I... I thought if I could give you something in return for the debt then I could... Then we could start afresh. Be together as equals.'

'Good God, Eliza, it was never your debt to pay back. And Ritton should never have used your ancestral estate to pay the damn thing in the first place. Don't you see? The estate has always been yours. Always.'

'What about the debt?'

He pulled her close to him and looked down at her. 'That will now pass onto the new viscount. And if he promises never to come within a hundred yards of you then I might consider it paid.'

'But, Sebastian...'

'This is not up for debate, my lady,' he murmured, brushing his knuckles down her cheeks. 'Don't you see? All I have ever wanted is you, unencumbered by any land, debt, castle or even treasure. Just you, Eliza.'

'I want you, too,' she murmured as her eyes filled with tears.

'Good, because I'm yours. I have been from that first moment you came tearing into my office. And if you'll have me, I want to be yours in every way possible.'

'You want to marry me?'

'I want to marry you.' He nodded, catching her lips with his before lifting his head, his eyes glittering with such tenderness. 'Will you have me?'

'Yes… Yes, I think I shall have you.' She felt her heart might burst from happiness. 'I love you, Sebastian.'

'I love you, too, Eliza. Always.'

As Sebastian bent his head to kiss her, Eliza pressed her finger on his lips. 'There's just one more thing you might like to know. I believe I might have found something under this tree.'

'Oh, God, Eliza.' His shoulders shook from mirth. 'Whatever am I to do with you?'

'Love me.' She grinned. 'But in the meantime, help me retrieve the box I found.'

'Gladly.'

Under the same tree where her ancestors had pledged to be together hundreds of years ago, they eventually unearthed a box buried deep within the earth. Inside the box, they discovered a small pouch tucked into the furthest recesses and within that, they found two gold-and-emerald rings that must have once belonged to Simon and Elowen. Smiling up at one another and using the same rings, Eliza and Sebastian made a similar promise beneath the same old oak tree. They promised to love and honour each other until the end of their days.

* * * * *

HISTORICAL

Your romantic escape to the past.

Available Next Month

Only An Heiress Will Do Virginia Heath
The Duchess Charade Emily E K Murdoch

The Unexpected Duke Julia Justiss
Winning His Manhattan Heiress Lauri Robinson

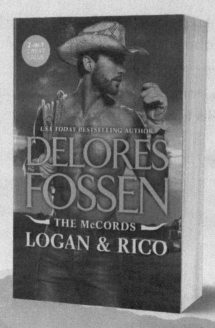

Subscribe and fall in love with a Mills & Boon series today!

You'll be among the first to read stories delivered to your door monthly and enjoy great savings.

MILLS & BOON